Burning
Island

BOOKS BY SUZANNE GOLDRING

My Name is Eva

SUZANNE GOLDRING

Burning Island

bookouture

Published by Bookouture in 2020

An imprint of Storyfire Ltd.
Carmelite House
50 Victoria Embankment
London EC4Y 0DZ

www.bookouture.com

ISBN: 978-1-83888-179-5
eBook ISBN: 978-1-83888-178-8

For Paul and Jacky who first showed us the beauty of Corfu.

We owe respect to the living;
to the dead we owe only truth.
Voltaire

This is a work of fiction,
but the events it depicts in Corfu in
June 1944 are inspired by eyewitness accounts.

Prologue

Amber

June 2007

Now I know the truth, I can never look at Corfu with innocence again. For me it is no longer a place just of sea and sunshine, for everywhere in the cobbled streets and dark alleyways I hear echoes of the past. Looking out over the sea I can hear the pleasure boats and the laughter of holidaymakers, but I also see shadows of the slow, rotting barges, packed with the sobbing people of the Evraiki, the Jewish ghetto of Corfu, leaving their homeland for the last time.

But I know James will never see this island the way I do. He sees ripe peaches, fragrant lemons, glistening fresh seafood, all the tools of his trade and the secret to his successful restaurant, but never the sorrow at the heart of Corfu.

I look across to the ancient fort, crumbling on its rocky promontory on the edge of Corfu's old harbour, then shade my eyes and look out across the sea. The mainland is but a shimmering haze in the distance, and that isn't even Greece – it's Albania. I try to imagine the journey of despair those people took so near to the end of the war and it makes me shudder. A journey they made in dread to the unknown, with just the slightest shred of hope, a journey that would be the last nearly all of them would ever make.

When I turn back towards the town, I pass rows of cafe tables draped with white cloths, shaded by awnings striped yellow and blue, filled with tourists drinking chilled beers and wine, eating moussaka and spiced meatballs with Greek salad. They know and care nothing of the hundreds who stood here all those years ago beneath the scorching sun that June, clutching their few possessions, fighting back their tears while the Germans issued harsh orders, scorning their pleas for rest and water.

And all around this beautiful island, when the Judas tree bursts into flower each spring, I cannot enjoy its blossom; its lurid fuchsia-pink flowers remind me of betrayal. Now I know the truth behind the lies, the facts behind the facade, I have to strive for truth everywhere. Wherever people seek carefree happiness and idle pleasures, there are shameful hidden stories, and this is just one of them.

PART ONE

THEY DEPARTED

Chapter One

A young girl stumbles in the rubble of the bombed houses as she runs through the dusty cobbled streets of Corfu Town, while the sun begins to set behind the tall tenements. Rebekka Nikokiris, thirteen-year-old daughter of Isaac, honourable cobbler, and his wife Perla, devoted mother of three girls, hardworking housewife and seamstress, is very afraid.

She clutches a small package close to her chest. Although the early evening air is still warm, she hides her head beneath her shawl, so no one will see her dark eyes and long lashes. Her boots are too large for her and chafe her ankles. *But you are lucky not to be barefoot like most children.* That's what Papa had said when he salvaged the old boots from the pile of uncollected pairs at the back of his shop.

The streets are empty, but she can still hear the soldiers shouting and laughing as they kick lemons across the road in a coarse game of football. The fruit is ripe, falling from the trees that line the squares, free to anyone in Corfu Town who needs a lemon for their avgolemeno lamb or to dress a salad. Some collect basketfuls of fruit to make limoncello, or preserve them for the wet days of the island's rainy winters, but no true Corfiot has such careless disregard for the abundant golden fruit – no one plays football with the thick-skinned lemons, no one disrespects the people and the produce of Corfu like the greedy, heartless Germans.

Rebekka quickens her pace, anxious to put the cries of the callous soldiers behind her. *Mama will fret if she isn't back soon.*

She's always worrying these days. 'It was all right when the Italians were here,' she'd complained that morning. 'They may have been too friendly with our girls, but they didn't really trouble our people. But now, with the Germans…' She'd frowned and bit her lip. 'The humiliation. The roll calls on the Spianada. Every week, they make us go there. Why can they not leave us in peace?'

'Quiet, Perla, you'll worry the little ones.' Rebekka's father always comforted her mother. He was not like some fathers. He was gentle and kind. 'As long as we can keep them hidden, they will not be counted.'

Rebekka looks over her shoulder as she nears her father's shoe shop. No one is following her today, but the other week a well-dressed man appeared with two soldiers as she went through the doorway and shouted at Papa, 'Where's your notice?'

'Hanging on the door,' Papa had answered, 'right there in that frame.' He'd pointed to the printed, signed poster, proclaiming his premises were 'Jewish'.

'You can't hang it inside. It can't be seen there. You have to put it out the front. You know it is forbidden for Germans to go into a Jewish shop and buy from you.' They'd stood there till he had rehung the notice in the approved place, then they'd marched away.

Rebekka had cowered in a corner of the shop until they left. 'That was our mayor,' her father had said in disgust. 'Mayor Kollas. He is responsible for this. He collaborates with them. See, his signature is on the notice. And it is even printed here, in Corfu.' He'd hammered his fist on the workbench; once piled with shoes to be soled and boots to be nailed, it was now bare, just like her Mama's sewing table.

When Rebekka opens the door to her home, she can hear soft murmurs from the family rooms above the shop. These days there is always muttering and tears. Before, the narrow alleyways and shops of the Evraiki had echoed with the tapping of the cobbler's hammer, the trundle of the tailor's sewing machines and the ever-cheerful cries of children's laughter. Their businesses may have been poor, but they served their people and were appreciated by the Corfiots, who accepted them and their religion.

Rebekka runs up the stairs, brandishing her precious package and calling, 'Mama, Kostas still had some chestnuts for us, maybe you can make your special stuffed cabbage tonight.' But as she enters the family kitchen where they have always gathered and eaten together, she is not greeted with grateful smiles. Her mother is slumped at the well-scrubbed table, her head in her hands. Matilde and Anna, Rebekka's little sisters, cling to Mama's apron, their fingers in their mouths. They are thin and pale-skinned from months of hiding from the German headcount inside the house.

Papa is frowning. 'It has come at last,' he says in a quiet voice filled with sorrow. 'From tomorrow we will not be able to leave the house, and I fear soon we will have to leave Corfu for good.'

Mama dries her tears on her apron and fetches plates of tomatoes and bread for their supper. Then she glances at her husband and, in a low steady voice, says, 'Isaac, I think now is the time for you to call on Doctor Batas. He will be expecting you.'

Rebekka does not understand. First, her father's announcement about staying in the house, now her mother is telling him to visit the doctor. Is he unwell? Or are her sisters ailing? They are both thin, but no thinner than many of the children in the town since the war began, and their heads have not been shaved like those of the homeless orphans that roam the streets. They have not ailed like the little ones her mother bore then lost before them; in spite of their hunger they look as if they will thrive. She wants to ask what might be wrong, but her mother hands her a knife and tells her to slice the tomatoes for the young ones.

Papa crams a corner of bread in his mouth, chews quickly, then kisses all three daughters on the head before kissing his wife on her cheek. 'Be good for your mother, all of you,' he says. 'I will not be long.' And he runs down the stairs and out into the street, locking the shop door below on his way out.

Rebekka looks at her mother and is about to ask a question, but Mama cautions her with a look and says, 'It has been such a tiring day. I want all of you in bed early tonight.'

Chapter Two

James

June 2006

It was the start of the summer season, soon after the late spring storms had finally blown away, when the first visitors began arriving. As the days grew hotter, lemons were falling from the trees every day. There were lemons in the garden of the restored villa where Ben was letting us stay, until paying guests arrived, and more ripe fruit was scattered in the grounds of the properties we were helping to manage. Large, pitted, yellow lemons with thick skins littering the hard earth – we couldn't bear to leave them to wither and rot.

'The guests will never use all these,' I said, throwing the ripe fruit into a bucket late one afternoon. 'We can take as many as we want.'

'But what will *we* do with them all?' Amber asked, peering at the pile of unmarked fruit. 'We can't drink that many gin and tonics, however hard we try.'

'We could make lemonade,' I said, dusting the soil off one of the fruits and smelling the fresh scent of the peel. 'It's not difficult. And we could make sorbet and water ice as well. Just what we'll need when the weather gets hotter.'

So we grated the tangy zest, squeezed juice and boiled sugar syrup to sweeten the lemons until we had jugs of cold lemonade in the fridge and iced boxes stored in the freezer. It became Amber's principal task in the kitchen, as I was always experimenting with another new recipe, or preparing an unusual fish from the market which I hadn't cooked before. We collected lemons whenever we could, so there was a cool drink waiting for us when we returned to the villa after a day of checking holiday homes for breakages and lost property and briefing new arrivals on car and boat hire.

'I do hope we have our own lemon tree when we eventually find our house,' Amber said one evening, moving the bottles of beer and wine in the fridge to make room for more freshly made lemonade.

'Of course we will,' I reassured her. 'Have you ever seen a garden in Greece without at least one citrus tree? They're everywhere. I went through the town the other day and the lemon and orange trees there were full of ripe fruit, free for the picking. I could have helped myself to bagfuls, right there on the street.'

'But would you, though?' Amber said, with a small frown. 'I always feel we aren't allowed to, as we aren't locals.'

'Don't be silly. Anyone can pick up fruit on the street. They just fall and rot otherwise.'

'James, it's different when we collect lemons from the villas. They sort of belong to us then, don't they? Out in the street, I wouldn't feel entitled. I think they belong to people who were born here.'

'Oh, they wouldn't care,' I said, kissing her cheek. 'Anyway, you can get away with anything with your charm and cheeky smile. They all love you to bits.'

'No, they don't. Spiro's old mother gave me a very funny look when I was getting bread in the shop yesterday.' Amber pulled a face, biting her lip the way she always did when she was worried.

'Maybe she thought your skirt was too short again. You know what these old women are like.' The younger women were friendly, and many wore shorts and T-shirts to work in the local shops or go about their cleaning jobs, but I could picture how the older generation stared with their knowing black eyes in their wrinkled prune-like faces, as they sat, hands folded in laps, on their chairs stationed in the doorways of the family shops and tavernas, monitoring all who came and went. I was never sure what they were thinking, but when their eyes followed Amber in her denim shorts or tiny sundresses, I could tell it wasn't good. The old men were all right. I knew what they were thinking as they watched me walk past, holding hands with my lovely wife, while they sat with their cronies, drinking ouzo in the shade. But the old women, the women in their black dresses and their black stockings, made me feel uneasy. I felt sure they were judging.

'Maybe now I'm an old married woman I should dress like all the other old bags,' Amber said. 'Make them realise I'm perfectly respectable.' She picked up a tea towel, folded it into a triangle, then spread it over her hair and tied it round the back of her head. 'What do you think? Does it suit me?'

I burst out laughing. 'Covering your hair isn't going to make any difference when the rest of you is half naked.'

She looked down at herself. We had changed in a hurry when we came back from a long hot day of checking guests into their accommodation, and Amber had stripped off the sensible blouse and skirt she wore to work and was dressed only in bra and pants, starkly white against her dark skin. She laughed at my remark and turned round, still holding the tea towel over her head, then wiggled in mock catwalk fashion through the doorway.

I threw a wet sponge at her back, then chased her upstairs.

Chapter Three

James

November 2005

We had talked about a change in lifestyle before, but I think it would be true to say it really began in November 2005. That's when we realised we didn't have to wait any longer to have a more satisfying way of life.

Amber and I, like so many of our generation, at least those of us who had benefited from a private education, had always felt that our lives had been mapped out for us and that with our undoubted privilege had come an obligation to those who provided it. From before the time we said our first word we were registered for nursery and had our names put down for prep schools. Later, we had private music classes, swimming lessons and extra maths tuition, then in the long summer holidays we went to junior sailing clubs in St Mawes, Bosham or the Isle of Wight. At Christmas, our hesitant voices warbled at Messiah from Scratch at the Royal Albert Hall, and we learnt to ride and play tennis. Like our contemporaries, we were educated to succeed within strict parameters, with clearly defined goals and, in the case of both of us, with traditional career paths expected of us. Amber's family were all involved with the Law, so it was only natural that she and her siblings – all adopted as infants – should aim to be barristers too.

I started out reading History and Economics, with the expectation that I would follow my grandfather and father into the family accountancy business. 'We Youngs have been well respected in

Chichester since well before the war,' my father always said. 'You can't go wrong if you join the firm. People are always going to need good accountants and with that behind you, anything's possible.' So it was a bit of shock to him when I announced, halfway through my degree, that I wanted to go into advertising – and not even the suited account director side. To be fair, he'd always thought that if I didn't join the family firm I would choose law, or maybe business, banking at worst, but he'd never imagined something as unstable and unconventional as advertising.

I'd attended a student union debate on what is more creative, advertising or art, and from that moment I'd been hooked. Dad thought I'd never make it, but I got into a top London agency despite the hundreds of other hopefuls and I was really quite successful. I loved the buzz of pitching for new business and throwing ideas around with my creative team partner Rob – a short angry Scot who'd fought his way into the agency from art college. He fought me too, but only when I wanted food for lunch and not just pints of lager in the local pub. Because that is my other passion. Food. I'd always loved food, and now I love sourcing it, preparing it and tasting it. I badgered my parents to let me do a cordon bleu course as a reward for my excellent GCSE results; I spent my gap year as a chalet boy in Val d'Isère and I applied to do *MasterChef* just before I started my degree. I'm pretty sure I could have gone all the way too, but my parents put financial pressure on me to concentrate on my studies, so with great regret I let that opportunity slip past me.

But Amber, my lovely Amber, knew all about my secret dreams, and she had her dreams too – of a life where she would never again have to work through the night and never have to travel on stifling Tube trains during the summer or shiver on freezing station platforms in winter. She dreamt of having the luxury of time to catch up on films and theatre, of evenings when we could enjoy leisurely dinners and one day having time to write. And then came that particular November, when for the second year running, winter began in earnest quite early.

It wasn't so bad for me – I could travel later than the majority of commuters and I only had to cope with thirty minutes of Tube trains crowded with damp winter coats, the rumbling of the carriages masking the rattle of coughs and the constant blowing of noses. I could hide behind my newspaper or book, or, being over six feet tall, hold my head above the crowd, hanging onto the rail and hoping the germs fell rather than rose in the fetid atmosphere. And whenever I had to work late on an urgent pitch, I would avoid the evening rush by staying long into the night then slumping in a taxi well after the crush had gone home.

But Amber was always lumbered with a heavy briefcase full of documents to drag out to another case in Guildford or Chelmsford, or wherever her clerk sent her next. She left before dawn in the dark winter months and was never home before me, having returned to chambers after a long journey back into London to collect her next brief. She hardly ever complained, but I'd noticed her caramel skin turning greyer, the hollows under her eyes deepening. She'd started coughing too, a sure sign that she would be stricken with a debilitating infection for weeks.

Yes, I remember exactly how it happened. It was that November, at the end of 2005. I was chopping carrots and celery for a bolognese sauce and sipping Merlot when she returned that particular evening. Slicing and stirring are soothing after a day of arguing and that day had been particularly fractious following the rejection of a campaign for a mayonnaise brand. Rob and I had been handed the brief at the last minute, and after two solid days of working into the night, we'd thought we'd cracked it. So had our creative director, but the client had been stony-faced when we presented that morning and Rob had not returned from the pub at lunchtime. I joined him for a couple of drinks, but getting home early and cooking was my best therapy. I went to the Italian deli near the office in Soho for more of their peppery olive oil and treated myself to some of their fat green nocellara olives, slick with oil and sweet as butter.

So I was in a good mood that night, despite the disappointment of the working day, waiting for my lovely wife to come home. I'd opened the wine to breathe, set the table with candles, sliced fresh ciabatta bread and poured some of my favourite oil into a little bowl for dipping. Then, while I cooked, I hummed and listened for the distant sounds of Amber's arrival.

Our flat was on the top floor of a tall Edwardian house in West Hampstead. We'd cursed the long flights of stairs when we moved in, hauling IKEA flat packs and boxes of books up to our eyrie, but our compensation was the sunset over the surrounding rooftops and sunbathing on summer weekends, lying on the flat roof of this attic conversion. On hot sun-baked days, we both lay there naked, burning in the heat. Amber's burnished limbs deepened from light mocha to caramel, while I obstinately sweltered my way from buttermilk to strawberry milkshake, never even getting close to a dark shade of bronze.

Amber would kiss the sweat away from my forehead, but she refused to make love on the roof in daylight, however much I tried to persuade her. 'No one can possibly see,' I would say, yet she insisted she felt watched and that would be her cue to leave the baking roof and return with cold water or ice cubes to throw at my roasted skin. But there was one memorable summer's night, when the flat roof held its heat, the air was soft and warm, and we made love under a velvet sky of stars.

And now it was no longer summer and I could tell, when I heard the flat door slammed and Amber began dragging herself up the stairs, that she was exhausted from her day. There was a series of thumps as she dropped her heavy briefcase and kicked off her boots. Halfway up the stairs, she called out, 'I can cope with rain, but not snow. It's too early. I can't take another freezing winter with cars in drifts and trains on ice.'

Her black curls were sparkling with melted snowflakes. Her cheeks were bitten with the cold, not rosy with health. 'It took me forever to get back to chambers. I thought I was going to be stranded in Guildford all night long.'

I handed her a glass of wine, which she usually gulped straight away, but as she took it she drooped against the doorframe, groaning with tiredness. 'Train after train was cancelled and then it started snowing. I can't bear it.'

I gave her hummus with crudités and pistachios and she began shelling the nuts and dipping carrots, while I sliced tomatoes and onions to make a salad. As I tore basil leaves and poured olive oil, I said, 'I've spiced up the sauce, but you can have carbonara if you'd rather.'

'No, it's fine…' She was dabbing at the dip with a carrot stick. 'I've been thinking,' she said, 'you know how we've often talked about not doing this for ever…'

I stopped stirring and looked at her. 'One day, yes, but you're only just getting started. You've worked so hard to get this far.'

She looked up at me. Me, standing there with a wooden spoon in my hand, her little flower-sprigged apron over my jeans. 'I really don't think I want to do it anymore,' she said. 'I can't face another wet, cold winter of early starts, cancelled trains and long journeys. We've talked about it before, haven't we, so maybe now's the time?'

It was true. We had talked, often. We called it our 'master plan' and in drunken moments we talked about where we would go, what we would see and how we would live a simple life that didn't involve London, commuting or long tiring hours, dark mornings and cold late nights. We envied friends who had continued travelling after gap years almost as much as we admired others who'd bought sensible little houses in the suburbs to breed babies and grow vegetables.

On the rare evenings we were both at home and didn't have early morning starts, we curled around each other on our sofa, drinking wine and dreamt of careers that would suit country towns. I'd be a private chef cooking for weekenders and filling hampers for opera lovers, Amber would offer legal advice or work part-time for a local solicitor. We'd have time for a garden, maybe a dog to accompany us on walks in the woods and eventually, there would be children. We'd be a proper married couple at last, not like flatmates who passed each other on the stairs now and then and slept in the same bed.

'I absolutely hated today,' Amber sighed. 'My feet froze waiting at the station this evening. Then when the train came, it was hot, it was crowded and just about everyone on it was coughing or sneezing. I was squashed into the middle seat between two enormous men. I could hardly breathe.'

'Just as well,' I joked. 'You'd have been breathing in all manner of germs if you had.'

'It's not funny.'

I looked at her. She'd put her head in her hands and I couldn't see her expression.

'Are you feeling all right?' I switched off the ring simmering the sauce and bent down to put my arms around her. Then I realised she was crying. 'Amber, darling, what's wrong? No one made any nasty remarks today, did they?' She usually shrugged off the casual racism she frequently encountered, but sometimes when she was particularly tired and couldn't get a seat on the train, she said it was a burden she shouldn't have to bear and came home feeling bruised by sullen looks and harsh remarks.

Her reply was muffled by her sobs, but eventually I heard her. 'No, they didn't. Not this time. Anyway, it's not that. I'm just tired. I'm so tired. I can't live like this anymore. I just want it all to stop and leave me alone.'

'See how you feel in the morning,' I said, thinking as I did so that I sounded just like my own mother, then went on to sound even more like her. 'A good meal and a good night's sleep and you'll feel much better.'

'I doubt it,' she sniffed. Then she pushed me away and sat up straight, wiping her eyes and nose with the back of her hand. She rummaged in her pocket for a tissue and blew her nose, then walked across the kitchen to the sink. She splashed her face with cold water, dried it on a tea towel, then turned towards me. Her eyes were still red and her mouth was trembling, but she was trying to smile. 'Is there any garlic bread?'

I laughed. 'I can make garlic bread, just for you.' And then I hugged her.

Chapter Four

7 June 1944

It's not fair, Rebekka thinks. *Mama knows I always like to tell my little sisters a story at bedtime. I wanted to do it tonight as well. And they like me to sing to them.*

Mama's firm words still rankle with her. 'Do as I say. Go to your room. We are all going to bed early tonight. There is much to be done tomorrow.' As soon as Papa returned from his visit to Dr Batas, she was impatient, rushing the last of their supper, hurrying the children upstairs to their bedrooms.

Rebekka lies in her bed, trying to sleep, listening to Mama crooning to Matilde and Anna in the room next door. Mama's voice grows softer and softer until there is finally silence, and then she hears footsteps on the stairs.

Rebekka sits up in bed. *They must be asleep now*, she thinks. *But I didn't give them a goodnight kiss.* She waits until she hears sounds in the kitchen below her bedroom. Dishes are being stacked, water splashes and her parents talk in hushed voices. Rebekka creeps from her bed to the door. She listens for a moment, then tiptoes out of her room and opens the door to where her sisters are sleeping.

They are lying side by side in the one bed, their curly dark hair fanned on the white pillows. They look so still, their breathing so faint it barely shows. A cup stands on the bedside cabinet. Mama must have given them one last drink before she sang them to sleep.

Rebekka leans forward to kiss each child on the cheek and as her lips touch their pale skin, she thinks how much they look like the expensive china dolls in the only toy shop in Corfu Town. She has gazed at the richly dressed dolls with longing since she was as young as Matilde, knowing that she could never possess such a fine mannequin with real blonde hair and a painted porcelain face. But she has had two little sisters instead. Matilde, now five, and Anna, only three.

Since they were tiny, she has helped Mama bathe them and dress them in clean clothes. As they grew and no longer fed at Mama's breast, she helped to prepare their meals and feed them soft rice, eggs and mashed fava beans. She has laughed at their clumsy antics and held their tiny hands as they learnt to walk with tottering steps. She has taught them words in songs and stories. These children have been her playthings, her dolls, and she loves them very much, certainly more than the grand but stiff dolls her father might have bought for her had they been a wealthy family.

She strokes their hair, then turns to the door to slip back to her bed. 'What are you doing there?' Mama hisses from the stairs. 'Get back to your room and stay there.'

Rebekka runs to her room, but stands against the door, listening. She hears Mama creeping around her sisters' room, and then the door closes. Mama rarely tells her off, and she was doing nothing wrong. She was only delivering forgotten kisses.

Chapter Five

Amber

November 2005

How quickly and easily we made that decision, that momentous, life-changing decision to leave our demanding but well-paid careers, sell our first home and escape from London. And not just London, but icy, grey, snowy England, where we had once thought we would live forever.

If it hadn't been for Ben, I don't think it would ever have happened so soon. I'd have blown my nose a few times and told myself to get a grip, resigned myself to taking regular doses of cough mixture and wearing thermal socks inside my boots, but then he came to stay with us, just for a night, only days after I'd had my tearful outburst. Ben Dawson is James's best friend from school; they'd shared detention for smoking at the far end of the playing fields, stood by each other at the school disco when neither of them had the nerve to speak to the girls from neighbouring St Hilda's; and Ben had also helped James recover from a broken heart long before I came on the scene, by downing shots and having all-night viewing sessions of box sets in the flat the two of them were sharing at the time. He performed the role of best man at our wedding with both humour and humility. Dependable, conscientious Ben, who, after behaving exactly as his parents had planned throughout school, university and as an intern with one of the biggest management consultancies in London, had sacrificed his promising and lucrative career to run off to Corfu and marry his childhood sweetheart.

No, that's not quite right – he'd been to the island many times on family holidays and had returned for what he thought might be one last summer with his parents. While there, he realised that the chubby, mischievous daughter from their favourite taverna, who'd beaten him in swimming and diving competitions every year when they were children, was now the lithe and silken-haired Eleni. 'She glowered at me at first, when she recognised the arrogant kid who'd always teased her,' Ben said, laughing when he described how they met again. 'Then, when she realised I was melting before her very eyes, she gave me this smouldering look and soon I was totally smitten and head over heels and so was she. Since then, I've never looked back.' It was such a romantic story, and it was obvious how much Ben loved Eleni and his life when he talked with a glow in his eyes.

Ben never returned to his job in London; he married Eleni and learnt everything there was to learn about her family's tavernas and property rentals. As Eleni's ageing parents were looking to take a back seat, he had put his business acumen to good use by expanding the enterprise – hiring out boats, renovating the rundown family villas into profitable apartments and acquiring a long list of mostly British-owned holiday homes that he managed and rented through an impressive website. James and I had looked through it a couple of times in idle moments on wet, bored weekends, picking out our dream holiday villa, complete with infinity pool and a view of the calm, blue sea.

Ben was only staying with us for one night. He was meant to be visiting his parents and Eleni had refused to leave the island as she was pregnant for the second time. James and I had debated where we should take Ben for dinner that evening. When James suggested going for Greek food in Camden Town, I thought that was the last thing Ben would enjoy. 'He won't want that, he needs a change,' I said. So we decided he should meet us at the flat and we'd start the evening in The Black Lion, our local pub, then go to Chang's Lodge, our nearest Chinese, where the pre-cooked buffet dishes were displayed at a bacteria-cultivating temperature for hours and were best avoided, but the freshly prepared crispy duck with pancakes and plum sauce was the best we'd ever had.

'Why don't you stay another night with us,' I said when Ben was bemoaning the lack of variety in Corfu's restaurants. 'We'd love it and we could go to the Bengal Lounge tomorrow and give you the best curry in London.'

'Yes, do,' James said. 'Remember how we tried to beat the uni Curry Club phaal challenge and you chickened out after only one mouthful?'

Ben laughed. 'How could I ever forget? No amount of water or lager could quench that fire. But one night in London's enough for me, thanks. I only came up here to see you guys. Too many journeys on that stinking Tube and I'll be heading back to the airport like a shot.'

Of course, that only encouraged me to repeat my complaints about longing to escape the stifling Underground, delayed trains, bad weather and germ-laden passengers.

'Then why don't you both do what I did?' Ben said. 'I could never go back to commuting in London after living in Corfu. So why not get away from it all? You should come and work with us for a season or two.' He helped himself to another pancake and packed it with duck and crispy seaweed. 'You could see if you liked the island and give yourselves time to look for a place of your own.'

'We're going to need more pancakes,' I said, nudging James, who was already waving at the waiter and ordering another round of Tsingtao beers. I needed a second or two to think about this proposition, but it already had its attractions when I looked at the icy sleet outside, beating at the steamy windows.

'Are you serious?' James asked, when Ben repeated his offer.

'Totally.' Ben gave a vigorous nod of his head as he rolled himself another fat duck pancake. 'I know you guys really well and trust you, and we could do with a couple more Brits in the business, given how most of our clients come from here. It's manic though, especially in the height of the season. You've got to be prepared to turn your hand to everything. You could be answering the phone one minute, meeting guests at the airport the next or updating the website and helping out in the restaurant.'

I looked at James. He was smiling. 'What do you think?' I asked.

'It sounds great. Could be just the opportunity we're looking for.'

I caught sight of my reflection in the mirrored wall, engraved with bamboo groves and flights of birds, opposite our table. In the half-light of the restaurant the hollows under my eyes and in my cheeks seemed deeper than ever, my complexion looked dull and grey. Such a contrast to Ben, whose golden skin and bleached-blond hair were clear evidence of the many long, hot summers he had enjoyed.

Ben was smiling back at us. 'I could really do with some reliable help next year. With another baby on the way, Eleni isn't going to be able to work half as much next season and the business is growing fast.'

'I wouldn't want us to commit to working with you long-term,' I said. 'Though it would be a great help to start with, so one summer might be all right.'

James hugged me. 'I agree. And you know how I've always been mad about cooking.' I could see he was feeling he needed to justify his reasons for leaving his present job and turn this opportunity to his advantage. He hesitated, then went on, 'And I've often talked about doing it for a living one day… well, I was thinking… so how would you feel if I worked some of the time in your kitchen as well? Not permanently, mind, as eventually I'd like my own place. But would you have a problem with that?'

Ben laughed. 'The kitchen's Eleni's domain, so you'd have to contend with her. But it's fine by me, as long as you don't set up shop next door to us.' He gave James a playful punch. 'And there's plenty of scope for higher-end restaurants now. We're getting more sophisticated visitors year after year, who demand more than the same old Greek salads and moussaka. The locals don't always take to us pushing in, but you should go for it, mate. It's a great idea and I'll help you find premises, if you like.'

'Just somewhere to live, at first,' I said, 'James's restaurant dream might have to wait for a while, till we're absolutely sure.'

'Oh, I can help you with a place to stay, no problem. We're already doing up some apartments ready for next season. If you don't mind a bit of decorating as well, you can have one of them. Or you can camp out in some of the villas, when they're not occupied.'

I think it was the first time in our lives we had made an impetuous decision. And I remember we toasted our future in beer, then laughed about two high-flying professionals packing it in to work odd jobs for Ben. There would be so many new skills to learn, but little did we know then how much more we would learn about ourselves.

Chapter Six

7 June 1944

Doctor Batas is normally a cautious man. He knows that he is risking his life. This is not a decision to be taken lightly. He and Isaac Nikokiris have talked about this moment many times, ever since he delivered Isaac's youngest daughter, Anna, three years ago. And when the Germans invaded the island in the autumn, imprisoning and executing the Italian troops who had occupied Corfu for over two years, their conversations took on an even more serious tone. The Italians hadn't complied with the German deportation policy and had told the Jews to escape while there was still time, but the community refused to believe that the Germans would ever come to the island and make them leave. They had always lived harmoniously with their Greek neighbours, but gradually, when they saw how the island's mayor collaborated with the Germans and news filtered through from other parts of Greece, their fears grew.

'Perla and I cannot thank you enough,' Isaac says when he and his wife finally bring the sleeping girls to the doctor's house in darkness. 'You are a brave man to take such a risk. We hope we will return to repay you, but if we do not come back, then surely you will be repaid in Heaven.'

'There is no time for speeches,' Batas says. He is fully aware that he would be shot for helping this innocent family, shot for depriving the Germans of just two little Jewish children, shot for depleting their tally of Jews. 'I have been afraid it would come to this, ever since we heard what happened in Salonika last year. They took everyone, promising work, but they have not been heard of since. If the rumours are true, there is no time to waste. I must leave immediately, while the children are sleeping.'

He is sure he can deliver his special cargo safely to Georgiou further up the coast, as long as he isn't stopped. The children are fast asleep. Perla has dosed them as instructed, so they shouldn't make a sound for several hours. But what if his car is searched? The Germans have some respect for his profession, but following the recent bombing by the Allies, the guards are more nervous and there are patrols all around the island. He will have to say he is on his way to a serious accident at a village the other side of the mountains, and that he must be allowed to proceed without delay or there will be consequences.

He daren't take the straight and easy coast road to the north, so he heads out of Corfu Town in a westerly direction, away from the port where most of the troops are gathering to ensure the frightened people don't escape from the island on fishing boats. He knows this is his only chance to get the girls away. Once they wake, they might cry for their mother – they wouldn't understand why they have been spirited from their bed in the middle of the night and are trapped in the boot of a car.

The roads along the west coast are the most likely to have patrols, watching for signs of Allied planes and ships arriving from Italy, so he drives along the back roads, passing fields of maize and wheat that have not yet been seized by the Germans. But he has only got as far as Gardelades when he sees lights ahead of him. Two guards step out into the middle of the road, guns pointed towards the car. 'Halt!' they shout, advancing on him.

Batas winds down his window but keeps the engine running in the hope that if the children stir, the slightest sound will be masked by the rattling of his old car. He holds out his authorisation from Mayor Kollas, permitting him to drive anywhere on the island to save lives and limbs.

'*Guten Abend,*' he says. 'I have been summoned to Ano Kora-kiana. There has been a serious accident at the olive press there. I must attend as a matter of urgency, to ensure they can continue with the pressing of oil. Supplies are running short at the garrison in Corfu Town.' The Germans know nothing of the island's seasons; he is sure they don't realise olives are harvested and pressed in late autumn, they just greedily recquisition supplies wherever they find them, leaving nothing for the local people. Corfu is lucky, with its abundant winter rainfall ensuring good crops, but in the city of Athens and on other less fertile islands, people are starving to death on the streets and in their homes because of the invaders' demands for resources.

The soldiers both study the permit. Most of it is printed in Greek, which he guesses they probably can't read, but they recognise the signature of the mayor and their commandant and wave Batas on his way. He resumes his journey slowly so they won't suspect his heart is beating so fast he feels breathless. Then once they are out of sight, he begins to drive faster, praying he won't be apprehended again.

Having given the guards a false destination, he judges it safest to head in that direction, then take the winding mountain roads through Sokraki and down through the village of Spartilas, where people used to gather in the old days for the walnut festival under its ancient trees. The hairpin bends of these hilly tracks will cost him valuable time, but then he can risk picking up the less-watched coastal road past Barbati and Nissaki to speed his journey to the north-east corner of the island, where Georgiou is waiting for this very special delivery.

Chapter Seven

Amber

March 2006

Rain was still falling on the flagstones of the town's narrow alleyways and pouring from bulging awnings and balconies, but it wasn't cold and grey like English rain; it was fresh, bringing the promise of new growth as the island came back to life after the winter. We ran between the high tenements, laughing, dodging the torrents that splashed us every time a broom emptied the stretched wet canvas above us.

It was early March when we arrived in Corfu, and at first James was afraid I might grow despondent in the damp weather, but while only a short time ago I had been cursing the English winter, here, despite the rainstorms, I was optimistic. It wasn't really cold, there was no snow and I'd been told the island's winter rains are a vital part of Corfu's life cycle – to be celebrated, not bemoaned.

We had driven into Corfu Town on one of the wettest days that spring, to visit an estate agent recommended by Ben. 'I want lemon trees and a pool, at the very least,' I told James, as we drove along the coastal road overlooking tiny Mouse Island, with its white chapel and tall dark cypress trees.

'Absolutely, and we want a terrace where our guests can eat under a shady vine in the summer,' James said, 'as well as a view of the sea.' We had high hopes of finding the perfect property after seeing some of the beautiful homes Ben managed and let out to holidaymakers. And when we reached the estate agent's office, slightly damp and breathless from running through the rain, we found the windows full of bright pictures of white villas draped with vines, lush with grapes and garlands of purple bougainvillea, cushioned sun loungers arranged around sparkling pools overlooking the deep blue sea. But our hopes fell when Katarina, the plump but glamorous proprietor, handed us a dog-eared list of less impressive properties, once we had told her our budget.

'You English are responsible for the prices,' she laughed, brushing her shoulder-length bleached hair aside with a waft of heavy scent and a clatter of bangles. 'It used to be known as the Durrell effect,' she added, in reference to the author of *My Family and Other Animals*, as she rummaged in her filing cabinet to find more particulars. 'Now it's often called Kensington-on-Sea, because of the number of well-to-do English visitors who come every year.'

'But that's just along the north-east coast,' I said. 'I've heard the south of the island is on a par with Faliraki, isn't it?'

Katarina frowned. 'In parts, it would seem so. And you English certainly don't help! We are very shocked at the outrageous behaviour of some of your young people, especially the girls, who drink as much as the boys. But the older visitors and the families who have been coming for years, those we like.' Her frown then changed to a smile. 'And I am sure we can find you just the kind of property you want.'

We looked through the details of various houses and existing businesses, none of which were as splendid as the spacious villas displayed in the window. Anything within walking distance of the sea, especially near the popular resorts, was wildly expensive, even the properties that were only half built. Most houses further inland didn't have the potential for us to develop both the restaurant and guest accommodation, and many were owned by families unwilling to fully relinquish control of their property.

We had also noticed, on our frequent drives from Corfu Town along the north-east coast, how many of the older buildings were interspersed with concrete foundations sprouting rusted scaffolding. When we asked Katarina about those sites, she waved her hands with their heavy gem-set rings. 'The owners, they build when they have money and when they don't, the work just stops. Some of them will stay like that for years, but they'll never sell up. They like to keep it in the family.'

'Now is perhaps not the best time to look,' she added, when she had finished running through the properties currently available. 'You will have to be patient. Owners want to make the most of the summer lettings and at the end, especially if they have had a poor season, they may be more willing to part with their property. Late September, October, there will be more choice, I am sure. In the meantime, you should get to know the island thoroughly, explore the areas away from the tourists.'

We left the office feeling a little deflated. We had left London with such high hopes of finding our perfect place in the sun quickly, and even though we knew we would have to work for a while before we could open the restaurant, we had been quite convinced it wouldn't take very long.

'Let's get a coffee before we head back,' I said. 'We don't have to do any more painting straight away.' On Ben's instructions, we were giving The Lemon Grove's bedrooms a fresh coat of white paint, obliterating the stencilled patterns the owner had thought would enhance the rooms.

'And then I want to stop off at the market,' James said. 'I want to try cooking lamb with prunes. I think it will be similar to that Moroccan dish you like with the dried apricots.'

'Sounds good. At least you're not going to force me to eat rabbit again.' I grabbed James's arm as we began running through the narrow, wet alleyways in the old quarter of the town. We were beginning to find our way through the maze of back streets, crumbling doorways and arches and knew where to find the best butcher, an old bakery with a flaking green door and the pharmacy.

The festering odour of dank drains, overflowing from the rain, was punctuated by the pungent cleanliness of doorsteps freshly scrubbed with bleach.

In the warren of high stuccoed buildings, painted terracotta, yellow and green, shops that would soon open for the hordes of summer tourists were still quiet and shuttered, but we could hear the life of the town all around us – children laughing as they ran home from school, mothers calling to each other from doorways, a lone scooter spluttering towards the main square and a caged bird trilling from a window far above us. At one point, we lost our bearings in the narrow alleyways. 'I think this is the old Jewish quarter,' I said as James was trying to find the way to our favourite cafe looking out towards the town's main square, where Ben said cricket was played in summer.

We found our way there again, and few of the outside tables on the sheltered Liston Terrace were occupied on that rainy day, but there were several people inside sipping the strong Greek coffee. 'Actually, I don't really mind the rabbit,' I said, once we'd ordered. 'I'm just not convinced it's something you should have on the menu.' I couldn't bear the sight of the skinned bodies, still with their heads, ears and paws, lying on the butcher's slab, awaiting the crash of a cleaver. I thought many English tourists would feel the same way.

'Menu?' James shook his head. 'There won't ever be a menu if we don't find a site for the restaurant. All I've got at the moment is ideas. I'm just exploring what's seasonally available and tweaking it to suit modern tastes. Rabbit is something the islanders would traditionally have hunted and cooked, and it's such an underused meat these days. It might become a regular feature, or it might not.'

I held his hand. 'I know, darling. I understand what you want to achieve. And you will do it, eventually.'

James smiled at my concern and, as he stroked my hand while he talked, I noticed tiny flecks of white paint sticking to his cuticles and knuckles. 'I think we've got to be different to the hundreds of tavernas all offering the same fare,' he said. 'I don't want us to be yet another anonymous place dishing out moussaka with pizza, steak and chips and fried calamari on the side. I want us to really celebrate the produce of this beautiful place, like the local lamb, the tremendous variety of fish and the wonderful fresh vegetables. Remember the taste and colour of those big tomatoes Eleni served the other night? They could never make their way into a super-market in England. Far too misshapen for our customers, much too tasty for English housewives.'

'Enough, James, enough. You don't need to lecture me, of all people. I understand exactly what you want to achieve and I'm wholly in favour. Modern Macedonia. Ideal Ionian. Whatever you want to call it, I'm with you, one hundred per cent.'

That night, despite our lack of house-hunting success, Ben was exuberant. 'Limoncello,' he cried. 'We must toast your new career with limoncello.' He waved the frosted glass bottle above the table and poured shots into four glasses, which we all had to toss back in one quick gulp.

It wasn't fiery like Metaxa, the Greek brandy, nor did it taste of cough mixture like the local ouzo; it was strong, but sweet and fresh like the whole island, which had been revived, after the scorching heat of summer, by the heavy rains of winter. We sat at a table on the terrace of the family restaurant, shielded from the cold wind blowing in from the sea by the waterproof rain shield that enveloped the building all winter, just like one of those clear plastic rain capes sold at music festivals. Inside this rattling raincoat, we could see and hear the choppy waves breaking onto the beach, still littered with driftwood and debris from several months of wintry storms. Soon the restaurant would reopen for business and throughout the whole summer every table would be booked for lunch and dinner by visitors who had heard of Eleni's prowess as a chef, but during the winter it was only open at weekends, when local families left Corfu Town to visit the beach and the countryside.

'I hope you don't mind mucking in and doing menial tasks,' Ben said when we'd downed our drinks. 'We all have to be prepared to turn our hand to everything and anything to keep the business going.' He turned to his dark-haired wife, glowing in the seventh month of her pregnancy. 'Even Eleni here. She cooks, but she's more than capable of refurbishing the villas or picking up a paintbrush if needs be.'

Eleni laughed and pushed her still-full shot glass towards her husband. 'And Ben, he thinks he can do everything himself, but he can't. He is not, how do you say, the Jack of all things.'

'Jack of all trades, you mean,' I said. Eleni smiled and snapped her fingers, as if to say *So close.* 'And nor are we,' I went on, 'but we're both more than happy to try and help in any way we can. We're just so excited to be here.' So far we had helped with spring cleaning, checked sun beds for rust, swept terraces of fallen leaves and cleared branches from driveways. We'd rolled paint over walls, drained swimming pools and cleared dishwashers of broken glass and washing machines of lone socks. We'd collected abandoned lilos from pool houses, discarded snorkels from cupboards and forgotten sex toys from the back of wardrobe drawers. Nothing was too much trouble.

'You both have clean driving licences, I take it?' Ben said. 'Because once the season starts I might sometimes need you down at the airport, meeting and greeting, that sort of thing.'

'Holding up a placard,' James laughed. 'Like taxi drivers at Heathrow?'

'Exactly. You'd be very good at it. I can see you now, doffing your cap.' Ben gave James a friendly shove on the shoulder. 'But seriously, when we're in the middle of the season it's manic. You might need to go to the airport, you might have to step in and help clean on a changeover day if the maid is sick or I might need a hand settling newcomers into the properties. You won't believe how busy it gets, all of a sudden.'

'That's all right, mate,' James laughed. 'We can do whatever you want.'

'Well, I think that calls for another drink then,' said Ben, reaching for the bottle again.

It was one of many friendly dinners, lunches and meetings. As the holiday season got into full swing, there was less time to socialise and we all had to work flat out. But that spring we got to know the layout of the island, especially the north-east coast where the majority of Ben's holiday villas were located, and we began to know characters we would never be able to forget.

Chapter Eight

7 June 1944

Georgiou is waiting in a rough wooden shack beside the road, at the very top of the narrow stony track that zigzags through the neglected olive groves clinging to the steep hillside. Only someone born on this rocky coast knows that this treacherous path leads to a hidden bay of plenty, where there are fish in the sea and abundant vegetables in a fertile garden. And so far, Georgiou crosses himself, the Germans have not ventured away from the main road and discovered his secluded house surrounded by olive and fruit trees, overlooking the clear waters of the sea.

In the good days, before the war, the simple shelter where he waits was used as a communal collection point for the area's olive harvest. Here they weighed the fruit each smallholder gathered in nets spread beneath their trees, so everyone would have the correct allocation of precious golden olive oil to see them through until the next harvest. Then the olives were all taken to the Batas press near Nissaki.

Georgiou has known and trusted the Batas family since he was a boy, sailing and fishing in the bay with the lad who became a respected doctor and who has continued to visit every summer, when the waters are warm and the peaches are ripe. And when the doctor asked if he and his wife Agata would help to hide two children, if their fears about the Germans were proved not to be unfounded, he readily agreed. Children would make Agata happy, whatever their origin.

In the old days, before each person left the roadside weighing station after delivering their olives, they would say a prayer at the nearby shrine dedicated to St Spyridon, who has saved the island from plague and other disasters four times, according to local legend. *Much good he is doing us now*, Georgiou thinks. *Prayer alone could not save us from the Italians, and certainly not from the Germans.*

He peers out of his shelter and down the main road. Is that a car he can hear? Every night since he received word from Dr Batas a week ago, he has waited up here, trying to sleep on the rough floor on a thin bed of sacking and straw, waking with a start every time he thinks he hears a sound. Usually it is the chiming call of the scops owl, but now he is sure he can hear the low whining of an engine and he sees a faint arc of light sweeping across the winding road. Please let it be him and not a German patrol.

And then the familiar car appears, its lights on half beam, and as it slows down, Georgiou steps forward to greet the doctor. 'You have them with you?'

'They are still fast asleep, my friend,' Batas says. 'With luck they will not wake until you have them safely in bed.' He jumps out of the car and opens the roomy boot. It is hard for Georgiou to see them properly, but he and the doctor each pick up a sleeping child, bundled in a blanket, then gently place them on a cushioned bed of straw in the handcart waiting beside the shack.

'Are you taking them down to your house all by yourself?' Batas asks.

Georgiou shakes his head. 'I have help. My donkey is grazing a little further down the path. I keep him out of sight of the Germans. They do not care what they use for target practice. I can pull the cart myself for a short stretch and he will take us the rest of the way.'

'Their mother gave me this as well,' Batas says, handing over another bundle. 'Clothes and shawls, I believe. I hope there will be enough to keep them warm if this goes on through another winter.'

'We shall do our best. There will always be a meal for them and Agata will find a way to clothe them. Have the parents left yet?'

'They'll round them up very soon. Maybe tomorrow, with the older sister, unfortunately. The Germans are telling everyone they will be going to work in the East. But I fear the worst. Since they confiscated all the radios we cannot know for sure, but there are rumours of extermination. Those taken from Salonika have not yet written home about their good fortune. Thank God we have rescued these little ones at least. Now go, before they wake and cry.'

Georgiou shakes the doctor's hand and begins pulling the cart down the steep path. Before he disappears out of sight, he turns and salutes, saying, 'God go with you.'

Chapter Nine

James

July 2006

I well remember the first time I met Greg. It was Ben's fault that we met. I find myself attributing some element of blame to everyone connected with that time in our lives, and Ben was responsible for the idea of us having a financial backer.

We were chatting late at the very end of a particularly busy day in early July, when the season was already in full swing. Flights from the UK had been delayed, so introductions at the airport, car handovers and the delivery of the welcome hampers included in the villa rental had all collided with each other. Amber had already gone back to the apartment to catch up on sleep before yet another early start, Eleni was settling the new baby and Ben and I were sitting in a corner of the restaurant terrace with cold beers, drunk straight from the bottle. One of the regular waiters was standing on the jetty smoking a cigarette, its tip glowing in the dark, while a second waiter was shooing away a stray cat hunting for crumbs, as he swept underneath the empty tables. A small group of diners was still lingering over coffee and glasses of limoncello, but most of that evening's guests had left to walk back to their nearby villas in the warm dark of the evening, the crunch of their steps on the stony path harmonising with the sound of whirring cicadas and the soft swish of the sea on the shingled beach.

'I'm beginning to realise,' I said, 'that the kind of place we can afford is going to need a considerable amount of work. Anything up to spec is way beyond our budget and thriving restaurants simply don't seem to come onto the market.'

'Those sorts of properties tend to stay in the family,' Ben sighed. 'And you're not about to marry into a local family, like I did, are you? That's the only other way in.'

'I don't think Amber would like that idea,' I laughed.

Ben roared with laughter, and we clinked bottles. 'I think what you could do with,' he said, as we recovered from our gusts of hilarity, 'is talking to someone with a bit of an inside view on managing a project.'

'What do you mean?'

'Someone who knows their way round, knows what might be coming up and maybe could even be interested in helping you get the business going.'

I leant my chair back against the balustrade around the terrace and stretched out my legs. 'I wasn't planning on going into part-nership with anyone else. Amber and I were thinking it would be just the two of us.'

'Of course. But here you are, new country, different customs, it could help. That's all I'm saying.'

'Do you have any suggestions?'

'If I had the time to help you, I'd do it myself, but seeing as I don't, and Eleni would kill me if I took my eye off the business here for even a second, I think I should introduce you to Greg Richards. He's been coming here for years, he's dabbled in a few local enterprises quite successfully and he's built his own house here. He pretty much knows what's what and he's a sociable kind of a guy and likes helping start-ups get off the ground.'

'Greg Richards? The name kind of rings a bell. He's a very successful entrepreneur, isn't he?' I sat up straight, suddenly interested.

'That's right,' Ben nodded. 'He eats with us here quite often. You should've met him by now, but he's been away recently. I'll introduce you next time I know he's coming over.'

We met briefly a week or so later. Greg was shorter than I'd imagined. He must have been in his early sixties, maybe even a little older. He had a good head of silvery hair and was slim – from regular games of golf and tennis, so I was told. His wife, Pam, had probably always been blonde, but had grown more platinum with age. Her figure was sturdy but still attractive in a turquoise sequined tunic over her white trousers.

They were meeting friends for dinner, so Greg invited us to join him and his wife for lunch on our day off. Amber and I usually liked to use that day for swimming and relaxing, but when I explained that Greg might be a useful contact, she was happy to join me.

I was anxious to make a good impression, so we allowed plenty of time to find the villa and actually arrived about ten minutes early. The turning off the main road led down a steep lane through groves of olive trees. The large barred gates to Ocean View House were open, surprisingly, and we turned into a long, gravelled driveway lined with pink and white oleanders, which stopped a couple of hundred yards short of the house. A jeep and a white Mercedes were parked in the only shaded areas, so I had to leave our dusty Citroën in full sun, hoping that by the time we'd finished lunch some cool shade would have fallen across the car.

Amber and I made our way down to the house. We'd visited a number of beautiful villas on the island since we'd started working for Ben, but this was far more luxurious than anything we'd seen to date. For easy maintenance, most of the holiday properties had stony, sparse lawns and very little ornamental planting. But here, small lemon trees stood as sentinels in swagged stone urns along the path, classical statues posed in shaded niches and a fountain in the shape of a gilded dolphin splashed into a marble bowl set in a carpet of lush grass. A gardener was even sweeping leaves from the far side of the lawn. Clearly no expense had been spared on the property or its surroundings.

As we neared the house, we could hear raised voices and we hovered briefly, wondering if we'd come at an awkward moment. I was holding a particularly heavy potted geranium Amber had insisted was an appropriate gift, while she was carrying a couple of bottles of good wine. But after a minute or two all seemed quiet, so we continued our approach and made our entrance.

'Hello,' I called out. 'I hope we've come to the right place. Sorry we're a bit early.' We stood on the edge of the wide terrace, which was shaded with the grapevines common to all of Corfu's houses, but here there were also colonnades and sculpture, and the charcoal-grey rattan chairs and sofas were spread with plump white cushions with not a single rusty sun lounger in sight. However, the pristine limestone paving was littered with pieces of timber. Greg looked red and cross, Pam flustered.

'James, Amber,' Pam greeted us with open arms, then stopped when she saw we were burdened by the plant and the wine. 'Lovely to see you both. We're all ready for you, aren't we, darling?' she said, turning to Greg, whose face suddenly adopted a wide smile.

'Just got to clear this mess up.' He gestured at the pieces of wood and used his foot to slide them to one side of the terrace.

'Getting on with a spot of DIY?' I asked. 'I'm quite partial to doing a bit of woodwork.'

'Really?' said Greg, looking alert and pleased. 'Tell me what you think of my idea, then.' He took the potted plant from my arms, placed it in a corner of the terrace near other similar pots of geraniums and roses and steered me to one side. I looked over my shoulder to see Pam taking the bottles from Amber, then guiding her inside the house, where a maid hovered in the doorway with a tray of glasses.

Greg and I stood at the edge of the terrace, facing the sea. 'That's why I built this place,' he said, waving at the sparkling blue bay of calm water with a distant view of Corfu Town. 'You can keep your effing sunset on the other side of the island. Too bloody obvious. The moon and the dawn, that's what this place is about. Until that effing freak show erupted!' He pointed at the towering white hotel a little further down the hillside. I could see bright umbrellas, an infinity pool and flat roofs studded with air conditioning vents.

'What a marvellous spot.' I shaded my eyes as I gazed at the view. 'Can you get down to the sea from here?'

Greg pointed to a wrought-iron gate on the far side of the villa's swimming pool, where large urns on all four corners were filled with trailing geraniums and a satyr trickled a cornucopia of water onto the pool's placid surface.

'Through the gate,' he said. 'Goes right down to a private beach. Well, it would be private if the effing government and effing police didn't insist that every inch of the coastline was public property. There's another locked gate at the bottom though, so the bloody tourists can't get beyond the rocks.' He laughed. 'I've made damn sure they can't come ashore easily anyway. If there's nowhere for them to moor their bloody boats they go away and pester some other poor sod.'

'So you don't keep a boat down there yourself?'

'Nah, why would I want to? Without a decent jetty the ruddy things are too hard to board. And jetties aren't permitted either and if they were, they'd get wrecked every winter with the storms. No, we nip along to Kaminaki or Nissaki if we want a boat when we've got people staying.'

He drew breath and seemed to be contemplating the view. 'Until they built that sodding monstrosity, I had it all to myself. Wouldn't have built this place here otherwise.' His face was red again, not with the heat of the day, but with anger.

'That's a shame,' I muttered, not sure how much to say at this stage.

'Too right it's a shame,' he spat, flecks of spittle flying from his mouth in his vehemence. 'It shouldn't bloody be there. And if you think it's an eyesore now, you should hear it at night. Discos, karaoke. Effing birdie song and chirpy chirpy cheep cheep shit for hours on end.'

'That doesn't sound very upmarket,' I said – it was the only thing I could think of saying, but I felt inclined to agree with him. I hate intrusive noise.

He didn't seem to hear me. 'Bloody lawyers are useless. I've got to put up with it or sell up, they say. Well, I've got other ideas. And then we'll see how they like it.'

I didn't hear any more at that point as Pam and Amber came out of the house, followed by the maid bearing dishes of salad and bread. But I did hear about it later, when I got to know Greg better.

Chapter Ten

Amber

July 2006

'What a pair of terrible show-offs,' I blurted out when we were a safe distance from the house after lunch. 'Have you ever seen anything so ostentatious?'

'They aren't that bad,' James said, switching on the car's air conditioning, then shutting the door so we could wait outside in the shade while it cooled down. 'Some of the clients we had at the agency were far worse.'

'But all those statues? Surely you could see they were just expensive reproductions and they're in such bad taste. And you didn't even see inside the house properly. It was just as bad. Huge gaudy paintings on the staircase, hideous chandeliers and every kitchen gadget you can think of, none of them ever used, I bet. They've spent a fortune on that place. There's even a cinema in the basement. Honestly, why would you need a cinema when you've got such a wonderful view?'

We'd eaten lunch out on the terrace, under a vast angled umbrella, which supplemented the mottled shade cast by the vines. Salade Niçoise made with freshly seared tuna, just the way I liked it, in a heavy pottery bowl and a platter of tricolore salad drizzled with green olive oil. With fresh bread and the local spinach pie, it was simple but substantial.

'I thought the lunch was quite good,' James said, as if reading my thoughts. 'And they were both perfectly pleasant.'

'Honestly, James, Pam's all right, but he's awful! I'm sure he chose all those pretentious sculptures himself. She's much more down-to-earth.'

'I quite liked him, actually.'

'I know you did. I heard the two of you killing yourselves laughing when I was dragged inside to chat with Pam. And again, when I was taken on the guided tour afterwards. You were sniggering at everything he said all through lunch too. Just what was so funny?'

James didn't seem to hear my question, he just said, 'Come on. The car's cooled down now. We can get going.'

We climbed in and I drove off in silence, but after a while I couldn't resist returning to the subject; they'd made such an impression on me. 'I know Ben thinks Greg would be a useful contact, but you don't honestly think you'd value his opinion, do you?'

'Okay, maybe not on decor perhaps, but on managing a project, on construction, yeah, I think I would respect his judgement. He's done a ton of work on the island. There's a lot to be said for that.'

As I drove, I fell silent thinking again about the house we had just seen. Pam was obviously proud of her home and was keen to show me the whole interior. All seven bedrooms had marble en suite bathrooms, there was a mirrored wet room accessed from the garden for quick showers after swimming, and every bedroom had its own flatscreen television. The basement utility room had two washing machines, which she pointed out, saying, 'I told Greg we had to have two if he wants the maid to cope with his demand for freshly laundered shirts all the time. And when Lavinia and the boys are here, the number of towels they get through, you wouldn't believe. And as for the bed linen, well, I insist it's changed twice a week and the girl wouldn't keep up with that if we didn't have the facilities. There's nothing I like more than fresh sheets, especially in this climate.'

I couldn't help smiling to myself as she spoke, thinking of the crumpled unmade bed in our temporary home on the island and how bedding was lucky to be changed once a month back in our London flat, when we were both busy working long hours. But despite the cleanliness and the immaculate order of the villa, I didn't warm to it at all. It had quiet air conditioning in every room, neatly rolled towels on shelves in every bathroom, electrically controlled blinds in all the bedrooms and music piped throughout the house; it felt like a shiny modern hotel, not a comfortable, much-loved home. Now and then there were occasional glimpses into Pam's character, such as the collection of porcelain and pottery frogs in her bathroom ('I happened to say how much I liked Paul McCartney's frog song once and now everyone buys them for me all the time'), and a scattering of family photographs in every room, which she pointed out, saying, 'Lavinia and her darling boys. Look, isn't this one of Anton when he was skiing just adorable? I gave him that red bobble hat for Christmas so he'd stand out if they lost him in the snow.'

Despite the frogs and the photographs, it was a cold, gleaming show house, designed just for that purpose, to show off its owners' wealth and influence. I pictured all the villas James and I had stayed in since we'd arrived in Corfu. We'd envied some for their views, others for the size of their pool and some for their sympathetic restoration of ancient buildings, but my favourite was the simplest of them all. Poised above a stony beach, there was a little gardener's cottage, bordered by low white walls, over which there was a clear view of the open sea. It only had one bedroom and no air conditioning, there was a tiny kitchen and a simple shower room, but it was secluded, surrounded by lemon and orange trees that we could smell even when we latched the green shutters fast at night. Ben said it wasn't suitable for winter accommodation as it was so close to the sea, with its high waves and storms, but I loved the thought of being inside with a blazing olive wood fire, hearing the winds batter the barred shutters and the sea crashing on the shore.

I knew what Pam would say about my little cottage. She'd say it would do for the maid. And as for Greg, well, he'd pull it all down and develop the site as another soulless edifice to his wealth.

Chapter Eleven

8 June 1944

When Rebekka wakes, the house is much quieter than usual. Why are her little sisters not crying for their breakfast or calling to her to help them dress? They are always awake early, saying they are hungry, clinging to Mama in the hope of an extra crust. She can hear footsteps below her bedroom and low murmuring, then the scrape of a pan and the sound of water, but not the high-pitched voices of children nor the scampering of little feet.

Last night, after their poor supper, she had argued with Papa. 'Let me stay with them please. I am old enough to look after Matilde and Anna on my own.'

'No. It is no use,' Papa had said. 'We have to go. They know we live here. Everybody is going to the square and we must go too. They have a list and all our names are there. They want us to work for them. That is all. We are going away to work for them.'

Rebekka had reached for her father's hand. Her mother looked stern but her eyes were brimming with tears. She was folding the younger children's few clothes into a large shawl. 'But Matilde and Anna are too young to work for the Germans. They are only little children. They cannot be sent away to work. Please, Papa, let me stay with them. We will be very quiet and then they will think we have gone with you.'

'No, my child, they would come for you all the same. Remember, they know we live here. Every week they have checked our names in the roll call on the Spianada. But they do not know about Matilde and Anna and I have made arrangements. Come, be calm, do not be afraid. They will be safe.'

Rebekka throws on her dress and runs downstairs to find Mama furiously scouring a pot in the kitchen. 'Where are Matilde and Anna?' she asks her mother.

When Mama lifts her head from the sink, Rebekka can see she has been weeping. 'Your father and I have done what we think is best. You must not ask us any more.'

'But I could look after them. I could stay with them.'

'Your name is on the list, Rebekka. Matilde and Anna have not been counted in the roll call. It is better this way.' Then Mama turns her back to her, scrubbing hard, angrily scraping and cleaning so her tears cannot be seen or heard.

Rebekka runs downstairs to the shop and is about to run outside when Papa grabs her by the arm. 'No, you cannot go out. We are not allowed to leave our homes today. The Germans have ruled that everyone from the Evraiki must stay indoors all day. You would be in danger if you break their curfew.' He takes her in his arms and holds her in a warm embrace. 'Please, my daughter, your mother and I need you to do as we say. It is better that way.'

Rebekka knows she cannot argue with him. She turns away and crouches in a corner of the shop, next to a heap of dusty, forgotten shoes. She pulls Katya, her skinny white cat, onto her lap and strokes her fur, finding the purring soothes her. The cat is thin, but her belly is bulging again. Perhaps this time she will be allowed to keep the kittens in place of her little sisters.

Chapter Twelve

James

July 2006

While I could understand Amber's dislike of Greg's villa, I was thinking more about the character of the man I'd just met, not his taste in decor. He had a boyish sense of humour I liked, a sense of mischief which reminded me of a boy in the year above me at school who'd always devised imaginative and hilarious escapades, such as pinning comic moustaches on all the portraits of the school's former headmasters lining the grand staircase leading from the main entrance hall. Greg had listened with interest when Amber and I outlined our plans for the restaurant, but I could also see myself enjoying a drink with him and playing practical jokes on anyone who crossed us.

When Amber had gone inside the house with Pam after lunch, Greg had suddenly said, 'Are you a cricketer?'

'I've played a bit in the past.'

'Any good at bowling? Or any kind of throwing?' He looked impish, a smile creasing his eyes, then he beckoned.

I couldn't imagine what he had in mind. He led me back to the edge of the terrace and pointed towards the hotel's roof. 'Think you could reach that?'

'Maybe. Might stand a better chance down by the pool, perhaps.'

'We're higher up here. I was thinking the angle might help. Let's both try.' He reached down behind a tall urn and brought up a plant pot filled with large pebbles. 'Here, take your pick.'

I selected a stone, weighed it in my hand, leant back and then threw. It landed in the bushes that marked the boundary between Greg's garden and the hotel grounds. Then Greg tried, with a similar result. We both tried a couple more times, then we walked down a flight of steps to the pool and stood there in full sun, trying to decide on the best vantage point for another attempt.

'Perhaps we'd have a better view further down the path to the beach,' I said, so we both went through the iron gate and onto a stony path cut into the hillside, with short flights of rough steps every few yards.

The track was overhung with thickly entwined juniper and myrtle, their dark branches shading us and making it difficult to see the hotel. I climbed up a tree near the boundary and found it offered a good view of the hotel's pool, surrounded by sun loungers underneath large umbrellas. 'You'd have no trouble hitting the water from here,' I called down to Greg. We inspected another couple of hundred yards of the trail, then made our way back up to the terrace.

We stood there, contemplating the hotel. Greg was tossing a stone from hand to hand, deep in thought. 'It needs more power,' he said. 'I was having a go at making some kind of contraption just before you got here. A kind of catapult, on a grand scale.'

'Catapult? Now you're talking. Though mine got me into some hot water at school.'

'Me too,' he smirked. 'Maybe we'd better not go there, eh?'

'It's a good idea though.' We both fell silent again, until I said, 'Why are we doing this, exactly?'

'Closure,' said Greg. 'I want the effing place closed down. I want it to fail big time. If the sodding lawyers can't find a way to do it, then I will.'

'So how will the stones help?'

A wicked smile crept across his face. 'That was just the test run. I was thinking more like say… cat shit.' He turned and pointed to the skinny tabby scraping at the thin dirt of the flowerbed below the terrace. 'The bloody moggies are everywhere. We've probably got twenty cats crawling all over the place, crapping on every square inch of bare earth, so that's a lot of ammunition. I was thinking a lot of cat shit in the air vents and the air con on the roof would sour the atmosphere for them down there.'

I couldn't help myself. Although the idea was disgusting, he looked so mischievous that I laughed and laughed. Part of me was shocked, but the other half, the half that had enjoyed a good lunch and several glasses of wine and appreciated a prank, said, 'Then it's obvious. Forget the roof, you've got to concentrate on the pool. If it gets polluted, they'll have to keep draining it out. That should soon put people off all right.'

Greg liked the idea and that was the laughter Amber heard. But I didn't explain it to her. I didn't think she'd appreciate the joke.

Chapter Thirteen

Amber

July 2006

As I opened the car door, the air buzzed with heat and I felt the dry dust rising from the track. We had managed to park in a sliver of shade, but with the morning temperature already well over 35°C that offered little relief from the oven-like heat. It was late July and the island was getting steadily hotter by the day.

I closed the door on the cool interior of the car and I knew I was going to find this an ordeal. James was keen to see the old village and was already striding ahead on the stony road, a small dust cloud marking his progress.

'Get a move on,' he called, turning round, taking a couple of steps backwards as he walked, rather than stopping and waiting for me. 'Let's see as much as we can before it gets any hotter.' He adjusted his cap and resumed his stride.

'Hang on a minute,' I called, clutching the large bottle of water I knew I'd soon need. I'd only taken a few steps when my sandal caught a sharp stone and I stumbled. I cursed and called for James, but he was already far ahead. 'I've hurt my foot,' I cried, although I knew he could not hear.

I hopped to a low wall beneath a prickly bush. By now James was out of sight and the track was empty. I took off my sandal and rested my injured foot on my knee. Gritty dust filled the bleeding cut on my big toe, so I poured a little of my precious water over it. The wound stung and I couldn't help a sharp intake of breath. Then, as I stared at my injury, I heard footsteps crunching behind me.

'James, you could have waited,' I started to say, and turned round to look at him. But it wasn't my husband. It was a tall bearded man, wearing a white shirt and blue trousers.

'May I be of assistance, madam?' His English was excellent, his tone educated. He removed his sunglasses as he spoke, revealing dark brown eyes.

'Oh, it's nothing. Just a stone, that's all.'

'Allow me.' He knelt in front of me, peering at my bleeding toe, then pulled a clean white handkerchief from his pocket. 'May I?' He took the water bottle from my hand, then poured a little onto the clean cloth before wrapping it around the wound. 'There. It is clean and it will heal soon.'

'Thank you,' I said, still looking down at his large hand holding my dusty foot.

He stood up and looked down the track. 'Would you like me to escort you to your husband, madam?'

'Amber Young,' I said, shaking his outstretched hand. I stuffed my bandaged foot back in my sandal, then allowed him to help me to my feet.

'Dimitri Barberis.' He gave the slightest bow of his head as he said his name. It was an old-fashioned gesture, which made me like him all the more. 'At your service.'

After a few faltering steps on the stony track, I almost stumbled again and threw my arms wide to save myself.

'Please, madam, take my arm. For your own safety.' He took my hand and tucked it around his forearm. My skin looked darker than ever against his white shirtsleeve and the tips of my fingers glowed with the bright orange varnish I'd chosen that day, like a little cluster of black and tangerine marigolds.

Walking slowly, with me limping and him guiding, I finally caught sight of my husband standing in the shade of a dilapidated building. 'James,' I called out, 'I've hurt my foot.'

He turned and didn't seem very surprised that I'd acquired a male companion. 'Honestly, Amber, I only left you alone for a few minutes.'

'I know. It was my stupid sandals. I should have worn something sturdier. This is Mr Barberis. He found me and helped me.' I slipped my hand from my rescuer's side and reached for James's arm.

'Thank you very much for looking after my wife, Mr Barberis,' James said, shaking the man's hand.

'My pleasure. Is this your first visit to the island?'

'Yes and no. We've been here a while and we're actually working for a friend. But we've come to see the village because we've heard there's some property for sale here.'

'Then let me help you. I know many of the local owners. I can show you around.' Dimitri produced his wallet and handed James a card. 'But perhaps first some refreshment, to help your wife recover from her accident.'

James looked at me and I nodded my acceptance. 'Thank you,' he said. 'We'd like that. But we shouldn't take too long. It's already getting very hot.'

Minutes later we were sitting on a shaded veranda, where vines shielded us from the sun. Cool water and traditional coffee were served by the moustachioed owner, who evidently knew Dimitri well, for they embraced and spoke rapidly in Greek.

'My cousin Costas tells me there is a beautiful farmhouse on the edge of the village which would be perfect for you. I will take you there shortly.'

'That's very kind of you,' said James, taking a slip of paper from his pocket. 'But a friend told me about another house here too. Do you happen to know where this one is?'

Dimitri studied the note and passed it to the cafe owner, who studied it then shrugged, exclaiming again in his rapid manner, the speed of his Greek way beyond our basic comprehension. Dimitri turned back to us. 'Costas thinks it is not so good, my friends. But if you wish, I will show you this house as well.'

We sipped our water and coffee while he talked. 'My profession is surveyor. I build new but also I make good the old. Many people are now interested in acquiring our oldest homes here. It is good for us and it will bring business back to the interior of the island. There is much development on the coast, but that life is not for everyone. So it is excellent you have come here to see what you can find.'

'It's so very peaceful up here,' I said, looking across the valley where sheep were grazing on the steep rocky hillsides. 'No scooters, no jeeps, hardly any people.'

'But remember, those who come are here because they appreciate the beauty and solitude. We get many people walking, studying the flowers and the wildlife. Especially in spring. Ah, that is the best time to be here. When the winter rain has finished, the hills are covered with the most beautiful flowers. It is like a garden everywhere.' He spread his hands in a gesture encompassing all the surrounding land and I could imagine a botanical tapestry of many colours, freshly painted.

James was frowning. 'So it's totally empty up here in the winter months. At least the resorts on the coast still have a few visitors then.'

'But that is a good time for us too. We reclaim it for ourselves. People can relax when the visitors go home after the summer. We walk and cycle, hunt and shoot, and we can enjoy the beauty for ourselves. And my friend,' he patted James's shoulder, 'if you can become like a Kerkyran and adapt to the seasons, then you will be successful always.'

'Sounds like you still have to make the most of the tourist season though,' said James. 'Right, we'd better go and look at these properties.' He stood up and waited for me to follow.

I tried to stand, putting weight on my injured foot, and James heard the sound I made as I winced.

'Oh really, Amber. We've come all this way specially. We don't get another day off for a week.'

'It's all right. You go ahead, I'll follow. I don't want to hold you up.'

'Perhaps you will permit me?' Dimitri offered his arm again in support.

'Thank you, but I'll be fine. You go with James and show him round. I'll just take my time.'

The men set out along the rough cobbled street, Dimitri gesturing at buildings on either side as they went. I sat down again and watched them. James, with his bare legs, rubber flip flops and cap, looked so juvenile compared with Dimitri in his well-washed but clean shirt and trousers. I sipped a little more water and looked around me. Large white butterflies were flitting over the oleander and I could hear a cockerel calling in the distance. It really was very peaceful, and I began to think we had found paradise.

Chapter Fourteen

8 June 1944

Agata hears their cries early in the morning. 'Mama, Papa,' they call over and over. She runs upstairs to the little room where she had tucked the two comatose children into bed the night before, when Georgiou returned with his secret cargo. The girls had hardly stirred in their drugged sleep and she had laid them down back to back, so each would be comforted by the solid warmth of the other.

'Shh, don't cry, my little ones. You are safe here with us.' She kneels down by the bed so they won't feel threatened by this strange woman. The little girls are sitting up, their eyes fearful, cheeks stained with tears. They are pale from their months of seclusion; hidden from prying eyes and the tally of the roll call since the Germans invaded last September.

'Where's Mama?' the eldest says. But the younger child has no words to express her bewilderment, she just wails and rubs her eyes with her little fists.

'You are Matilde, are you not?' The older girl nods. 'And your little sister is Anna?' They both nod and their crying ceases. 'Your mama and papa have had to leave Corfu for a time. They have gone away to work and they have asked me to look after you here until they return. You are going to live here with me and my husband, Georgiou, and grow big and strong. We shall feed you well and your parents will be so pleased to see how much you have grown when they come back.'

Matilde manages a small smile. 'Has Rebekka gone with them as well?'

'Yes, she has, my dear. Your sister is a big strong girl and old enough to work hard.' Agata tries to return the child's smile. She knows Rebekka is not yet fourteen, not yet fully grown, not yet a woman. God willing she will survive and come to no harm.

And how old are these little children? Five and three? What will they be able to remember of their parents, their sister and the life they once had before they were smuggled away in the night?

'Bread,' demands Anna. 'Hungry.'

'Of course you are, little one. You can't have eaten properly for ages. Come with me and you shall both have bread, milk and peaches for your breakfast.'

As both girls scramble out of the bed Agata realises the little one's dress is wet and there is a large damp patch on the mattress. 'Here,' she says, holding out her hand, 'let's take off those wet things and get you clean and dry.' She pours water into the basin on the side table, rinses out a cloth and mops both the children clean. They are so thin; every rib is visible beneath their translucent skin after their poor diet this last year. Then she dresses them in fresh clothes from the small bundle that arrived with them the night before. They are not the babies she once hoped to have, whose tiny folded garments will never leave the scented drawer she rarely opens, but they are children in need and she will protect them with her life and show them loving care.

'Now you are both clean and ready to come and eat a good breakfast.' They show they trust her by reaching up for her hands as she leads them down the stairs. Their little legs make for a slow descent, so Agata talks to them with every step. 'When we've eaten you can go outside. It is safe here and you can play in the sunshine on the beach. And I'll take you to see the chickens and we can see if they've laid any eggs yet today. And we'll pick tomatoes in the garden.' The children listen quietly to every word and then Matilde says, 'Mama doesn't allow us to play outside. We have to stay indoors all the time and be very quiet.'

'I know, my dear. Your mama is very wise. But here you can play outside every day, as long as I can see you. And you can make as much noise as you like.'

Chapter Fifteen

James

August 2006

It was the swallows that convinced Amber this was the right place. Screeching, swooping, they dived under the tiles and into the ruined house. There, in the shadows, in a scooped bowl of hardened mud, were five gaping yellow mouths, awaiting the beakfuls of insects their parents were delivering every few minutes. With black eyes they gazed at Amber and she stared back in amusement.

'I love it here,' she said. 'This is where we should live.'

I remember I laughed at her. 'In this tumbledown hovel, in the middle of the island?'

She gripped my hand. 'Maybe not this particular hovel, but somewhere in this lovely old village. Just imagine how we could bring it back to life.'

We had been back to the village several times since our first visit. Amber remembered to wear more sensible shoes and we explored the ruins, the few houses still standing, the remains of barns and the overgrown gardens and orchards.

She looked at me with her dark eyes and then turned to look again at the baby swallows, tucked side by side, tight in their cot of daub. 'It feels so right,' she said. 'Up here in the hills, I feel we're closer to the heart of the real Corfu and its past. It's not like the crowded beaches with their tacky bars or the marinas with the expensive yachts. It seems more earthy and genuine somehow.'

I put my arm around her and kissed the springy curls on the top of her head. Then we started walking again along the partly cobbled path where wildflowers and grasses grew among the warm stones. The once well populated village had been abandoned for many years, but recently, as more tourists hired cars and explored the island's interior, a handful of Kerkyrans had returned and there were now a couple of tavernas and a souvenir shop in the previously derelict houses. Some of the old buildings lacked floors and roofs, but others were largely intact and I was beginning to see that these could, with a lot of work, become habitable again.

'It could be right for us here, couldn't it?' She squeezed my hand. We stopped outside one of the less dilapidated of the crumbling houses. The heavy wooden door had flaking green paint, but there was still a roof and stairs. Slatted shutters were bolted over the lower windows and inside was a rough table, splattered with bird droppings, in front of the open fireplace. Outside, the ground was overgrown, but we could just see the outline of paving slabs marking the remains of a terrace and upright beams which had once supported a healthy vine, now wizened and unwatered.

I still had my doubts about the location, so far away from the main mass of tourists, but Amber's conviction was beginning to persuade me. I waved my hand over the hidden stones and could picture it transformed. 'I suppose this would be the main area for the restaurant. We'd have tables inside as well, of course, but I'm sure we'd have many days, even out of season, when everyone could eat outside. And it's big enough for us to do bed and breakfast as well.' I looked up the stairs. 'There must be at least five rooms up there.'

'We might not want to do bed and breakfast in the height of summer though,' Amber frowned. 'We'd be busy enough running the restaurant. But I know there are lots of walkers and cyclists in the spring when the flowers are at their best and then again in the autumn, so we could easily do rooms then.'

'But what about the winter, when the visitors have gone? It might seem very bleak up here at that time of year.'

She giggled and nudged me with her elbow. 'Then we'll have time for the repairs, making the garden wonderful and sitting by the fire,' she nudged me again, 'or on a rug in front of it.' She took a few steps across to the edge of the camouflaged terrace and gazed down at the land below, then across to the view of the hills beyond. 'If this belongs to this house too then we'll be able to grow all the melons, courgettes and tomatoes we need. And in the summer we'll have that astonishing blue morning glory that grows everywhere here, climbing all over fences and the pergola.'

'Morning glory and a vine. We've got to have a vine.'

'Of course we have,' she said, laughing again. 'We'd never be accepted around here if we didn't have a vine. And look, see down there? We've got lemon trees and olives too.'

Then she took my hand and we stood watching the scrubby bleached pasture around the village, where an old man was leading his sheep home for milking. As they trotted along the narrow path their bells tinkled with different tones.

'It's like a dream. London seems a lifetime away.'

'Only a few months, but another life. Another time.' I kissed her head. 'We can start again now.' I continued looking around the empty house. The walls were sound, the floors were intact, as was the staircase, and the rooms were spacious. There were even steps leading down to a cellar, which smelt dry and still had some dusty barrels in a corner.

'Maybe we should ask that Dimitri Barberis to look at this one with us. It would help to have a local give us an idea of the renovation costs. You've still got his card, haven't you?'

My arms slipped from her shoulders. 'I'm not sure about him. He was quite pushy about the farmhouse.' I remembered our first expedition to the village and the tour of the property on its outskirts. Dimitri had sung its praises till I'd felt uncomfortably pressured and had insisted on returning to the cafe to check on Amber. I found she had not moved, staying in the shade with her sore foot, and had used this as an excuse to leave promptly.

'Oh, come on. I thought he seemed really helpful. He'd have been happy to take us to lots of places we could never have found on our own. And though in the end we've found it for ourselves, it would still be worth having a second opinion.'

'Okay, but I think I'll ask Ben who he uses to work on the villas as well. It makes sense to get more than one quote.'

'Sure. But you like this one, don't you?' She was excited. Smiling at me. Keen for me to agree.

'I do. But just remember one swallow, or even half dozen, doesn't make a summer. I'm not sure how that's appropriate, but I think it means just because you've been captivated by those baby birds, that doesn't mean that this is the place.' I took her arm and tried to turn her towards the street.

'There were five. Babies, I mean. Then two parents as well. That's seven. My lucky number.'

'Secret seven.'

'Secret?'

'Like magpies? You know, one for sorrow, two for joy, seven for a secret never to be told.'

Amber glanced at the old fireplace and the steps leading to the cellar below. 'I expect there are secrets here too. What's eight?'

I laughed. 'Eight for a wish and nine for a kiss!' I lunged at her and caught her round the waist. She twisted away from me, squealing with delight, then clasped my hand and pulled me outside into the bright sun.

'How come you know all that nonsense, anyway?'

'My nanny used to sing to me and tell me all those old rhymes. I'm full of such rubbish.' I laughed again and began to sing, '*You shall have a fishy,*'

'*On a little dishy,*' she responded, and then we both sang, swinging our hands together as we walked along the old stones in the late afternoon sun, '*You shall have a fishy when the boat comes in.*'

It must have sounded strange to the man, watching unbeknownst to us in the shadows of the ruined house nearby; the man who was taking a close interest in our pleasure.

Chapter Sixteen

8 June 1944

Late in the day, Rebekka watches the swallows returning to their night-time roosts in the town. *Why must we leave our homes tomorrow*, she thinks, *while the swallows are allowed to stay. Every year, they come back to Corfu to mate, build their nests and feed their young, but we cannot stay because of who we are. And today, we were not even allowed to walk through our own streets. The Germans made us prisoners in our own homes.*

She leans out of her bedroom window at the very top of the house and watches the birds swirling above the roofs as the sun fades in the sky. The homes in the Evraiki are so close to each other, she feels she could almost touch the green shutters of the house across the alleyway. Lower and closer the swallows dive, screeching their greetings to one another. By day they fly high in the air, but come the evening they gather over the terracotta-roofed houses of the town, crying and swooping, finding their way back to their homes for the night.

Rebekka tilts her head to see their acrobatics. Now and then one ducks beneath a gutter, another flits through a broken roof tile. There must be hundreds overhead, circling and dipping, never colliding, calling to their mates, their chicks and their neighbours.

I wish I could fly like them, Rebekka thinks. *I wish I could hide in the tiniest gap in a roof then fly away with my children when the summer is over, knowing our homes will all be here when I return next year.*

When the Germans bombarded the Italians in the autumn, many people and birds lost their homes. The Evraiki was badly damaged and the homeless have been reduced to sleeping in the damp tunnels of the Paleo Frourio, the Old Fortress. *We were lucky, we still have our home and shop. But where did the swallows go*, she wonders. What did they think when they returned this spring and found their old nests had been destroyed?

And the swallows have not had to part with their children, they still have mouths to feed, young ones to snuggle under their wings. Rebekka misses her little sisters. If they'd been here with her, they'd have played together and told stories.

Rebekka wonders if they, too, are watching the swallows come home tonight. Her throat aches with unshed tears as she thinks of the two girls, how she brushed their curly dark hair and sang to help them fall asleep. She hopes someone is singing to them and kissing them goodnight.

The sudden slamming of a neighbour's window shutters across the alleyway disturbs her thoughts. It must be getting late. A sign that birds and people must rest and prepare for whatever will come tomorrow. She closes the shutters and the window, hoping the Nikokiris family will all return to their home one day, just as the swallows always will.

Chapter Seventeen

Amber

October 2006

James didn't tell me Greg was coming with us until we were having breakfast. I was spooning thick Greek yogurt over sliced fresh peaches, as I did every morning, when he said, 'Oh, by the way, I've asked Greg to meet us there.'

I was so surprised, I didn't speak at first. I just looked at him. We were going to look at the old furniture at the Mill of the Mountains for the property we were restoring. 'Why is he coming along?'

'I thought it might be helpful, having a second opinion. He's got an eye for style and he's a good negotiator. Plus, people like Greg could be our target market if we want to develop a high-class, Michelin-starred restaurant. Think of it as a kind of market research.'

I think I replied with a dismissive snort and then began to eat my breakfast.

On the drive along the coast we passed the turning to the bay where we had come across the Mill à la Mer, sister shop to the Mill of the Mountains. We'd discovered it on one of our many excursions to rented villas that first hot frantic summer. I think we'd been replacing beach towels and an umbrella that had been blown away in a seasonal storm, and then decided we'd earned a drink before heading on to another property up in the hills. As I sipped iced coffee and James had cold beer, we'd noticed the shaded interior of the cavernous shop opposite the cafe, so different to its neighbours with their novelty inflatables, sunglasses and plastic sandals. I remember holding my icy glass to my cheek so the condensation could cool my skin, as I stared at the enticing entrance through which I could just make out carpets, cushions, lanterns and pottery.

James had drained his beer glass and was standing up ready to get back to work before I had even half finished my drink. 'I just want to take a quick look in that shop over there,' I'd said, leaving my coffee and walking towards the Mill. I didn't ask if he wanted to come, but he followed as soon as he'd paid the bill for our drinks.

Since that day, we'd returned many times, buying gifts for family back home and browsing through the goods, imagining how our own home was going to look. I loved the feel and the smell of all the textiles, impregnated with the scent of patchouli, and James exclaimed over the colours and patterns. As the shop was usually open until sunset, we often called in on our way back after a day of fretful holidaymakers' complaints and petty problems. We'd stroke the intricately woven rugs and weigh the heavy glazed pottery in our hands, discussing which pieces would create the right atmosphere for our future home and for the business.

And then we'd sit at a table in the restaurant where we'd had that first cooling drink. Gradually we began to share our dreams with Inge and Marian, the owners of the shop. They never tried to persuade us to buy anything, although we often did. They just seemed content for us to appreciate their varied stock and enjoy their company.

It was obvious to me from the start how much they loved each other. Inge must have been in her mid-sixties, and I thought Marian was about ten years younger. They finished each other's sentences; Inge with a still-pronounced Northern European accent and Marian with a hint of the Estuary twang that betrayed her Essex roots.

They must at one time have looked very similar, as both were slender, long-legged and fair-haired, but Marian was still strong and energetic while Inge's wrinkled skin had an unhealthy grey tinge, and she spent less time refolding the heavy rugs or unpacking hefty pottery and more of her days sitting at a table in the front of the shop, taking payments, writing price labels and untangling beaded necklaces, a cigarette ever smouldering in her lips.

'You must come out and see our other shop one day,' Marian said one evening, when we'd been talking about our plans for the business. 'We call it the Mill of the Mountains. You might find it gives you some idea of what you can do with these old country properties.'

'Yes, do go,' said Inge. 'I hardly ever go there now, but Marian is so clever the way she is always finding such unusual pieces around the island and elsewhere. She says she has a pair of marble fonts sent over from Paxos. Who will want them, I don't know. Do go and tell me if you think she is going quite mad.'

Marian laughed. 'Someone's going to absolutely love them. Maybe they'll turn them into hand basins or garden ornaments. I don't know, but they're just beautiful and were a knockdown bargain.'

We didn't think she was at all mad. We saw the fonts the first time we visited the shop in the mountains. It was a cluster of old farm buildings around a cobbled yard, where a central fountain slowly trickled cool water. The main structure, once an old barn, Marian said, had been converted, but the rest of the buildings were ramshackle, with terracotta-tiled roofs patched with corrugated iron and barn doors wedged shut with heavy bars. The original farmhouse was long gone, a low rugged line of stones marking where it once stood. And in the courtyard were the fonts, filled with a sculptural arrangement of pebbles and succulent green and purple sedums.

On that first visit, Marian showed us long tables of elm and olive wood, scored by heavy kitchen pans and sharp knives, their silky patina created by years of honeyed pastries and the slick of olive oil. We stroked the scarred wood with the flat of our palms, as many hands had done over the decades before us, sat on sturdy benches, peered in carved cabinets with iron hinges and latches, and admired groups of plump reddish-brown pithoi. We'd talked about selecting key pieces to give the restaurant character and authenticity and I'd imagined James and I doing this alone, together. But now, we were on our way to meet Greg and I had my doubts.

Chapter Eighteen

James

October 2006

I did my best, as I drove, to placate Amber. She clearly wasn't happy I'd asked Greg to come along with us. I started by trying to distract her and break her mood, by telling her a terrible joke I'd heard from Ben a few days before. But she was silent. So then I thought I should work harder and convince her that Greg could be an asset.

As we passed the melons piled by the roadside and turned the hairpin bends at Kassiopi, I maintained a monologue singing his praises. 'Ben thinks we're jolly lucky, being able to tap into Greg's expertise. He doesn't exactly take a shine to everyone, you know. He's had his finger in a lot of pies over the years and has done really well with his property investments.'

'Not so well with his own place, if I remember correctly,' Amber said, finally breaking her stubborn silence, adding, 'And I wouldn't call that an astute investment, now that awful hotel's gone up nearby.'

'True, but he's made a bomb elsewhere and he knows lots of useful contacts. We should take advantage of that.'

'Fine, but don't expect me to trust him. I know you like him, and his awful jokes crack you up, but he's just not my type. There's something about him.'

'He's a good bloke. He can be a bit crude sometimes, I know, but you've got to admit, he's very successful. He must get some things right.'

She was silent again for a couple more miles, then spoke again as we began the winding ascent into the mountains. 'I quite like his wife, though. She must put up with a lot. But this time, you've got to make more of an effort to involve me in the conversation.' Amber slapped my arm as I gripped the wheel on yet another tight bend. 'I'm your main business partner, not him.'

'Of course, of course.' I was already straining to hear her over the grinding noise of the engine struggling on steep slopes and tight bends, and that seemed the likeliest response to end the conversation. She continued talking, though, and while I was paying token attention to her remarks, my mind drifted to the conversation I'd had with Greg when he picked me up one afternoon, after I'd finished meeting and greeting at the airport.

In a dark, smoke-filled bar in one of the town's back streets, he'd said, 'I don't know how silent a partner I would want to be, exactly. I'm used to having some say in my investments. And you've got to admit I know the island extremely well, better than the two of you do. After all, I've been coming here for nearly thirty years and I've dealt with a number of developments here.'

'Point taken. But I'd have to think about it very carefully. Amber and I already have enough capital to set ourselves up all right.'

'Ah, but do you have the cushion to see you through the dead times? And what if it takes a while for the business to get going, eh? Have you thought about that?'

'Sure I have. That's why we're interested in talking to someone like you. It could take a lot of the pressure off us.' I'd stirred my coffee. 'What I'm trying to say is, we don't actually need to have an investor to get ourselves off the ground, but I have to admit it would make things easier.'

'Okay,' Greg had said. 'I understand, but if I invest in a project I like to be sure what I'm getting into. I don't necessarily have to be involved in a hands-on kind of way, but I do like to be kept informed. And I can bring a lot of experience to the table. The restaurant table, get it?' He'd laughed at his own joke, slapping the table in front of him, then added, 'I can advise on business structure, forecasts and also contacts. And don't forget that I also know a lot of influential people, the sort who like good food and good service. If that's what you're going to be offering, then you can charge whatever you like. You become the Heston of the Hesperides and you've got it made, my boy.'

I smiled at that. 'Well, I don't know how quickly I can aspire to such heights, but I'm certainly going to try. I'm convinced there's a need for top-notch dining here.'

'Too right. There's great food here of course, but I don't think there's anywhere on the island that can truly claim to be offering innovative high-class cuisine. But hey, what about doing some market research? What do you say to you and me checking out all the supposedly fine-dining establishments here? Would you like that?'

'Very much so. It would certainly make sense.'

'Could we make a start next week?'

'I think I could fit in a couple around my regular duties. They usually leave me free at lunchtime.'

We'd met for several fact-finding missions since then. We went to restaurants hidden away in the alleyways of Corfu Town, where wizened aged proprietors stirred bubbling casseroles of fish and herbs, and we visited harbourside cafes, which specialised in octopus in vinegar; we tasted salted fish, dips of spicy garlic-ridden mashed potatoes and sampled honeyed pastries served with bitter coffee. Sometimes Greg drank more wine than he ate, sometimes I had to drive him home, but Amber was never involved and I still hadn't revealed to her how much I had already discussed with him or how much money had already been committed.

Chapter Nineteen

9 June 1944

'It's better that you don't know,' Papa says when Rebekka asks again where her sisters have gone. 'Then you cannot be forced to reveal their whereabouts. They are safe and well. That is all I will tell you for now.'

'We took them to stay with good friends, while they were sleeping,' Mama says. She glances at her husband and Rebekka suddenly feels afraid. She has overheard neighbours saying they would rather smother their children in their beds than let the Germans take them. Mama notices her look of alarm and puts her arms around her daughter, a young girl on the edge of womanhood, but still little more than a child to her. 'Don't fret, my dearest. I gave them a draught from good Doctor Batas to keep them asleep until they were far away from the town, so they would not be afraid. They are quite safe, my love.'

'The Germans will not come searching for them,' Papa says. 'They do not know about Matilde and Anna. Their names never went on their list.'

'But they could have stayed here with me,' Rebekka protests. 'I could have cared for them perfectly well.'

'I know you would have looked after them,' Papa says. 'But remember, the Germans know that you live here.'

Rebekka is quiet for a moment. She misses her playful little sisters, their bouncy skipping and their giggling as they chase each other around the kitchen table. 'And what about Katya?' Rebekka bends down to stroke the skinny white cat, its belly swelling, its fur grubby from roaming the dusty rubble in the streets. 'Who will look after her?'

Papa shakes his head and sighs. 'Katya must stay here, to kill the mice and rats which will want to move into our house when we've left. She will have an important job to do, keeping the house ready for our return.'

From outside the house, Rebekka hears many voices. A dull wave of murmuring and the thud of reluctant, shuffling feet. She pulls back the shutters and peers out of the window at the crowd in the street below. With slow, heavy footsteps they are trudging towards the Kato Plateia, where the whole community has been ordered to assemble. Everyone, man, woman or child, has a sack or a bundle slung over their shoulders or carried like a baby in their arms.

'I will take my suitcase,' Rebekka says. 'I don't want my clothes to get creased and wrinkled. I will want to change into fresh clothes when we get there.'

'The Germans have said we cannot take cases,' Papa says. 'There won't be enough room for everyone to sit on the boats and trains if we have pieces of luggage. Whatever we want to take must be put into a sack.'

'Here,' says Mama. 'Take my thick shawl and wrap it around your clothes. That will make a good cushion for you on the journey.'

'Then I am going to wear my best dress today,' says Rebekka. 'The white one with the blue and red embroidery. I would like to look respectable when I arrive.'

Mama's smile is faint at this confident assertion and she says, 'The most important thing for us to carry is supplies. We must take provisions and as much water as we can manage. They may not realise how hot the month of June can become in Kerkyra. We must be prepared in case the Germans have not ordered enough for us all.'

Chapter Twenty

Amber

October 2006

I suppose if I'd known then just how much James and Greg had been talking in my absence, I would have felt even more unsettled. But when we met Greg at Marian's shop in the mountains, he was amusing, charming and attentive, and I began to warm to him. He made me feel that my opinion really mattered. He greeted me with a hug and a kiss, and as we walked across the courtyard to the barn, where most of the furniture was displayed, he made a point of flattering me.

'I can tell you've got a real instinct for this,' he said, as I pointed out the pieces I liked best and took some quick shots of them to add to my ideas file. 'You're very organised, and you've got a good eye. You remind me of a designer I know, who worked on the show flat for my last development back in the UK. She keeps telling me rustic chic is the next big thing.'

I remember responding to that remark, feeling he understood what I wanted to achieve. 'You mean unsophisticated, but it's still got style and simplicity.'

'Exactly. You don't need too much of it. And you can save money on the rest of the basic furnishings and keep them quite simple, if you have some signature statement pieces here and there.'

As we wandered around the barn, James was a few steps behind us, looking thoughtful and smiling to himself. I grabbed his hand and pulled him towards a large dark coffer adorned with curling brass inlay. 'What about this gorgeous chest? Wouldn't it look great in the entrance to the restaurant? And it would make such useful storage.'

He came closer and squeezed my shoulder. 'I love it all. I think we're going to find everything we need up here.'

'And look,' I said, happy that we were in agreement once more, 'couldn't we find some way of using these old doors and window shutters as well?' I pulled him closer to the peeled and faded frames stacked in rows against the end wall. Their cracked blue and green paint revealed older colours as well as scratched patches of bare wood and spoke of days of blistering sun, winters of teeming rain and years of keeping village houses safe and dry.

'Your wife's a natural,' Greg said, coming over to look at the old frames, with us. 'I doubt many people would see the potential in this kind of salvage.'

'We don't actually have to use them as doors and windows for our property, but I love the age of them and the distressed paint.' I pulled a couple away from the wall and looked at the backs of the frames. 'Maybe we could adapt them and use them for cupboards, or to make mirrors? They've got such character.'

I think that was the point when Marian joined us. She'd been talking to some people outside while we wandered around the barn on our own. 'I hope you'll be telling Inge about their potential. She thought I was crazy buying up a job lot of frames and doors. But underneath the peeling paint, the wood is still hard and in good condition.' She rapped the frames with her knuckles. 'Those architectural salvage places back in the UK would go mad for them.'

'Too right,' Greg said. 'Have you thought about shipping some of this stuff back there? Could be an interesting little venture. I know someone who might like to do a deal with you on this sort of thing.'

'Thanks, but no thanks.' Marian didn't look at Greg or smile as she answered. 'We're happy with the way things are.'

I didn't really think much of her remark then, but I did notice that she seemed worried – her clothes were damp and her eyes were a little red. Then Greg walked away and began inspecting a wooden trough on short legs that must have once held feed for pigs, or maybe it was used for grinding chickpeas or olives, and James was hugging my shoulders again and saying, 'We should be making a move soon. Greg's suggested we get a bite to eat on the way back.' Marian had drifted off to her desk by then and although I wanted to ask her if she was all right, I didn't. I should have done. I don't know if it might have made a difference to all that came to pass, but it might have done.

As we drove away, following Greg's open-sided jeep, I couldn't help but wonder why she had been so offhand. We knew her reasonably well by then. Perhaps she had other worries, I thought. Perhaps Inge was ill. I knew she wasn't in the best of health, but she had seemed reasonably cheerful the last time James and I had met with the two of them.

'Do you think Marian's all right?' I asked James, as we bumped along the mountain road. He was driving fast to keep up with Greg and I held on tight to the edge of my seat.

'What? I don't know. I'm trying not to lose him. I don't know where we're meant to be going.'

So I kept quiet and let him concentrate on his driving. I didn't like the mountain roads when we took them slowly and I certainly didn't like them at this speed. The tight bends and loose surface made me very nervous – I shut my eyes as we spun round each turn and concentrated on the view across the valley on the straight stretches in between.

I thought about the little we knew of the two women. Marian had told me something of her past, while Inge was more reticent. I'd spent an evening drinking with them in the cafe opposite their shop while James was meeting a delayed flight at the airport. If he'd been with us, she might not have talked as openly as she did.

After I'd told them about my home life, meeting James and about my recently abandoned legal career, I'd asked Marian what she had done before Corfu and she surprised me when she said, 'I ran away from home when I was in my teens.'

I was shocked and glanced at Inge, but she just looked at Marian with her gentle smile and stroked her hand. She had obviously heard the story before. 'Go on,' I'd said. 'I'm listening.'

'I didn't despise my parents, I just ran away to stop them despising me. I think they had always been ashamed of me. They never told me I was pretty, that they loved me, or said well done whenever I brought home my school reports. Perhaps I didn't do well enough for them to praise me.'

She'd run her fingers through her short blonde hair, pushing it back from her tanned forehead. 'I thought I was pregnant. I had disappointed them enough already, but I could not face any more of their disappointment. That's why I left.'

'How old were you then?'

'Only sixteen. The boy I was seeing told me if I was ever "in trouble" I should take ephedrine. It's used in a lot of hayfever preparations apparently. But I was too scared to ask the chemist in our town. Too many people knew my parents. So I ran away. Three weeks later it was all over anyway, without me doing or taking anything. My period came. I could have stayed after all. But by then it was too late. I knew I couldn't ever go back.'

'So where did you go?'

'London. It wasn't hard to find work in those days and I rented a pokey bedsit in West Hampstead. I couldn't afford the Tube or buses, so every day I walked to the pub where I was working in Camden Town. I told them I was eighteen and they never questioned it. I did everything from washing up to pulling pints and making fried egg sandwiches. The Vic, the locals called it. It had stained glass, ceilings yellow with smoke and a long bar. It was an old-fashioned London pub, but there was a big advertising agency nearby whose staff gathered in the bars every day, so it was young and alive. At weekends we only served local residents. There were semi-intellectuals from the once-grand houses that looked towards Regent's Park and workmen from the Peabody Buildings that overlooked the train line from Euston. But in the week it was filled with clever young men and women laughing. Camden was changing fast then, getting quite hip and trendy.'

Marian had paused and sat back; she twisted the silver rings she wore round and round her middle finger and looked down at her hands. After a few moments, she'd said, 'Do you ever feel that you were born in the wrong place?'

I was quiet for a second, because of course I'd been too young to remember my birth mother, but my childhood had been happy and my adoptive parents were kind and wonderful. 'I don't think I feel it as such,' I said, 'but I do sometimes wonder what would have happened to me if life had been different.'

'I used to envy those smart advertising people. They seemed to be having so much fun. They enjoyed their work, while I was in a dead-end job doing nothing of lasting value. I wished I could be one of them. I wished I could find a way into that kind of life.'

'James was recruited by one of the big agencies from university,' I said.

She went quiet and looked dreamy, remembering her early years, then said, 'I went out with one of the guys for a while. Charles. Charlie, I called him. He invited me to some of their parties, but I knew it wouldn't last. One time we went back to a house owned by a couple that worked together. He was an art director at the agency and she was a copywriter. I thought they were so cool and glamorous, so clever and creative. They had a room where the walls were papered with sheets of brown wrapping paper. I'd never seen anything like it. All I'd ever known was red flock in the local Indian and anaglypta at home. The room was newly papered, all fresh, and they invited everyone to write on the bare walls.'

'So, what did you write?'

Then she was quiet for a moment and hung her head, before saying, 'I didn't. I couldn't. Everyone else was writing such witty stuff, even poetry. I just said I'd wait till the others had finished, but really, I was too scared, too afraid whatever I wrote would look pathetic. They'd all been to university and art college, and what had I done? Nothing, not even the local tech.

'And then it was all forgotten and no one noticed, because there was music playing and people were dancing and that was something I knew I could do well. I could really dance.' She jiggled her shoulders as if recalling a beat from long ago. 'I knew I looked good, better than any of them. So it no longer mattered that I couldn't bring myself to write on their walls.

'I asked Charlie once if he thought I could get a job in the agency and he just said, "Well, what can you do?" And that's when I realised I couldn't do anything. I couldn't type, I wasn't educated, I couldn't understand figures; I was useless. I was just the girl from Romford who worked behind the bar in their local.'

I felt so sorry for her then, seeing in this competent successful businesswoman the timid girl she had once been. 'But you could have gone to night school and got some qualifications, couldn't you, if you'd really wanted?'

Marian smiled and shook her head. 'Not at the same time as holding down a job to pay my rent I couldn't. You have to work evenings in a pub. So eventually I decided that I would save hard for a year and then do what I was best at.'

'Which was what?'

She gave a sad little laugh. 'Running away. No, not exactly running, but getting away. I had no ties, nothing to keep me there, so I could travel. I wasn't afraid of taking a job wherever I landed up. By the time I left London I was twenty, and I went to Australia. I'd stayed in touch with one of the agency secretaries who'd gone back home there, and she said I could stay with her if I ever decided to see the world. So I did. I worked there for a bit, bars again, saved up, then hopped over to India and eventually back to Europe.'

I'd thought of my own family and how distressed and worried they would feel if I disappeared. 'Didn't you ever think you'd like to go back home?'

'Oh, sometimes I thought about it, but every time I did, I saw their disappointed faces and heard their questions. No, I've left it too long now. They would never understand that I left because of them.'

I could see in her eyes distant memories of dull suburban streets, wet with cold English rain, and almost knew the answer before I'd asked my next question: 'But do you ever feel guilty?'

'For leaving them? Sometimes. I can't put it right, but if I thought I could explain and they would understand, I would want to let them know. Sometimes I think I'm like a cat we once had. He was away for about a month, then we heard he'd been found on the other side of town. He stayed with us for about a week before disappearing again. I used to think he came home just to let us know he could cope on his own. So sometimes I think I'd like them to know I'm well and happy.'

'So why don't you?' I'd asked, thinking of that family who, if they had any feelings for her at all, must have fretted and wondered about her fate for years.

She'd hung her head, then said, 'I'm afraid of the questions. I wake up in the night, hearing their voices, and anyway, it's too late now. They must be long gone.'

I'd thought it was the drink talking, but deep down I knew she was telling the truth.

And Inge hugged her close. 'Don't have regrets, *liebchen*. Your home is here now.'

Chapter Twenty-One

James

October 2006

Greg was showing off in his speedy jeep and although I put my foot down, I didn't risk it as much as I would have done if I'd been on my own. I could hear the tension in Amber's voice and out of the corner of my eye I could see her gripping the seat and sometimes shutting her eyes. I'd have enjoyed the race if she hadn't been with me.

The jeep finally screeched to a halt in a cloud of dust and scattered gravel outside a taverna with iron railings, where tables were set under an awning. Although it was late in the year, there were still times when the sun was hot in the middle of the day and it was more pleasant to sit outside in the shade. By the time I'd parked, Greg was talking vigorously to the owner, a stout, balding man in his fifties, clapping him on the back as an old friend. 'Good news, good news,' he announced as we approached. 'My very good mate, Adonis here, says another acquaintance is due here shortly. So we shall have a bit of a party!'

Amber was very quiet and hung back, but there was nothing we could do. It was lunchtime, Greg was being friendly and hospitable and we needed to eat, but I assured her we would try to make our excuses and leave once lunch was over.

'This is the best cuisine the island has to offer,' Greg said. 'This guy, this wonderful guy, looks after his lovely elderly mother, and she does all the cooking! And such cooking as you have never experienced before in Corfu. Recipes that she has cooked for years, and her mother, her grandmother and her great-grandmother before that. Just you wait. You are in for a rare treat.'

I was immediately sold. I love authentic dishes and I'm inspired by simple traditional ingredients. 'I can't wait,' I said. 'Where's the menu?'

'There isn't one. You're getting whatever Mama feels like cooking today.' Greg laughed and poured a jug of robust red wine into tumblers. 'That's what I love about this place. It's full of surprises. There's something different to eat every time I come here.'

I clinked glasses with him and then Amber slowly did the same. We sipped the wine – well, Greg and I drained our glasses almost immediately, so it was Amber who was sipping. She switched to iced water pretty quickly too. Adonis brought dishes of homemade tapenade and little black olives, spiced balls of minced lamb, aubergine dip, tzatziki and freshly baked pitta, the like of which rarely appeared in the local restaurants. It was so unlike the sanitised cardboard seen in English supermarkets; the flatbreads were soft golden pillows of dough, charred here and there from the wood oven, glistening with a slight sheen of oil.

Then we heard the screech of another car pulling up, and Greg waved in the direction of the driver. 'Over here,' he called, and a tall bearded man strolled across to join us. When he removed his sunglasses I recognised him immediately from our very first visit to the abandoned village.

'Now let me introduce you to the most useful man on the island,' Greg said, after shaking hands with his friend.

'Actually, we've already met,' I said, and I could see Amber smiling in recognition too. 'But I can't quite remember your name, though. It was back in the summer.'

'Of course, my friend.' He bowed his head and shook my hand. 'Dimitri Barberis, at your service.' Then he turned to Amber and as she went to shake his hand, he bent his head and gave it the lightest of kisses, causing her to smile, making her more attractive than ever. 'I trust your foot has healed well, Madam,' he murmured.

She laughed. 'Yes, thank you. It was such a stupid thing to do. I've learnt since then to keep my sandals for the beach and the evening.'

'May I?' He gestured to the empty chair at the table and looked at Greg, who nodded and waved at him to sit down, then poured another glass of wine for our visitor.

'I didn't know you all knew each other,' Greg said, laughing. 'It's just like a family reunion.'

'We only met briefly,' I said.

'All because I tripped,' Amber said.

'Whatever.' Greg waved his hand around. 'I asked Dimitri to join us because he's got some very useful contacts and experience. He might be able to help you get things moving more quickly.'

I wasn't totally surprised, because Greg had told me a couple of times that once we found the right property he would advise us how to stay on track and I was anxious not to waste time or money. The house Dimitri had shown us, when we'd first met back in July, hadn't been suitable, but the one we had finally bought would be perfect for our business if we could only get the work finished on schedule. It was already mid-October and I wanted it completed by Easter at the very latest. If we didn't meet that deadline we wouldn't be taking any bookings once the main tourist season started.

'I will be honoured to assist you,' Dimitri said.

Greg was pouring more wine but Amber put her hand over her glass. 'Maybe we should take a detour on the way back,' Greg said, through a mouthful of bread and tapenade. 'Give Dimitri an idea of what you're up to.'

Amber shook her head. 'I'm afraid I need to get back. I promised Eleni and Ben I'd help look after the children this afternoon.'

Then the main course arrived. Great plates of sumptuous, tempting food. Mama never made an appearance, but Adonis brought golden courgette fritters and *dakos* – a salad of bread, tomatoes, feta cheese and olive oil. Then he fetched a platter of grilled lamb, pink inside, charred outside, flavoured with rosemary, thyme and garlic, the very scent and flavour of the island, served with wilted spinach tossed in lemon and pepper, with a bowl of crunchy roasted potatoes.

I piled my plate and began to eat, relishing the juicy meat and the delicacy of the fritters. Amber touched my arm and whispered, 'Let's go soon.'

My mouth was full and it was a minute before I could reply, but when I could I didn't whisper, but spoke so the whole table could hear. 'I think I should take Dimitri over to see the house. It's a pity to miss an opportunity. Why don't you take the car back?' I glanced at her and her lips were tight. I looked across the table to Greg and said, 'Would that be okay with you? Can you give me a lift later on?'

I think Amber left soon after that. But the three of us lingered all afternoon at the table, Greg drinking more, Dimitri drinking very little, until it was agreed that Greg should leave his jeep behind and we would go with Dimitri.

We reached the building site late in the day, while there was still just enough light to make out what progress had been made. All was quiet, apart from the distant clang of sheep bells, harmonising with a church bell tolling over the hills. The cement mixer was still, a wheelbarrow lay on its side, the men had gone home and I had no way of knowing how much work had been done that day. 'Your men should not leave at this time. There is still light.' Dimitri looked stern. 'I would not permit such a short day of work.'

I sighed and shook my head. 'I thought they were going to be good. Greg's used them before and Ben employed them on one of the villas and told us they were reliable workers.'

Dimitri puffed his cheeks and surveyed the scene. 'There is much to do here and there will be much rain in the winter. They must make work while, what do you say, the sun shines?'

'Yes, hay, that's it. We're not going to be ready by the spring, are we?'

'That depends,' he said. 'If you have a project manager, they will work harder.'

'A project manager? And where will I find one of those?'

'Right here, my friend,' Dimitri tapped his chest. 'Right here. I would be honoured and happy to assist.' He looked beyond the outer reaches of the old village across to the far side of the valley, now merging into deepening purple shadows. 'You have chosen well here. This location has great promise. It will be a pleasure to work here with you.'

I laughed with relief and shook first his hand then Greg's, and we all laughed and clapped each other on the back.

'Sounds like we have something to celebrate,' Greg said.

Chapter Twenty-Two

As she carries her bundle down the stairs, Rebekka pauses to look around the kitchen, where the family has enjoyed so many happy meals together. One last look to memorise it all before they finally leave their home with all their neighbours on this journey to the East and into the unknown.

Until the recent hardships of the war, the ceiling was always garlanded with strands of dried mushrooms and peppers, bunches of thyme and oregano. Jars of rice, flour and beans had filled the shelves, but now stand empty, as every last grain has gone to feed this hungry family. But even though food has been in short supply in recent weeks and months, Rebekka is sure she can still smell the garlic that enriched her mother's potato *burekas* sprinkled with sesame seeds, and the savoury aroma of her aubergines stuffed with rice, herbs and pine nuts and stewed with tomatoes. It is a long time since Mama cooked meatballs with walnut sauce, but perhaps the family will all be together again before too long and she will prepare a grand dinner in celebration and they will all laugh, sing and eat their fill.

She watches Mama give her favourite copper pan a final polish with a rag, then hang it on its rightful hook, where it has always hung, below the carved blue spice cupboard which still holds a few grains of fragrant cumin, coriander and paprika. Then Mama stacks the plain earthenware bowls from their last breakfast on the shelf and wipes the worn, much-scrubbed table, where they have always talked, laughed and celebrated Pasach.

When Rebekka was younger and didn't have to run so many errands for her parents, she played under that very table, pretending it was a secret cave, a ship at sea, or a house of her very own. At first, she played alone, and then later with her sisters, each imagining their own worlds.

The whole room is as neat and spotless as the rest of the house. The floors have been swept and the shelves dusted. All the family's bed linen is folded, the rugs are rolled and dishes have been washed and put away in cupboards.

'We cannot delay any longer,' Papa says. 'Come, Perla, you can do no more here.' He takes his wife's hand and removes the duster she holds tight in her fist. She wipes her hands on her apron, then unties the strings and hangs it on a hook on the back of the kitchen door. She picks up her bulging bundle and he throws his sack across his shoulder. Like many of the men trudging past the shop, he is wearing a dark jacket and trousers – his best suit, brushed and pressed for this very important journey.

'What will happen to all our belongings and furniture?' Rebekka asks as she follows her parents down the stairs to the street. 'We are leaving nearly everything we own behind here.'

'It will be fine,' Papa says. 'We will lock the door to the house and the shop and it will all be here waiting for us, ready for when we come back from working for the Germans.'

Chapter Twenty-Three

Amber

October 2006

I was so cross when I left James at the taverna with Greg and Dimitri that my driving almost rivalled the speed of our earlier journey. I felt like I'd been dismissed from the room, so the grown-ups could go on to discuss more important things. I knew that wasn't really the case, I knew they were more likely to continue drinking and joking, but that was how it felt as I drove away.

By the time I reached Ben and Eleni's house I was calmer and was happy to be distracted by the gurgling of their baby, George, and the chatter of their toddler, Maria. Eleni had begun cooking again in the restaurant in the evenings and just needed a couple of free hours at the end of the afternoon for essential preparation, even though they were entering the quiet winter season. 'You must tell James,' she said, as she handed me a bottle for the baby and a beaker and biscuits for Maria, 'a good chef always plans and always prepares. A dish may only take a few minutes to cook in the end, but the chopping, the peeling, the filleting, that is where a real chef does their work.'

When, after two hours in which I'd cuddled and played with both children, she returned, I still hadn't heard from James. I went back to the villa we were using until our new place was habitable and decided I was not going to waste my evening wondering when he might eventually turn up; I would drive down to the Mill à la Mer and see if Marian was there.

The beachside shop closed earlier, now that the season was over. No more long, drawn-out days when they had to remain open until the last roasted tourist walked off the beach and the sun was beginning to dip behind the hillside church. I climbed the long flight of stone steps from the beach terrace to the upper levels of the shop, where the women lived and from where I could hear the murmur of their voices and the crunch of a knife on a chopping board.

Inge was sitting back in a chair, smoking as usual; Marian was slicing into a crisp lettuce. 'Darling,' Inge said. 'Come and join us. How wonderful to see you.'

Marian looked up from her preparations. Her eyes were no longer red, but she looked very tired. 'Hello again,' she said. 'How was the rest of your day?'

'You don't want to know. I haven't seen James since lunchtime. I just thought I'd drop in and ask how you were. I got the impression you weren't too happy when we left you today. Was anything the matter?'

Marian rolled her eyes at me then looked at Inge, who spoke on her behalf, 'The poor girl had a nasty shock today.'

'It's nothing. Don't make something of it. It was just an unfortunate accident, that's all.' Marian was shaking her head, then glanced at me. 'Are you staying? There's enough for all of us. It's just baked pasta with meatballs.'

'I'd love to, if that's all right.' I sat down at the table and Marian slid a tumbler and a bottle of wine towards me. 'But what happened? Do you mind talking about it again?'

'Of course she doesn't mind,' Inge said. 'It will do her good to tell you everything.'

Marian sprinkled cheese over the pasta, put the large dish in the oven, then sat down at the bare table and poured glasses of red wine for herself and Inge. 'Oh, I don't know,' she sighed. 'It's really nothing, just a cat that's died, that's all.'

'I'm sorry to hear that,' I said. 'It's always so sad losing a pet.'

'No, she wasn't really a pet. But what's happened is rather odd.' She sipped her drink then continued. 'You know what Greek cats are like – scrawny, riddled with parasites, constantly hungry. Most people here don't look after them, but they manage to survive, hunting vermin, pestering visitors for scraps.'

'Like all the cats that hang around the tavernas,' I said. 'They're all very well fed when the tourists take pity on them.'

She nodded. 'She was a shy little tortoiseshell. I don't know how long she'd been coming to our shop in the mountains, but gradually she became friendly and I'd leave her food and milk.' She shrugged and gave a little smile. 'Yes, I know, she was meant to be catching mice, but she looked so thin, I felt sorry for her. I even gave her a name – Tabitha. Then I realised she was pregnant and she had her kittens in one of the outhouses about eight weeks ago. Two ginger and two black and white. Such pretty things, and I've been leaving extra food out for all of them.

'Then this morning when I checked the dishes, the food had gone but none of the cats were around. They're usually always there to greet me in the mornings, but I had things to get on with and I knew you were coming over later, so I didn't think too much of it. Then, after you and James arrived, while you were browsing inside, I went round the outhouses and found the kittens sleeping in a crate in a shed at the back of the barn. Mum was still nowhere to be seen, so I left the kittens food and water and got on with sorting out the urns that came yesterday.'

She turned to Inge at this point. 'I'd tried grouping the urns around the courtyard in order of size, then decided they look better scattered about in random groups.'

'Yes, my darling,' Inge said. 'I'm sure it all looks splendid. Now get back to the rest of your story.'

Marian sipped her wine, then continued. 'It was one of those mornings when there were a few visitors roaming the village and coming to browse. And that's when it happened. A white-haired couple came up to me and said, "Excuse me, but did you know there was a cat in your fountain?" They were part of the group that was milling around, all coach party types, you know the sort, here to do the main tourist sights. Then they said, "We thought you ought to know. We think it's dead." So I rushed over to the fountain and there she was in the water. I thought there might be a sign of life, so I felt her wet chest and her limp pink paws. There was a little trail of blood oozing from her nose. But it was no good.'

Marian paused for a moment and I could see how shaken she still was by what she had seen. Then she continued, 'And then the stupid woman who'd called me over said the cat must have been thirsty. And her husband, if it was her husband, told me I should cover the water in case it happened again. Stupid people.'

'They weren't to blame, darling,' Inge said. 'They didn't know her, that's all.'

'Then I watched them walk away and I was just standing there with a totally wet shirt, water dripping from the body down to my feet. I couldn't understand how it had happened. Didn't I leave the cats enough water?

'I left her in a box in the barn and once you'd all gone, I realised I had to bury her quickly. So I carried her round to the back of the barn, wondering how was I going to dig a hole. There were no tools, no spade, and no pickaxe to break the rocky ground. It's all boulders and scrubby gorse round there, no soft earth. So in the end I laid the body on the ground and pushed one of the larger stones out of the way. It was really heavy, but I managed to roll it aside and the earth was damper and softer underneath.'

Marian paused again and took a gulp from her glass. 'I had to scrape away at the grit and dirt with my bare hands, till it was large enough for her.' I glanced at her hands clasping the chunky glass tumbler. The nails were torn and grimy, her knuckles grazed.

'I picked some wild oregano and lavender, crushed the leaves and laid them over her.' She brushed her tears away with her fist and sniffed loudly. 'And when I'd finished, I made her a promise. I promised to look after her babies and told her to go to sleep. I scooped the earth over her body and gently replaced the stone. I didn't want to crush her. And then, as I got up, I thought I saw a movement beyond the barn, where the visitors park their cars. There was a bearded man watching me. I had the feeling he'd been watching the whole thing all along. And I'm not sure, but I think I've seen him before.'

Chapter Twenty-Four

James

October 2006

It was late when I returned to the villa after that long afternoon with Greg and Dimitri, but Amber wasn't there. I assumed she was still with Ben and Eleni and would maybe eat with them, but I was hungry, even though I'd eaten plenty at lunchtime. So I looked through our supplies and decided to make a mushroom and butternut squash frittata. It takes longer to cook than an omelette, as the squash has to be peeled and roasted, but it's much more interesting, especially if you add a dash of chilli and cumin to the roasting dish.

I was just starting to peel the squash when my phone rang. I assumed it would be Amber, but it was Greg. He sounded drunk and shouted, 'Hey, I just did it. I got the crap in the pool!' His laugh was loud and then it was distant, with clattering noises and muffled words. 'Dropped the bloody phone,' he spluttered. 'Bullseye!'

'Brilliant,' I said, rolling my eyes. 'You'll definitely be on form by next summer. But they'll be draining the pool for the winter soon, won't they?'

'Yeah, probably. Shame, I'll have to keep my hand in some other way though.'

'You do that, mate. Gotta be ready for the start of the season, eh?' There was no response. Whether he'd dropped the phone again, lost reception or fallen into a drunken stupor I couldn't tell, but there was silence. I couldn't help smiling to myself as I prepared my supper.

Greg was a couldn't-care-less, fuck-you, one-off individual and I couldn't help but find him highly entertaining. I could see that his mischief-making could be dangerous, but that was part of his charm for me. And when it came to talking money, he was deadly serious.

We hadn't exactly talked figures after Amber had left, but it would have been clear to Dimitri that Greg was an equal in the enterprise. Handing the project over to a site manager, even someone clearly as experienced as Dimitri, was going to add to our costs in the short term, even though it might save us money in the end, but Greg was totally in favour of the idea. 'You can't be there on site yourself, all the time,' he kept saying. 'And just think what an advantage you'll have over the workforce with Dimitri cracking the whip. He's a real taskmaster, aren't you, Dimitri?'

And Dimitri had nodded with a slight smile and simply said, 'I will be very attentive. It is a great responsibility and I am honoured that you think I am worthy of such a task.'

'Don't be so damned modest, man,' Greg said. 'You could do it with your hands tied and your eyes shut.'

'But I will maybe keep my eyes open,' Dimitri said. 'Keep them plucked, don't you say?'

Greg couldn't stop laughing at this. 'Very good,' he chuckled. 'Here's to a productive partnership. Tell you what, let's go back to Adonis and drink to a successful project.'

Back at the restaurant, Greg's glass had clanked against mine and red wine splashed over the tablecloth. 'Here's to…' He'd paused for a second. 'What the hell are you calling the place?'

'We haven't actually decided yet. Amber and I have had a few thoughts, obviously, but nothing's clicked with us so far.' I'd given a small embarrassed laugh. 'One idea we had, well, it sounds totally stupid now, was to combine our names and call it Jamboree.'

Greg had almost choked on his drink, then spluttered and said, 'Definitely not. Sounds more like a bloody kids' nursery, not a fine-dining establishment.'

'Yeah, I know. Not right at all, is it?'

'Name, we've got to have a name,' shouted Greg, slamming his glass on the table. 'We've got to make that a priority. Come on, everyone, let's get thinking.' He was quiet only for a second, then he'd thumped the table again, saying, 'I know, we should all put our ideas into a hat and pick one.'

I laughed and said, 'Who's got the hat? You got one handy, Greg?'

He'd laughed too, and held up his empty hands. 'Okay then, the bread basket will have to do.' He tipped the remaining pieces of pitta bread out onto the table, then tore the paper napkin lining the basket into pieces. 'Right, one name per slip, fold them up and put them in the basket.'

I think we were all laughing by this point, especially when Greg waved to Adonis and called him over to join in as well. 'This isn't exactly what you'd call a professional brainstorm,' I said, 'and I'm not guaranteeing we'll go with whatever crap name you come up with. It's bonkers, but come on, let's do it.'

This was what I liked about Greg. It felt just like we were a group of kids secretly writing dirty jokes or composing coded messages. It reminded me of messing about in a den in the woods with my child-hood mates in the summer holidays, but here we were, four grown men, frowning, chewing our pens and scribbling on scraps of paper.

'Right, all finished?' Greg was the first to stop, then me, then Dimitri and lastly, Adonis, who contributed only one folded slip of paper. Greg stirred the little pile with his finger and then held the basket out to me. 'Go on, pick one.'

I'd hesitated, sniggered, then rummaged through the pile and picked out one slip from the bottom of the basket. I unfolded it slowly and stared at the writing, utterly baffled by the Greek characters. Then I held it up so the others could see it.

Greg was the first to speak. 'You Greek bastard,' he'd said, laughing and leaning to one side to clap Adonis on the back. 'You stupid Greek bastard.'

'Why, what does it say?'

'He's written Mama's Kitchen! Fucking idiot!'

We were all laughing, Adonis included, and even more when he'd said, 'My mama, she is the best. I cannot think of a better name. There is no one like her.'

'Of course there isn't, you daft bugger.' Greg had wiped the tears from his eyes and pulled out a large handkerchief to mop his brow. 'James, have another go. He only did one, so the rest should make more sense. Bloody Mama's Kitchen, I ask you.'

I'd picked another slip and opened it. 'No, this one isn't right either. It's one of mine.'

'Well, tell us then,' Greg said. 'Let's hear it, whatever it is.'

'Swallows Rest.' My words were met with silence and I'd grimaced. 'Amber and I had played around with that one because we saw the swallows nesting there when we first found the place. But I know it's not right. Sounds like a stupid pun, totally inappropriate for a high-end restaurant. No, it sounds even worse now I say it and see it written down.'

'Chuck it,' said Greg. 'Try again.'

So I did, rejecting one after another of the slips we'd written until I unfolded the final one. 'Mountain Thyme. I like it. Is that yours?' I'd looked across at Greg, who shook his head and pointed at Dimitri, who was holding up his index finger and smiling. 'I really like it. There's something so right about that name.'

'Told you he was our man,' said Greg, tossing back the last of his wine.

Chapter Twenty-Five

9 June 1944

Rebekka steps out of the shop doorway and looks along the high-sided alleyway, still in shade even though the sun is nearly at its height. No longer do bright strands of freshly washed clothes and sheets flutter overhead like carnival bunting, and the caged birds that once trilled from balconies have all been set free, unlike the people. All around her, with their heads lowered, some faces wet with tears, the residents of the Evraiki – dark-haired children, women wrapped in black scarves, men in dark suits – are creeping like a trail of black ants from every crevice of the Jewish quarter.

German soldiers stand with ready guns slung across their bodies at the corners of the streets as the entire community streams into the main square of Corfu Town. Most of the people follow this migration obediently, too afraid to break away from their families, but now and then a young man or boy darts into a dark passage and in seconds has vanished.

'Good luck to them,' mutters Papa. 'The Germans daren't enter the Campiello.' Rebekka wishes she could run after them and hide there. Even the Italians never dared to penetrate that dense warren of alleyways where the lurking Resistance conspired and deadly steel knives were keenly sharpened. She overhears muttered conversations all around her. 'Josef, look, your friends have escaped, go now, go quickly,' and 'No, Mama, I can't leave you and the others.' The ties of the Jewish family are hard to break as she knows only too well.

She slips a hand through her mother's arm as they take one sorrowful step after another towards the Kato Plateia, the square where the horse-drawn carriages used to wait, where the Germans now lounge in the cafes of the Liston Terrace and where row upon row of frightened people are ordered to line up in groups of five in the harsh, scorching sun. She longs to ask after her little sisters, but she is afraid to speak their names in case someone overhears their conversation and thinks there would be some advantage to be had in revealing that *Here, look, over here, this family is incomplete – there may still be hidden children to flush out.*

Looking back towards the Evraiki, she can see soldiers searching the empty houses. Soon the air is filled with a haze, like a cloud of drifting dandelion seeds. It is puzzling until she notices that they are dragging mattresses out onto the streets, slashing them with knives so the cobbles are covered with tufts of white kapok. And she realises the men are ransacking the homes where the families lived and loved for hidden valuables. *We are poor people*, she thinks, *but they want to take everything from us.* She clutches her mother's arm tight, hoping she won't turn back to see the home she once proudly kept so neat and clean defiled by the looting soldiers.

Four long tiring hours they stand in the fierce sun, some fainting, some crying, while the Germans bark orders in harsh voices. To amuse themselves, the soldiers direct a group of men to squat and jump like frogs, their hands held above their heads. Rebekka wants to look away, horrified that her people are being ridiculed, but she cannot stop watching the humiliation. Then, above the general shouting and murmuring, above the lines of frightened people, there comes a rallying cry. Startled, Rebekka grabs Papa's hand. He strains to hear the words. 'It's the Resistance. They're trying to help us. They're calling for our people to fight back and run.'

'Should we go, Papa?' Rebekka is afraid, but more afraid of the unknown. Then they hear shots. 'Are the Germans shooting them, Papa?'

He is stretching his neck to see above the crowd. 'No, it's not the Germans. Oh, I can't believe it! It's one of ours. It's Patrikios. He's the right-hand man of the police chief, Dedopoulos. He's grabbed one of the German machine guns and turned on our people. Now no one will be able to escape, and the Germans will be even more vigilant than before.'

'But he should have helped us, Papa. He is a Greek police officer. He should be on our side.'

'I know. A hundred of us could have gotten away, but now no one dares.'

Rebekka clings to her parents' hands, fearful of what might happen next. Then, after standing for maybe another hour, she becomes aware that those on the farthest side of the square are beginning to move forwards. They are going somewhere at last. But where? There is only the harbour and the open sea ahead of them and then there is Albania, a wild country populated by a race all the Corfiots consider to be peasants and bandits. Papa squeezes her hand and says, 'At least we are moving. And they won't send us to Albania. The Italians are there now.'

Chapter Twenty-Six

Amber

October 2006

'That's a really good decision,' I said, when James told me that Dimitri had agreed to be our site manager. 'He's polite, he understands the problems and he's available at just the right time. You don't have any doubts about him, do you?'

'No, not at all now. I've grown to like him. I'm just aware that it's another cost, that's all.'

'But if in the long run he saves us money, what have we got to lose?'

'You're right. It's a winner all round.' James was grating courgettes to make fritters. He wanted to recreate the dish we'd had with Greg at Mama's, but was working with some difficulty as he'd cut his finger rather badly the night before chopping butternut squash. 'The knife wasn't all that sharp,' he said when I asked how he'd managed to do it. 'But the squash was very hard and the board was wet and slippery.'

'I see, so it was nothing to do with the amount you'd had to drink with Greg then?' I'd come home late in the evening to find the kitchen in disarray with bloodied chopped squash and a bowl of beaten eggs left out on the worktop; James was slumped on our bed with his hand wrapped in a tea towel soaked in blood that had seeped over the duvet.

'I should have asked for the recipe while we were there.' James was sprinkling salt over the courgettes and holding the colander with his good hand. 'I'm not quite sure whether to go for an eggy sort of batter or something with more of a tempura consistency. What do you think?'

'No idea,' I said. 'Why don't you do one version tonight and try it another way next time?'

'Yeah, I'll do that,' he replied distractedly, which meant he was composing the recipe in his head as we spoke and it didn't matter a jot what I said.

I left him alone for twenty minutes or so, then returned to the kitchen to open wine. 'How's it going? Can we talk now?'

'Course we can talk. I'm not stopping you, am I?' James was patting the courgettes with a clean tea towel to remove as much moisture as possible.

'I was thinking it would be an idea to take Marian up to see the site. If we're going to buy some of her furniture, it would be helpful for her to see where it's going. And maybe we should take Inge too. They've both got a good eye and they might give us some ideas of how it could all work.'

'If you really want to, I suppose that'd be okay.' He went back to stirring his saucepan. 'Maybe best to wait a while though, till there's a bit more progress. It's early days after all. Wait so we can show them more of the whole finished layout.'

'I suppose you're right. That's probably best.' I finished patting the courgettes. 'Do you think these are dry enough now?'

He leant over me and put his arms through and under mine, nuzzled my neck, then dabbed at the vegetables. 'They're fine.'

'What do you want me to do now?' I wiped my hands on a dry tea towel and he returned to making his batter.

'Just pour me a drink and wait there. This is the easy bit and I can talk and cook at the same time.' He stirred the courgettes into the batter, then heated oil in a pan. Once it was hot he began ladling spoonfuls of the mixture into the frying pan. He let each fritter set before flipping it over, revealing a golden surface freckled with green herbs. As he cooked, he said, 'I've been thinking some more about possible names for the restaurant.'

'Good. We could do with making a decision soonish, if we're to plan our advance publicity and the website. Can't have the thing going live without the right name. So what have you come up with now?'

He flipped another fritter and lifted the first one out onto kitchen paper to drain. Then he turned to me and smiled. 'What do you think about calling it Mountain Thyme?'

I thought for a minute, then gave him the biggest smile. 'James, it's absolutely perfect. Yes, I can see it working. It's great.' I hugged him, nearly making him drop the next fritter as he lifted it out of the pan. 'It's relevant to its location and the environment. It's about the natural surroundings and the scent of the herbs on the mountainside. And it's about spending time relaxing in the mountains, enjoying all they have to offer. Well done. I think it's simply wonderful.' I threw my arms around him and hugged him again and kissed his cheek. 'You clever old thing. I knew I could rely on you to think of something brilliant.'

'I thought you'd like it,' he said.

Chapter Twenty-Seven

James

January 2007

I was never all that keen on having the two Mill women visit the restaurant site, to be honest. Okay, I admit their shops were full of interesting pieces and I was happy to do business with them, but I didn't like them the way Amber did. She always seemed to be making excuses to visit them, saying they had some new stock she wanted to see or Inge wasn't well and needed company.

So every time she brought the subject up, I'd say, *oh no, not this week, the builders are doing the drains*, or *why don't you leave it till the lighting's done*. But by January I couldn't put her off any longer. Despite the heavy rains of December, work had progressed quickly and the building had reached the stage where we could begin to imagine exactly how each room should look. The fresh plaster still had to be painted and bare bulbs lit the restaurant, but it was beginning to look like a real living breathing house and business at last.

'Bring them over on Thursday if you really want to,' I'd said. 'All the kitchen appliances are arriving on Friday, so it might be rather chaotic then.' So all three of them turned up together. Amber was armed with a camera, notebook and tape measure, Marian was carrying a plastic folder of photographs of stock in their shops and Inge just coughed and kept fumbling for tissues in the canvas bag slung over her shoulder.

'James, we've had a wonderful idea,' Amber called to me, after she'd shown them around the whole site. 'See these large pots,' she tapped at a picture in the folder of some typical Greek pithoi. 'We should have a really big one in the middle of the courtyard entrance. They can be adapted to make water features. Wouldn't that be wonderful?' Her face was glowing with excitement.

'And over here' – she dashed across the courtyard area to the main doorway – 'we should have a similar pair of pots, planted with something blue and trailing that echoes the water.' She stared down at the spot and then looked again at the photograph of the urns. 'Not lobelia in this climate, something that will last.' She frowned, then said, 'Oh, I've got it. My mother used to have a wonderful cascading rosemary – Sea Waves or Blue Waves, I think she called it. That's what we'll have to plant here.'

Marian was smiling at Amber's infectious mood as she followed her round. 'She's really making this place come alive with her ideas, isn't she?'

Then Amber was walking through the main door, into the restaurant area and out onto the terrace, which we knew would have the most desirable tables in the summer, with its shady vine-draped beams and view of the whole valley. 'And we've got to have thyme growing everywhere. We'll plant it in troughs here' – she marked the edge of the terrace with a wave of her hand – 'and in window boxes' – she turned, sweeping her hand towards the windows – 'and we'll have individual pots of thyme on the tables.' She stared at a corner where one of the tables would eventually sit, covered with a white cloth and sparkling glasses, then said with a shriek of excitement, 'Ooh, I know, I know! Each pot will have an enamelled plant label standing in it and the label will have the table number on it, not the plant name. Isn't that a good idea?'

I loved her being this excited; seeing her happy mood I could forgive her for bringing the two women along. They were laughing too, enjoying her carefree enthusiasm. 'That all sounds great,' I said. 'It's all coming together, isn't it? Now all we need to do is get the website going and pray for bookings.'

'You will do well, I am sure,' Inge croaked in her husky voice, before coughing again.

'And we'll send visitors across to you once you're open,' Marian added. 'You must make sure we have a good stock of your business cards. If you decide to have the pithoi, I'd really like people to see them in situ and get an idea of how to make the most of them. See? We're going to really be able to help each other.'

I had to agree with that. With so many businesses competing for trade during the main season, it was vital that complementary enterprises were mutually supportive. Ben had promised to promote us as well, although most of his visitors wanted to stay near his restaurant for the beach and all its various watersports. But I couldn't deny that Marian's shop could be useful. 'And we'll make a point of supporting the Mill too,' I said. 'We could have some cards to hand out and maybe put a note about you in the menu and on the website.'

Marian and Inge nodded at each other, then Marian said, 'We'll see what kind of deal we can offer you once you've finally decided which pieces you want from the shop. I'm sure we can come to some advantageous arrangement.'

We shook hands and then I suggested we warm ourselves in the temporary kitchen with fresh coffee. Down on the coast the climate was temperate, but up here in the mountains the high altitude meant temperatures were low at this time of year; that morning there had been a frost, and some of the older villagers said there could even be a light covering of snow soon.

The kitchen still wasn't very warm, but we huddled around an old picnic table and sat on scratched white plastic garden chairs, which Ben was throwing out of one of his villas. I brewed coffee and apologised for the chipped mugs, which were all we had on the site. 'It won't be like this when we finally open,' I joked. 'I want everything to be clean and perfect by then.'

'This is good enough for now,' Marian said, blowing on her steaming mug. 'And we have brought something for you here, to go with the coffee, haven't we, darling?' She turned to Inge, who bent down to retrieve a parcel of tin foil from her shoulder bag. As she unwrapped the package, Marian said, 'It's plum cake and it's delicious at any time. I'm always begging Inge to make it for me and she hasn't baked any for ages, so you're in luck today.'

Inge laid the opened foil on the table, revealing pieces of crumble-topped cake, scattered with toasted almonds. 'It's not quite how it should be made, but this is the way I do it now.'

I took a bite. It was sweet, then there was the taste of sourer plums, a hint of cinnamon and the crunch of almonds. I held it out in front of me and examined the structure.

'Is something wrong?' Inge looked concerned. 'You don't like it?'

'No, it's delicious. I was just trying to work out how you made it.'

Her face relaxed and she smiled. 'My mother used to make it for us all the time. It's called *pflaumenkuchen* – which is really just German for plum cake.'

I took another bite. 'It's really good.'

'She makes a great apple cake too,' Marian said, with a broad smile at her friend.

'You'd better not start selling this in your shops,' I joked. 'I don't want any more competition.'

As we were laughing, there was a knock at the half-open door and Dimitri looked in. 'Excuse me,' he said, looking directly at me, 'when you're free, may we talk?'

'Of course,' I said. 'I'll come right away.' I slurped the last of my coffee and brushed the crumbs from my jacket. 'Forgive me, ladies, I must get back to work.'

Chapter Twenty-Eight

9 June 1944

'I want Mama,' cries Anna, curling up on the bed and turning away from Agata to face the wall.

'And I want Rebekka,' sniffles Matilde, chewing the hem of her dress, exposing her skinny bare legs.

Neither child has a nightdress, they only have one clean dress apiece and neither has knickers. Maybe their mother had bartered cast-off clothes for food, or perhaps the town's traders are no longer allowed to deal with the Jews. Agata resolves to raid her store of linens to see what can be adapted. And if the girls are to stay with her through the winter, then she will have to prepare warmer clothing. Even though the coast is milder than the mountains and never sees frost and snow, it can still be cold when the winter storms begin and rage until late into the spring.

'There there, my dears,' she says in what she hopes they will take to be a soothing tone of voice. 'Try to settle down to sleep now. You will feel better in the morning.' She had hoped they would be tired after their day of new experiences. They had watched her milk the goats and collect eggs, then helped Georgiou pick beans in the garden. They had eaten well and squinted in the bright sunshine. She had held their hands on the beach and shown them the rock pools they were allowed to splash in. Surely they should sleep well tonight.

Anna rolls back towards her, colliding with Matilde, 'Want song. Rebekka sings at bedtime.'

'Can you sing to us?' her sister asks, taking her damp, chewed dress from her mouth and looking up at Agata with pleading eyes.

Agata smiles and agrees, but she has not sung to any children for many years. A long time ago, when she was the older sister, she had little brothers and sisters who liked her singing to them, but she has never had children of her own to hush to sleep.

She takes a deep breath and then begins to sing the only song she can remember from those times: '*Kouvelaki...*' As the song about a little rabbit wiggling its ears and playing hide-and-seek among the cabbages continues, the children begin to giggle and look very wide awake and Agata realises this is too lively a song to settle the girls at night-time. So she lays them down again, covers them with the cool sheet and resumes her singing. But her words grow softer as she strokes their hair until she is sure they are finally asleep.

She tiptoes from the room, hoping they will not wake till morning, and resolves to ask Georgiou if he can remember any songs from his childhood, ones more suited to a quiet, peaceful bedtime. But before she goes downstairs to prepare their evening meal, she lifts the heavy lid of the carved wooden chest, the chest that she and her mother filled with linens in preparation for her marriage. Scented with sandalwood and lavender lie folded white sheets, bedspreads and tablecloths, hardly used in this simple life just the two of them share. If their family had grown as they had hoped, all of this would have dressed their beds and their table, but it was not to be. She sighs and lifts out a large white cloth with bands of red and white embroidery. It will never cover her bed again, but she can put it to good use in clothing the little ones now in her care.

Chapter Twenty-Nine

Amber

January 2007

I couldn't quite put my finger on it. The visit to the site went well, I thought, but there was an undercurrent that didn't feel quite right. Whether it was because I was bubbling over with enthusiasm, which I can be sometimes, or because Inge clearly wasn't, well, I could not be sure, but there was definitely an atmosphere in the car as I started driving us back down the mountain roads to the coast.

Marian finally broke the silence, saying, 'Who was that man who came in to talk to James?'

'You mean Dimitri? He's our project manager.'

She was quiet for a moment then said, 'How did you find him?'

I couldn't be bothered to tell her the full story, about my injured foot back in the summer and the lunch in the autumn at Mama's Kitchen, so I just said, 'A friend introduced us. He's been amazing. I don't think we'd ever have got on with the development so quickly without his help.'

'Really,' Marian murmured.

We drove on for a while without talking, then I said, 'Why were you asking about Dimitri?'

She took a moment to answer. 'He looked rather familiar, that's all.'

I didn't think any more of it and continued driving, dropping Inge off at the beachside shop first, then continuing the journey up to the Mill of the Mountains. Marian was still fairly quiet and I was doing my best to encourage normal conversation. 'I'm so pleased you could come out to see the site today. It was really good of you to bring that file of photos. It helped so much. All these original touches are going to give Mountain Thyme such character and atmosphere.'

Then, finally, she spoke. 'I've never told you about the opposition we've faced, have I?'

I was startled by these words and began driving more slowly. 'No, what do you mean?'

I heard her take a deep breath, then she said, 'You mustn't think that everyone in Corfu will want you to succeed, you know. They may seem very friendly, but they may have their reasons.'

We had reached the mountain shop by now, so I parked. It was cold here too, but the morning frost had mostly gone, lingering only on corners of roofs untouched by the sun. I turned to her and said, 'Marian, what are you trying to say?'

'Let's go inside. Can you stay for a while?'

I followed her towards the barn and the almost fully grown kittens she cared for ran alongside us, mewing for food. 'I must feed these little monkeys first,' she said, walking to the outhouse they'd come from. She unlocked the padlock fastened to the door and went to a box of tins in the back. Soon the kittens were purring loudly and eating canned tuna.

Marian was smiling at them and bent to stroke their skinny backs and tails. She shook her head as she petted them. 'I will have to get them all neutered. There's two boys and two girls, so there could be trouble ahead. But I think four cats should be enough to deal with all the mice around here.'

We left them to their breakfast and crossed to the barn. Marian lit the wood-burning stove and we sat on wooden stools, close to the heat, drinking more coffee. 'Right,' I said, 'now tell me what's going on. You're obviously bothered about something.'

She sighed and put a heaped spoonful of sugar in her cup. 'They're very keen on family ties on the island, and even keener on hanging onto what they consider to be family property. Has Inge ever told you how she came to own the Mill à la Mer?'

'No, she's never said anything.'

'It was left to her by the old couple who gave her a job when she first came to the island, many years ago. They didn't have any children of their own and Inge not only worked for them, but she also cared for them in their old age. Apparently, they said she was like the daughter they never had and she was very fond of them too. In the end, they rewarded her devotion by leaving the entire property to her, both the shop and the house.

'Of course, the original business wasn't quite what it is now – in those days it was just another beach shop. It's Inge's talent that has made it so successful and so original. She is so clever.' Marian smiled and sipped her coffee.

'That was a real stroke of luck for her, inheriting the property.'

'Yes, very lucky for her, but not so lucky for the handful of distant relatives. They weren't at all happy about her good fortune. They tried to get the will declared invalid, but didn't succeed. At first, they made life rather unpleasant for Inge, but in recent years they've been quiet and we thought they'd forgotten about her.'

Marian paused, as if wondering how to proceed with her story. She put down her cup then continued, 'But now I'm wondering if perhaps they or someone else has decided to rekindle their resentment.'

'Why do you think that?'

She looked thoughtful, then said, 'About a year after we opened the mountain shop we got an offer.'

'You mean someone wanted to buy it?'

'So they said. But I think it was more that they didn't want us to succeed. You've heard of constructive dismissal? Well, it was more along those lines.'

'I'm not sure I know what you mean.'

Marian was smiling a little, but it was not the warm smile of pleasure and delight, it was the smile of one who is weary, tired of worrying, tired of fighting. 'We had such high hopes when the second shop opened. Inge wasn't sure about it at first, but I'd persuaded her that because so many people were buying properties on the island, we needed premises that could offer more for their homes than we could stock in the shop by the beach. We were getting such a great demand for the rugs and pottery there and people were always asking where they could buy furniture and larger pieces. That was what made me confident we could make a success of it.'

'But you're saying Inge had her doubts?'

Marian shook her head. 'No, I'd just say she was a little more cautious. But when we found this old place and saw the huge millstone in the courtyard, with the oregano growing through it, she was as committed as I was. But then,' Marian looked sad and sighed, 'back then, Inge was well. She was so strong, so healthy when we first met. And now,' she sighed again, 'now she is but a shadow.'

I put my hand on her shoulder and patted her. 'But she's having treatment, isn't she? There's every chance she'll get better?'

Marian shook her head. 'Not a chance.' She sniffed and wiped her nose on the back of her sleeve. 'And I don't want her to know how worried I am, so please don't say anything to her.'

'I won't, I promise.' I wasn't sure where all this was leading, so I said, 'But the business here, the Mill of the Mountains, has done well, hasn't it?'

'It has.' Marian was smiling properly now. 'We were absolutely right to expand up here. We had steady sales during our first season and we have had every year since. We advertise it with posters in the beachside shop and also with local estate agents, who are keen to support their new clients and convince them they can easily find lovely pieces to furnish their properties.'

'You must have found yourselves stretched, running two shops at the same time.' I was full of admiration for Marian and Inge's enterprise and in awe of their industry.

'Obviously we needed extra help in the season. So from the start we decided we would employ another person during the busiest time over the summer. That first year we hired Joanna. She was in her second year at Exeter, studying Classics and Ancient History, and she left at the end of the summer to visit the Roman ruins in Turkey. We've never had a problem finding bright kids to manage the beach shop, while we came up to the mountains.'

'It sounds like you had everything under control,' I said.

'Yes, I think we did. That first season went well and we both enjoyed coming here to take delivery of new stock and arrange displays. It was such a refreshing contrast to all that burnt flesh on the beach.'

I couldn't help laughing at that. 'I know what you mean.'

Marian laughed too. 'But then, after a year, with Inge not feeling well, she didn't want to come up here so much. She preferred to stay at home. She pottered around the beach shop and spent some of her time talking to customers, but she was no longer fit enough to come up here and haul heavy pots into cars. So I've been managing the Mill of the Mountains on my own for the last four years.'

'And you said you received this offer about a year after you'd opened?'

'That's right. It was summer, but it was early in the season. I'd left Inge rearranging sunhats and sandals down by the beach and I remember joking about it as I left. She's always been very particular about how she displays them.

'Then late in the morning, around the time the first tourists usually start arriving in the village, I'd just finished filling a large stone jar with stems of gladioli on that lovely old table' – Marian gestured towards the piece of furniture in the middle of the barn

– 'when I heard steps on the gravel outside. I turned to see a large man with dark sunglasses holding his hand under the trickling water of the fountain, which we'd only installed in the courtyard that spring. I remember him looking up and smiling. Then he wished me good morning and asked if I was open for business.

'So I asked him to come inside. It was already getting very hot and it was cooler in here. Then I asked him if he was looking for anything in particular.'

'And was he?'

'Well, he didn't answer right away. He started wandering around, picking up bowls and pots and turning them this way and that.'

I looked across to the tables displaying various pieces of pottery as she was talking.

'Then, when he finally spoke, he said, "Actually, I'm looking for a house." I can hear his voice now. It was soft and his English was good, but he wasn't a native speaker. "I would like to buy a house just like this one," he said. "Are you interested in selling?" Incredible.' Marian shook her head as if she was still astonished at his audacious question.

'So what did you say to that?'

'I couldn't quite believe what I was hearing, so I said, "What, you mean sell this house, where we have our business?" And then he said, and I remember this so clearly, he said, "Yes. This one. It is a very attractive property. I like it very much."'

'But there was no harm in that, was there, if he said it politely?'

'Oh yes, he was perfectly well mannered. So then I told him the answer was no. I said we had not had it all that long and we'd searched for quite some time to find the right place for our business. So the answer was definitely no.'

'So how did he respond to that?'

'At first he just smiled at me. He stood there' – she pointed to a spot in the middle of the barn – 'he stood there, rubbing the beard on his chin, staring at me. And then he said, "I believe you

might want to think carefully about your decision." I didn't like
that at all.' Marian frowned.

'That sounds rather like a mild threat.'

'It was a bit unnerving. But I felt I could handle it. I said we
didn't need to sell and had no intention of selling in the near
future. So, goodbye.

'Then I turned away from him and started to walk to the back of
the shop, to the counter where the phone is. I felt I wanted it near
me, just in case. Then, behind my back, I heard some shuffling steps
and I could feel my neck prickling. You know that funny feeling?'

I nodded.

'And then I looked round and he was standing right there in the
arched doorway, his figure black against the bright sunlight of the
courtyard. He stared at me for a few more seconds, almost as if he was
waiting for me to change my mind, and then he finally walked away.'

'And then what happened?'

'Oh, I rang Inge right away, just to hear her voice, but I couldn't
tell her about him. I didn't want to worry her. But all morning
I kept thinking I was going to hear the crunch of gravel again.'

'But is that all that's happened to worry you? That and your
poor cat?'

'Mmm, no, not quite all. There have been other petty incidents
– broken pots in the courtyard, rubbish in the fountain, that sort
of thing. But I suppose nothing major.'

'And have you seen that man again?'

She looked directly at me. 'I think I've seen him hanging around
from time to time. And I'm sure it was him when I was burying
Tabitha. And then,' she paused for a second, 'I thought I saw him
again today. In fact, I'm sure it was him. I knew his voice, too.'

'You saw him today? Where?'

'At the building site. At your restaurant.'

'What, you mean one of our builders?'

'No. Your site manager. Dimitri.'

Chapter Thirty

James

January 2007

I was more than happy to leave the women in the kitchen when Dimitri called me away. I rather enjoyed the muscular bustle of industry around the site as well as seeing how much progress was made each day. I hankered after helping with some practical task, like tiling or the fitting of new windows, but I'd absolutely no experience of any such handiwork and knew I would be a hindrance rather than a help, so I limited my input to making encouraging noises, offering regular cups of coffee and samples of any dish I'd been developing, and asking Dimitri how we were doing.

'Two more weeks,' he said. 'I think paint, lights, plumbing, all finished in two weeks.' He turned over a page on his clipboard, checking the list with his pen. 'Yes, I am sure nearly everything will be done by then.'

'That's marvellous. We're ahead of schedule. I wasn't expecting it all to be completed until the end of February at the earliest.'

He smiled, looking very proud of himself. 'We have been most fortunate. The rain, it has not been so hard this year.'

'So do you think we'll be able to start moving up here at the beginning of next month?'

He shrugged. 'Probably yes. Maybe we shall have to deal with a little problem here, a little problem there, but I expect so.'

'That's great news. I can't wait to start living up here. I've been wanting to move in for ages, but Amber wouldn't consider it until everything was finished.'

'Ah,' he smiled, 'the women, they like a home where all is in order.'

'They most certainly do. And they like it properly furnished too, so we need to get all our orders and deliveries confirmed and scheduled very soon.'

He looked down at his checklist again and finished making notes, then I heard Amber calling out that she was leaving with Inge and Marian. We watched the car rock its way along the bumpy cobbled street until they were out of sight. Dimitri stood next to me in silence until they were gone, then said, 'The ladies here today, you are buying all the furniture for the restaurant from the two ladies?'

'We're planning to buy some of it from them. Amber's very keen, and I quite like the goods they have in their shops as well.'

He was looking down again at his clipboard and nodding.

Sensing he had more to say on the subject, I said, 'Are you familiar with their shops? The Mill of the Mountains and the Mill à la Mer? The mountain shop is further south, nearer Pantokrator.'

'Yes, I have some idea of their business.' He glanced down at his notes again. 'May I ask, have you placed an order with these ladies yet?'

'No, not quite, but we're close to doing so. They know we're very interested in their stock. That's partly why they were here today, to help us finally decide which pieces would really work for us. Why do you ask?'

He tilted his head and grimaced a little. 'I just think perhaps you may find better prices elsewhere. I can put you in touch maybe with a very good man.'

'I see... Well, I think we've more or less decided on what we want to buy from the Mill shops, but I suppose there's no harm in taking another look around. Do you think we should go and see your chap?'

'I will call him for you. I will personally take you there and make the introduction. He has much excellent furniture and very reasonable prices.'

'Well, thank you. Cost is such an important consideration. This project is a huge investment for us, as you know, so I've got to keep my eye on every area of the budget.'

'Of course, you must spend wisely. Some of these people take advantage and charge too much. My man, he is very fair. He is a businessman and so are you. I think you will prefer him. He is an honest man of Corfu.'

I could have left it there. I mean, there was nothing wrong with us looking at another supplier, just as we had felt we should get more than one quote for the building work, but there was something about the way Dimitri spoke that made me wonder if he was holding something back. I wandered out to the terrace, where we would one day have our tables for lunch and dinner and where guests would breakfast on local yogurt and peaches on early summer mornings. Then I turned back and saw Dimitri was still standing in the doorway to the room where we would eventually have a reception area and bar.

'Dimitri, is there something you're not telling me?'

His eyebrows rose. 'Not telling?'

'Yes. Is there anything else I should know about the Mill ladies? What have you heard?'

He shrugged and looked a little sorrowful before giving a slight shake of his head. 'I hear things in my business. People talk to me. I meet many people who furnish their houses and many are not satisfied.'

'Well, in what way? What do they say?'

He shook his head again. 'Some say it is the price, some the quality, some there is damage and some are unhappy that their purchases are not delivered in good condition and on time. But' – he waved his hand in the air – 'that is just what I hear.'

'And is that all?'

He frowned. 'It does not matter to me,' he said, tapping his chest, 'but there are some who say it is because the older one, she is German. That is reason enough here. People do not forget what happened.'

'That's daft,' I dismissed this comment with a wave of my hand. 'I'm not interested in prejudiced gossip. Now, is there anything else we need to discuss before I go?' I walked across the terrace to look at the view over the surrounding olive groves and orchards. Some of the almond trees were already dusted with a haze of green from the first buds of spring.

Dimitri came and stood beside me, his clipboard closed and tucked under his arm. 'You have chosen well here,' he said.

'It's beautiful, isn't it? I love looking out on these trees, with the hills in the background on the far side of the valley. When people come to the restaurant, they're all going to want to sit out here on the terrace and enjoy this wonderful view when they're eating.'

Dimitri coughed, then said, 'Such beautiful land should be shared. Then you would have many more visitors for your restaurant.'

'What do you mean?'

He swept his hand across the vista, now darkening as heavy black clouds began to gather over the hills. 'Such an opportunity you have here. Top-class villas, here, here and here.' He jabbed his index finger at points in the landscape. 'Rich owners, high-paying guests, where do they go to eat in the evening? There is nowhere but this place. Your restaurant.' His hand swept the imaginary customers towards us and he nodded his head in satisfaction at this pronouncement. 'You will do very well here.'

'Yes, I see,' I said, gazing at the empty pasture and the groves of trees as the rain began to fall around us. 'I see what you mean.'

Chapter Thirty-One

9 June 1944

Rebekka is silent, but her mother is complaining. 'They have herded us like cattle. There's far too many of us here. One bucket of water and another for the business. It is not right to treat decent people like this.'

'Shh, Perla,' Papa says, keeping his voice low. Armed guards are watching, some move among the crowds – kicking a man in the back, tearing a bundle from a mother's arms, hitting an old man over the head with a rifle butt. 'Do not draw attention to us. We may not have to wait here very long.'

The entire population of the Evraiki has been crowded into the vast open quadrangle of the Paleo Frourio, the sixteenth-century Venetian fort built on a promontory jutting out into the sea on the eastern edge of Corfu Town. This secure island citadel has been used as a prison for centuries, separated from the town by a deep-sea channel still known by its Italian name – the Contra Fossa. When the cowering community crossed over the drawbridge, the Germans demanded their jewellery and the keys to their properties. Anyone who could not offer them valuables was beaten. 'I was afraid of this,' Papa says after handing over the key to the shop and a gold watch. Mama's hands were bare; her ring was sewn into the seam of her dress.

After that shameful parade in the main square in the relentless heat, the frightened people are at last able to sit or lie down. They are tired, they are hungry, and the Germans offer them nothing to eat, nothing to drink but a few buckets of water shared between hundreds.

There can be no escape for any of them now they have been marched into this barren place. To one side is the towering bare rock face leading to the fort's highest point, on the other, beyond the ancient low battlements, a sheer drop to the rocks and the sea. A baby and an old man have already met their fate in the waters below, and more may join them soon if exhaustion, hunger and the bored guards claim victims.

Within this arid, open ground, the Germans can see their captives clearly and there is no shelter. Everyone is exposed to the heat of the sun and the occasional shower of summer rain. As the sun moves across with the waning day, some people receive a little shade from the fort's ramparts and some have been crammed into the damp tunnels below, but the majority are fully exposed to the burning rays until evening approaches.

Rebekka sits cross-legged, her finger tracing a circle in the dry dust of the pebbled enclosure, studded with tufts of parched grass and weeds. The clean smell of hay is now overlaid with the tang of urine and stale sweat. She buries her face in her mother's sleeve. 'I've eaten all my bread,' she whispers. 'But I'm still hungry.'

'Try not to think about it. We have some more hidden, but we must make it last. Who knows how long it will be before we have proper food?'

'I hear they are waiting for boats,' Papa says. 'They are taking us to the mainland. There will be adequate supplies there, for sure. They are taking us away to work. They need strong, healthy workers, so I am sure they will feed us well.'

Rebekka clutches his hand. 'And what about Matilde and Anna? My little sisters are always hungry. Will they be given plenty to eat?'

'They will have the best,' Papa says. 'They will fatten up like little bunnies. Our friends will feed them well and they will grow big and strong.' Then he hugs his eldest daughter close to his chest, his greying beard brushing the top of her dark head, and she can't see his eyes filling with tears.

Chapter Thirty-Two

Amber

January 2007

'What did Dimitri want with you today?' James was home before me that evening and was already busy in the kitchen. I could smell crushed garlic and frying onions and there was steam from something simmering on the stove.

'Oh, nothing much,' he muttered, chopping carrots into tiny dice with rapid sweeps of the enormous sharp knife from his chef's collection. He was so proud of his expensive professional knives. His artillery, he called it. Then he looked up with a big smile on his face and laid down his tools. 'But the good news is, Dimitri thinks we're going to be able to move in very soon.'

'That's wonderful. When? Do you have a date?'

'Dimitri says a couple of weeks should do it. Isn't that exciting?' He returned to his chopping then scraped the diced vegetables into a pan.

I frowned. 'That's not far off. We'd better confirm the furnishings from the Mill. I don't want to get caught out.' I picked up my mobile phone to find Marian's number.

'Hang on a minute,' James said. 'I wanted to talk about it first.'

'But I thought we'd decided on what we wanted.' I was confused. We'd spent a lot of time visiting the Mill, measuring and photographing the furniture stocked there, and I'd felt our visit today had finally confirmed that the characterful pieces we'd selected were absolutely right for the project.

'Yes, but…' James was wiping his hands on his trousers. I had bought him a striped apron which he never used. He said chefs never wear aprons, so his normal clothes always needed an extra rub with washing-up liquid or stain remover before I did the laundry. And it was always me who did it.

I handed him a tea towel, which he left crumpled on the worktop. 'But what?' I said.

'I'd just like to think it over before we finally commit ourselves. All the basic stuff – the mattresses, the bedding, the bed frames and so on – you can go ahead with. That's all bog standard. But the more expensive key pieces, well, I'd like to think about them a bit more.' He turned to the large fridge and began sorting through the drawer where we stored the salads.

'But James, those special individual items are our most important pieces of furniture. They are crucial to the look of the whole place. I can't begin to take photos for the website without things like that lovely carved chest. Those pieces are the essence of Mountian Thyme – it's the basics, as you call them, that can wait. They're not hard to source. We can get those any old where. It's the signature pieces we need sooner rather than later.' I was confused by his prevarication. It seemed obvious to me that we had to have them as soon as possible.

'Listen, Amber,' he said, 'I do understand how you feel. You're absolutely right, of course. And I'm as anxious as you are to get the website up and running.'

'It's not a question of being anxious, it's about being ready in time. You've had your fun playing around on the building site and toying with your menus while I've been working on the promotional material, but I can't launch it without good pictures. The sooner I get the right shots, the sooner we have a chance of getting solid bookings this coming year. You do see that, don't you?' I put my mobile phone down on the worktop and stood facing him, hands on hips.

'Of course I understand. I know how efficient you are. You'll do a great job.' He wrapped the chicken breasts he'd just taken from the fridge in cling film and began hammering them with a wooden mallet to flatten them into thin escalopes. I couldn't continue the conversation with that noise, so I turned away from him and went upstairs to look at the partially constructed website and other material I had been writing and developing for the last month or so.

The restaurant name had been the catalyst for the design of the whole project, and I had been liaising with Lorna, a graphic designer friend back in London, on the logo and layout. We had incorporated images of the island, the views, the plant life and the local livestock, but pictures of the actual premises were still missing. We didn't even have a photograph of the exterior yet, let alone the interior showing the rooms where guests would sleep and eat. I couldn't make any further progress until at least some of the rooms were furnished and I knew that the website was the vital spearhead for our promotional drive.

I went back downstairs to find the kitchen was quieter, with only the noise of frying and simmering. James was stirring a sauce and looked up as I came in. 'Won't be long now. I've made *pollo cotoletta* with *melanzane alla parmigiana.*'

'I just had another look at the design for the website. Lorna and I have really gone just about as far as we can. It can't go live without photos of the rooms and I can't even begin printing business cards or leaflets until we sort out the interiors. I don't mean we need to have every single room finished, but I simply have to have a couple of them fully decorated and furnished as soon as possible.'

He stood beside the stove, leaning back against the worktop. 'Stop worrying. I promise you we'll make it a priority. Just bear with me and let's look around just a little bit more before we finally place the order. Just to be absolutely sure.'

'If you really think we must, okay, but I don't understand why you're suddenly so reluctant to go ahead with the Mill order. What's brought all this on?'

He turned back to his frying pan and was quiet for a moment as he lifted the cooked chicken out and slid it onto kitchen paper to drain. 'Oh, it was just something Dimitri said today, that's all. He's got a good contact in the furnishings trade who might be able to save us some money. So I said we'd go and take a look. You can't object to me wanting to watch the bottom line now, can you?'

I huffed. 'We'd better go there damn quick then. But I suppose if Dimitri thinks it's worth us going, then we should do it.' I was well aware of how helpful his advice and support had been. He had encouraged us and calmed us throughout the project, in fact, ever since I had stumbled on our first visit to the village early the previous summer.

'Great, I'll call him after dinner and fix it as soon as.' James lifted the baked aubergine out of the oven, then turned to mixing his favourite salad dressing.

'I had a funny conversation with Marian today, after we left you,' I said as I gathered cutlery for our meal. 'It seems she and Dimitri may have crossed paths before.'

'Really?' James was distracted, holding the glass jug up to the light to check how much vinegar he'd added to the mix.

'Dimitri didn't say anything to you, did he?'

'No, he didn't. We were too busy talking about the work schedule and a completion date.'

'Well, she doesn't seem to like him very much. But you don't think we've got any reason to feel worried about him, do you? He's been such an asset, hasn't he?'

'I have no qualms about him whatsoever,' James said, drizzling his concoction over a variety of green leaves in the olive wood bowl. 'I think we've got a lot to be grateful for and I'm not going to listen to any gripes from either of those two old dykes.'

'Don't talk about them like that. They're good friends and they have some wonderful stuff in their shops. But if you really feel we must weigh up the options, then of course we can go along and see how this other place measures up.' We carried our plates to the table and as we sat down I said, 'But it's going to be rather embarrassing if we let Marian and Inge down after all the interest we've shown, and they've both been so helpful. We've virtually promised them a substantial order. I wonder if I ought to let them know we might have to rethink. I'll ring after we've eaten and say we need to hang on for a couple more days, say we're checking our finances.'

'Oh, you don't need to worry about that,' James said, his mouth full of chicken. 'I've already told Marian.'

'What do you mean, you've told her? When?'

'Earlier. While you were upstairs.'

'You mean Marian rang you?'

'No, she rang your mobile, so I answered and said you were busy. She said she has to take Inge to the clinic tomorrow, so if you wanted to discuss the order and reserve some of those pieces, could it wait till the following day. So I said that's not a problem, we're having second thoughts anyway.' He took another large mouthful of food.

I dropped my fork onto my plate with a clang. 'You said *what*?'

Wolfing his food, he took a second or two to answer. 'She was fine about it. I told her it wasn't personal. She's a businesswoman. She understands how these things work.'

'But you had no right to do that.'

He frowned at me. 'I only answered the phone, for God's sake. Since when did that become a crime?'

'I can't believe you did that. You shouldn't have answered my phone, for a start. And you shouldn't have told her we might not be placing an order when we hadn't even discussed the possibility at that stage.'

'But we have discussed it. And you've agreed to look elsewhere.'

'I've agreed to look, but that doesn't mean I'm cancelling the order we might be giving to the Mill. How dare you assume it's not going to happen?'

'Well, what's the problem? So now she knows we're weighing up our options. There's no harm done. We can still go back to her and give her an order, if we change our minds.'

I was silent. I cut my chicken into small chunks and stabbed at a piece with my fork. It scooted off my plate and onto the tiled floor. As I bent to pick it up with my fingers, James said, 'You don't have to throw it all over the floor, if you don't like it.'

'It's fine,' I said, putting the fallen chicken on a side plate. 'I'm just not very hungry anymore.' I laid down my knife and fork. 'I think I'll go up and take another look at the website. I need to work out exactly how many photos we still need.'

'All right then.' James reached across the table for my plate. 'If you don't want it, you won't mind if I have it, will you?'

'Eat the whole bloody lot, why don't you?' I stomped up the stairs and slammed the door, muttering, 'And serves you right if you choke on it.'

Chapter Thirty-Three

James

January 2007

Greg rang again the following night. He wasn't quite as drunk as the last time, but he was still triumphant. 'I got one into the air con,' he shouted. 'What do you think of that?'

I couldn't help laughing and said, 'Well, that should cause a stink.' Then I added, 'Seriously, if you can possibly be serious for a second, are you free for a quick chat tomorrow?'

We arranged to meet for breakfast at a cafe Amber never went to in Corfu Town. I didn't want to take her along, even though she knew Greg was taking an interest in the restaurant and would be backing us, so I told her I had to get there early to meet a potential supplier. 'You're welcome to come with me if you want, but I'm meeting him in the harbour where they land the catch and it will be very early.'

'No, you go off on your own then. I don't need to see loads of smelly fish. Lorna's sending through another proof for the business cards, so I want to spend the morning dealing with that before we go off to meet your Costas guy.' We had arranged to meet Dimitri's furniture contact at his warehouse in Perivoli at two that afternoon. Amber had already grumbled again about it being a waste of time and she was still annoyed with me for speaking to Marian. She was also disgruntled about the location too, saying, 'Why is he all the way down there, the tacky end of the island? It doesn't give me much confidence this is going to be worth our while.'

It didn't give me much reassurance either, but I'd arranged it through Dimitri and, even though he wasn't coming along with us as suggested, I felt, having pushed Amber into agreeing to look at alternatives, that I had to follow through with the appointment.

I left our villa at seven thirty in the morning and parked in the car park on the harbour. In summer I always tried to be there early to grab a spot shaded by one of the oleander bushes, but today it was raining again and I splashed through puddles across the shining wet flagstones and up the steep steps to our rendezvous. Although the rain brought the promise of spring in the depths of winter, I detected the odours of sewage and rubbish lurking in the old alleyways.

Greg was waiting for me, already sipping from a small cup of strong Greek coffee. 'You want one of these as well?' he asked as I sat next to him.

'No, thanks. I don't need that kind of kick up the arse this morning. You feeling a bit the worse for wear today?'

'Don't ask. Pam's already read the riot act.' Greg shook his head in a weary way, then yawned and looked sorry for himself. 'She's a wonderful woman, but she doesn't have our sense of humour.' He yawned again.

I ordered eggs and bacon and milky coffee. Greg said he might eat something once the caffeine had worked its magic. 'Don't want to upset the old guts before they've woken up properly. So, what are you up to today?'

I told him about our afternoon visit to the furniture dealer Dimitri had recommended, saying, 'I don't know if it'll be any good, but it's a chance to check our options.' And I didn't say that Amber wasn't at all keen, nor that we'd had harsh words about it.

'I doubt he'll offer you the genuine article,' Greg said, 'but there's nothing wrong with having a look. Though bear in mind, you don't want to go spoiling the ship for a ha'porth of tar, as they say.'

'If it's not right for us, I'll be very diplomatic. I don't want to go putting Dimitri's nose out of joint.'

'Good plan,' Greg said. 'Best to keep on his good side. He's invaluable.'

'Too right. I'm beginning to realise that. In fact, he made an interesting observation the other day, about the potential of the land around the restaurant. You know, the undeveloped areas we look out onto from the terrace at the back?'

'Oh yes,' Greg murmured. 'I'd noticed that too. It's a very attractive area. Pasture and orchards mostly, isn't it?'

'Yeah, on the whole. There's some grazing and a large number of old trees that haven't been pruned in ages, so they won't even be very productive now. It's pretty rough land altogether. But a bit of development up there could be to our advantage. It could open up a whole new market.'

Greg took out a large white handkerchief and began blowing his nose. When he'd finished mopping up, he said, 'You don't think it would spoil your view?'

I shook my head. 'I've been thinking about it. There's plenty of space and loads of trees all around us. It could be very discreet. And,' I was getting excited, because I'd been thinking about the idea ever since Dimitri had mentioned it, 'if it was an upmarket development, it would bring us an equally upmarket clientele, wanting a first-class restaurant.'

Greg was looking serious and nodded in agreement. 'Could be just the leverage you'd want by then. The jump from lowly bistro to fine dining, you mean?'

'Exactly. There's no point in aiming for a Michelin star if there's no one to appreciate it, is there?'

'You're setting your sights high, my boy. Very high.' Greg waved at the waiter and ordered scrambled eggs with chorizo, saying, 'I need some spice as well as caffeine to pick me up today.'

'Well, you agree with me, don't you?'

'About the Michelin star or the development?'

'Both. All I've ever wanted to do is create a beautiful restaurant with amazing, original food. But I need to reach customers who will appreciate it. This way we could be on to a winner. But I don't know how to set the ball rolling. Do I have to invest more myself, find other investors or talk to potential developers? What do I have to do to make it all happen?'

I'd finished eating but Greg's breakfast hadn't yet arrived. He picked up the piece of crisp bacon I'd left on the edge of my plate and began chewing it, looking thoughtful. 'It's not that easy here,' he said. 'Undeveloped land up there might not be that straightforward. You don't know quite what you're getting into.'

'But it's not out of the question, is it?'

'Course not,' he said, suddenly choking on the dry bacon shards and reaching for the water that had been left on the table when the coffee was served. After a couple of gulps his coughing had subsided and he gasped, 'But you don't want to go getting involved in all that yourself. Could be all sorts of tricky complications. Family land, restricted covenants, that sort of thing.'

'Sounds like it could be messy. You don't think I should investigate it further?'

He shook his head and sipped more water from his glass.

'You don't think that development there could be worthwhile?'

He cleared his throat. 'I didn't say that. I just meant you don't want to go getting tied up in that sort of thing personally. You've got your hands full already, finishing the restaurant, setting up your guest accommodation, launching the business, securing suppliers. Don't you think you've got enough on your plate?' He laughed at those final words and added, 'Plate, restaurant, funny eh?'

I laughed with him. He was such a likeable rogue, even though his jokes were terrible. 'But if someone else spots the possibilities with this land and the wrong kind of properties are built there, it would do just the opposite. It could actually have an adverse effect on our business. You do see that, don't you?'

'Course I do,' he said as his eggs arrived. He scattered them with ground pepper and Tabasco, then continued, 'I'm not saying it shouldn't happen, I'm just saying keep your eye on the ball, or restaurant in this case, and don't worry about it.'

'But if I don't worry about it, who will?'

'Leave it to me,' he said, with his mouth full. 'I'll put out some feelers. Don't you worry. I won't let a little gem like this pass me by.'

I leant back in my seat, relieved he had seen it my way. 'So you might take an interest then?'

He nodded and when he'd finished eating, he said, 'You just concentrate on fretting about your fritters, my boy, and leave the finances to me.'

Chapter Thirty-Four

11 June 1944

'You have to tell them,' Georgiou says. 'It is for their safety. The Germans have left us alone here so far, but who knows what could happen? Our steep valley with its narrow track should keep us hidden and safe from vehicles. But one day there may be a plane overhead, or a boat could be patrolling the coast and down anchor in our bay. There could even be a motorbike or a patrol down the track. We must tell them what they might have to do to be safe.'

'I will explain,' Agata says. 'I am so afraid of scaring them, but you are right. They must be told.' She glances across to the little beach from the shade of the terrace, where a grapevine curls its tendrils and bunches of fruit are already beginning to swell. The girls are playing on the sand, gathering shells and stones, laughing and chattering as children should, as if there has never been a threat to their lives. Already, after only a couple of days of fresh air and sunshine, their cheeks, once pale from months of imprisonment, are flushed and golden.

As long as they have each other they don't seem to be distressed. They had both cried out again in their sleep last night, but now they seem content and are both eating well. Georgiou will cast his net in the rocky bay again tonight, as fishing is no longer permitted on open waters. And if they are lucky, he might spear another octopus in the shallows.

Agata kneels down on the sand and holds out a handful of shells to add to the swirling labyrinth pattern they are creating. 'Such clever girls,' she says. 'Your mama and papa would be proud of you.'

'And Rebekka,' adds Matilde. 'She's our big sister.'

'Of course, and Rebekka. She would be proud of you too. And because you are both so clever, I know I can ask you to keep a very special secret.'

The girls pause in their game and gaze at her, their eyes and mouths wide open.

'You know how Mama and Papa asked you to always be very quiet in your home in Corfu Town? Remember how you hid indoors like two little mice, so no one knew you were there?'

'Because of the bad men,' shouts Anna.

'That's right. They didn't want the bad men to ever see you.'

'And now we are here, there aren't any bad men, are there?' Matilde says.

'That's right, they're not here. But if they did come here, what do you think you should do?'

'Hide,' shouts Anna, then drops her voice to a whisper, 'and be very very quiet.' She lays a finger across her lips.

'Very good,' Agata says, giving her a quick hug. 'And I have the best secret hiding place for you. No one will ever find you there. Would you like to see it right now?'

Both girls jump to their feet and hold her hands. 'If we ever hear a plane or a boat, or strange men come down here,' Agata says, 'this is where you must run and hide straight away. You don't even have to ask me first, you must just run there, fast as you can. Then I will always know where to find you, won't I?' She leads them up the stairs to the upper terrace, through the house and up the next flight to the room where the girls sleep.

'Shall we hide under the bed?' Matilde says. Anna giggles and throws herself on the floor, ready to wriggle beneath the bed frame.

Agata laughs with them. 'I have a better idea,' she says, and opens the wardrobe door and shows them the little doorway at the back, leading into the cavity beyond, set into the thick walls of the house. 'Shall we all try and get into it together?' She crawls into the hiding space with much puffing and groaning. 'Oh, I'm far too big for such a tiny hidey-hole. It's not meant for fat old ladies like me.'

Matilde and Anna skip up and down, laughing, then crawl in after her. It is dim inside, but not totally dark, with light and fresh air filtering through the grille above them in the wall. Agata pulls the little door shut.

'See, here is a catch, so you can make sure the door cannot be opened from outside. Try it for yourself.'

They take it in turns to open and close the door till they are both satisfied they won't be locked in forever.

'And just in case you have to stay in here for a while, I think we should make it comfortable, don't you? So what do you think you will need in here?'

'Breakfast,' shouts Anna.

'Water,' says Matilde. 'And blankets.'

'Anything else?' says Agata. 'There will always be water and food waiting in here for you, just in case you suddenly have to run and hide yourselves. I will make sure of that.'

'We must have a bowl for us to wee in,' shouts Matilde, and both girls laugh and roll over, kicking their heels in the air.

Agata joins them in their laughter. 'All right, I'll leave a big bowl in here, in case you ever have to stay hidden for a while. But maybe that will never happen.'

Let us pray it will never be needed, she tells herself.

Chapter Thirty-Five

Amber

March 2007

As James and Dimitri pushed the heavy elm chest into place, I breathed a sigh of relief. I had always known it would look perfect and bring Mountain Thyme's reception area to life. The wood gleamed from the many hands that had touched its surface over the years and as I stood back to admire it, the coffer seemed to breathe with relief and settle into its new home as if it had always been there.

'You see?' I said to James. 'Doesn't it look wonderful? I never had any doubt the Mill would give us just what we wanted. There was never any need to look anywhere else.'

'You win,' laughed James. 'Now we'd better unload the rest of the stuff.' Dimitri was silent and I was reminded that he had initiated the visit to the warehouse filled with expensive, ornate furniture, which was nothing like the simple rustic pieces we were now putting into place.

While the men talked loudly about what should be brought in next and how they were going to manipulate the heavy table and chairs through the narrow entrance, I tenderly polished the chest. Its deep interior would make perfect storage for all the table linen we planned to use; we'd both agreed that we'd never have paper napkins on our tables. And although we'd want to open the chest at least once a day, I thought I could still display a pottery bowl filled with business cards on top.

The van driver and his mate came shuffling onto the terrace with a long narrow table. Its rich dark top was made of cherry wood and the legs and struts were oak. 'No, not inside,' I shouted. 'Over here, over here.' I dashed to the side of the building, where the terrace was sheltered and dry under a tiled roof. 'Put it right there, please.' Grunting all the while, they settled the table against the roughly plastered wall, where I planned it would hold baskets of cutlery, a pile of white linen napkins and bottles of local olive oil. Underneath, between its sturdy legs, there would be a display of large earthenware bowls and flasks. And above, I planned to hang the carved blue cupboard, still impregnated with the scent of ancient spices.

James and Dimitri returned, both carrying heavy chairs with tall carved backs under each arm. I directed them to place a chair either side of the table and to put the other two in the reception area. These were not meant for use as everyday seats, although they could easily take a substantial weight and probably had done so for 200 years or more; they were decorative features, adding character to the bare rooms which had been given a fresh coat of white paint, in traditional Greek style.

I was longing to shoo the men away and begin adding the finishing touches to our new interior so I could take photos. In the last couple of weeks we'd taken shots of some of James's dishes: his duck ragu with orange, herb-coated grilled lamb and braised rabbit garnished with olives. I'd photographed the olive trees below the terrace and the wild garlic at the foot of the steps to the ruined church, but the website still lacked images of our premises.

When the last urn had left the truck and I was satisfied everything was in the right position, I went to the car to fetch my camera. I wanted to take the pictures and send them across to Lorna immediately, because I knew I was going to be busy with other deliveries for the next couple of days. Dimitri was talking to the van driver, but as I approached he slapped him on the back and turned to me, saying, 'You have made excellent purchases, madam. Such authentic craftsmanship is so hard to find these days.'

'Thank you, I'm really pleased with everything so far, but I'm sorry if we put you in rather an awkward position, not giving the order to your friend.'

He shrugged, saying, 'It is of no consequence. Your husband maybe had some doubts, I think, about your lady friends. It was good for him to see that you were right in your choices.' He gave a slight nod of his head when he'd finished speaking, a gesture that felt almost like a subtle acknowledgement of my superior judgement, then I thanked him and went to my car.

I spent the following hour taking pictures and looking at each of the five bedrooms, trying to decide which one should be featured on the website homepage. I planned to take this photograph after the beds had been delivered. Although the frames and mattresses would be new, I'd insisted on carved headboards to add character and each one was slightly different: one had curling acanthus, another animal heads looking like a cross between a camel and a goat, while the others were more architectural with solid carved bands around the frame. I finally decided to focus on the bedroom at the back of the hotel, with its view of the far mountain. I was dying to begin snapping pictures, but knew I'd have to wait for the next delivery of furniture and until I had made up the bed with crisp white linen and the blue and white traditional bedspreads we had chosen for all of the guest rooms.

I wandered back across the upper landing and through the other bedrooms to satisfy myself that the headboards were in the right places. I stood and looked out of the windows at the front of the house, down onto the terrace, which would be laced with vines in the summer. The room at the corner of the house also had a side window looking down the street. It wasn't the best view we had, but the almond trees were still in flower and there was a dusting of pale petals over the dark cobbles, which made me reach for my camera. I took a couple of shots and as I took a third and a fourth, two men came into view, talking with harsh gestures, one jabbing the other's shoulder. This time there were no jovial slaps on the back. They were arguing face-to-face and one pushed the other in the chest. Then I saw a wad of money being exchanged. I thought one of them might have been Dimitri, but from above, and half turned away from me, one dark Greek head looks much the same as another.

Chapter Thirty-Six

James

March 2007

I had to give Amber credit. She had been absolutely right all along to order from the Mill women. Their furniture was perfect for our kind of business. But although I could respect Marian and Inge for their discerning eye and ability to source original pieces of furniture, I couldn't really warm to them as people. 'You're not off to see them again, are you?' I'd said to Amber. 'We're not buying anything else from them, so why bother?' Maybe it was Inge's coughing, which exposed her yellowed smoker's teeth, or Marian's ever-solicitous attitude that irritated me. They turned to each other constantly, completing each other's sentences, stroking each other's hands.

'I find them fascinating,' Amber said. 'They've both led such interesting lives. Anyway, you're always off meeting Greg and I don't complain about that. I may not like him much, but I can respect him and his contacts and I'm very aware of how helpful he is to us.'

'Well, don't let them persuade you to buy anything else today,' I said as we finished breakfast on the terrace. It was still early in the year and most days it was too chilly to sit outside, but today, the sun was shining with a promise of glorious summer mornings to come, when we would share breakfast with paying guests and fill the restaurant with appreciative customers at lunch and dinner. I was still working on finalising my menus for the spring and summer, but that particular day, once Amber had left to visit her women friends, I was expecting Greg.

'What's he coming over for today?' Amber was dabbing at the croissant crumbs on her plate with a moistened finger.

'Just a catch-up. I thought I'd give the lamb with baby artichokes a trial run. But don't worry, there'll still be some left for us tonight.'

She smiled. I loved her smile. 'Well, just you make sure there is. I'm looking forward to trying that dish.' She picked up her plate and cup and shivered. 'It's still a bit chilly out here this morning, even though it's lovely to sit outside again at last.' She gazed out across the orchards to the other side of the valley. 'I just love this view. We are so lucky to have found this place.'

'I'll clear up,' I said. 'You need to get a move on.'

'Okay, I'll go. I want to pop into town first. Do you want anything? I need some pants from M&S.'

'No, thanks. I've got my deliveries all sorted.' I loved using the local suppliers for all the meat, fish and vegetables and hated the reminders of the British high street in the centre of Corfu Town. 'Get some lacy ones, won't you?' I called as she ran down to her car.

'No chance,' she shouted back. 'I need them big, white and comfy.' She laughed and waved to me.

I watched her go then checked the time. She would be gone until mid-afternoon, giving me plenty of time. Greg was coming soon, so I had to get to work on lunch. The lamb had been alive the day before yesterday, but now it was marinating in wine, herbs and garlic. It didn't need tenderising, but the flavour was improved with those additions. The artichokes had been grown nearby and if they were picked at just the right time, while they were still young, they were small enough to cook and eat whole, before the core had grown into a choking, hairy thistle.

I was absorbed in my preparations, dicing garlic, when Greg arrived. He crept up on me in the kitchen, with its new gleaming workstations and huge fridges, and I suddenly felt a clap on my back and caught the edge of my finger with my knife. 'Bastard,'

I yelled. 'Look what you've made me do.' I held my finger under the cold tap then wrapped it in kitchen paper.

'You'll need another of those blue plasters.' He laughed and laughed, staggering to the opposite worktop to support himself in his mirth. 'Chef's badge of honour, aren't they?'

I dried and taped my finger then started laughing with him. 'You won't find it so funny when all my fingers are cut to pieces, you idiot. Anyway, an experienced chef shouldn't have any blue plasters.'

'Come on, man up. What's a scratch between friends?' He started lifting the foil on the roasting tins, inspecting the contents. 'This lunch?' he said, bending and sniffing the dishes.

'It will be if I can get it done in time. And don't go poking your dirty fingers in there.' He snatched his hand away and pulled a face at me. 'I'm going to have to ban you from the kitchen once we're up and running. I won't be getting any kind of star if we're not up to standard on the hygiene front as well as with the food.'

He gave me a mock salute, 'Yes, chef. I'll certainly follow orders. Now, can we get on with business or do you want me to finish peeling spuds and washing-up first?'

'You can sit over there, out of my way,' I pointed to the little table with four chairs to one side of the kitchen, which I planned would one day become the so-called chef's table, where guests would pay a premium to dine in the heightened atmosphere of a working kitchen and sample a tasting menu of my latest creations. 'Just sit down and stay put while I finish this off.' I sprinkled oil and seasoning over the artichokes and wiped down the countertop. I was meticulous about cleaning work areas and had to clear away as I finished each task. It helped me to feel in control and concentrate. Then I brewed coffee and brought it to the table with a plate of little sugary madeleines I'd made earlier.

'Any luck?' I said, looking at the fat file Greg had just opened. It was full of documents, copies of old deeds by the look of it, and faded maps.

'I've asked Dimitri to join us. With his help, we should be able to throw a bit more light on this stuff. It's as I suspected, all very complicated. A whole tangled mess of land transactions over the years. All interbred, like most of the peasants round here.' He showed me a rough map, very similar to the one we'd seen when buying our house. 'This is you,' he said, stabbing at a section which someone had coloured in with a red pen, 'and over here, this is the area we're thinking about.'

'What are all those lines criss-crossing over it?'

'That's the problem. Are they historic or are these parcels of land still owned separately?' Greg sighed and showed me the stack of papers accompanying his maps. 'My guy thinks the land isn't registered to anyone actually still alive now, and that something similar to common land rights has been exercised in the past. But we can't be absolutely sure, so that's why I've asked Dimitri over.'

'Are you sure he'll be able to help?' I looked at the documents, with their faded handwritten scribbles. 'It's all in Greek.'

'Yeah, it's all Greek to me too.' He thumped the table with a whoop of delight. 'But it won't be to him, will it? Hah!'

Chapter Thirty-Seven

11 June 1944

'Papa, wake up. Some people are leaving. Where are they going?' Rebekka stands up, stretching on the tips of her toes, trying to see what is happening. There is a commotion on the far side of the fort quadrangle, where steps and slopes carved into the rock lead down to a harbour.

Soldiers are pushing groups of people forward and shouting. When a woman drops her sack and tries to turn back for it, she is hit with the butt of a rifle and the soldier kicks her possessions to one side as she stumbles forwards.

Papa groans and shakes himself awake from his uncomfortable sleep. They have been lying on the hard dirt floor of the fort for two nights and lumpy sacks and bundles make poor pillows. The cool night air has been a welcome relief after the scorching heat of the day, but their bones ache and their stomachs growl with hunger.

'Sit down, child. I will try to see what's happening.' He crawls to the side of the terrace, between the tightly packed half-sleeping bodies. Some grumble as he kneels on a foot or a hand, some are already awake and on their knees swaying, eyes closed in prayer. A weeping woman is clutching an unresponsive grey-skinned baby to her breast and another group is singing softly.

'What can you see?' Rebekka calls, as he peers round the corner of the wall in the direction of the departing crowd. He doesn't reply, but creeps back, and she can tell by his expression that it isn't good news.

'I can't really see anything, but I heard them say that they have to wait for more boats,' he says. 'The first groups are being loaded onto boats now. Let us hope we won't have to wait much longer and wherever we go will be better than here.'

Rebekka huddles closer to her mother. She doesn't like being imprisoned in the Old Fort and already there are signs of sickness and death. But now she fears leaving. All her short life she has lived in their house in Corfu Town, in the rooms above her father's shop, where swallows nest in the eaves and call to each other as they return each night. She has attended the synagogue in Vellissariou Street, fetched provisions for her mother, called on the baker and delivered repaired shoes for her father, but she has never left the island, never travelled by boat and never been parted from her family. She hopes that whatever happens she will never be parted from Mama and Papa and she prays she will see Matilde and Anna again one day.

Chapter Thirty-Eight

Amber

March 2007

Much as I loved our new home, delighting in all we had achieved, I still relished escaping to visit Inge and Marian. Mountain Thyme was wonderful but it wasn't yet peaceful, with workmen still completing various jobs around the place. As I left, one builder was hammering at the pergola over the terrace and another was drilling with an angle grinder into a slab of stone, filling the air with piercing screeches and blue smoke. But when I finally reached the Mill à la Mer early in the afternoon – after the long drive down through the hills, the straight road into Corfu Town and a successful shopping trip in which I purchased not only sensible comfortable white pants but also less sensible black lace – I knew I would find peace.

As I climbed the long flight of stone steps to their living quarters, I saw that they had hung their birdcage outside on the wide balcony to catch the sun. The two little green and yellow parakeets chirped and hopped, then nuzzled each other. Marian had told me they used to keep a rabbit on the balcony, but that the birds were less trouble, and Inge had added, 'She means they don't bite through the wires. Our naughty *kaninchen*, she loved to chew the telephone wire. And we wondered why we never had any phone calls.'

Inge was resting on the balcony terrace, her thin legs stretched out on a faded cushioned lounger, her shoulders, despite the spring sunshine, wrapped in a shawl. 'Darling,' she croaked, letting her cigarette smoulder in her fingers, 'how wonderful to see you.' She waved her hand, smoke trailing. 'And I have you all to myself. Marian is working at the other shop today.'

'I can go if you want to rest,' I said. 'I know I hadn't warned you I was coming, but I just thought I'd drop by on my way back.'

'No, stay, please. I'm tired of resting. Stay and talk to me. Talking will stop me smoking any more.' She stubbed out her cigarette in a dish already filled with half a dozen fag ends. 'What refreshment shall we have now? Did you eat?'

'Don't worry about me. I already grabbed some lunch in town. But I can get you something if you want. Just tell me what you'd like me to do.'

But she was already easing herself off the lounger and getting to her feet. 'Come with me. Let us see what we can find.' She led the way into their kitchen and dining area and opened a large cupboard, then took down a dented and scratched green cake tin. '*Gut*, we are in luck. Marian always takes some cake with her to work, but there is still enough here for us two.' She showed me the contents of the tin. '*Apfelkuchen*. It is quite good cold, but we shall have it warm, just as my mother used to.' She switched on the oven and pushed the pieces of cake inside on a baking tray, then looked inside the little fridge. 'We should really eat it with *schlagsahne* or crème fraîche, but here,' she picked up a plastic tub, 'Greek yogurt will do just as well.'

Then Inge began to cough, holding onto the back of a chair for support, so I made her sit down while I boiled water to make coffee for her and tea for me. She told me where to find cups and plates and soon we were sitting with warm cake in front of us, each piece dusted with icing sugar and crowned with a dollop of yogurt. The moist sweet cake was better for the sharpness of the apples and had a hint of cinnamon. 'I remember Marian praising this,' I said, 'when you came up to see the restaurant early in the year.'

Inge smiled as she broke the cake into pieces with her fork. 'Such an exciting project, for you both. I understand how very special it is to share love and work. Marian, she is my partner in business as well as in life.'

'You've been together a long time, haven't you? And Marian told me about how when you came here, you worked for the old couple who originally owned the shop. How long ago was that?'

'So many years,' Inge murmured, half closing her eyes. 'Dear Agata, darling Georgiou. They were so sweet, so caring, and I shall never forget them. I owe everything to them and will do my best to respect and honour all they did for me and for others. And when I am finally gone, Marian will take over everything.'

I knew I shouldn't pry, but I couldn't resist. 'Do you mean you'll leave the shop to her?'

'Of course. It is hers now anyway, I have seen to that. And the mountain shop is all hers too. She is the one who has had the ideas and the energy in recent years. I owe it to her to make sure she will be able to continue after I've gone, which will not be much longer now.'

'Oh, you mustn't talk like that.'

Inge shrugged. 'But it is true. I have to accept that. And one day, when you know you don't have much longer either, you too will want to think about what you will leave behind. You will give your favourite jewellery to your children; you will want a cousin to have your silver hairbrush and a friend to have the vase she has always admired. It is a time to be truthful and tell those you care about how much you love them.'

'Is that what you feel you are doing now?' I'd eaten only a little of the cake; I couldn't manage to eat while she was in this mood.

'There is only Marian. She is the one I care for most and she will have everything I possess. But,' she hesitated and looked at me, 'I worry that she will be alone, and the fact is I know she will almost certainly be on her own, for it is most unlikely she will find another partner to share her life. So I hope she will always have good friends around her.'

I nodded. 'Of course she will. You mustn't worry about that.'

She smiled. 'And I hope she will have someone who can share with her my legacy in telling the truth.'

I was puzzled. 'Telling the truth?'

'Telling the truth about the past.' She sighed. 'For a long time I couldn't do it. Tell the truth, I mean. Then, as I came to realise that time would disappear, I decided I should face it.'

'I don't understand what you mean.'

She smiled at me. 'Eat, *meine kleine Mädchen*, and I will tell you. I'll tell you the story of how I came to live and work here, how I learnt what it means to be good and how I have tried to honour the memory of two brave people, Agata and Georgiou.'

Chapter Thirty-Nine

James

March 2007

While Dimitri and Greg were hunched over the documents, I peeled potatoes to roast next to the lamb and rinsed freshly picked greens to wilt in garlic and oil. There was intense discussion between the two men and, what with the noise of both the boiling water in the pan on the hob and running water from the tap, I caught very little of what they were saying. When I finally sat down again, Greg said, 'It seems we might not have a problem here after all.'

'Why's that?'

'Because it appears that nobody actually owns the land.'

'But there are fruit and olive trees out there. Surely someone must own them?'

'They used to.' He paused and smiled. 'But not any more.'

'How come?'

'Dimitri, tell James what you've just been telling me. You'll do it much better than I can.' Greg got up from the table. 'All right if I help myself?' He was already standing by the wine rack, pointing to the bottles, so I just nodded.

'The old families, the people who once lived here and owned the land, they moved away, long times past.' Dimitri spread out the map and pointed to various sections. 'See, here is written their names, but these people are no longer here. I know all of the families in this region. The old ones, they leave. They do not care for the land any more, so it does not belong to them now. And here and here,' his finger circled other areas on the map, 'the land has never been owned.'

'But what does that mean exactly?'

He shrugged. 'It means anyone can claim it.'

'And can they then develop the land? Use it for building?'

Dimitri nodded. 'Agricultural land, yes.'

I stood up and looked out of the window over the land in question. The gnarled groves were thick with weeds and scattered with rocks, but there were other areas of scrubland, dotted with tussocks of grass and thorn bushes. 'And what about the uncultivated land around here? Have its owners disappeared too?'

Dimitri smiled. 'That is not a problem either,' he said. 'It is, how you say, up for grabs.'

Greg sat down again with a large glass of red wine, holding the bottle in his other hand, and I could see he'd helped himself to one of the better vintages. 'Didn't I tell you this guy was great? He knows just about everyone and everything on this island. I knew he'd get to the bottom of it for us.'

'But I don't understand how this can work. It seems far too easy.'

Dimitri coughed, then said, 'There are some restrictions to development, but in certain circumstances, if perhaps…'

He hesitated, as Greg put a hand on his arm. 'Enough of that. We don't need to go into the boring details. We know where we stand and that's enough to be going on with.'

'So what happens now?'

'First things first, my friend.' Greg stood up again and went to fetch two more glasses. 'We have to toast this guy's brilliance.' He poured the wine and we clinked glasses. Greg then knocked back his drink and poured himself some more. 'And our next move is getting this little lot,' he tapped the papers on the table, 'all registered correctly. And once it's all above board, we can start making some proper plans.'

'Will that cost much?' I was suddenly worried that after all the expenditure involved with the restaurant, I might be expected to chip in after all.

Greg began to laugh and Dimitri joined him. I couldn't understand what was so funny, then Greg said, 'Just leave it to me. I'll sort it, don't you worry.'

He raised his glass again, and so I responded to his toast. Why should I question the details, when I just wanted to concentrate on running Mountain Thyme and making it a huge success? So my only comment was, 'How long do you think it might take to start building, once you've got it all sorted out?'

'Well, it ain't gonna happen overnight, that's for sure,' Greg pulled a wry face. 'I'll need to sort the money side first. But I should think two years down the line we'll certainly have started. I've done new build before and you get the money in before completing, so it becomes self-funding in the end.'

'Two years? That's not so very far away,' I said. 'If we get off the ground with our first season, we could be doing really well by then. We've already got a stack of bookings for this year and Amber's working on more publicity for the restaurant too.'

I went to check the food. 'You must tell me what you think of this,' I said, fetching plates and cutlery. 'I'm still developing the menu and I can't afford to get it wrong.' I took the lamb out of the oven and moved it to a platter to rest with the potatoes and artichokes, while I deglazed the pan with red wine.

The papers and maps were stowed away in their file and we settled down to eat. I squeezed lemon over the artichokes and spooned the reduced juices over the meat. As Greg and Dimitri tucked in, I said, 'It's a variation on a traditional Greek recipe. Lamb and artichokes, usually done with stewing lamb and served with an egg and lemon sauce. But I'm not sure that would suit a modern palate.'

Greg had his mouth full and just nodded, but Dimitri said, *'Arni meh aginares meh avgolomeno.* My mother, she make for us for special occasions. But this is very, very good too.'

'I want to capture the essence of real Greek food,' I said, 'but bring it up to date a bit.'

'I've had that greasy stuff before,' said Greg. 'You can't go giving sophisticated diners peasant food.'

'That's exactly what I think. I've got to start as I want to go on.'

'I mean,' said Greg, getting into his stride and waving his fork towards the file of documents, 'if we get this development idea off the ground, we're not going to build fucking pig sties and cow sheds, are we? If we started putting up authentic peasant dwellings, that wouldn't bring you clientele wanting fucking fine dining, you'd just get riff-raff wanting chips and burgers. No, what we want are villas with wall-to-wall air con, infinity pools and Wi-Fi. That'll bring in your Michelin-starred customers, not your Michelin men.'

'I'm glad you think so, sir.' I was always amused by Greg's turn of phrase. 'And is the food to your satisfaction today, sir?'

'Fucking fabulous,' he said with a big smile.

Chapter Forty

12 June 1944

They are beginning to look like normal healthy children again, Agata thinks. The sunshine, playing on the beach, helping to water the vegetables in the garden and collecting the eggs, have touched that pallid skin with gold, brushed away the shadows beneath their eyes. They are filling out too. They weren't exactly starving when they arrived, but it was clear that their unfortunate parents had not been able to give them much nourishing food for quite some time.

Agata sits in the shade of the terrace, stripping chickpeas from their stalks, watching the girls chase each other, running towards the water then back again, not dressed in clothes but bare-skinned, like all healthy little children of the island should be. Rosy, golden girls with black hair, they could easily be taken for any Greek's children, but still she is always alert, ever listening for the ominous sound of a boat or plane. Georgiou says the Germans have probably been scouring the island by car and motorbike, searching for missing Jews, but so far, no soldiers have ventured down the steep rocky hillside to this secret haven.

She turns her head at the sound of her husband's singing. He is watering the melons and courgettes and she smiles. He loves hearing the children laughing, loves seeing them eat well, be happy and grow strong. 'What if their parents never come back when the war is over?' she asks him. 'I keep telling the girls that they will stay with us until they return, but what if they don't?'

Georgiou frowns. 'Isaac and Perla made it clear to Doctor Batas that if they did not survive, we should make contact with their relatives in Athens. He has an address for them. They said they would write to him once they had settled into their new place of work, but I do not think it is wise just now to go looking for news. It is best we stay away from the villages and the town.'

Agata's eyes fill with tears. She is growing to love the two little girls. And when she glances up and looks at Georgiou she can tell that he is affected as well. 'They are Jewish,' he says. 'We have been elected to care for them for the time being, but it is right and proper that they should be reunited with their own people one day. They have their own heritage and that is what their parents want for them. We must respect that.'

And Agata knows that much as she can watch them, feed them and care for them, they can never be hers – one day, when it is safe, they must leave this place of peace and safety and leave her too.

Chapter Forty-One

Amber

March 2007

Inge didn't smoke while we ate the cake and had our drinks, but she lit another cigarette as we talked later, drawing the deadly vapour deep into her sick lungs and closing her eyes. I wondered how much pain she was suffering; by this stage of her illness another cigarette could not harm her any more than she was hurt already. I finished the last crumbs of cake while she settled herself in an armchair near the wood-burning stove that had glowed all winter and which still warmed the house in those early days of spring.

After a couple of drags on her cigarette, she spoke in her rasping voice, 'It's a story of two halves, really. Their story and mine. Without them, mine would have no end.' She shuffled in her chair, adjusting the cushions behind her back, and I could sense she was weighing up how to begin, then after a long pause, she spoke.

'I imagine everyone despises their parents at some point when they are growing up. The trouble is, I never learnt to love them again. I don't know exactly when it started, perhaps when I was about fifteen or so. It was the start of the sixties. Wasn't that when life began for all Western teenagers? Our eyes and senses were awakened by the new music, by the freedom and the free-thinking. And that was when we began to ask the questions.'

'What do you mean, questions?'

She laughed, a dry laugh that developed into a throaty cough. Once it had subsided, she drew on her cigarette again and shrugged.

'It is funny, don't you think? So funny that one little question can lead to so many more. Oh, so many questions, but never any answers. What did you do in the war, Daddy? And no one would ever tell us. Sometimes, they would simply say, *Oh, it was very hard for us. We had such a hard time in those years. We don't like to talk about it.* And some of my friends had older relatives who even denied the camps and the atrocities.

'So then my friends and I began to talk and ask more questions. We said they had been responsible. They had let it happen. It was their fault. And those of us who thought about it, who asked why, began to hate them for it. How could they not have known? How could they have destroyed their country and the respect in which it had once been held? How could we ever be proud of our nation? So we began to want a better way. And we felt they could not be allowed to have control again. We did not think they were capable.'

'But surely you couldn't think such terrible times could ever happen again? The worst culprits were either dead, disappeared or tried for war crimes, weren't they?' I was gripped by the thoughts she was stirring in my head, the images that her words provoked, and felt a cold prickling at the back of my neck. Any slights I had experienced so far in my life were as nothing compared to those committed in the years to which she was referring.

'*Ach so*, that is true, but the rest had been complicit. Because of indolence perhaps, but mostly through fear, they had done nothing to stop it. So they could not be trusted with our future. We felt we had to make a stand. Make them take notice. We wanted to show the world that we were not like them, that we could create a better country.'

I thought as she spoke of how my grandparents and James's all talked with pride of their role in the war. 'I can see how difficult it must have been for you,' I said. 'Being British, I've only ever heard older people talk about us winning the war.'

Inge gave that feeble, sickly laugh again. 'It wasn't the losing we minded, it was the shame. Don't you realise how ashamed we were? How very ashamed we were, when we were old enough to understand what they had allowed to happen?' She closed her eyes for a second and I felt this emotional subject was tiring her too much.

Then she rallied again and said, 'Why, we could not talk about it even to the smallest degree. You know, when I was at school I had an English penfriend – Anita, her name was. She came to stay with me one summer in Reutlingen, when I was about seventeen. Then one evening my friends and I met with her school friends, who also had pen friends in our town, and we were laughing and talking in English and one of them used the word "gentile", I can't remember why now. And I naively asked what that word meant. I had no idea that the answer would make me feel so uncomfortable. Without any trace of embarrassment, my innocent pen friend answered, in perfect German, *"Das ist wenn man keine Jude ist."* "That's when you're not a Jew." She had no hesitation in uttering these words, because she bore no guilt, but the rest of us, me and my friends, we all fell silent. A dark shadow we could never escape was cast over our happy little gathering.

'With those few words, in the middle of our simple, happy group, we were reminded yet again of our country's enormous sin. And we could not discuss the rights and wrongs, because we could not ever know precisely how our fathers, our mothers, our uncles, our aunts, our older cousins, our grandparents, our neighbours and even our teachers had acted during those times. We felt that their entire generation was tainted with guilt. That was how it started.' She gave a great sigh, then leant forward to grind out her cigarette stub in an ashtray next to the fireplace.

'How what started?' I was totally mesmerised by her story. I had never before considered the feelings of post-war German youth.

'How we began to think of making them wake up,' she said in a quiet voice.

'I don't understand.'

She sighed, then coughed again and when she had caught her breath, she continued, 'We all felt it was the only way we could make our parents see that we were different to them. We would not be like them and blindly accept the rules. We would not be unquestioning. We had to take a stand. We had to shock them.

'I think it began when I was still at school. And then I went to university in Göttingen, which had a lot of radicalised students. That was when I met Günther – he made me see that mere disapproval of our parents was not enough. It was essential to act, and I agreed with him.'

'And how did he persuade you?'

'Oh, it was the oldest story in the world. I fell in love with him and I thought he loved me.' She stopped for a moment and stirred the grey ash and the white stubs in the ashtray with her fingertip. 'I think maybe he did love me for a while. I thought he was the most handsome boy I had ever seen. Like Paul McCartney but thinner, with bony wrists and a little beard.' Inge's finger whisked around the edge of her chin as she said this, then she reached for another cigarette. 'But he didn't really care for me as much as I cared for him. He used me.'

I could see how this faded grey woman with the gaunt face had once been a lithe, long-haired blonde, turning heads and said, 'You mean used you because he just wanted you for sex?'

She nodded, a matter-of-fact nod. 'That, but other things too. It was good for his image to have a pretty young girl by his side, adoring everything he said. And it was good later for him to have a devoted servant, washing his jeans, making his bed and cooking his food, when he decided to come back to our flat, that is.'

'So he wasn't faithful to you, then?'

Inge laughed and sounded so tired. 'He was faithful to his principles, to his cause. When I became pregnant and wanted to keep the baby, he said that would not be very much use to him or to the movement. He said if I loved him and all he stood for, I would get rid of it. He wouldn't even discuss it. He told me where to go for the abortion and that was that.'

I shook my head. 'That must have made you very unhappy.'

'The abortion? No, not particularly. I was only twenty. Why would I have wanted a child at that age? I only wanted Günther and I wanted him to love me and our child. But his response,' she nodded to herself, 'that was what made me unhappy. I think that was when I fully realised for the first time that I meant nothing at all to him, not in terms of love, that is. I had the termination in a dirty room with no one to hold my hand. That was what hurt, more than the pains in my womb. He didn't even care about my health or my safety. And afterwards, I cried, not for the child, but for myself, and he simply didn't want to know.'

'But you could have been very ill. You could have even died.'

'I know. I didn't know that at the time, but I could have. There was a lot of blood afterwards. And then, while I was lying in my bed, in such pain with a blood-soaked towel between my legs, a friend came and told me that Günther had a new girlfriend. I challenged him when he came back and he just said, "Well, what do you expect? I need someone who is fit for duty, not an invalid." And I told him I would not help him any more and that we were finished.'

'How did he react to that?'

'He said he was going to tell me to go anyway, even before my latest little problem, as he put it. He said his new girlfriend was more than capable of taking my place, because she was as committed to the cause as he was. She was prepared to take action, unlike me.'

'Was that true? I thought you meant all you and your friends wanted to do was protest, take a stand.'

'We did. But I never wanted to hurt or threaten anyone. I could not do that. And it seems she could. So he had what he wanted and I left.'

'And is that when you left Germany and came to Greece?'

'No, not straight away. I decided to finish my degree elsewhere and moved to Heidelberg, then when I graduated I started travelling. I worked for a time in England. I stayed with my penfriend and found a position in a school where I could teach a little, with conversation classes. I supplemented that with work in a bar, where I always pretended I was Swedish to avoid any embarrassment or questions.'

She looked exhausted, leaning back against the cushions and closing her eyes. And then I heard steps outside and Marian was there. Inge looked up at her with a smile and said, 'Amber has been keeping me company this afternoon.'

'I've been hearing all about Inge's fascinating life.'

'So she's been boring you with tales of her revolutionary past, has she?' Marian laughed and bent to kiss Inge's head. 'Quite the little rebel, wasn't she?'

'But there's more,' I said, turning back to Inge again. 'You haven't yet told me about Agata and Georgiou and where they fit into your story.'

Inge's smile was weary as she gave me her hand. 'Another time, *liebchen*. I will still be here another time. We will talk again soon.'

Chapter Forty-Two

15 June 1944

'I don't think you should go,' Agata insists. 'The soldiers might see you and stop you and ask questions. And if they follow you back, then they will know we are hidden away down here.'

'Don't worry so. I won't be gone long. We need to know what is happening up there.' Georgiou puts a flask of water and a wrap of fava in his sack. He doesn't intend taking any longer than is absolutely necessary, but the booming noise they've heard from the other side of the headland is worrying. Could the Germans be creating an outpost so close to their home? And why now, facing Albania, when surely they must still be more concerned with the advance of the British from Italy, on the other side of the island?

'I will go up as far as the main road and wait there for a while, hidden, in case there are troops or convoys. Then I'll come back through the olive groves and keep undercover to get a better look at the headland.'

Agata knows he cannot be deterred. He has watered the vegetables, irrigated the melons and tethered the goats. She can manage till he returns and she watches him trudge up the steep narrow track as the first light glimmers through the trees before the full heat of the day. God willing, he should be back before sunset. And if he does not return, she knows the soil as well as he does and could provide enough for this little hidden family. She laughs to herself. She might not know how to cast a fishing net out on the open waters, but she could wade through the rock pools looking for octopuses, sea urchins and mussels. She and the children will not starve, no matter what today brings.

And then she hears childish laughter on the stairs. The girls wake early every day and are full of life from the moment they open their eyes. They are growing in both strength and confidence, with fewer tears and many more smiles.

'Aggie,' they call as they run to her, throwing their arms around her legs. She will not let them call her Mama or Yaya, as she is neither their mother nor their grandmother. She knows her role is only temporary. She is their protector and provider, but that cannot stop her loving them, as she washes their faces and brushes their tangled hair.

'Georgy,' giggles Anna. 'Want Georgy.'

Agata laughs whenever she hears the little girl's attempt to pronounce her husband's name. 'Georgiou has had to go away for a while today, but he'll be back soon. And you can help me collect eggs and tomatoes. He'll be very pleased to know you've been helping and made yourself useful.'

'And me,' says Matilde, hopping up and down beside her little sister. 'I want to help too.'

'Yes, you too, but first, we must all have breakfast. Then we'll have the strength to work hard. And after we've done all our jobs, I am going to measure you each for a new dress with this material.' Agata holds up a long white bedspread of heavy linen with rows of blue and red embroidery at either end. 'You are both growing so fast we shall soon have nothing for you to wear.'

The girls pull the cloth from Agata's hands, draping it over their heads, and dance around, laughing. Agata laughs too. The bedspread was stitched by her own mother, embroidered by her as a gift for her wedding chest. But as it has not helped her produce the children that she expected to have, she feels sure her mother would not object to her using it to clothe two little girls who may never see their parents and older sister again.

'Here, let me take it,' she says, pulling the cloth from the sisters' hands. 'We don't want it to get dirty before I've even started. We want to make lovely white dresses for you both, so your Mama will be proud of you.'

Chapter Forty-Three

Amber

April 2007

'How's the restaurant coming along?'

Pam was the last person I'd expected to see that day, though I shouldn't have been surprised. All the British ex-pats shopped in M&S in Corfu Town when they were missing home comforts. I'd dashed into the store for their pillows. They really are the best, and quite inexpensive. And suddenly, there was Greg's wife, in the same department, browsing through the towels only a couple of yards away from me.

'It's all on schedule,' I said. 'We open for business at Easter. We've got our first bookings then.'

'Lunch or dinner?'

'For bed and breakfast.' She looked perplexed. 'We're offering accommodation as well as the restaurant, but that will be open by then too.'

'Oh, really? I didn't know that.' She seemed to glaze over, and then turned her attention back to the towels. 'What do you think? This charcoal or the cobalt blue?' She pointed at both stacks on the display with a manicured hand adorned with large rings and red varnish.

'I always prefer white, myself. But dark colours are very practical.'

'That's what I was thinking. Lavinia always leaves so much make-up all over the towels when she comes to stay with us.'

'Is she coming here for Easter, with the children?'

'Yes,' Pam murmured, still hovering between the colour choices. 'You know, I think the charcoal really would be best, don't you? It won't show the make-up stains so much. I'm always telling Lavinia she shouldn't bother with foundation when she's here, but she won't listen, insists on using it, even when she's starting to get a tan.' Her eyes flicked across to me. 'Not that you need to worry about that sort of thing, dear, with your lovely natural colour.' I let the comment bounce off me, and was just about to leave with my pillows when she turned to me. 'I'll have to bring Lavinia and the boys up to see you. We could come over for lunch one day while they're here. That would be such fun for them, before you get too busy.'

'Do that. Let me know when you want to come. And let me know how many too. We've had quite a few enquiries already and I expect we'll be very busy over the holiday, so we'll have to make sure you're booked in.'

'Well, I'm sure Greg will want to join us as well – he's been full of praise for your husband's wonderful cooking. Always coming home and telling me what an inspiring meal he's had.' She was weighing a towel in each colour in her hands, looking at them in turn. Then she said, 'You know, I'm so pleased he met you two. It's giving him such an interest. He loves helping to launch new businesses, and of course he's got such valuable experience to share. And I hear you could be very busy in the future if this villa development goes ahead. Could be just what you two need up there.'

'Villas? In our village?'

'I think so, dear, or is it another village I'm thinking of? I'm sure I heard Greg talking about it to someone.' She turned away to return one of the towels to the display stand, murmuring, 'No perhaps I will get the blue after all. The charcoal's really rather depressing.'

'I must go,' I said. 'I've got to get back. Call me when you want to make that booking.'

On the drive home I kept wondering about her remarks. Maybe she was mistaken. Maybe she'd misheard. Her mind was rather full of her daughter and the towels, after all. But it was strange after that conversation with James the previous month. I couldn't think of a way to ensure our lovely peaceful view remained unspoilt, but I did hope it would never be scarred by diggers and concrete mixers.

James was busy in the kitchen as usual when I returned, simmering a large pan of passata. I asked why he was making so much and he said it was a very useful base for many dishes, so he was going to freeze it in small quantities. And then when I said I thought he was meant to be cooking entirely from fresh produce, he gave me a filthy look, so I disappeared to the bedrooms with my new pillows. I'd already made up the beds and sent Lorna photos for the website, but I'd suddenly thought that some people might want extra pillows, so I'd decided to keep spare ones in the wardrobes. I stowed them away then stood by the windows, looking out across the valley. Maybe a sensitive upmarket development wouldn't be so bad. At least it would be better than the wrong kind of building.

Then I thought I'd check on the website. Lorna had suggested some minor changes and we had a good selection of pictures of the completely finished interiors. I'd sent her all the photos I'd taken, thinking it was helpful to have a detached eye making the final selection. And she had chosen well. There was our terrace, not yet hung with vines, but with pots of thyme on the tables and shafts of sunlight striking the textured paving stones. The bedrooms looked fresh and peaceful, with pale-blue curtains matching the spring sky; the front of the restaurant seemed welcoming, with its bay trees and stone troughs of herbs and the images of James's dishes looked enticing, promising succulence and flavour.

But there was an intriguing message from Lorna, too. *Thought I'd skip the pics with Mr Angry.*

I couldn't be bothered to look back at all the photographs I'd sent her, so I quickly typed: *What do you mean? Are you talking about James?* She'd suggested including a picture of us together, the proud and smiling proprietors, but I thought we'd both looked friendly and welcoming, certainly far from angry.

She was never far away from her iPhone or iPad, and her reply came back almost immediately: *Not James. The guy who looks like Simon Cowell meets Antonio Banderas.*

I couldn't help laughing to myself. She'd got him spot on. I knew instantly that she meant Dimitri. But I couldn't remember sending her any pictures of him. I was sure I hadn't. *Show me then*, I typed.

It took her a bit longer to respond this time, but in minutes she'd sent them. There were three photographs of different aspects of the restaurant and premises, and I hadn't noticed that Dimitri was in the background in all of them. And I certainly hadn't noticed he was facing the camera and scowling.

Chapter Forty-Four

15 June 1944

As the sun reaches its height, Agata realises Georgiou has been gone for at least seven hours. He left just as the first misty glimmer of dawn appeared through the trees.

The girls played on the beach for a while in the morning, but once the heat was at its fiercest, Agata encouraged them to stay in the shade of the house. Their limbs, once so pale and translucent from months of hiding and poor diet, are now brushed with sepia and gold, but they do not yet have the tanned skin of island children who have been exposed to the harsh Greek sun since birth.

While Agata cuts then stitches the linen for their new dresses, Matilde and Anna play a game with shells and stones under the table. She can hear their voices and laughter, muffled slightly by the draped cloth she has spread across her work table to ensure the white dress fabric remains spotless. Seated at her work, in this cool, shady room, with its view of the calm sea, Agata feels contented and peaceful until she hears a shout. The cry of a male voice. She starts. It cannot be Georgiou, can it?

She stands up from her sewing and looks through the open doors towards the bay. And there, rising from the waves, is a man, dressed only in black swimming trunks, shaking the water from his dark blond hair.

Without even looking at the children, keeping her eyes firmly fixed on this figure striding through the water towards the beach, Agata says, 'Girls. Go quickly, like I've told you. You must hide, right this minute.'

Matilde and Anna dart from their den in silence and scamper up the stairs. Agata can hear their bare feet slapping the stone steps as they run, but otherwise they make no sound at all.

She lays down her needlework and quickly folds it away. It would not do to let anyone see that she is making dresses for little girls when there are no children to be seen around the house. She moves towards the open doors and stands on the threshold, steadying herself by holding the doorframe. The man sees her as he reaches the sandy beach. He is tall and bronzed, like an Aryan Adonis, and brushes his hands over his slicked-back hair.

'*Gnädige Frau*,' he calls out. '*Guten Morgen*.' He comes closer and she can see diamond droplets of water sparkling on his tanned, muscular frame. '*Ich möchte ein Tasse Wasser trinken, Bitte*.' He gives a little bow and then smiles. 'You must forgive me for this intrusion. I felt like a refreshing swim on this hot day and had no idea this beautiful bay was also your home.'

His gracious tone and manner persuades Agata that he is probably an officer, not a foot soldier, and it would be wisest to be courteous and offer him hospitality. She gestures to the table and chairs just inside the cool and shady house, but he chooses to sit on the bench outside in full sun.

He leans back against the wall and closes his eyes against the glare of the sun's beams. Spreading his arms along the back of the bench, with his legs widely splayed, his firm flesh is offered to the fierce rays like a shoulder of lamb on a charcoal grill. And as he settles himself, Agata catches a glint of silver on the ring finger of his left hand.

In the kitchen, she sets out creamy fava, tapenade and some sliced tomatoes on a plate, with a piece of the flatbread she made at breakfast time. She pours him cold water, not wine. They have not had coffee for months, so she also boils water for mountain tea made with wild herbs.

Her movements are quiet and measured and all the while, as she prepares these simple refreshments, she listens. She holds her breath and listens for the sounds that might indicate that the German is curious about her home, that Georgiou is returning unaware of this unexpected visitor and, most importantly, for any hint of childish voices that would betray the hidden presence of the forbidden Jewish children.

He gives no hint, when she returns with the food and drink, that he might suspect anything untoward. Then, as she bends to set the tray down on the small table before him and he reaches for the water, she finds herself transfixed by his silver ring, the ring she had assumed might mean he was a respectable married man. But this is no ordinary wedding band; adorning the ornate design is a gruesome skull, and Agata tears her gaze away. She doesn't understand its significance, but the ominous symbol chills her, despite the warmth of the midday sun.

Chapter Forty-Five

Amber

May 2007

Once we were open for business, it was more hectic than I could ever have imagined. Our rooms were fully booked during the Easter holidays and we had a steady flow of customers for lunch and dinner. Service ran smoothly on the whole, apart from the evening Pam and Greg arrived with their daughter Lavinia and her sons. James nearly lost his patience over Lavinia's questions about his ingredients and special requests.

After the Easter break we only opened the restaurant on Fridays, Saturdays and Sundays, as these were the busiest days and the time off in the week gave James time to continue developing his menu. He said we could make as much in these three days as we could by opening all week.

Spring also brings many serious walkers to Corfu, particularly those interested in the flowers which suddenly burst open after the winter rains, smothering the hillsides with the deep blue of wild muscari and iris. There were so many ramblers calling by, even on the days when the restaurant was meant to be closed, that I began to wonder if we should rethink our opening hours and, after a bit of persuasion, James agreed we would open for lunch midweek with a limited set menu.

The second time we did this, a group of ramblers came in for lunch and one of them was keen to show me the photographs he had taken that morning. He said March and April were really the best months for spring flowers, but he'd found pink tulips and geraniums growing wild on his walk that day. Then I remember pointing to the tree below our terrace, thick with clusters of deep pink flowers, and saying, 'Isn't the peach blossom wonderful too? It's everywhere at the moment.'

And he stared at me with a look of total surprise, saying, 'But that isn't a peach tree, my dear. That's a Judas Tree.' I'd never heard of it before and asked him why it had such a strange name, then he said, 'Judas Iscariot hanged himself from such a tree, so the story goes. Legend has it that the tree originally had white flowers, but they turned pink and blushed with shame, because of his betrayal of Jesus.'

I remember how I gazed at the magenta clusters, then shuddered. It was no longer a fresh innocent symbol of spring and fruitfulness; it suddenly signified death and deception and I began noticing the trees everywhere on the hillsides, shameful reminders of that terrible sin.

Our full launch, the first week in May, was a huge success. James prepared ten dishes, including his rabbit stew and braised octopus. I concentrated on giving out leaflets and business cards, along with small sample bottles of the house olive oil James had finally selected, labelled with both the name of the producer and Mountain Thyme. Lorna had done such a good job on the website and promotional material that we'd asked her and her partner Rob to join us, and their online review resulted in several more bookings for both the restaurant and accommodation almost immediately.

I'd invited Inge and Marian as well; I felt so grateful to them for giving our premises such authentic character and showed them round all the finished rooms to see what they'd helped us to achieve. But they didn't stay very long, as Inge tired very easily, so as they left I promised to visit very soon, before the summer season was fully underway. I was fascinated by Inge's stories and wanted to talk to her at length again.

There are days in May and early June when rain still pelts the island and waves throw themselves onto the beachside tavernas, but before long all is hot and calm again. The day I went to the Mill was one of those stormy days, and I didn't expect to find Inge stretched out in the sun; I knew she would be wrapped in a woollen shawl beside the stove, cigarette in hand. The beach shop wasn't yet open for business and their summer help was not needed for several more weeks, so it felt like the souk was still slumbering in its winter hibernation when I arrived.

I'd made James make me some more *churros* from the batter he'd prepared that morning for the restaurant – I couldn't expect Inge to always offer me homemade cake when I visited.

'I don't see why you have to keep going over there,' he'd said. 'We don't need them; we've got all the furniture now.' But he'd made me some *churros* all the same. They are so quick to make, and he'd made plenty of the batter.

'How charming,' Inge said, when I presented her with the little cinnamon sugared doughnuts and told her James had made them specially that morning. 'You must thank James. He is so kind and generous. We shall eat them with hot chocolate.' She reached for mugs and a chipped enamel saucepan to boil the milk. 'Marian has eaten all of our cake. I tell her she will be *eine Knödel* if she eats any more.'

'What does that mean? *Knödel?*' I stumbled a little over my pronunciation.

'I think you say "dumpling" in English. A great big dumpling.' She laughed, an affectionate laugh of love for the woman who shared her life and was her almost constant companion.

I pictured Marian's dimples, her pink cheeks and blonde hair. 'Has she changed much over the years?'

Inge gave a hoarse laugh again. 'No, she is still the lost girl I found in the harbour many years ago. Still the babe in the woods, you know. Has she told you how we met and how she came here?'

'She did once,' I said, remembering Marian telling me about their first meeting. *I'd been backpacking around the islands and I was checking the ferry times at Corfu harbour when I noticed a beautiful blonde woman staring at me. And now we've been friends for over thirty years and lovers for nearly as long.*

I sat while Inge poured the milk into the pan, and asked, 'Marian came to help you one summer, many years ago, didn't she?'

'*Ja*, my student help had changed her mind that year. But as soon as Marian came here and saw my shop she fell in love with it. I sometimes think it was the Mill rather than me that convinced her to stay.' She gave another little croaky laugh.

And again I could hear Marian's words in my mind: *When Inge unlocked the mesh shutters at the front of the Mill and waved me inside, I loved the place. It looked and smelt like a casbah, hung with caftans, rugs, lanterns and joss sticks.*

'People thought we were sisters then,' Inge said, standing by the stove. 'We looked so alike, even though I am ten years older than her. But now she looks much younger than me. I am fading.'

The milk was boiling, and I told Inge to sit while I made the hot chocolate. 'Have you got help coming again this summer?' Now that Inge was so frail, the women had gone back to having a student help them at the beach shop during the busy season.

'Josie is coming back to us this year. It is not hard to find good help. They have their own room and enough free time to enjoy the beach and see friends. I should know. It is how I started here too.'

And then I remembered she had been travelling through, just like the other students, when she had come to Nissaki and found her home. 'You were going to tell me about Agata and Georgiou, weren't you? How you came to live with them?'

'Ah yes, that is so. Such dear people. I came to think of them as my grandparents, but they were grandparents I could respect, especially when I came to know them better and knew what they had done. They always said I was like the child they never had.' She looked sad and dipped her sugared *churro* into the hot chocolate and nibbled, like a sickly rabbit.

'How old were they, when you came here?'

'Oh, seventies, eighties. I was never too sure. They were very old, but they still worked hard. Every morning, Agata washed down the steps and swept away the sand on the terrace. Georgiou grew tomatoes and courgettes in the plot of land at the back, which we now rent out to the taverna and their donkey. But back then it was full of fruit and vegetables – corn, squash, aubergines and melons. He was always bent over the earth, hoeing, weeding, and watering. They were simple people, like many here were then, brought up to provide for themselves. A chicken here, a goat there, a little bit of land – they could feed their families well on what they grew.'

'And had they always had a shop here?'

'By the time I came here, they'd had the shop for maybe nearly twenty years. Visitors started coming back to Corfu and then the track down here became a road, so people could get down to the sea. But the shop was very simple when I arrived. Just beach mats, towels, some sun lotion, plastic shoes, just basic things people might need for the beach.'

'Well, it's certainly not simple any more. You've made it into a virtual Aladdin's cave.'

She smiled. 'It was what people began to want. I had already begun importing from Morocco and then Marian and I went to Rajasthan one winter and began to bring back goods from even further afield. It is all so very different from its simple beginnings.'

I looked around the kitchen – the furnishings and the pots and pans had probably barely changed since Inge came here all those years ago, and I thought of the richly stocked exotic shop below. 'Do you think Agata and Georgiou would be proud of what you have achieved here?'

She gave me the gentlest of smiles, then said, 'Perhaps, I hope so. But I am more proud than you can imagine of what *they* achieved here. They did something greater and more important than I have ever done.' Suddenly she was struggling to get to her feet and I put out a hand to steady her, but she waved it away, saying, 'Come, I will show you, then you will understand.'

She began to shuffle out of the kitchen towards the staircase and then, with great effort, climbed the stairs, one slow step at a time. When she reached the top, she turned to a room on the right. 'In here,' she said. 'We use this room now for our summer student. When they are here it looks quite different. Not at all tidy.' The room was sparsely furnished, with just a bed heaped with folded bedding, a chair, a desk and a tall, carved wardrobe against the wall opposite the door. 'Open it,' Inge said, pointing at the heavy furniture, then sitting down on the bed to catch her breath after the tiring climb.

It was a large dark cupboard with an ornate cornice and an iron handle, which I twisted so the door creaked open. It was totally empty inside apart from a few skeletal wire hangers swinging from a rail. Then Inge pointed to the interior, 'Can you see the catch right at the back?'

I couldn't see anything, it was so dark, but I fumbled around the edges of the back panel until I felt a small metal catch. 'Now turn it,' she said, so I did.

The catch was stiff, so I suppose it hadn't been moved for years, but eventually it turned and the back of the wardrobe creaked open to reveal a deep alcove, with a little bit of light filtering through an upper ventilation grille. 'What is this?' I asked, leaning forwards inside the wardrobe and peering into the dark space, which was probably no more than twice the size of the cupboard which concealed it.

'It's where they hid the children,' Inge said.

I turned towards her and saw she was smiling.

Chapter Forty-Six

Amber

June 2007

I never did find the right moment to tell James about Inge's story. I came back that day wanting to tell him and yet feeling I'd been entrusted with a secret too precious to be tossed away in an idle conversation, with him only half listening as he busied himself in the kitchen. I wanted to savour it, hold onto it until he could appreciate the importance of what had been entrusted to me. And in the days that followed he was utterly preoccupied with prepping dishes and cooking for the restaurant, so I knew it would be some time before he could listen and fully appreciate the danger and bravery that story entailed.

But, in the heat of the market in the centre of Corfu Town, I couldn't help remembering what she had said. I hadn't really wanted to go in that day, but James had insisted, saying, 'On top of sending snails instead of sea urchins, they haven't delivered the samphire. I've got to have some today. You'll have to go into the market for me again.'

The days were getting hotter. At the beginning of June, there was still a freshness in the air each morning, but the sun soon grew fierce, so I preferred visiting the market very early in the day. I parked near the harbour in a sliver of shade cast by the oleander bushes, then looked for a moment at the Old Fort that towered above the sea. Now I knew its terrible history, as told to me by Inge in her husky, smoker's voice, still echoing in my head since my visit, I could no longer visualise its romantic Venetian past, only its more recent, more terrible function.

Although it was only 8.30 a.m., the market was already crowded with local people buying the best of the fish and fresh vegetables. Before I reached the covered stalls, I passed an old lady in black, waving me to piles of garlic in baskets at her feet. Next to her was a man with plastic flagons of golden liquid. I used to slow down to look more closely, wondering whether it was oil or vinegar, but James always pulled me away, saying, 'I wouldn't touch it. There's no way of knowing what he's put in it.'

My favourite olive stall lay in the centre of the market, where the different olives were piled in trays, some large and black, others green, marinated with garlic, chillies or various herbs. Bunches of dried oregano and thyme were always stacked at the back of the stall. And after I'd bought James's vital sea urchins, I saw the woman with the samphire. She had a large plastic tub of the green fronds, smaller than those we're used to eating in England, and she threw handfuls into clear plastic bags, charging what always seemed like pennies.

I found her so quickly, I thought I had time to stop at the market's little cafe. It consisted of nothing more than a ramshackle veranda with a simple canvas awning, but nevertheless offered shade and a vantage point from which to survey the market's early morning business. This was no high-street coffee chain with a bewildering array of concoctions; there was just Turkish, espresso or Nescafé, which was our usual choice, as the others offered such immensely strong charges of caffeine.

I sat on a white plastic chair, elbows on a clean aluminium table, watching the people of the market. Local women picked out cherries one by one, squeezed and sniffed melons, and examined enormous, bulbous tomatoes. A stallholder sat back in his chair, supervising his stock of cucumbers, all dark green, all fresh, but with more bumps and curves than would ever be permitted in supermarkets back home. He put his feet up on the edge of his stall, took a large knife out of his pocket and began to peel and eat some of his produce. The peel fell to the ground in slivers, then one by one he cut chunks of the vegetable with his knife and speared each one with the point of the blade before popping them in his mouth. It was a masterclass in market table manners.

The cafe owner brought me a white cup with the instant coffee frothed, looking remarkably like cappuccino, and when I asked for extra milk, he poured it from a can. It was thick and creamy, so I was sure it was evaporated milk. Watching the busy scene, I noticed a stall with a pile of courgette flowers. I couldn't remember whether James had ordered any, but I loved them so much, I decided to buy some before leaving.

I bent over the box of flowers, some with courgettes the thickness of a man's thumb, others with only a vestige of fruit, no bigger than a baby's little finger. A wasp was crawling over the flowers but lazily crept away as I selected the ones I needed. 'Take more,' the female stallholder urged when I handed her the bag with only half a dozen flowers.

I resisted the urge to buy cherries and giant radishes and began the walk back to the car. It was getting hotter all the while and I was reminded again of Inge's story. As I walked, I glanced around at the people and the streets. A moped zoomed past; its owner was bare-headed, like most of the local bike riders. I passed a group of English tourists debating whether they could safely buy fish from one of the many market stalls piled high with their silvery catch, iced water pooling with flaked scales in puddles at their feet, and I wondered how many of them knew about the Old Fort.

I reached the car and let the air con run for a few minutes before beginning the drive back. And all the while, my memory was replaying everything that Inge had told me that day. I had turned to her from the wardrobe with its secret and said, 'But I thought you told me that Georgiou and Agata didn't ever have any children of their own.'

'They didn't,' she'd said, shaking her head. 'But they hid other people's children here.'

I'd peered into the dim, hidden space again, imagining little bodies huddled in the corners. 'When and why?' I said.

'Late in the war, in 1944, they hid two children here. My dear old friends, they were so brave. They could have been shot themselves for doing that. But they chose to save them.'

I'd crept forward a little more and poked my head inside the refuge. 'I suppose it's similar to a priest's hole.'

'Priest's hole?'

'Where a priest would hide during times of religious persecution. They've been found in some old English country houses, and I expect similar things have happened elsewhere.'

'And this is like a little rabbit hole. For two frightened little bunnies.' Inge sighed. 'Georgiou and Agata were so brave, so honourable.'

'Why were they hidden?'

'They were Jewish. You do not know this part of Corfu's history, I think. Very few do.'

'I don't know anything about it.'

'That is what is so sad.' She sighed again. 'The tourist guides, well, the ones distributed by all the tour companies that is, they don't mention it at all. There is a monument in the town, but so few visitors know what happened when they come here. They have come to enjoy the beach, the blue sea, to eat and drink, and they do not care to know about the past.'

'Tell me then. Tell me what happened.'

So then she told me. She told me how in June 1944, when the end of the war was in sight, the Jews of Corfu were rounded up by the Germans. Those who escaped only did so because they were given refuge by local Greek families, like Inge's Agata and Georgiou. 'Those poor people, almost the entire Jewish population of the island, were imprisoned in the Old Venetian Fort. Nearly 2,000 men, women and children, the sick, the dying and the old, all herded in together and left on dirt floors, open to rain and sun for five days. And it was so hot that year. Finally, they were marched out, pushed into barges, towed by motorboat to Lefkas and kept there for a day, where the locals who tried to feed them were beaten or shot.

'It was five days in all before they got to Athens, where they were then loaded onto the trains to Auschwitz. Their journey took over twenty days in all, with almost no food or water. Many of them were dead on arrival, the rest so far gone that they were sent straight to the gas chambers. Three hundred of them were subjected to forced labour. The Mayor of Corfu at that time was a known collaborator and he issued a proclamation, when they left on their terrible journey, thanking the Germans for ridding the island of the Jews so that the economy of the island would revert to its "rightful owners". That was not a sentiment shared by many local people, who had lived peaceably with the Jews for many, many years. And of the Jews of Corfu who were deported, only a handful came back.'

'I feel quite ashamed,' I said, shocked. 'Ashamed of not knowing, of not even thinking about what might have happened here during those awful years.'

'Not as ashamed as I feel,' Inge had said. She looked sad and weary. 'Now you can understand why I turned away from my countrymen. The war was coming to an end, the Allies had entered France, yet two days later the Germans still considered their greatest priority was to cleanse this island of a peaceful community which had never done any harm and had always lived in harmony with their neighbours. I thank God there were people like Agata and Georgiou who could make a difference, even a tiny one.'

'There's a saying, isn't there, about saving a life and saving the world?'

Then Inge looked up at me and said, '*Whoever destroys a soul, it is considered as if he destroyed an entire world. And whoever saves a life, it is considered as if he saved an entire world.* It is from the Talmud.'

So Agata and Georgiou saved two worlds when they hid those two children, and I thought of them again as I sat in the cooling car, looking towards the rocky isle where the fort crumbled. I thought too of those frightened people, crowded together, hungry and thirsty in the roasting heat, that summer long ago.

Chapter Forty-Seven

15 June 1944

'People are saying the Germans cannot find proper boats for us. They have only been able to get hold of rotten barges, not motor-boats,' Papa whispers. 'They are towing the barges to Lefkas, then on to Patras. It will take days to get us there. We must conserve our supplies.'

Rebekka hides her crust in her bundle. She is very hungry, hungrier than she has ever been during the months since the Germans first came, but she understands. Her stomach is shrinking and if she stays still and tries to sleep more, she will not think about food so much. She longs to take great gulps of the water they still have and splash her face and hands to rinse away the dust of the arid quad where they sit, hour after hour under a merciless sun, but she knows it is precious and must be used sparingly.

Although some of their community departed the day after they had been brought to the Old Fort, most of them have been held here for nearly five days now. The fresh water has been refilled once, but the overflowing latrine buckets have not been replaced. And in that time there have been deaths and births. Bodies have been thrown over the harbour walls to join those of the Italian officers who were shot when the Germans took command of the island. They might soon be joined by the wizened babies of mothers too exhausted and dehydrated to feed their newborns.

'Papa,' whispers Rebekka, tugging at her father's sleeve, 'tell me again about Matilde and Anna. Tell me more.'

Isaac puts his arm around his daughter. She is his eldest, but she is still his child, even though she is already showing signs of becoming a woman. 'They are living in a fine house and can cool themselves in the sea whenever they wish. They are eating fresh sardines and sea bream every day, cooked with tomatoes,' he says. 'They will help our friends grow maize, courgettes, aubergines and melons. There will be chickens for eggs and goats to give them milk and make cheese.'

'But what if the Germans steal their crops? They take so much from all of our people. What will they do then?'

'Our good friends live far away from the towns and villages. There is no proper road to their home, only a rough track down to a beach. When the Germans have learnt how to ride a donkey they may bother to search these hidden places, but until then I think your sisters will be quite safe.'

Isaac manages a hoarse laugh at this thought, then adds, 'And if our friends fear that the Germans will come to search their home and may find your sisters, our friends will run away with Matilde and Anna, up to the mountains, where they will catch rabbits and pick wild greens. They will not starve, my dearest. Your sisters will grow big and strong and they will be waiting for us when we come back home after working for the Germans.'

Rebekka is comforted by these thoughts, and dreams of the little ones paddling in the sea or running through mountain meadows, chasing rabbits.

Chapter Forty-Eight

Amber

August 2007

The temperature climbed day by day. It peaked at 35°C in late July, but in early August it reached 42°C. Those who managed to endure the drive into the mountains during the day flopped into the chairs on our terrace and picked at little more than salads and iced tea. By the evening it was a little cooler, and we usually had a handful of guests for dinner, but I began to see how much more we would benefit if there were customers from a nearby development, as few people were willing to drive far after the roasting-oven heat of the day. They preferred to spend the evening sitting by their pools, or on the edge of the sea where there was the chance of a cooling breeze.

And yet again I had to drive into the town early in the morning for supplies. James was short of fresh tuna. 'Everyone's asking for it and I haven't nearly enough. Get me a dozen steaks, will you? In this heat they all want salade niçoise or tuna tartare.'

The town was busy even early in the morning, with everyone trying to complete their shopping before the temperature rose even higher. I couldn't park anywhere near the market and on my way back to the car park beside the harbour, having resisted the temptation to linger over the stalls heaped with peaches and cherries, or sit and watch the bustle over coffee, I stopped for a moment's rest in a church. In a corner of its dark interior I hid and thought and cooled off. There was no service and a priest sat reading beside the entrance.

It was peaceful and soothing, an oasis before I would have to rush back in my hot car to face more dramas at Mountain Thyme. Then, while my eyes were closed and I was almost meditating, I heard the murmur of familiar voices. I opened my eyes and saw two figures shuffling through the door, walking towards the altar. At first, with the bright light of the day behind them through the doorway, I wasn't too sure, but then I saw it was definitely Marian supporting Inge, guiding her and gently holding her arm.

Inge stepped up to the icon at the altar, clutching the rail. Marian sat on a chair at the end of a row and watched her. Inge was so thin and she had chosen to wear pale grey, which echoed the parchment tone of her fragile skin. Despite the heat of the day, she wore a crocheted cardigan covering her bony arms. Sprigged cotton hid her skeletal legs and a misshapen felt hat disguised the remains of her hair.

From behind she looked so old, so much older than her sixty-plus years. I saw her veined hand shaking as she made the sign of the cross. She had to hold the altar rail with both hands to bend to kiss the sarcophagus, below the gilded image of the saint. Then she attempted to kneel and Marian stepped forward and whispered, 'Careful, Inge.'

But Inge waved her away, saying, 'It's all right. I can do it myself,' then she shakily lowered herself, gripping the rail tight, while Marian hovered behind her. I supposed she expected to have to lift her weakened partner to her feet, but after a few minutes, in which Inge bent her head then looked up at the golden haloed face, Inge pulled herself up and I heard her whispery voice say, 'Thank you. My suffering is nothing compared to His.'

Marian put her arm around Inge's shoulders and they walked slowly towards the open door, then halted before the priest. He stood and offered Inge his hand. She bent and kissed his ring. Then Marian pulled Inge away and out into the sunshine, as if afraid she would be obliged to do the same.

I didn't want to intrude, but I was curious to know where they were going next in such heat, so I rose from my dark corner and followed them. They were heading back towards the market and I thought they must have come, like me, to buy food before the day grew too hot. But they passed the turning to the market and headed for the main square. I thought perhaps they had parked there under the trees, as I often did, but instead of heading for one of the many cars lining both sides of the road, they carried on and crossed over the road towards the entrance to the Old Fort, then sat down on a low wall in the shade. Of course, Inge must be tired from her exertions – she tired easily, I knew. But she didn't look weary, she was smiling as I approached and greeted them both.

'You've made an early start, like me.' I held up my bag of fish. 'I've got to get back soon or James will be frantic.'

'Don't let us keep you,' said Marian. 'I've just got one more errand to run.' She turned to Inge. 'Are you sure you'll be all right for a bit? I won't be very long.'

'I can stay with Inge for a few minutes,' I told her. 'I'll wait till you get back. The fish will be all right. I've got ice packs in there with it.'

'If you're sure,' Marian said, then waved to us both and set off.

I sat down beside Inge and fanned myself. 'This bit of shade isn't going to last very long. You've picked just about the only spot on this street.'

'Oh, I always sit here,' Inge said.

'You're one of those people who always knows the best spots,' I laughed. 'I bet you always have your own favourite tables in restaurants too.'

'No,' Inge said. 'I always sit here, because this is where they came when they left the island.'

And then I suddenly knew what she was talking about, and looked at her weary face with its gentle smile. The sign to the fort on the lamppost was insignificant, almost apologetic. The many tourists who came to gaze across the sea or enjoy a cool drink at one of the many nearby cafe tables would never realise that this was a pathway to hell, that this was the way those thousands of men, women and children walked at the start of the journey to their deaths.

'Then,' she said, 'if visitors are not sure whether to go in or if they ask about this place, I tell them what happened here. The fort does not talk about its history. It has nothing to say about that time. I have been coming here often, ever since Agata and Georgiou were gone. They did their duty and were proud of what they had done and I owe it to their memory to make sure others learn the truth. It cannot make it right, but it helps, I think.'

I was in awe of her. Despite her frailty she was still true to herself and her beliefs and I didn't know what to say in response, so I just clasped her thin, veined hands. Then she said, 'At one point I was tempted to daub graffiti in Kollas Square, thinking it was named after that terrible mayor during the years of the war.' She gave a little wispy laugh at herself. 'I was all ready with my paint and my brush, but then I found out just in time that it was named after an earlier dignitary.'

I laughed with her then. 'You rebel, you. I can see you haven't quite thrown off your revolutionary streak.'

'I feel as passionate now as I did when I was a student. There was so much denial, so much turning away in my youth.' She tilted her hat to shade her eyes and said, 'When I was a child I loved my grandfather, he was so kind to me. But when I was older I found out that he printed propaganda for the Nazis at his press, and posters condemning the Jewish businesses in our town. Yet he denied he had any responsibility for all that happened.' She shook her head sadly. 'He did not think he had done anything wrong. And then my friends and I learnt that even our own home town, our beloved Reutlingen, had employed slave labour. It was everywhere, you see.'

I put my arm around her. There was little I could add, but I said, 'You are so strong. So principled. I really admire you.'

'And when I am finally gone, Marian has promised me that she will come and take my place. It is such a comfort to me to think that my darling Agata and Georgiou's work will continue.'

'You really feel you have to do this, don't you?'

And her reply was stark and simple. 'I am merely a witness to the truth. I cannot do much, but I can do this.'

Chapter Forty-Nine

James

August 2007

I can still remember the first time we saw a fire in the hills. It was one summer evening, the year we arrived on the island. We were driving back after taking my mother to Corfu airport. She had been staying with us for two weeks in the stifling heat of August and it was time for her to return to the wet cold summer days of England. I kissed her goodbye at the terminal, and then waved from the car as she wheeled her suitcase inside to the check-in desks. Amber said we should have stayed with her, but the airport parking was so limited I refused. I'm glad we left, because the flights were very delayed that night and we'd have had a long boring time waiting on hard seats with little refreshment.

We drove through the back streets of Corfu Town, then hugged the glittering bay, garlanded with lights, as we began the drive further north, back to the beachside villa Ben had lent us that month. Above the resort of Agios, with its clusters of hotels, Amber said, 'I don't ever remember noticing lights up there before, do you?'

I glanced towards the black mountain but couldn't look long enough to see anything. I had to concentrate on driving those winding roads in the dark and slowed down as we approached the treacherous bends where the big coaches swung out into the road, their side mirrors like the claws of a praying mantis. Then, as we began our descent into Ipsos, where bars and discos were strung close to each other, parallel to the beach, I looked again, peering harder at the darkness, and Amber said, 'There's a string of orange flickering up there. It looks rather like fire. High up on the hillside, just above the bay.'

I didn't think anything of it at first and said, 'Farmers, probably. Maybe they burn the old crops. Like they used to be allowed to do back home, before EU health and safety started laying down the bloody law.'

I remember seeing those orange lights, dancing on the black hillside. It was wildfire, not crop burning, but so distant, so far away from the sea, nowhere near our villa or the rental offices where we were working that first summer. But later that same month, fire crept down the hillside, approaching the main road near Barbati and threatening the highly combustible olive groves.

We smelt the smoke all that night and charred vine leaves were still drifting onto the terrace when the sun rose, leaving a delicate dusting of ash over the awnings, the sun beds and tables. It reminded me of our visit to Herculaneum, when we spent our honeymoon on the Amalfi coast. All that morning sea planes scooped water from the bay to drench the still-glowing cinders and fire forces ringed the scorched groves to prevent any stray sparks and embers spreading and causing further damage.

It was just as hot and dry a year later, and Amber was taking forever to come back from the market. I was waiting to prepare lunch in the restaurant, and getting impatient for the tuna. I could sear steaks to order, but the tartare had to be made in advance and I was sure there would be demand again that day. Eventually she rushed in.

'I'm so sorry I'm late. The road was closed. I had to come all the way round from Sidari. There's a big fire over on our side and the fire brigade's out dealing with it, but they've closed that road off for now.'

'Bugger!' I shouted. 'That's all we need. The heat's enough to put people off already without a sodding fire as well.'

She handed me the dripping bag. 'I'm sure the tuna will be all right. It's still really cold with those ice packs, even though they've melted a bit.'

'I don't mean the bloody fish. I mean the people, stupid. They're not making the effort to get here in the heat. We had three no-shows yesterday. We can't afford any more.'

She grabbed a cold bottle of water from the fridge and held it to her forehead. 'I'm going. I need to cool off, then I'll be on the front desk.'

It wasn't her fault, I knew that, but it was frustrating. The busiest time of the year, and we were missing out. I began to pray for a drop in the temperature, then thought what I needed was some sympathetic company, so I rang Greg and told him to come the long way round.

'Mate, I need a bit of light relief up here. I know I'm always saying we're too busy to fit you in last minute, but I'm sure we'll have space again today if it's anything like yesterday. Fancy coming over for lunch?'

He did, and he fancied sitting at my kitchen table with Dimitri, who, though sober and serious, was always a good foil for Greg. 'They don't know what they're missing,' Greg said when I told him about the no-shows. 'Give me their names and I'll sort them out.'

I laughed. 'If it's anything like what you're doing to that poor hotel, I'd better not.'

Greg slapped his knees, doubling up with laughter. 'I'm nearly one hundred per cent foolproof now. Get 'em in every time. Dimitri here's going to get me an inside mole. He knows someone who's a seventh cousin of a cousin twice removed or something. He can find out what the management's saying and what effect it's having.'

Dimitri was shaking his head and looking sorrowful. 'I tell Mr Richards I have cousins at this hotel. We must be very careful – I do not want Mr Richards to be in big trouble.'

'He's already big trouble,' I said. 'You want to watch yourself, Dimitri, associating with the likes of this character. He could get you into hot water.'

Dimitri looked puzzled, then said, 'The hotel swimming pool, it is cold water, not heated, no?'

Greg doubled up with laughter again, and then I distracted him with a plate of tuna tartare, thinking I had to use it now we had it, plus a dish of salt and pepper squid. As I turned my attention back to the courgette flowers I'd stuffed, I said, 'Was the road still closed on your way round?'

Greg shook his head, his mouth full, but Dimitri said, 'These peasants, so careless.' Greg had a coughing fit and I passed him a glass of water, which he waved away in favour of the wine glass. Once he'd sipped some of the rich boutari and recovered, Dimitri continued, 'Ignorant peasants, they do not think what they are doing.'

'I suppose the undergrowth and grass are just tinder-dry at this time of year,' I said, lifting the fried flowers out to drain on paper before serving them. 'That's why barbecues are banned. Ben's always dealing with complaints about it from disappointed visitors, wanting to cook outside at their villas.'

'It's not the tourists. It's the locals. They're all bloody ignorant,' said Greg. 'Probably some dumb farmer or smallholder, trying to clear another bit of land. Stupid bastards.' He and Dimitri looked at each other and both began to laugh. I couldn't see what was so funny, but I didn't ask and just handed them the stuffed flowers.

Chapter Fifty

15 June 1944

Georgiou returns when the sun has almost departed and the cooling breeze of evening begins to drift from the sea. 'I don't think there is any need for us to worry,' he begins, dropping his sack on the stone floor. 'The explosions we heard before were just them blasting the rock. They're installing a gun emplacement, but just the one, so there won't be a large encampment nearby. I stayed long enough to see that there will only be a couple of soldiers there, three at the most.'

'It doesn't take many to find us,' Agata says. 'One is enough.' She stirs the tomato sauce for the roasted aubergines they are about to eat.

Georgiou is hungry. He hacks at a freshly picked cucumber with the knife he always carries in his belt and shoves chunks into his mouth. 'Why, what's happened? Where are the girls?'

'We had a visitor late this morning,' Agata says. 'I told the children to hide as soon as I saw him and they ran off and didn't make a sound. But I had to leave them there for the whole afternoon, till I was quite sure it was safe. They must have been shut in there for more than four hours. Luckily, they had the food and water I always leave there for them. I think they slept most of the time.'

'Where are they now?'

'Asleep in bed. They wake so early, they were still tired. And very frightened too. This is the first time I've been afraid since they arrived.'

'How many came here?'

'Just the one. He swam round from the headland. An officer, I should think. He was well mannered, courteous even. He didn't know anyone lived here and the girls had run upstairs before he was even out of the water, so he has no idea they exist.'

'And what did you do?'

'I gave him refreshments, he thanked me and then he left. He asked who else lived here and I said you were out checking the olive trees and would be back soon. He didn't ask many questions and I don't think he will give us trouble.'

Georgiou shakes his head. 'He may have left us alone for now, but he could easily come back. And he may talk about the beautiful bay he has found and about the kind hospitable host.' He stabs at the cucumber, skewering a chunk on the end of his knife. 'It's too great a risk. We must leave. We must leave tonight.'

'If I pull the blanket over your heads you must stay very still and be very, very quiet,' Agata tells the girls. 'We don't want anyone to see you. Anyone at all.'

Matilde looks fearful, but Anna curls up into a ball, saying, 'No bad men can see me. I'm not here.'

Agata laughs as she settles them into the handcart on cushioned sacks of straw. The moon has risen over the dark cypress trees at the top of the hill, lighting the track that threads through the twisted olive groves and up to the main road. She has packed dry goods, preserves, clothes, blankets and provisions for their journey. Georgiou has harvested all the ripe produce from the vegetable garden, tethered the goats to the cart and crammed the hens into a wicker crate. He has also assured his wife that he has carefully packaged seeds as well, in case they cannot return to their home and productive garden for some time.

'Where are we going?' Matilde asks. 'I like it here.'

Georgiou pats her head. 'We're going up to the mountains, my sweet. That's where our ancestors once lived, far away from Albanian pirates. The air is cool and fresh up there and no one will ever find us.'

'Do you think any of your family could still be there?' Agata asks him.

'Perhaps. An old aunt and a cousin were still living at the farm long before the Germans came, but the village has not been fully occupied for many years. And if we cannot stay in the farmhouse we will still find shelter there, I am sure.'

Then he turns to Agata and says, 'I'm not sure the girls should be hidden on our journey. If we are stopped by a patrol, they will not hesitate to rifle our goods and the children will be found and then they will wonder why we've tried to hide them. It will look much less suspicious if we treat them like ordinary children.'

Agata clutches his arm and looks at the girls, tucked up in the cart, arms curled around each other and beginning to fall asleep again. 'I suppose you're right. If we didn't have to conceal their parentage, we would let them be seen. But we must always have a hiding place for them if needed. They are used to hiding.'

'Of course, my love. But for now, they are Greek children. We are their guardians, that is all. We shall keep them safe – I think this is the wisest course of action.' He looks at the sky. 'We must leave now, while the moon lights the path.'

Agata locks and bars the doors of the house, pulls a shawl around her shoulders and picks up a bundle of clothes. As the donkey begins to pull the cart up the stony track, Matilde's head pops up from her bed of straw. 'What about our dresses?' she calls out. 'You said you were going to make new dresses for us.'

'I haven't forgotten, my dear.' Agata laughs and holds up her bundle. 'I have it all here. You will have your lovely new dresses as soon as we are settled into our new home. Now sleep, little one, for later you may have to walk with us.'

Matilde settles down once more, murmuring, 'New dresses…'

PART TWO

THEY SURVIVED

Chapter Fifty-One

Amber

July 2008

It was our second summer since opening Mountain Thyme and I felt like an enormous whale. In fact, I would have preferred to be a whale, swimming in a cool, blue ocean, gliding through waves and diving fathoms deep below. But I was a beached whale. There was no ocean, there was no sea, just heat – merciless, baking heat – and I was eight months pregnant.

The days had become so hot I longed to float in cool water, like one of the giant comical inflatable creatures sold in all the beach shops. Then I could be a dolphin or an octopus slowly swimming in circles, if I could only float in cold water. The beach was forty-five minutes away and we didn't have a pool, up here in the mountains, so I rehydrated with glasses of water, cold showers and sometimes, when I couldn't bear it any longer, I even sat with my feet in a bowl of water, run straight from the tap.

If I could have planned it better, I would not have chosen to be pregnant right in the middle of the searing heat of summer in Corfu. But then I had never actually made a conscious decision to have this baby, in Greece or anywhere. Even in an English summer it would have been hard, bearing such a burden, such a huge sack of kicking potatoes on hot humid days, but in Corfu, as the sun heated the rocky soil to roasting temperature, it was almost unbearable. I could only sleep at night if the air conditioning was switched on, but James said it made 'too much of a racket' for him to sleep soundly. I could rarely sleep during the day because there were guests to check in and out, rooms to clean, beds to change and the restaurant to manage.

Marian had been to see me a few times, but Inge was not feeling up to the long drives up here. 'Maybe she'll feel more like coming to see me when the weather is cooler,' I said, but Marian had just nodded and replied, 'She wants to spend as much time as she can down at the Old Fort during the summer season, while all the tourists are here.'

And I remembered how Inge had said, 'I am merely a witness to the truth. I cannot do much, but I can do this.' So while I puffed and complained then cooled my swollen ankles in a bowl of cold water, I reminded myself of Inge's purpose and how she was using her limited strength and energy. I hoped she would improve with the new treatment Marian said she was receiving, and that I could talk to her again soon, show her my new baby and give her hope.

Pam very sweetly invited me to visit her, saying, 'You're more than welcome to just come and sit by the pool all day, darling.' But I declined; even though the thought of her blue infinity pool with its gushing fountains was tempting, Lavinia was there too with her boisterous boys, shattering the peace. Luckily, we had more tables booked than ever, so I hadn't had to fob Pam off with excuses every time she asked if we could find room for them all. And that meant one less argument with James, who said he never wanted to serve that 'awful girl or her brats' ever again.

Oh dear, arguments with James. Did I ever expect us to disagree as much as we did then? Certainly the news of my pregnancy wasn't received with any of the delight I had so often fondly imagined. I think it was February when I realised what had happened and had to tell him.

'You're sure? Well, it's bloody awful timing.' Those were the first words with which my once so tactful, sensitive husband greeted my announcement. I had expected words of tender concern, a reassuring arm at my elbow helping me to a comfy seat, a peppermint tea and a cream cracker to ease my nausea, excited speculation about the baby's sex, which one of us it would most resemble and intense but enjoyable discussions about suitable names. But no, the overriding concern was not for my health, or where I would give birth and how I would get there, but the sheer inconvenience of this development for the business.

Up until then, despite the challenges of my career and then the demands of moving away from London and establishing the restaurant in Corfu, my life had always proceeded according to plan, as if it had been mapped out on one of those gigantic wall planners with coloured pins and magic markers. I'd aimed for straight As in my A-levels, set my sights on Cambridge, picked up a pupillage in a reputable chambers, qualified, met my future husband, bought a flat, and so on. The next step was going to be a baby at the age of thirty-six, so although suddenly finding myself pregnant at thirty-four wasn't quite in keeping with the grand plan, to my mind it was only a little premature and unexpected, and I felt sure we could cope. After all, the last couple of years had shown how flexible we could be. I certainly didn't expect James to be as displeased with the situation as he obviously was.

'When did you say it was expected again?' His face had gone white.

'They reckon my due date is August fifth, but it could happen any time a couple of weeks either side of that.' I was nibbling a dry digestive biscuit, fighting another bout of nausea. 'Babies aren't always totally predictable, you know.'

'August.' He'd given a great sigh of exasperation. 'Great. That means you'll probably be out of action for most of July and the whole of August. And they're the busiest months of the year.' He was pacing the kitchen, running his hands over his hair.

'I know it's our busiest time. I didn't suddenly think, ooh, I know, height of the season, that's the best time for us to have our first baby, so let's go for it.'

'Of course not, I mean, I know you didn't.' He'd shaken his head. 'But think back to how busy we were in our first year. It's going to get even more hectic now we're getting a name for ourselves.'

'I should hope so,' I'd said. 'It's what we've been working towards.'

'But you've always been around to deal with the enquiries and the bookings and everything else. I'm totally relying on you. I can't handle the calls and the questions as well as all the ordering and chefing.'

'And I will still be around. I won't be disabled or ill, you know. Pregnancy isn't an illness.' The nausea hadn't subsided, so I drank sips of water, hoping it would pass.

'But August,' he'd moaned. 'Why did it have to be August?'

I sighed. 'Because we drank too much at New Year?'

James looked at me. 'That night? How could it…? You're on the pill.' We'd celebrated rather enthusiastically, drinking far too much, and I'd been very sick in the early hours of the morning. If I hadn't felt so fragile I would have remembered to take another pill, but I didn't, and this was the somewhat inevitable result.

I'd hesitated to answer. I didn't see why I should take the blame, it takes two after all, so I only said, 'It's not foolproof. Anyway, we've always said we'd have children one day. It's just a bit earlier than we thought.'

'A lot earlier.' He was scowling. 'I thought we'd have the place running smoothly by the time we had kids. Now you're telling me that just one year after we've started, you'll be changing nappies and smelling of baby sick instead of helping me. You couldn't have chosen a worse time. Even out of season would have been better.'

'It's not deliberate,' I'd said. 'You're talking as if I've chosen this date specially to annoy you. I know it's not convenient, but it's happened now and we have to think about how to cope. Hopefully, I'll be fit and well all the way through and we'll manage.'

He looked even more worried after I'd said that. 'What do you mean, "hopefully"? What on earth am I going to do if you're not well?'

'We'll have to think about getting some more help in. It wouldn't be forever, after all.' I'd turned on my heels and stomped upstairs. This wasn't how it was meant to be. We should both have been thrilled at the prospect of our first child, he should have been protective and I should have been calm. Instead, I was shaking with anger and felt sick.

We didn't have that conversation again. It was almost as if he chose to forget that I was even pregnant. Later, I told him I planned to have the baby at the hospital in town and warned him that he might have to drive me there, but we didn't speculate on our baby's future or discuss names. I carried on with my duties as normal through the spring and early summer, but by July, as the days grew hotter, I grew slower and larger. We brought in extra help to lay tables and make beds, James already had assistance in the kitchen, and whenever it was quiet enough in the afternoon, I retreated to our room to lie down and imagined I was floating in a pool of cool water.

Chapter Fifty-Two

James

July 2008

I knew we needed the overnight guests for the extra income, but I wasn't half glad we had spare rooms some nights and I could have a bed to myself. Those were the times when I slept well and wasn't disturbed by Amber shifting around in bed, or her frequent visits to the bathroom. She usually switched on the air con and overhead fan once I'd left our room. I couldn't bear the noise, so I preferred sleeping alone in one of the empty bedrooms. If we'd had more guests staying it would have been a problem and I'd have had to put up with her shuffling about all night long and tossing the sheets to one side. She wasn't at all sympathetic when I said I needed a good night's sleep, even though I was the one who had to be up early to prep all the dishes for the day and check the deliveries. Luckily, we had a local girl to take and serve the breakfast orders when we had guests, and another to cook them, otherwise I'd have been even more stretched.

Greg was on my side though. 'You've got to keep your eye on the ball,' he announced on one of the days he dropped by. 'Lose your grip now, just when you're building up the business, and you'll set yourself back at least two years. I know it's tough, but you've got to keep at it.'

'I wish Amber could see it that way.'

'Hormones,' he said. 'Stops them getting things in perspective at these times. But she'll thank you for staying focused in the end. It's her future too, you know.'

'And I can't even sleep in the same bedroom as her any more. What I'll do when we're fully booked, I don't know. There's nowhere else to go for a quiet night. I'll be on my knees before long.'

'Then come over to me. Finish up here, zoom down to our place, get a good night's kip, pop back in the morning. You'll start the day fresh as a daisy.'

'Thanks, mate. I might just take you up on that.' The thought of escaping was a revelation.

'Any time,' Greg said, slapping me on the back. 'Can't have you falling asleep over your souvlaki, can we now? Might have a nasty accident.' He wandered round the kitchen, picking up utensils, and halted in front of my block of professional knives, sliding one from its slot. He ran his index finger along the sharp blade then looked at me. 'Don't want a dozy chef chopping his fingers off, do we? Tools of the trade, they are.'

I laughed at his attempts to cheer me up. 'All right, I'll remember that. I think we're fully booked for the second half of July, so I could be taking you up on your offer quite soon.'

A few days later, when every room was occupied, I slipped away at midnight, having texted Greg earlier in the evening to say I was coming. I found him alone, sitting on the terrace, chilled wine on the table. He turned his head when he heard my steps. 'Pull up a seat and have a glass,' he said.

I was relieved to sit down after such a long day in the kitchen. I stretched my legs and held the cold glass to my forehead before downing it in one. The outside temperature had soared to 38°C during the afternoon, but it must have been even higher in the kitchen while I was cooking.

Greg poured us both another glass, then said, 'Cool off down in the pool, then we'll go and take a look at the enemy.'

I knew exactly what he meant. The neighbouring hotel was quiet by this time of night, but he'd told me there was still loud music most evenings. 'How bad was it tonight?'

'Bloody awful. If I hear "(Is This the Way to) Amarillo" one more time, I'll be showing them the way to get off.'

I did a couple of lengths then heaved myself out. Greg was sauntering down the lit path. 'Take me to the action,' I said, as I slid my feet back into my espadrilles.

We crept in silence along the track we'd walked down two years before, on my first visit to the house, and Greg showed me a rickety platform he'd hammered together from rough timber. It was dark, but the moon was bright overhead. Putting a finger to his lips, he turned and climbed the ladder. I followed, and realised that from this vantage point, we had a clear view of the hotel swimming pool. Like Greg's, it was illuminated, and we could see the whole expanse glistening in the artificial light.

'Isn't there ever anyone here at night?' I whispered.

'Not allowed,' Greg whispered back. 'Health and safety. Management are too scared drunken guests will fall in and sue them.' He sniggered. 'I'm all for health and safety.' He picked up two pairs of thin rubber gloves and handed me a set. 'Better wear these. Health and safety,' he whispered. Then he passed me a catapult and offered me what he called 'ammunition'. It stank. I picked out a piece of hard, dry cat shit with my gloved fingers and fired it off. My first shot missed the water and landed on the pool's tiled edge, then rolled underneath a sun bed.

Greg took aim after me. He was bang on target and it bobbed on the water. We both had about five shots each, then he hissed, 'Don't want to overdo it. They might get suspicious.' We crept back to the terrace, stifling snorts of laughter, and he poured more wine.

'Don't they suspect anything yet, after all this time?' I asked him, when we were sat in the rattan chairs, looking down the garden.

'Apparently not. My mole tells me the hotel management is in two minds about who's to blame. Is it cats or kids crapping in the water?' His cackling laugh rolled out into the night. 'Kids or cats?' He shook his head as he laughed. 'Serves them right for not attracting a better class of clientele is what I say.'

'Surely they can tell though, can't they?'

'Who knows? Maybe all turds look the same after a night swim.' He roared again, thumping the table, and I began to laugh with him.

'What do you think they prefer,' I said, 'crawl or butterfly?'

'Doggy paddle,' he shrieked, bending over with laughter.

I suppose we must have both been quite loud, as I suddenly heard Pam's voice behind us, saying, 'Keep the noise down, you two. And Greg, you've had quite enough drink for one night.'

Greg put a finger to his lips again and I nodded at him in agreement. 'My personal health and safety,' he hissed, tapping his nose. 'Looking out for me.'

Chapter Fifty-Three

16 June 1944

Rebekka's heart jolts again when she hears the splash. Not the splash of oars or an anchor, but the sound of another body being thrown overboard. After five days in the Old Fort without extra provisions, they left Corfu in the open, creaking barges, towed slowly due south by a motorboat, towards the mainland. All day they sit, huddled in the leaking boats, the relentless sun baking their salt-crusted clothes and roasting their skin.

Surely they must be nearing their destination now. She sucks the orange she had hidden in her bundle, holding it under her shawl so she can't be seen. Papa has told her never to give in to temptation and lick the salty droplets of seawater, however thirsty she becomes.

And then a cry goes up and she feels both her parents stir. 'Land at last,' Mama croaks. 'They will surely give us water now, for pity's sake.'

'This is far from the end of our journey,' Papa says. 'We have only reached the island of Lefkas. I am afraid we are still far from the mainland.'

But when the barges are hauled alongside the dock, guards appear with guns and order everyone to climb out onto dry land. They are impatient and brutal – everyone is so slow and stiff from the time they have spent packed into the cramped boats. And as Rebekka and her parents stumble forwards, still clutching their bundles and sacks, damp from the salt spray of the sea, they hear the people of the island shouting in Greek and throwing loaves, dried sausage and fruit across to them. Everyone tries to grab what they can and some succeed in concealing a small portion of food in their pockets, but then they hear gunshots and see guards beating off the kind well-wishers with the butts of their rifles, kicking anyone who falls with their heavy boots. Rebekka manages to grab a bruised peach and Papa snatches a sesame seed loaf from the dusty concrete path, but others are not so lucky, as guards kick the good food into the waters of the harbour. Soldiers keep pushing the tired hungry people forward and herd them into a barren hot square, with no shade from the burning sun.

'The Germans are worse than I feared,' mutters Papa, squatting on his damp bundle. 'They will not even allow good honest people to share what little they have with us.'

Rebekka doesn't want to look, but she sees men and women running away, some falling to the ground, their clothes soaked in blood. 'They are only trying to help us,' she whispers. 'Where is the harm in that?'

She feels her mother's arm around her shoulders. 'Thank God I packed well. If there is water we shall survive,' Mama murmurs.

And Papa says, 'They are keeping us here for a day before the boats are towed to Patras and then on to Athens. When we reach the mainland, they will surely transfer us to trains for the rest of our journey. That has to be better than these old barges, I am sure.'

'We will travel in comfort,' Mama says, putting her arm around her daughter. 'No more seasickness, and plenty of space for us all to sit down.'

Rebekka has never even seen a train, let alone travelled on one. But she knows from her schooling that trains travel faster than slow old barges, so their journey will surely soon be over. She bites into her bruised peach, taking care not to waste a single drop of sweet juice.

Chapter Fifty-Four

Amber

July 2008

I knew James didn't always spend the night at Mountain Thyme and I realised I simply didn't care. I used to think I would miss the comfort of his presence in bed, but during the hot stifling nights of that scorching July all I cared about was having a few hours of proper sleep if I could. He had told me a couple of weeks before that he might sometimes stay the night with Greg and Pam, when we were fully booked. I said as long as he didn't expect me to be up early, making breakfast, it didn't matter to me one bit. But after a while I began to realise that he left Mountain Thyme even when we didn't have any overnight guests occupying the other rooms. He left when he'd finished cooking for the day, because he wanted to relax and unwind with wine and amusing conversation. I was not good company for him, I was a tired swollen lump, so he left me alone and went to have fun with Greg.

The first time he left he came and said goodnight first. He kissed my cheek and stroked my hair, almost like he used to, before I expanded into a gigantic balloon. But there finally came a night when I was sure he'd gone even though he hadn't come to our room to say goodbye. There were empty beds in our house that night, but I knew he would rather seek Greg's company than drink alone.

At least it meant we didn't have to change the sheets in one of the guest rooms again. If he slept in a spare room and we had bookings the next day, it made for more work. When we first opened for business, I used to do all the housekeeping myself, but once I became so bulky and clumsy I could no longer bend down to tuck the sheet tightly around the mattress, Adrianna did all the bedrooms after she'd finished the breakfasts.

Those nights in July were particularly hot and still and although I knew I shouldn't open the windows, because of the mosquitoes, I told myself there weren't so many around that year and I could allow myself just a brief breath of fresh of air before I lay down on the bed each night. I often stood by the open shutters, smelling the cloying scent of the last of the white jasmine winding its tendrils around the balcony. It was utterly quiet apart from the whirring cicadas and a distant scops owl, its cry chiming in the night.

One night, in the lemon groves below, I heard the faint sounds of night creatures rustling, cats or more probably rats, scavenging the rotting fruit. There was no moon that night and all was dark, apart from what looked like a flickering light on the far hillside. I hoped it wasn't another fire. There had only been a couple so far that summer and luckily, they hadn't caused much damage, but the scrub vegetation was so dry a single spark could set a blaze roaring in an instant. Open fires are banned from May to October, but a careless cigarette stub or a piece of broken glass is all it takes to set hectares of dry brush alight.

Ben said he had made sure all his villas had notices banning barbecues, but when the holidaymakers arrive and see the purpose-built brick grills on the terrace, they think a few chargrilled kebabs can't possibly hurt. His staff had already dealt with a couple of scorched gardens that season, but luckily the careless fires did little more than singe the nearby shrubs. If the flames had reached the oil-rich olive trees and spread to the undergrowth, the fires could have rapidly spread through the groves and then become impossible to douse without firefighters.

I leant against the window frame wondering if I tucked the mosquito net tight around the bed, whether I could sleep with the windows open, the night air cooling me instead of the noisy fan. But I knew that if the insects invaded the room I would become a swollen, bitten mass, with bites in places I couldn't even reach to scratch. I closed the shutters tight then heaved myself onto the bed, and lay down with a pillow supporting my ungainly, lumpen belly. The baby was kicking and I was suffering from heartburn again.

Despite James's misgivings, and although the heat had made me slower, I was still able to make a contribution to the business. That day I had arranged tall stems of blue agapanthus in vases in the restaurant, folded napkins and polished glasses, then checked bookings for both lunch and dinner. I answered emails and responded to enquiries for the following year; I phoned suppliers and took calls from diners wanting to eat with us in the coming weeks. But I had to lie down on my bed in the middle of the afternoon, swollen ankles raised on pillows, so I could smile and greet guests in the evenings as they arrived for the wonderful dinners that were gaining such a wide reputation.

I could no longer rush into town so easily if James was disappointed with a delivery of fish or a vital ingredient was missing, but I could still supervise the running of the restaurant and our accommodation, with help. Adrianna and Ariadne arrived early every day and took it in turns to stay until the dinner service was finished. They worked alternate afternoons, so whoever was doing the evening shift didn't have to work right the way through the day. They were reliable friendly girls, and both lived in villages at the coastal end of the mountain road, several miles away.

I remember how one day, around that time, Adrianna very kindly asked me if I would like her to stay behind at night. 'For when your time comes,' she said with a small smile. I wasn't sure why she was saying that at first, then realised she meant when I went into labour. 'It is no trouble for me,' she insisted, when I declined her offer.

I didn't think she knew that James left me there alone most nights, but now I wonder. One day, he hadn't yet come back when she arrived to help make the breakfasts for our guests. 'Mr James is always in the kitchen in the morning, but not today,' she said. 'He has gone out early?' She had knocked at my bedroom door and brought me tea and a fresh croissant, which had just been delivered with the bread and rolls we ordered each morning. James was usually downstairs early every day, prepping the lunch dishes and checking what supplies were left over from the day before.

'Oh, he had to see someone urgently,' I'd said, knowing that he had probably been drinking till late with Greg. 'He said you'd be able to manage this morning.' I'd thanked her for the tray she left on my bedside table and hoped she did not notice that his pillow was uncreased. The rest of the bed linen was crumpled, but his pillow bore no impression of his head, so I pulled it across to my side and propped myself up to eat.

Marian also offered to drive up to Mountain Thyme if I needed company, even though both her shops were busy till late during the hectic summer months. She visited me now and then, as I preferred not to drive too far on my own in late pregnancy, and I hadn't been to either of the Mill shops for a few weeks. I didn't like to tell her that James wasn't always by my side overnight. She was so attentive in her care of Inge that I felt sure she would look at me with an accusation of neglect, if I told her he couldn't bear to sleep with me any more.

That night, as I tossed uncomfortably in my hot bed, then propped myself up again on the pillows, I wondered how James would behave when the baby finally arrived. It would have to sleep in our room until the holiday season petered out as we couldn't be guaranteed spare bedrooms every night until October at the earliest. And although by then I hoped I'd be sleeping soundly, when I could, I imagined he wouldn't take kindly to waking to a hungry baby's cries in the middle of the night. I planned to put it down to sleep in a basket on the floor, on my side of the bed. I didn't have a cradle or a cot, nor a pram or a buggy – I only had a basket padded with folded linen and half a drawer in my wardrobe, filled with little vests and nappies. No knitted layettes or poppered Babygros for this baby, as it would arrive in the high temperatures of summer and be quite warm enough.

I closed my eyes, and once again imagined floating in cool water, as I did every night to lull myself to sleep. I was floating in a pool and the baby was floating inside me.

Chapter Fifty-Five

James

July 2008

The guest rooms were all empty that particular night, but I still didn't want to stay at Mountain Thyme. I'd been cooking all day and talking to diners who wanted to meet me. After hours on my feet, hours of chatting and hours of working hard, I needed to relax. It was midnight and I knew Amber wouldn't miss me. She'd gone to bed at ten and I was always back by seven in the morning. She understood. Her job was to carry on doing whatever tasks she could still manage and look after herself so this pregnancy didn't turn into even more of an inconvenience than it was already. My job was to grow the business and make sure we built on the reputation we had acquired in our first year. I told myself I was doing it for her and the baby and that she understood that, or at least she would eventually.

It was quiet when I finally left and quiet when I reached Greg's place. I pulled over into my usual parking spot and noticed that as well as Greg's jeep and Pam's white Mercedes, there was a third car parked under the trees. *Please don't let that stupid woman still be here*, I thought.

Lavinia had arrived the previous week for a girls' holiday, to cheer herself up over her separation from her Russian husband, Vladimir. When I'd come over a couple of days previously for a peaceful night's sleep and a matey chat with Greg, she'd been larking around in the pool with a couple of drunken friends, shrieking and splashing, all three of them vying for attention in their skimpy costumes.

She'd sauntered across to the terrace and stood there, hand on hip, blonde hair dripping over tanned shoulders, sunburnt flesh dark against the clinging white fabric of her tiny bikini. Pouting, she'd said, 'Don't be so boring, James. Come on down for a late-night swim. You'd like to cool off with all of us girls, wouldn't you?'

The water was tempting, but she and her beautiful but vacuous friends weren't. She soon lost interest when she saw I wasn't coming out to play, and Greg and I had resumed our conversation. We hadn't walked the trail or fired missiles that night, preferring to creep away early to our beds.

I decided that if she was there again, I'd go straight up to my room and catch up on my sleep. But then I realised it wasn't her car, although I was sure I recognised it. Then I saw a man coming towards me, walking up the gravel path. At first I could only see a white shirt and light trousers, luminous against dark skin, but as he came closer, I saw it was Dimitri. 'Fancy seeing you here,' I called out. 'You're not usually here this late.'

'Mr Richards has many big worries,' he said with a shake of his head. 'Much on his mind, I think you say.'

'Well, I'm sure you've been able to help him sort them out. He's always saying how much he relies on you.'

Dimitri gave a small nod, a gesture that was almost a token bow. 'I do my best, Mr James, I always do my best.' He turned to go, then looked back over his shoulder. 'He is waiting for you on the terrace.'

'Yes, I mustn't keep him. Good night.'

Dimitri saluted, '*Kalispera*,' he said and turned away, his distant steps crunching the gravel as I approached the house, where Greg was sitting in his usual chair, examining his phone and cursing.

'Effing thing,' he swore, slamming it down on the table. 'These arsey fairies don't design these gadgets for real men's fingers.'

I laughed. 'You haven't gone and got yourself a smartphone at last, have you?'

'Pam made us both get one. Wants to keep track of me, I reckon. But she's got smaller fingers. I can't get the sodding thing to work for me.'

'You'll soon get used to it. It took my dad a while but he swears by it now.'

'Yeah, well, I'm swearing *at* it right now.' Greg laughed, then grabbed the yellow-labelled bottle on the table and poured us both a cold glass of Kourtaki retsina. 'Here, have some of the local crap. Pam says it's better for me than my usual stuff. Tastes like disinfectant, but hey, it's still alcohol.'

I sipped. I actually liked retsina anyway, but then I always did have cheap tastes. 'Do you want me to show you how to set your phone up?'

He tossed it over to me, saying, 'It's set up all right, but I buggered up the text I was sending Dimitri. I've probably told him to go and get lost now.'

I found Greg's messages and then the text to Dimitri. I shook my head as I tried to interpret it. *Ill Ave to yu*, it read. 'What?' I showed it to Greg, who picked up his glasses and peered at it, then exploded in laughter.

'At least I didn't tell him to go fuck himself.'

'Do you want me to rewrite it?'

'No, doesn't matter. He's got the picture anyway.'

'New project?'

'No, he's still dealing with the ins and outs of the land up near you. These old sites are a tangled mess of transactions going back years.' He yawned, as if the day had been exhausting for him too. 'But I think we're nearly there.'

'That's good to hear. We're getting enough customers as it is, but more quality business would be very welcome.' I leant back, holding my glass, and put my feet up on the opposite chair. 'I'm sick of these cheapskate tourists, dropping by and expecting a cut-price meal. It's not what we're about.'

'Stick to your guns, mate. You've got a vision, you should hang onto it.'

I finished my wine and Greg topped up my glass. 'I'm hoping we'll get more of the Brits in due course,' I said. 'They still seem to mostly stick with their old favourites down in Agios and Kalami, but a lot more of them have taken the trouble to drive up to us this year, and I think they'll gradually spread the word around.'

'What about the Russians? They're splashing the cash this year, aren't they?'

I nodded. 'They sure are. We had another group in for lunch the other day. Very ostentatious, all ordering champagne and handing out big tips for the staff. When they're having fun, they want everyone else to have fun too. But they can be very loud and rude. Not the sort we really want around the Brits we're hoping to attract.'

Greg sighed. 'They don't get it, do they? No finesse. Once a peasant, always a peasant. It's the same with Lavinia's ex. Told her when she met him, it wouldn't last.' He stared into his glass, swilling the wine around, looking morose. 'Always after the latest, flashiest model, that lot.'

'Are they still married?'

'Just. They'll be divorced once the money's all worked out. Got my bloke in London onto it, but that bastard Vladi's tight as a cat's arse. They all are.' He reached for the bottle again and held it up in disbelief. It was empty. 'Till then, Daddy's footing the bills, so I could do with a few good deals right now.'

I really didn't want to have to share another whole bottle with Greg, so I said, 'You need to take your mind off it. Come on, let's see who's the best shot this time.'

We walked down the garden in silence to the hidden platform. As we approached, we heard splashing and giggling. 'Sounds like we've got company tonight,' Greg whispered.

We climbed up and stood there, looking down on the brightly lit pool. On previous occasions this area of the hotel grounds had always been totally empty after dark, but that evening the pool's calm surface rippled as two figures, a man and a woman, cavorted in the water. They swam side by side to the end nearest to us and as they stood up in the shallows we could see they were both quite naked.

Greg nudged me and we loaded our weapons with stinking ammunition and fired simultaneously. The pellets landed about a yard away from the kissing couple, but there was no reaction.

Then Greg's next shot skimmed the girl's hair, piled up in a loose mass of tendrils on the top of her head. She must have felt the lightest of touches, like a large flying insect, as she broke away from her boyfriend and brushed her hair with her hand. She looked down at the water and, puzzled, held her hand under one of the little floating cat turds, looking just like a small pine cone or seed pod. She scooped it into her palm and stared then suddenly jerked back in disgust, throwing it far away from her into the water. She took a couple of steps back, then looked around.

Greg and I were choking back our laughter, trying not to give ourselves away as she clambered out of the pool, grabbing her abandoned dress from a nearby lounger. The man followed, stumbling into his shorts, tripping in his flip flops as he tried to run after her.

'Good idea of yours,' Greg laughed, when the couple had gone. 'Other people's misfortunes always cheer me up.'

Chapter Fifty-Six

16 June 1944

'How much further do you think it is?' Agata asks her husband. The steep winding trek from their home to the main road has already taken over an hour with their heavily laden cart. The girls have slept, despite the bumping of the wheels on the rough path, but the sure-footed goats and donkey have walked with a steady pace over the uneven stones.

Georgiou hushes his wife and makes her wait behind the roadside shack while he listens and checks the road is clear. 'We can cross over here – with luck we shall reach the farmhouse by the end of tomorrow,' he says on his return.

He has been familiar with all the paths to the mountains ever since childhood, when he would often take fresh fish up to the family farm. As a boy, unburdened by luggage, livestock and children, he could run there in a few hours. The tracks are rarely walked by men, more usually by nimble sheep and goats, so he is confident soldiers will not come their way. The Germans prefer to take the easy roads with their motorbikes, cars and tanks. Obscure trails twisting through thickets of juniper, myrtle and carob are not at all to their liking, and might hide the Resistance and resentful peasants.

They pause to listen again before crossing and Agata turns to the roadside shrine of Saint Spyridon. She holds two fingers to her lips and transfers the kiss to the chipped and peeling plaster effigy. She would have liked to light a candle, but daren't leave a sign that they were here recently. Instead, she whispers a hurried prayer, 'I pray you will bless us, my saint, and keep us all safe from harm, as you have done many times before.'

They cross the tarmacked road and are soon shielded by the dense growth of shrubs and trees. Then Agata pauses and turns back to the verge, where huge prickly pears grow like sculptures, small fruits bursting from their branches. She slips a knife from her pocket and, holding a basket underneath the towering plant, quickly slices off the ripe juicy pears, carefully avoiding the sharp spines. If their journey is long or they have to hide for a time, she will peel the spiky cacti to quench their thirst. *And if we are lucky,* she thinks, *we may also find a strawberry tree bearing ripe fruit.*

'Come on,' calls Georgiou, anxious to continue their trek. He understands her wish to gather whatever provisions they may need, but he is keen to move on and disappear, away from the danger of the open road and into the safety of the thickly wooded foothills, as soon as they can.

After two more hours, the girls are fully awake and keen to walk. Agata gives them each a sweet peach to eat as they follow the cart. The sun has been up for a while and although there is shade under the trees, it will soon be very hot. Their progress is slow on the rutted path, then Anna stumbles and cries, so Agata lifts her back onto the cart.

'We shall stop and rest at noon,' Georgiou says. 'We must conserve our energy and stay alert.' He leads on for another couple of hours, holding the donkey's halter until they reach another grove of neglected olive trees, where gnarled branches form a canopy of shade over crackling beds of dry leaves. Tiny fallen olives are scattered all around, ungathered and unwanted, but the children begin scooping them up, competing with each other to see who can find the most.

Agata spreads a blanket over the leafy floor and sets out a sparse picnic of tomatoes, hard-boiled eggs and cucumber. Georgiou gulps water from his flask and the girls run over to show him the handfuls of wizened black olives they have found. He laughs and helps them count the withered fruit, then leans back against the tree trunk and looks up through the twisted branches. A bird is circling far overhead. 'Look,' he says to the girls, 'that's a kite searching for food.' Both children look up and shade their eyes as they watch the bird gliding, wings outspread.

'What does it eat?' Matilde asks.

'Rats and naughty little mice,' Georgiou says, tickling her under her arms, making her shriek with delight.

Agata looks up too, and then she points to the high mountain they can see, towering over the wooded slopes. 'And there is Mount Pantokrator,' she says. 'Can you see the monastery at its very top?' The children peer at the white building they can just about see on the peak, and Anna says, 'Why is it there?'

'It's watching over us,' Agata replies. 'There has been a church there for hundreds of years. From that height it can see the whole of Corfu.'

'Can it see us now?' Anna asks.

Agata takes her in her arms. 'It can, my darling, and it is wishing us a safe journey to our new home.'

'Can it see the bad men as well?' Matilde says, sitting down on Georgiou's outstretched legs and looking up at the mountain.

'Of course it can. And it is praying they will leave Corfu for good very soon.'

Chapter Fifty-Seven

Amber

July 2008

In my dreams that night, I was sure I could smell burnt toast. James always liked his toast very well done, so well done that he often burnt it. He called it 'proper toast'. I like mine light brown, in thick slices, crisp outside and soft within. I dreamt I was telling him I didn't want to eat toast with charred crusts and then I woke up, knowing that the scent was real and not a dream. There was the faintest hint of smoke in the air, but it didn't smell like toast and I couldn't hear James downstairs, and it wasn't morning.

I switched on the bedside light and checked the time. Three o'clock. James didn't usually come back in the middle of the night and he certainly didn't come back in the early hours to begin cooking. I wondered if he might have left a pan on the stove in the kitchen, simmering till it boiled dry, or maybe a lantern had been left alight on one of the restaurant tables and had caught hold of a dry leaf, fallen from the vines overhead.

I heaved myself out of bed, then stood still and listened. The nights up there in the mountains were always so quiet when everyone else who worked in the village had gone home that the silence almost seemed to hum, the stillness broken only by the occasional cry of an owl or the bark of a far-away dog. But that night, although I could tell there was definitely nobody else in the house, I began to think I could hear something, a distant rustling sound, like dry leaves blowing in the wind or rain pattering on a roof. I pulled a shawl around my nightdress and lumbered across the landing and down the stairs, switching all the lights on as I went. The kitchen was empty and nothing was boiling dry. There was no haze of smoke hanging in the air in any of the rooms, and the alarms would surely have sounded if there had been, but I could still smell the faint trace that first woke me.

None of the candles inside the restaurant were burning and none of the lamps on the outside tables were alight when I stepped out onto the terrace. But I could still hear that curious rustling noise, and as soon as I switched on the lights that illuminated the steps leading down to the cobbled surface of the road, I could see why. The very stones that paved the street seemed to be moving. No, they weren't just moving, they were crawling. The cobbles were alive with wildlife, and birds that normally sleep in their nests at night were darting through the air. Mice, rats, rabbits and even a stone marten were running past Mountain Thyme, along with a slow scuttling hedgehog and many, many, creepy crawlies.

I crossed the terrace and looked out over the olive and lemon trees. I could hear more rustling from that side of the restaurant too, and although there was no light, I could see the undergrowth was full of creatures, running and crawling. And then I could see why. On the far side of our valley, almost reaching the furthest edge of the lemon, orange and olive groves, fire was advancing, driving the animals before the tidal wave of flames. Rivulets of fire were streaming ahead, threading their way around the twisted tree trunks, running towards the village.

For a moment I was mesmerised by the sight, the flickering flames beyond the trees, the orange threads trickling through the orchard. Then I realised I had to act fast, just like the fleeing wildlife. But James had taken the car and no one else ever stayed in the village overnight. Our property was the only one permanently occupied, so I was completely alone.

I went inside and rang James. He knew that I only had a couple of weeks left till the baby was due. I thought he must surely keep his mobile phone switched on and with him at all times. But there was only an automatic response. I tried several times but he didn't answer, so finally I left a message. 'Ring me as soon as you can. A wildfire's broken out up here'.

When I went back outside to the terrace, the trees were already encircled with a necklace of golden flames and I knew they'd soon catch fire. I called the fire service. Yes, they were aware of the situation and were on their way. But they couldn't tell me how quickly the fire would be under control and I knew that these mountain roads could quickly become impassable, with flames leaping from one side of the track to the other as sparks scattered from the dry grass and brush.

I tried calling James again, then Greg and Pam, but they too must have been asleep, their phones switched off. I called Adrianna and Ariadne but no one was awake at that time of night. We were the only ones, my baby and me.

I stood on the terrace, looking at the advancing flames, wondering how soon the fire service could reach the village and get it under control. The dry grassy scrub around the groves ran right up to the walls of our home, and drifting embers from burning trees could float on the wind and ignite new fires yards away. If sparks landed on the vines which clung to the walls and over the wooden beams that shaded the terrace, the fire could rapidly travel into the restaurant and the whole building could soon be blazing.

I tried to think where all our fire extinguishers were and found the first one in the reception area. But it was so heavy. I dragged it out onto the terrace and across to the balustrade overlooking the oncoming flames, but I couldn't lift it. Maybe I could have previously, but in the cumbersome state of late pregnancy, I struggled with the weight.

I then remembered we had a hose our handyman used for watering the vines and the pot plants, so I dragged that over too, linked it to the tap and checked that it was working. The spray was feeble, even when the tap was fully turned. It could douse a few sparks, but I doubted it would be any use if the whole grove caught fire.

And then the baby kicked me. It was telling me I couldn't fight this blaze alone. It was telling me I must find a safe place to shelter. But where? Was there anywhere safe, if the village was surrounded by burning olive trees? If I tried to leave on foot in the dark, I could fall, and I doubted I could manage to walk very far on the cobbled streets and rough mountain tracks. I imagined leaving Mountain Thyme, then stumbling and falling from the steep roads into a crevasse, giving birth under a thorny berberis bush and no one ever finding me in the wilderness.

And then I remembered the cellar; the deep cool cellar below the restaurant, where wine and oil were stored, along with preserves and dry goods. I moved as quickly as my baby would allow and filled a basket with bottled water, peaches, cheese and bread from the kitchen. I was only wearing slippers, a loose nightdress and a shawl. I would have preferred to be properly dressed, but there was no time to go back to the bedroom and worry about clothes.

I threw a torch into the basket with the provisions, and then went slowly down the steep granite steps, closing the door to the restaurant behind me. I hoped we'd be safe there, the baby and me, while every other living creature in the entire village was fleeing for its very life in the middle of the night.

Chapter Fifty-Eight

James

July 2008

One minute I was in a dead sleep, the next the light was switched on and Greg was shaking my shoulder. 'Wake up, quick,' he was saying. 'We've got to go, right away.'

I was groggy with sleep and the wine we'd drunk earlier, mumbling, 'Why? What time is it?'

'There's a fire up the mountain. Come on, hurry. Get dressed.'

He rushed away. I could see he was already dressed. I fumbled for my clothes, pulling them on in a stupor, and staggered into the bathroom to splash water over my face and brush my teeth. Then I felt for my phone. It wasn't in my pocket, nor on the bedside table. Where was it? Then I remembered. I'd had it when I was showing Greg how to use his new phone. I must have left it on the table out on the terrace.

I ran downstairs, where Greg was gulping black coffee. He held out a cup for me, but I waved it away and ran outside. Both phones were still where we'd left them and when I picked mine up and switched it on, I saw I had several missed calls from Amber and a message. Her voice was shaky and she sounded very scared. I ran back in to Greg, shouting, 'We've got to go. I have to get to Amber right away.'

'I know. Come on,' he yelled back and we ran to the cars. 'No,' he shouted, as I went to unlock mine. 'We'd better take the jeep. If the road's blocked we might have to go cross-country.'

'Has it reached the village?' I asked, as he pulled away in a spurt of gravel.

'It's very close,' was his terse answer. He was hunched over the wheel, accelerating around the bends.

'The fire brigade, we've got to call them,' I said, as I tried to ring Amber again. Every time I dialled she didn't answer, making me more and more frantic. She must have her phone with her, I kept thinking, she must have charged it up. She knew it was her lifeline. There was no answer from the restaurant phone either.

'Already done it,' he said, driving even faster.

'You called them?'

'Yup. They'd already had the call and were on their way.'

'On their way? They're not there yet?' The jeep swung wide round another sharp bend and suddenly Greg shot across the road, taking the tight turn up to the mountains. I hung onto the strap above the side window and steadied myself with one hand on the dashboard. As we climbed, there was a view ahead of the mountainside, normally dark and featureless at night, unless there was a full moon and a clear sky, but now it was jewel-like, wreathed in beads of orange, amber and red. 'My God,' I said. 'It's spreading everywhere.'

'Bloody fool,' Greg muttered, taking another sharp turn, tyres screeching and spraying gravel on the hairpin bends.

I was craning to look at the hillside, struggling in the dark to work out exactly how near to the village and the restaurant the blaze was. It seemed to be taking us forever to get there. Through the open window, as well as the growling whine of the engine, I thought I could hear something above us and suddenly, against the dawning sky, I could see a plane, carrying a bulging parcel. 'I think they're bringing in water,' I shouted to Greg. 'That should help.'

'Shit, shit, shit,' he cursed. 'It must be spreading fast. They only do that when they can't reach it with the hoses.'

Of course. I should have known. We'd seen it two years before, in our first summer on the island; the seaplanes dipping and

scooping over the turquoise waters, hauling great bucketloads up
to the burning hillsides.

'But the firefighters must be trying to deal with it too. They
must be. Amber's up there. She's all alone.' I punched the dashboard
in frustration. 'Damn it, I shouldn't have left her on her own. I
should never have left her.'

Then suddenly, just after we'd rounded another bend, Greg
skidded to a halt. A police car was angled across the road and an
officer came towards us, his hand held up to halt our progress. He
and Greg spoke rapidly in Greek, waving arms and pointing down
the road towards the village.

'What's he saying?' I shouted. 'Tell him I've got to get through.'

'He says no one's allowed any further. They all think the village
is deserted and no one's there overnight. But I've told him we're
sure Amber's still there, on her own.'

'She must be. I know she is. She couldn't leave without a car,
not in her condition. We both know that.'

'Calm down. The fire fighters are all around the village. They'll
get to her very soon. She'll be fine.'

I climbed out of the car, but I couldn't see or hear any activ-
ity. I could see the distant glow of the fire but I couldn't see the
village. It was half a mile away, tucked into the valley, shielded by
the mountain slopes. I felt frantic, not knowing how Amber was
coping. I cursed myself again for leaving her on her own. And I
knew I couldn't stand there doing nothing – I had to get to her,
right away.

'I've got to find her,' I shouted, and charged past the police car
and its officer. I heard him and Greg shouting after me, then more
shouts as I ran. It was starting to get light now and I could see the
road as a grey ribbon ahead of me, snaking round boulders on the
left and dropping down into steep gullies on the right. *Please don't
say she's tried to leave alone on foot in the dark*, I pleaded, *please let
her be safe.*

Before long, my breathing became laboured; I wasn't as fit as I used to be. All that time in the kitchen may have been hard on my feet and my fingers, but it hadn't prepared me for this kind of endurance race. My pace slowed and I had to catch my breath. I leant on my knees, easing the stitch that was gripping my stomach, and that's when I heard steps behind me. I looked round, about to start running again, thinking it was the policeman trying to stop me, but it was Greg. Despite his age and his drinking, he was fitter than me from all his regular tennis and games of golf.

'Catch me up when you can,' he called, as he jogged past. 'We'll get to her, don't you worry.' His voice trailed into the distance and he was soon out of sight, far along the track.

I began running again, but couldn't catch up with him, as I was soon reduced to stumbling with another agonising stitch in my side. Then, as I rounded the final bend, I could see the tiled rooftops in the hollow ahead of me. 'No,' I cried out loud. This end of the village was completely surrounded by fire, and flames were licking the doors and windows of the very houses.

Greg was nowhere in sight, but as I stumbled down the stony track and neared the burning village, I thought I could hear distant shouts from the far side. I hoped that meant the firefighters were tackling the blaze and that it might soon be under control. Flames were starting to trickle through the undergrowth on either side of the road, and the narrow lane into the village was littered with falling debris from houses and trees. I came to a halt at the entrance to the cobbled street we usually drove down to the restaurant. All I could see ahead of me was buildings ablaze on every side, with tiles crashing through roofs as timbers burnt and windows exploded, their glass shattering into the street.

I couldn't see a way to reach Mountain Thyme safely, so I decided to skirt around the perimeter of the village by following the thin worn path used by the local sheep and goats, winding through the scrubland dotted with thorny bushes. It made for slow progress, as I kept tripping over roots and rocks – not a problem for nimble, cloven hooves, but an obstacle race for my big clumsy feet.

Although the sky had lightened with the dawn, visibility was still poor because of the smoke, so I didn't immediately see the figure crouching a little way off behind the stunted juniper trees. But, as I came nearer, I noticed a man hunched there. At first, I assumed it was Greg catching his breath, then I suddenly realised it was Dimitri. 'What on earth are you doing here?' I called.

His head jerked round in surprise on hearing my voice. 'Mr James,' he said, pointing to the flames. 'The fire, it is a terrible thing. The whole village destroyed, I fear.'

I reached him, almost out of breath and gasped, 'Have you seen Greg? Did he come this way?'

'Mr Richards? Is here now?' He looked around from side to side, his eyes wide open.

'He came on ahead of me. I've got to find a way in,' I panted, trying to catch my breath. 'I must find her. Amber's in there alone. Is there any way of reaching the restaurant?'

But Dimitri just kept on staring at me. Why on earth didn't he answer? Was he numbed into silence by the ferocity of the fire?

'Dimitri, where's Greg? Come on, we have to get into the village and find them.' I turned away and resumed running along the narrow goat track, and then I stopped and looked back. He was still standing there under the trees, then, suddenly, he turned and began to run. He started running fast, but not towards me and not towards the village: he was running away, back towards the road. 'Dimitri!' I called. 'Where are you going? Come back. We've got to get to Amber. She needs help.'

He shouted something as he ran. At first, I couldn't quite catch his words, tossed away as he stumbled up the track. But as I turned them over, trying to interpret his distorted cry, I realised he'd shouted, 'None of it's yours. It belongs to us, not you!'

I began to run after him, my chest bursting with pain, my feet catching on the rough ground. He was faster than me and I saw he was heading for his car, tucked away under bushes in the shadow of a cliff, but then suddenly he tripped and as he staggered to his feet, limping, I caught up with him, grabbing hold of him by his collar. He swung back and lunged at me, but I dodged his fists.

'Hey, hold on!' I cried, ducking another swing. 'What's the problem? What's this all about?'

'You English!' he shouted. 'Always taking. It's not yours. It never was.'

'I don't know what you're talking about. We're in business, aren't we? We're all in it together?'

He pulled free of my grasp, stepped back, and then began to laugh. 'Never. It will never be yours. The fire takes everything and then it will be ours again.'

I was shocked into silence. I didn't understand. All I could comprehend was his contempt for all of us and his total lack of concern for Amber. And then he spat at me, his spittle landing on the ground at my feet. At that point I lost control and threw myself at him, knocking him off balance. As he lay there stunned, I fumbled in his pockets and found his car keys, then I threw them as far as I could across the dry scrub. 'I'll deal with you later,' I shouted, as I began running back again along the narrow track towards the fire. 'I've got to find my wife. You can wait.'

Chapter Fifty-Nine

16 June 1944

That night they sleep under the trees. The girls are sleeping in the handcart, dreaming of new white dresses, the donkey and goats are tethered nearby with a bag of hay and the caged hens mutter soft clucks in their feathery sleep. Georgiou and Agata lie on a bed of pine needles, looking up at the stars through a ceiling of airy branches. They ate a sparse cold supper of feta and cucumbers, not daring to light a fire in this tinder-dry clearing.

'I keep wondering about their parents and their older sister,' Agata says. 'Have they left the island yet? Have they reached their destination?'

'We've no way of knowing,' Georgiou says. 'We may not even know for some time whether the Germans have left Corfu, whether this dreadful war has ended, or if the Allied forces come here. Once we are up there in the mountains it's likely we'll know even less than we did before. But we shall all be safe, even if we are ignorant.'

'I've told them their parents are working hard, and so is Rebekka. I tell them that so they will have hope and so they will want to work hard too, when they are old enough. But I have such feelings of dread for their poor family and all of their people.'

'I know, my dear, I know,' Georgiou says, taking his wife's hand and holding it to his lips. 'But for now, we can at least protect their children and keep them safe.'

'We will. And I've also decided that although they are very young still, I must teach them everything I know. Little by little I will show them how to sew, how to make bread and how to grind chickpeas and beans for hummus and fava. We must both make sure they can survive if we are no longer here. We don't know if anyone else in the old village and around that region will help them. And we don't even know yet if anyone else is still living up there.'

'You are right, my love. And I will show them how to tend the garden, so they will always have vegetables and fruit to eat. As we learnt these skills from our parents and grandparents, so they must learn from us. You will soon have rivals for your cheese if you teach them how to milk the goats.'

'Such a pity we will no longer be able to fish, though. You could have taken them out in your boat if we had been able to stay.'

'There may not be fish, but up in the mountains I will show them how to set snares for rabbits and nets for small birds. We may also find dormice and tortoise. Our larder will be plentiful.'

'You are a good man, Georgiou…' Agata murmurs, as she finally closes her eyes and sleeps.

'Aggie,' Anna cries, tugging at Agata's skirt. 'I want a pet like Matilde.'

Agata shakes herself awake, stiff from her night under the trees. 'What did you say?'

'It's not fair. I want a pet too.' Anna turns and points to where Matilde is crouching by the twisted roots of an olive tree, dabbing at something with a twig. 'She says his name is Tomas.'

Agata gets to her feet to look. There, in among the dried leaves and pine needles, is a large black scorpion arching its tail. It is not enjoying the game as much as Matilde, who pokes him once more with her stick.

'Come away,' Agata shouts, grabbing Matilde's hand and waking Georgiou as well. She drags the child from the tree, ignoring her protests and those of her sister, who is clinging to Agata's skirts. 'You must never play with a scorpion. The sting could kill you.'

She knows it probably couldn't kill a healthy child, but she is taking no chances and neither child is as strong as they would have been had they not been deprived of exercise, fresh air and good food for months. If they were country children they would have known about the dangers of the wild from an early age, but they were born in the town and have only feared the cobbler's scattered nails, and the Germans.

She sits the children down near her husband and both girls cry. Not great gasping sobs, but with tears welling in their eyes. It is the first time Agata has had to admonish either of them. And she had not thought it would distress her as well as them, but she knows she must be firm for their own good. 'There are many poisonous, dangerous creatures in the forests. You must never touch them. If you are curious, you must come and tell us what you have found right away. Do you understand?'

Both girls nod and sniff away their tears. Agata puts her arms around them. Her words are true – there are vipers, spiders and scorpions all around them. And they are not the only hazards. Their trek has exposed the girls to thorny bushes, scratching their legs and arms, stony paths grazing their bare feet and insects biting their dimpled flesh. Agata has anointed them with lavender oil, but they still have red bites swelling on their skin.

I will do my best to keep them safe, she thinks, *but it will never be enough. I may be able to hide them away from the Germans, but I cannot shield them from every danger.* But aloud, she says, in a very stern voice, 'You must never play with a wild creature ever again. Never. What on earth would I tell your parents if you came to any harm?'

'Sorry,' says Matilde.

'Can we have breakfast now?' Anna asks, standing up and kissing Agata's cheek.

'When you've helped me milk the goats. Then we will have warm milk for our breakfast.'

Chapter Sixty

Amber

July 2008

I didn't think I would be able to sleep down in the cellar, but after I'd made myself a makeshift bed on the hard cushions of sacks of flour and rice, I must have nodded off. I remember waking suddenly, thinking I could hear distant shouts and crackling. I tried hard to listen, but couldn't determine whether I was hearing fire fighters tackling the blaze or the fire raging and gaining control. And it was almost totally dark in the cellar, although I was sure I'd left the lights switched on before I fell asleep.

I managed to get up, heaving myself to my feet with the help of nearby boxes and barrels, and find the light switch on the wall near the staircase. I flicked it twice, three times, but the lights still didn't come on, so I assumed the whole village was blacked out because of the fire. I shone my torch up the stairs, but didn't like to go up and open the door at the top. The fire might have crept inside the building and I was worried that opening the door could suck the flames in a devastating fireball down the steps. I just hoped that even if the whole restaurant was blazing, the cellar would still get enough fresh air through the air vents, and the old shaft originally used for the delivery of wine casks.

Then I checked my phone. It was still very early, not quite five o'clock, but I thought James should be awake. He usually set off around six to come back for breakfast and start preparing that day's meals. I hadn't received any messages, but then I realised I a flood of pee, I hadn't even wanted the loo, but I thought I felt a pop, like a small balloon, and a warm wetness trickled all down my legs and over my feet. *No, please not now*, I begged. *Not here, in the dark.* That wasn't good fortune; it wasn't meant to happen for another two weeks. And then the first vice-like pain gripped me and I steadied myself against the rough wall until it had passed.

I didn't have fresh towels, I didn't have hot water and I didn't have help. I'd expected the birth to take place in a clean hospital on a firm bed, wearing a white gown, with kind nurses and the best medical help available if needed, not sheltering in a dirty, cobwebbed cellar in a wet nightdress. I hadn't even been to any antenatal classes, just done some research online. My friends back in England and my mother all told me I should have gone, but there never seemed to be any time during my months of pregnancy. The classes were in Greek anyway, and I was still far from fluent. James and the business had come first, not me and the baby.

If we hadn't left London, I imagined I'd have had a nursery prepared, with tiny clothes, nappies, a cot and a changing mat. The little I had been able to lay by was in a drawer in my bedroom, and I didn't dare leave the cellar to go back upstairs, as I didn't know how much devastation I might find raging through the restaurant above my head.

I breathed steadily to calm myself. I tried to remember everything I had ever read or heard about the birth of first babies. How long could it take? Did labour normally begin immediately, once the waters had broken, and would I be able to give birth alone? I didn't know the answers to any of these questions and I didn't know how long I would have to stay in the cellar or whether I would even leave it alive, with a tiny baby in my arms. But I wanted to be optimistic and I knew I had to prepare for this as best I could.

It was cool in the cellar, compared to the heat of the raging fires and the dawning summer's day outside. But while it wasn't cold, I

didn't have a signal. Deep in the cellar there was no receptio
I had no way of contacting the world outside and James ha
way of reaching me.

I told myself I had to stay calm. I must keep myself an
baby safe. I sipped some water, bit into a ripe peach and nil
on a corner of cheese. I told myself that the cellar was the s
place to be; it was carved out of the very rock of the moun
and most of it ran underneath the flagstones of the outside ter
If Agata and Georgiou's little children could be brave enoug
hide in a crevice in a wall, then I could surely find the coura;
shelter in the cellar. Inge had not been able to tell me how (
they had been hidden, nor for how long, but when I comp
myself, a healthy confident woman, to two little girls, I told m
I could do this.

I shone my torch around, checking what else might be use
I was to stay down here for a while. We used the cellar for ou
goods, large canisters of olive oil and crates of wine. I assum
must have always been used for storage, and briefly puzzled ove
purpose of some chalked marks on the wall near the light sw

I wished I'd thought to bring candles and matches down
me in the night, as I needed to conserve the torch battery a
could barely see in the dim light. I heard a rustling over in a co
behind some crates of beer, and when I shone the torch, ho
it wasn't a rat, I found it was a toad, shrinking from the li
blinking. *That's a good sign*, I told myself. A toad is a sign of g
fortune. At least my mother always said so. I was about to sw
the torch off and leave him to hide in safety, when I realise
was crouching over a grated drain, just below a tap. It was r
but it turned and clean water gushed down over the toad, w
quickly retreated. *So you are good luck*, I thought. *I have a supp
food and now I've found fresh water. Things could be worse.*

I turned the tap off, and that's when it happened. While th
dripped water into the drain, my own waters broke. It wasn't

thought a newborn baby would find it chilly after the heat of my womb, so I folded my shawl and put it aside to keep it clean and dry.

In the torchlight, I looked around the cellar and found some empty paper sacks, which I laid nearby over the dusty stone floor and across the bed formed by the flour and rice bags. There were two buckets in a corner, so I decided to keep one to use as a toilet and the other one I washed out under the tap and filled with clean water. I ripped the damp hem of my long nightdress into rags, and then rinsed them for use later. Each task was accompanied by intense gripping pains, but I was determined to make these basic preparations. And then, when I had done all I could think of, I began to pace the floor, wondering what would happen first. A rescue, a birth, or death?

Chapter Sixty-One

Amber

July 2008

It wasn't very painful at first. Not much worse than a really heavy period, but after a short while the contractions became more intense, like a vice tightening and squeezing the whole of my insides and bruising my back.

I tried hard to think of everything I'd ever heard of to ease the pain. I walked up and down, I knelt on my knees on the pile of sacks, I crouched on all fours and arched my back and I breathed slowly. *If you'd paid attention*, I told myself, *if you'd gone to those antenatal classes, you'd have your favourite music playing and your husband would be reading you soothing stories*. I tried singing, but found I couldn't remember the words to most songs. I could manage part of 'My Favourite Things' from *The Sound of Music*, but when I got to '*warm woollen mittens*' I couldn't remember any more and got lost in the tune, repeating the same words over and over.

I burbled the doggerel of nursery rhymes, asking the baby to bear with me, saying I'd do better when this was over, but no matter what I did, the whole experience was bloody painful. In between contractions I collapsed and sat or lay down, resting until the next agonising surge gripped my entire being.

Because the cellar was cool and quiet and I couldn't see or hear the fire, I didn't feel frightened by what must still be happening outside, to the village and to our home. I knew I could be in danger, I knew help might be a long time coming and the restaurant might be burnt to the ground, but it seemed much less relevant to me than the momentous event I was in the middle of experiencing. I was strangely exhilarated, and each time I entered that private world of pain, the life outside, the fire, the destruction of the restaurant, departed from my thoughts. I sipped water when I could and told myself that this is what my body was created for; *This is what you have been waiting for. Soon your baby will be here and you will hold him or her in your arms.*

After an hour or so in which the pains were spaced out, giving me time to recover between each spasm, they began to come a little more frequently and I found I had to crouch and concentrate on breathing steadily till the grip slackened. When in this intense, crushing vice, I was aware only of my body, but as I surfaced once more from the depths, I thought I could hear some shouting and possibly banging, outside the cellar. I wondered if it was the fire crew, finally reaching the cobbled street, turning their jets of water onto the buildings. And then, when there were more thumps and knocks, I began to worry that the restaurant might be collapsing above my head and the exit would be blocked.

But, as I stayed still and listened, I slowly realised that the noises overhead were actually heavy footsteps. I tried to concentrate until I was sure I was hearing steps above me. It could be the firemen or it could be James. Please let it be a fireman; a muscular, well-equipped fireman, come to swoop me up in his arms of iron and carry me off to safety.

He would be strong, he would be trained, and he would know exactly how to care for a heavily pregnant woman in labour. I'd be carried away to a waiting vehicle, maybe a helicopter, and whisked off to a clean hospital, with fresh sheets, warm water, pain relief and smiling doctors and nurses. I fantasised for a moment about reclining on white pillows instead of dirty old sacks, and then I was hit by another belt of pain, squeezing me so hard that I struggled to breathe. I shut my eyes and concentrated on counting and breathing and then, as the agony faded and I came out of that deep place, I heard a loud crash and realised that the cellar door had been forced open and someone was coming down the steps.

I struggled to turn round from where I was crouching on my hands and knees, panting, to see who it was in the dim light. It wasn't a burly, uniformed fireman, and it wasn't James, it was the last person I expected to see. It was Greg.

Chapter Sixty-Two

17 June 1944

'Is this it?' Agata looks around at the old village, now a ruin of tumbling stones and broken tiles, with bougainvillea sprouting from paving stones. She thinks of the clean, well-ordered house she has left behind, but chokes back her words and determines to make the best of what they are now facing.

'It has been neglected for a long time,' Georgiou says. He shakes his head. He too is disappointed at how much the village has deteriorated since he last saw it, maybe twenty years ago. The villagers he knew as a boy left for an easier life on the fertile plains below the mountains, to fish the abundant waters of the sea or to work in Corfu's docks. Very few could endure the harsh winters and isolation of the mountains, nor make the thin soil productive. But through his disappointment he notices peach and citrus trees, cherries too, growing among the ruins. The birds have not left much fruit, but there is some. There will be enough for them to survive.

'Come,' he says. 'Let us see how things stand with the farmhouse. It may not be as bad as the other houses.' He leads the donkey forwards, down the cobbled street littered with leaves and tufts of weeds, past houses now inhabited by buddleia and birds. The children hold Agata's hands as they stumble on the uneven path in their bare feet.

'Are we there yet?' Anna asks, looking up at Agata. Her dress is stained, her feet are black and she is tired from their long hike through the forests and along the rutted mountain trails littered with twigs and harsh thorns.

'Nearly, my dear. We'll be in our new home very soon. How exciting that will be. You and your sister can help me unpack, and then we'll eat.'

It is early evening, the sun is beginning to drop behind the far hills and the soft light lends a golden glow to the waves of tall, dry grasses around the village. And then, in the stillness, above the clip-clop sound of the goats' and donkey's hooves on the cobbles and the trundling of the cart's wheels, they hear the tinkling of bells. Not a triumphant peal, nor the deep solemn toll of a church bell, but the dull, uneven ringing of sheep bells. They all stop to listen. 'Over there,' cries Matilde. 'I can see a lady with some sheep.'

Georgiou shades his eyes and sees a very old woman, bent over, supporting herself with a stick, leading a line of a dozen small, wiry sheep, all bearing brass bells around their necks, towards the village. He looks hard for a moment, then says, 'I can hardly believe it. It looks like Zenia Vasilakis. She must be well over ninety by now.' He hands the donkey's halter to Agata. 'I must find out if anyone else is still living here.'

He steps from the path and onto the scrubby grass. 'Zenia? Zenia Vasilakis?' he calls out. 'It's me, Georgiou Stefanopoulos. Remember? The boy who stole your cherries?'

The old woman lifts her head, straining to see him. As he draws nearer she drops her stick and raises her arms. 'You have come to make amends, you bad boy?' Then, tiny and bent as she is, she throws herself at him and squeezes him tightly to her. 'You have come back? For good?'

'For long enough, Zenia. And I am not alone. Look, here is my wife and our two little girls.' He needn't explain their relationship, not for now.

'*Mikro koritsi,*' she exclaims, clapping her hands with joy. 'We shall have children in the village again. It is far too long since I heard the sound of little children.' Tears begin to seep down her wrinkled cheeks and she dabs them away with her scarf.

'Tell me, Zenia,' Georgiou says, bending down to her diminished height, 'is anyone else still living here now?'

She shakes her head and continues to wipe her face. 'All gone. Every one of them. I am all alone these past five years.' She grasps both his hands and brings them up to her lips. 'You will stay? You will move back to your family's farmhouse?'

He takes her gnarled old hands gently in his hardened fisherman's fists. 'We hope to. We have come a long way and the children are very tired, but we'd like to stay. It is not safe for us now, down on the coast.'

She nods her head. 'I see them. I don't know who they are, but I know they bring trouble.'

'Have they been here? Have you seen any soldiers?'

'None. But I see them up there.' She shakes her fist at the sky. 'And I say, away with you. Leave us in peace.'

'Good for you. And how are you managing here on your own?'

'Life is hard, but it is simple. I have sheep, a garden and hens. What more do I need?' She glances across to where Agata and the two girls are watching and waiting.

'I will gladly share what little I have for the pleasure of your company and to hear the laughter of little ones again.'

Chapter Sixty-Three

James

July 2008

As I ran around the outskirts of the village, I was sure I could hear shouting. It had to be the fire crew tackling the blaze from another side, but it was hard to be certain of their location while the flames were still crackling and advancing. I had no idea what the crew might be saying and doing or whether they thought they had any hope of saving any of the buildings.

The blaze was creeping around every house and barn, but finally I came to a corner where the fire hadn't quite grabbed hold. It was at the very end of the cobbled street, far beyond the restaurant, and when I looked along the little lane, I realised I couldn't safely approach Mountain Thyme at ground level, but I could get there if I took to the rooftops, above the level of the fire –the houses were jammed close to each other, the village having grown organically over centuries without the interference of town planners.

I clambered up a flight of outside steps to the top of the nearest house, then scrambled over the tiles and jumped the narrow gap across to the next roof. Despite the smoke, I could just about make out the tiles of the next roof and thought that if I could leap from one roof to another I would soon see the recently tiled roof of Mountain Thyme; our tiles, mostly reclaimed and recycled, were redder and more evenly spaced than those stretching ahead of me.

I held out my arms to balance myself as I slithered across the sloping sections of roof and ran forwards confidently where they were more level. It was far from easy, as many of the old tiles were slipping, some crashing to the street the minute my feet touched them, and there were gaps where the battens were broken, revealing gaping holes into the rooms below. I was desperate to run to Amber's aid, but I knew if I didn't watch my step I'd fall through a roof or down to the cobbled street below.

After a few minutes' sliding and scrabbling, I was probably only a few hundred yards away from the restaurant. I heard a roaring sound overhead and looked up to see another small plane was circling the village and coming nearer, swinging its great trickling sackful of seawater. *Thank goodness they're still bringing in tonnes of water*, I thought. *We might stand a chance if they can get the fire under control soon.*

And then the plane and its whining engine came closer and closer still. It couldn't possibly have seen me; I was no more than a dot on the roof and smoke was swirling all around me. The plane dipped and circled overhead, its bulging cargo swinging out beneath the undercarriage. And then, suddenly, the water fell. It gushed and crashed down like a minor tsunami of salty water, and although I wasn't directly hit, the impact of the drenching made me lose my footing – I fell and slid down the roof, landing in an upper terrace of one of the houses.

I don't know how long I was unconscious. It could have been minutes, it could have been an hour or even longer. When I finally tried to sit up, my head throbbed and so did my right arm and leg. My clothes were soaked through, but the buildings nearest to me were no longer burning, they were just smouldering, and there was a thick smog of smoke curling in the morning air.

I managed to pull myself to my feet by hanging onto the balustrade around the terrace and realised there was actually another outer flight of steps leading down to the street. I hopped down, one painful step at a time, heaving myself along the wall, and then began limping over the cobbles using a branch for a crutch. I was only a couple of hundred yards away from Mountain Thyme by then, but the distance seemed like a marathon as I made agonising progress, supporting myself on walls and windowsills where I could, trying to avoid tripping over the debris caused by the fire.

There was a door hanging off its hinges, heaps of fallen tiles, some shattered glass from windows, fallen branches and a dead chicken, roasted in its dressing of feathers. In the porch of the old house that Amber and I had found in our first summer on the island was this year's swallows' nest. But the chicks were not calling for their parents any longer, with gaping yellow mouths spread wide; they had been suffocated by the smoke, and their parents were nowhere to be seen.

I called out, hoping there'd be a response from Mountain Thyme or I'd see Greg's florid face, grinning, letting me know all was well. 'Greg, Amber, I'm here. Where are you?' I cried, but no one answered, and I was just as abandoned as the baby birds in the shattered remains of the charred and smoking village.

Chapter Sixty-Four

Amber

July 2008

I could barely speak when I saw Greg come down the stairs; I was still panting with the effort of my labours. But finally, I managed to gasp, 'Where's James? Isn't he coming?'

Greg shone his torch towards me when he heard my voice. 'He'll be along soon,' he said. 'We drove up here together, but we had to leave the car half a mile away. He wasn't far behind me, so he shouldn't be too much longer.'

'It's started,' I groaned, as another intense pain began cutting into me.

'Any idea how long or how far apart?' He knelt down beside me and put a gentle hand on my shoulder.

'No. I'm not sure. Oh, I can't…' my voice tailed off as I dealt with another fierce contraction.

'I'm going upstairs to phone. There's no signal down here.'

'No, don't leave me,' I managed to cry.

'I'll only be a second, I promise,' he called, as he ran towards the stairs. 'Don't worry, I'll be back right away.'

I don't know how long he was gone. I didn't hear him climb the stairs and I didn't hear him come back again. I could only listen to my inner pain as it squeezed and tightened until it felt as if I didn't have a single breath left in my body. But then suddenly he was back. 'James, where's James?' I gasped.

'He's coming,' Greg said. 'Here, let me help.' He rolled a sack and wedged it behind my back. Then he held a bottle of cold water to my lips. 'Drink some of this. You'll be fine and I'm staying right here with you.'

'Get the car… hospital…' I croaked.

Greg put his arm around me. This was a totally different Greg to the braggadocio I had known before, he was far more gentle and quieter. 'How far do you think you could walk?' he said.

I tried to stand and he helped me by putting both his hands either side of my expanded waist. But as soon as I tried to take a step, a vice-like contraction gripped me once more and I couldn't move at all. I was made immobile, chained with agony, totally immersed in the pain, panting with every muscle, every nerve in my body.

'I think we're better off staying here,' he said, helping me sink back down onto the sacks. 'The cellar's quite safe and I've told the fire brigade exactly where we are. They'll find us very soon. You can't leave here now without their help.'

'But the baby,' I groaned. 'What about the baby? I don't want to have it in here. It's not right.'

'You might not want to, but you might have to.' He held my hand and stroked it. 'Don't worry. I'm going to stay with you the whole time until help arrives.'

Then he shone his torch over the makeshift bed I'd pulled together. The sacks were rumpled, slipping onto the hard floor. He pulled a small barrel up to one end and draped it with a folded sack, making a hard but firm backrest. He straightened the other sacks, then helped me to sit down again. It was more comfortable than before, with the support of the barrel and another rolled sack behind my back. He propped his torch on one of the upright barrels so my bed was partially illuminated, then sat down beside me and held my hand again. I felt calmer.

As another contraction began to sweep in, I squeezed his hand tight and heard him say, 'Go on. You can do it. Grip my hand as much as you like. You can't hurt me.'

'Thank you,' I panted, as the wave of pain receded. 'It will be all right, won't it?'

'Of course it will,' he said. 'You're young, healthy and strong. You'll be fine and so will the baby. I don't know much about childbirth, but I was there when Lavinia was born. She was so beautiful. Still is.'

I couldn't make out his expression in the dim half-light, but his voice was tender. 'You'd do anything for her, wouldn't you?' I said, wanting him to keep talking and to give me something to think about other than the next jolt of pain, which was already beginning to take hold.

'She can wind me round her little finger,' he laughed. 'And she knows it too.' Then he was silent for a second before saying, 'We always thought we'd have more, but she's the only one.' He sighed. 'My lovely Lavinia.'

I don't remember much of the conversation after that, as the contractions became more and more frequent, until it was nearly one continual surge of agonising pain, culminating in the most almighty desire to push, which I instinctively knew meant the baby was about to emerge. I didn't know whether it was the right thing to do, but I felt I had to be on my knees and I just about managed to hold back my scream to gasp, 'Not on a sack. Please not a sack.' And then I screamed. I hollered and bellowed and didn't give a damn who heard me.

But through my screeching, I kept hearing Greg's soothing voice, saying, 'Keep going, good girl. It's coming. Don't worry, I've got it.'

And then suddenly it was all over. I panted, catching my breath, and fell on my side, turning towards Greg. 'Is it all right? Can I see?' And I heard squawking as he passed the small bundle to me. I peered at the cross little face in the poor light, so scrunched, so tiny.

'He's perfect,' Greg said, rinsing his hands in the water bucket then wiping them on his trousers. 'You have a beautiful baby boy.'

And then I noticed Greg was bare-chested. I glanced down again; my newborn baby was squinting at me, wrapped in Greg's blue and white striped shirt. 'Thank you,' I whispered. 'Thank you so much for being here and helping me.'

'I'm glad I could be of service,' Greg said. 'But now I think I'd better see if there's any help nearby.' He started climbing the stairs. 'I won't be long. I promise.'

Chapter Sixty-Five

17 June 1944

'Go to sleep now, my dears,' Agata smooths the children's freshly brushed hair and kisses their cheeks. They are exhausted from their long hike and the excitement of reaching the village. Tonight, they have no need of songs or stories to bring sleep, which comes quickly as they curl around each other on their makeshift bed, the blackened soles of their feet peeping from under the blanket. In the morning, Agata will wash them and their clothes, but for now they must rest. She covers them loosely and goes outside to the terrace, where Georgiou is contemplating the overgrown garden while he sips his cooling mountain tea.

'There is much to be done,' he says, 'but I think we can manage here.' The farmhouse is in better condition than many of the village houses. The windows are cracked, but their shutters can be fastened and the doors can be barred and locked, and its walls are strong. But Agata will not allow the girls to venture up the staircase until Georgiou has checked that it is free of rot and that the floorboards in all the rooms above are sound. 'I will check the roof thoroughly tomorrow. Some tiles have broken away, but I can replace them. We must have a dry house before the winter rains.'

'We are lucky your cousins didn't take everything with them,' Agata says. 'A table, chairs and bedframes, all still here. In the morning, I will clean out the kitchen range and see if the chimney is clear. There is dry wood all around us, so we should be able to cook and keep ourselves warm.' She had gathered a bundle of dry kindling as soon as they reached the house and tethered the donkey and goats on the grass.

'It's not so bad, is it?' Georgiou says, putting a protective arm around his wife. 'We haven't done the wrong thing in leaving our comfortable home?'

She lays her head on his shoulder. 'We had no choice. We can't think of ourselves. These poor children have only us to protect them. We couldn't take the risk.'

'Then come and sit down and let us plan the work we must do. I will visit Zenia and see what help she needs in return for sharing her livestock. She has a pig as well as sheep and there will be milk for a while, as they lambed this spring.'

'Then we may have meat for our table, if she is willing. And although the garden is overgrown, I am sure I can see artichokes. They may have gone too far now to eat this year, but we can tend them and ensure they will be productive next season.'

'And we should also explore all the other abandoned houses here. There may well be furniture or tools that we can put to good use, as well as fruit trees.'

'But first we must make this house safe,' Agata says, 'and then I will clean everywhere, so we can use more than just the one room. I think birds have nested upstairs and there may be mice in the old kitchen. I don't want to put our mattresses on the beds until I am sure the house is free of vermin.' Agata had insisted the bedding they had brought on the handcart should remain rolled up until she considered it safe to make the beds. Tonight, she and her husband will make do with sacks of straw and hay, while the little girls sleep on blankets over a pile of dry leaves.

Georgiou laughs at his wife's high standards. She is proud of her industry and her housekeeping skills. She was taught well by her mother and will teach the girls all they need to know too. He throws another dry vine cutting onto the campfire they lit to boil water and cook eggs for their supper. It reminds him of his adventures as a boy, exploring the mountain trails and camping out on summer nights, while herding sheep and goats. He was happy to fall asleep under the stars after a meal of cheese and grapes. But Agata is not used to such a carefree way of life and much as it suits him, he knows he must create a more civilised home for her and the children as soon as he can. He looks up at the untended vine entangling the beams over the terrace. 'There are a few bunches of grapes here too, despite the neglect. But I'll prune it hard and we should have plenty next year.'

Agata takes his hand. 'You are a good man. I know you will do your best to provide for us.'

Chapter Sixty-Six

James

July 2008

Another seaplane roared above me, its cargo swinging beneath its belly, then it circled over the far side of the village. I watched the water cascade onto the furthest buildings and olive groves and hoped the fire was finally coming under control.

I had managed to hop no more than a dozen or so yards from where I'd fallen and was finding it exhausting as well as painful. I leant against a wall, trying to find the strength to continue, then suddenly saw the half-dressed figure of Greg emerging from the smoke-blackened walls of Mountain Thyme, further down the street. 'Greg!' I shouted. 'I'm over here. Is Amber there? Is she all right?'

He ran up the road to me, jumping over all the dead creatures and rubble in his path. 'She's fine,' he called, as he ran. 'She's had the baby.'

'The baby? Here already? But it's far too early.'

'Maybe, but she's just had a healthy boy. It looks fine and so is she. They're down in the cellar.' Greg grabbed me as I slumped, then helped me sit down on a low ledge. 'Mate, you're all done in. I was wondering what had happened to you.'

'One of the planes,' I said. 'Decided I needed a shower.' I was exhausted and in pain, but I knew I needed to see Amber. 'I've got to get to her. Can you help me over there?'

'Sure. Then I've got to find help so we can get her to hospital.'

'Hospital? But you just said she was all right.'

'She is. But she needs to be checked over. And so do you, by the looks of things. If this mess has calmed down, the fire brigade should be able to radio for an air ambulance now. I doubt they'll be able to get up here by road for a while yet.'

He helped me to my feet, then pulled me onto his bare back and stumbled forwards over the cobbles towards the restaurant. 'It looks bad,' he said, 'but the main structure is still intact. It should be salvageable.' I could see ash and debris everywhere, but it was still more of a building than many in the village.

'I can't believe this has happened. How could it have spread so quickly?'

Greg was silent apart from the grunts of his exertions as he carried me, then he gasped, 'I can't believe it either. Bloody fool.'

'Who's a bloody fool?'

'Nothing. Forget it.' He stopped and let me slide off his back, then bent down and stretched to ease his muscles. We were nearly there and the path was clearer than before. He stood up again, arched his back, took a deep breath, then said, 'Think you can make it on one foot now?' I put my left arm around Greg's shoulders and began hopping on my good leg. It was painful and slow, but we could get there.

As I hopped, I said, 'But how do you think it all started?'

'Started?' He was panting.

'The fire. How on earth did it start?'

He shook his head. 'It only takes a spark… someone careless… cigarette ends, glass maybe…'

'But there's never anyone up here at night. It's always deserted. I don't get it.'

Greg came to a halt and let me lean against a wall while he caught his breath, bending forwards, hands on his knees. 'Stupid idiot,' he muttered. 'Stupid fucking idiot.'

'What's that?' I said. He didn't reply, but stood up and turned away from me, running his hands over his hair. When he turned round again towards me, I saw from his face that he was distressed. He was shaking his head and saying, 'He just didn't think. Could've killed her. I'm so sorry.'

I stared at him, wondering for a second or two what on earth he was talking about. Then suddenly I had one of those lightning moments of comprehension. Various events and comments slotted together into one utterly clear but totally shocking pattern. All those times when Greg and Dimitri were discussing the land deeds and laughing; Dimitri leaving Greg's house when I arrived last night; Greg's inept text message; then Dimitri running away from the village…

'Dimitri,' I said. 'You're talking about Dimitri, aren't you? Did you tell him to start the fire? Tell him to raze the land? Please tell me you didn't get him to do that.' I could feel my suspicion and anger rising, like an indigestible, rich, spicy curry.

Greg backed away from me a little. 'No, I definitely didn't tell him to start a fire. Look, he just told me he would sort it out and I could leave it all to him. That's all.'

'That's all?' I shouted. 'You're saying that's all? All he's done is ruin my business and my property, and nearly kill my wife and child into the bargain. That's all!'

'I know, I know.' Greg spread out his hands in a placating gesture. 'How was I to know what would happen? I never wanted this. Try to stay calm. She's okay and so's the baby.'

'So he did do it then, did he? Dimitri started the fire that caused all this… this utter devastation?'

'Maybe.' Greg was shaking his head, still walking backwards. 'I don't know if it was him, for certain.'

'And you… you knew he might do something like this?'

'No, I didn't. Not for sure. I mean, I didn't know what he would do.'

'But you knew he was up to something, didn't you? You're to blame as much as he is. You paid him. You must've put the idea in his head.'

'Now hang on…' Greg took another step back as I hopped nearer, heaving myself along the low wall for support.

'All those times… the two of you… in my kitchen… plotting…'

'Not plotting, planning. Come on, James, you knew all about it. You knew development here would be to your advantage. You'd have made a tidy profit out of it. We all would.'

'But I didn't know this was how you'd get the land though, did I?' I was spitting with rage by now, all my pain forgotten. 'Did you know this was how he was going to do it? Did you?' I hopped closer.

Greg stepped back again. 'I swear I didn't know what he was planning to do. He just told me he would take care of things. That's all I know. I had absolutely nothing to do with it.'

And then it happened. I managed to get close enough to Greg to shove him in the chest with my good arm. 'How could you?' I shouted, nearly toppling over with the effort.

He staggered and took another step backwards and there must have been a broken trap door, or maybe it was a cellar chute under his feet, but there was suddenly the sound of splintering wood and he fell. He fell out of sight with a great cry followed by a crash, and then silence.

I shuffled towards the gaping black hole and called. There was no answer, and I could just make out Greg lying broken and silent on the stone floor below. I didn't dare go any closer in case I fell in as well, so, gripping the wall, I moved away and continued my unsteady progress towards the restaurant, hoping I would soon reach my wife and child. And with each agonising step I wondered whether I had just killed the man who had saved their lives, rather than causing their deaths.

Chapter Sixty-Seven

Amber

July 2008

I think I had fallen into a doze on my bed of sacking after Greg left. Then I suddenly woke when I heard a bump at the top of the cellar stairs. It was followed by more thumps and laboured grunts, and then, by the light of my torch, I saw long legs in torn shorts, sliding down the steps. Eventually I could see it was James, heaving himself down the staircase, inch by inch on his bottom, one step at a time, pushing himself along with his left arm, while the other was held across his body. He was clearly seriously injured.

'What's happened?' I called. 'You're hurt. And where's Greg?'

James just kept grunting and didn't answer till he'd reached the bottom step, where he tried to haul himself to his feet by pulling on the banister. He gave a cry of pain as he stood up, and then said, 'You've had the baby.'

'He's perfect. Can you see him?' I held the little face towards him. 'You'll have to come closer. It's hard to see in this light.'

James felt around for something to help him walk and found a broom propped against the wall at the bottom of the stairs. He tucked the brush under his arm and then made slow and obviously painful progress towards my bed. He looked down at me and our baby, then managed to sit on a nearby barrel, groaning with pain as he did so. He reached into his pocket for his mobile phone and shone its light over us.

'He's beautiful, like you.' Then he was silent for a moment before shaking his head and saying, 'Amber, I'm so sorry. I'm so sorry I wasn't here.'

'I know,' I said. 'But Greg was here. And he was wonderful.' There was silence between us and then I said, 'He told me he was going off to fetch help. He phoned earlier and thought the fire brigade would reach us soon. Didn't you see him anywhere outside?'

James cleared his throat. 'Yeah. I did.' He coughed again. 'He's had a bit of an accident.'

'What? Because of the fire? Did you see it happen? Is he okay?'

'I don't know.' He hung his head. 'I couldn't get to him.'

We were both quiet for a few more seconds, then I said, 'But he was going off to get help.'

'Don't worry. I think he'd already phoned again. And anyway, I phoned as well just before coming down here. They know where we are and they know there's a new baby. The fire's under control, so they should be able to get through. They said it won't be too long now.'

But it turned out to be a very long time. Maybe it was only a couple of hours, but it seemed to take for ever. I sipped water and made James have some too. I wasn't in very much pain by then, I just felt drained, battered and bruised, but James was clearly in agony and there was no relief for him.

I tried to distract him by asking him to help me decide on our baby's name. I was wavering between Theo, which means God-given, and Felix, which means happiness, but when I said I thought his middle name should be Gregory in honour of Greg and his heroism, James shouted, 'No, never. You can't. I don't want to be constantly reminded of that terrible man.'

'What on earth do you mean? He's not terrible. He was amazing. I don't know if I could have managed to give birth down here without his help.'

'I know.' James shook his head. 'I'm sorry I wasn't here.'

'But I don't understand. You really like Greg, don't you? I know I didn't warm to him before, but he was so different today. You should have seen him. He was so gentle and kind. I've got so much to thank him for.' I looked down at my sleeping baby, his head sticky with the mucus and blood of his birth, still wrapped in Greg's bloodstained shirt. 'Oh, I do hope he's going to be all right.'

'Of course, I know you're grateful to him. But you don't know him like I do.'

'What's that supposed to mean? I thought you were such great friends.'

'I know, but that was before.'

'Before what, James? Before he helped deliver your son? I think you should be eternally grateful to him for that. I know I am.'

James was groaning and I thought at first it was the pain of his injuries, but then I realised he was actually distraught. He was shaking his head and running his fingers through his hair, muttering, 'I thought I could trust him. I thought I knew him. But this disaster, this catastrophe, it's all his fault. Damn him. Damn you, Greg!' he shouted, lifting his face towards the ceiling of the cellar.

'His fault? How on earth could that be?'

He was still shaking his head and rocking backwards and forwards on his precarious barrel. 'He was the one with the big ideas. I just went along with it. I didn't know how they were going to do it.'

'I don't know what you're talking about.'

'Greg and Dimitri. Always scheming. I think he's been in on it right from the start.'

'You're not making any sense, James.' I paused to think what he might mean. 'Are you talking about that idea of developing the land around here?'

'Yes, of course I am!' he shouted. 'It's clear as day to me now. I was a fool to let them think I agreed to it. Letting them snoop around up here, sit in my kitchen, eat my food and drink my best wines whenever they felt like it. All that time they were taking advantage, letting me think we'd benefit from it in the end.'

'But we never agreed to any kind of development, did we? I thought we didn't want to see that happening? And anyway, what has all this got to do with the fire?'

'Don't you see? In the end they couldn't lay their hands on the land legitimately. It was no man's land. Nobody could be traced, nobody owned it. But it couldn't be developed unless it was cleared by fire. So they arranged to have one, conveniently. Hoping it would look like yet another accidental wildfire.' He was breathing heavily.

'You mean the fire was deliberate? That they started it?'

'Of course they did.'

'Greg came up here and started the fire?' I felt as if my breathing had stopped, yet my heart was pounding.

'No, not Greg. Dimitri. I came across him when I first got to the village hours ago. He's guilty, I tell you.' He thumped the barrel with his fist. 'Oh God, I wish I'd killed him and not Greg.'

I was stunned. It was as if he'd punched me and not the barrel. I gasped and finally managed to whisper, 'Greg? You're saying you've killed Greg?'

'No, I haven't. I mean, it was an accident. He fell. Oh, I don't know. I couldn't really see what had happened. Oh God, this is all so awful.'

I held my baby close to my breast and cradled his head with my hand. He was innocent, blameless and I wanted to protect him. Suddenly it seemed as if everyone around me, Greg, Dimitri and now even James, had lied to me and could not be trusted.

Chapter Sixty-Eight

19 June 1944

'You must kill him,' Zenia says. 'Years ago, I could do it all by myself, but it is too much for me now.' She waves at the large black pig, contentedly grunting in the shade of his wooden shelter, from which he can freely roam around a small grassy enclosure littered with leaves and windfall apples. 'When I was younger I collected acorns for our pigs in the autumn, but I cannot do that any longer. No, he must go. Besides, you will be in need of good ham and loukaniko this winter. And souvlaki – ah, I have not tasted fresh souvlaki in a long while.'

Agata looks at Georgiou. Her husband is resourceful and determined and he has caught many large fish in his time, from tuna to swordfish, but has he ever tackled anything as large as this pig? And she has never made loukaniko, sausages flavoured with orange zest, but she is willing to learn.

'I would be honoured to undertake the slaughter of your pig,' Georgiou says. 'You and he will be doing us a great service. But let us not be hasty. Let us prepare the house first and plan for this important event. We must not waste him. He will add greatly to our winter provisions.'

'In the old days,' Zenia says, 'we had a feast when we killed a pig. Such a celebration. The men did it all and there was much dancing and singing.'

'Perhaps we should make a smokehouse in one of the empty houses,' Agata says. 'There will be a lot of meat to preserve and that will be the best way to keep it.' She is glad the children aren't listening to this talk of killing – they're playing with a litter of striped kittens under the trees.

'We shall have plenty for all of us,' Zenia says. 'And when the rains come our tanks will be filled with sweet water again.' Agata was disappointed to find that the farmhouse did not have fresh water. The underground tank had acquired a layer of rotten leaves, souring the remaining water. Georgiou promised to drain it and clear away the sludge, but in the meantime they can fetch water from a nearby spring, which is still producing a clear trickle from the winter reserves.

'Are your sheep milking well?' Agata asks, keen to know as much as possible about the resources available to feed the children and keep them healthy.

'Five of them give a good yield, five are this year's lambs and two are old ladies, fit only for the table. But we get enough milk to make feta and kefalotiri, so we shall eat well.'

Agata has never made any cheese other than feta, but knows that the hard cheese kefalotiri will keep well, unlike the softer cheeses. 'Is there enough for yogurt too?' she says, thinking of how she can supplement the children's breakfasts with a thick creamy topping over fresh juicy peaches.

'But of course,' Zenia says, clapping her hands. 'The milk has been going to waste up to now. I cannot drink it all myself. You must come every day and collect as much as you need. It will be a pleasure, knowing it will be put to good use, making those children grow big and strong.' She turns to look at the little girls. 'They could do with fattening up. Have supplies been so very short?'

Agata glances at her husband. Maybe now is the time, now Zenia has offered to share so much with them, to share some of the truth with her. Georgiou nods, so Agata says, 'They've come from the town. Life has been very hard there, with the Germans and the bombing. We've adopted them and hope to give them a safe, happy home.'

SuzZanne Goldring

Zenia's wrinkled face creases even more as she frowns. 'They will be happy here. We will all make sure of that. And they need never go hungry again.'

They all watch the children for a moment, enjoying their carefree play, then Georgiou says, 'You said your sheep lambed this year, but I didn't see a ram. Did he pass over?'

'No, Gabriel went back to Lafki with Tomas. He has sired many lambs here. He came in November to cover the ewes and give me lambs for Easter and he will come back again on St Michael's Day.'

'In five months' time,' murmurs Georgiou. 'I look forward to meeting Tomas and his fine ram.'

Chapter Sixty-Nine

James

July 2008

They came for Amber first. Two strong firemen carried her and the baby up the cellar steps on a stretcher, and then they came back for me.

Outside, the morning sun was shining brightly on the devastation all around us. Although the walls of Mountain Thyme were blackened, the main structure was relatively unharmed. Our vine was scorched and ash as thick as fallen autumn leaves was strewn across the terrace and tables, where our guests usually enjoyed their morning coffee and orange juice. But today, instead of the smell of grilling bacon and freshly baked croissants, honey and bougainvillea, everywhere smelt of scorched destruction.

Faint plumes of smoke were still spiralling into the air all around the village, pierced by shafts of sunlight. But that morning there was no melodic birdsong or triumphant cockcrow to greet the day; all we could hear was the loud drone of the helicopter overhead, waiting to lift all three of us to safety. The way through the village was still impassable and this was the quickest route out.

As Amber was hauled up, the baby strapped securely to her breast, I watched them disappear into the arms of the medic reaching out from the body of the aircraft. She had not said a word to me since our rescuers had arrived and her main concern as she was preparing to be airlifted was her lack of clothing, so they wrapped her in a blanket for the sake of modesty.

I kept picturing her face, a grim mixture of utter shock and quiet determination. I couldn't blame her if she was furious with me. I had to admit I hadn't ever asked Greg to hold back on his ideas for a development, but I suspected he and Dimitri would have gone ahead even if I hadn't been compliant. If they had been successful, then I would have been celebrating with them. But I should have asked more questions, been more curious about how the land title problems were going to be resolved. It was a poor excuse now, but I'd been so deeply immersed in establishing the restaurant, its growing fame and my escalating reputation, that I'd not paid enough attention to their scheme.

'Please, we take you now.' The man from the air ambulance was gesturing to the harness, which had been lowered again, and offered his arm to help me stand up.

As he tightened the straps, I said, 'There's another injured man nearby, over there. He might still be alive.' I pointed across the road to the splintered wood around the pit where Greg had fallen. 'Can you check and see if you can help him as well?'

The crewman ran across and peered down into the vault, then radioed his colleagues. 'I stay here and you go up,' he said, tugging on the hoist which then began lifting me into the air. I watched him as I rose higher and higher. He was sitting on the edge of the hole, his legs dangling, and then he jumped down into the cellar.

As I was hauled up, I found myself praying that Greg would still be alive, that he would survive and that I'd have a chance to forgive him and thank him for all he had done for Amber and the baby. And all around and below me I could now see the full extent of the disaster that had engulfed the village. No more lemons, oranges, olives or walnuts grew here; their groves were charred graveyards of fallen fruit and twisted trees. As far as I could see, we were the only living creatures to have survived the conflagration and if Greg hadn't been there to help Amber, there might have been only two lives to lift to safety.

When I was pulled aboard, wincing and groaning, I was lifted onto a stretcher and strapped down, then a needle entered my arm and with it came the relief of oblivion. As I started to drift into a painless sleep, my head lolled to one side and I saw Amber staring at me. She was holding the baby tight to her breast, her face grim and fierce. She looked at me hard, stared at me unsmiling, then looked down at her child's dark head, cooing with softened features as she stroked his cheek, and I knew she would never smile at me with affection again.

Then her final words in the cellar came back to me, and even as I fought the drugged sleep that was now claiming me, I could not stop myself from hearing them echo in my head again and again: 'If you could have told me everything from the start, we might have seen the truth for ourselves together. But you thought only of yourself and your reputation.' She shook her head in disappointment and added, 'You are not the man I thought you were.'

Her words haunted me and her stern face stared at me as I lost my hold on wakefulness, and in the dreams that followed I was falling down stone staircases, chased by flickering flames, calling to Greg and Dimitri to quench the fires, while Amber was lifted into the air with our baby, leaving me completely alone in the ruined restaurant for ever.

Chapter Seventy

Amber

July 2008

I didn't see or speak to James again after we reached the hospital. He was sedated during the flight and was still groggy when we landed. We were both transferred to an ambulance and once we arrived, James was taken away for X-rays and I was wheeled to the maternity ward, where my dreams of a proper bed with clean white sheets and plump pillows soon became a reality. My torn and bloodstained nightdress was cut away from my body and, after a short examination, I was allowed to enjoy a long shower, while Theo was checked, weighed, bathed and wrapped in a clean nappy and gown.

I lay in my bed, in a fresh but unflattering hospital robe, watching other new mothers in the ward being kissed and hugged by husbands and relatives, all bearing colourful cards, balloons and bouquets. My bedside table was empty apart from a glass and a half-empty flask of water. I had no gifts and no visitors, but I had my healthy baby boy, sleeping in a bassinette beside my bed. Every time he snuffled I had to check he was breathing properly. I had already examined every tiny finger, toe and limb and could hardly believe that he was so perfect after the dramatic circumstances of his arrival.

And as I rested in my bed, I closed my eyes and found myself trying to re-examine all the events that had led to this disaster. How much had James really known about Greg and Dimitri's plans? When had they decided to clear the land and why on earth had they started the fire at the riskiest time of year, in the middle of summer?

I also tried to think clearly about what should happen next. Mountain Thyme, although it hadn't been destroyed like so many other buildings in the village, would not be habitable for months to come. And the restaurant could not open again for business this year, if ever. My home and my livelihood were both gone and so too, I suspected, was my husband. I could return to the UK and my mother would probably welcome me back with her first grandchild, but I wasn't sure I wanted to go back to the kind of life we'd had before coming to the island. If I even could return to my old career, I'd be working long hours, leaving my baby in a nursery for most of the day. I could turn to Ben and Eleni, but Ben was more James's friend than mine and I wondered whether he would feel he should remain loyal to his old schoolmate – I would find the situation with him too awkward.

I was lying there on my second day, just after feeding and changing Theo once more, when a flurry of turquoise and gold entered the ward. It wasn't another eager visitor for one of the other occupants, it was Pam. Her lipstick was patchy and her eyes were red and rimmed with black smudges. She had obviously been crying.

'Oh, my dear,' she exclaimed, rushing across to my bed. 'Let me see the little mite. Oh, thank goodness you are both all right.' She looked down at the cot, pulling the top edge of the sheet away with a long scarlet fingernail so she could see my baby's sleeping face, her jangling gold charm bracelet cascading down her wrist as she did so. 'Oh, what a perfect little darling. And he's such a lovely colour, not as dark as you, but still lovely. You must have been so relieved to get out of that dreadful place in one piece with him. What a nightmare for you.'

She pulled a metal chair from the other side of the ward towards my bed, scraping it across the worn lino floor, then threw herself down on it and reached for my hand. 'My dear, I've just come from seeing Greg.' Tears began to well in her eyes again but she shook her head and sniffed a little to chase them away.

'Greg? Is he all right? James wasn't sure…'

'He's black and blue and plastered from head to foot, but he'll live. He's tough as anything.' She smiled through her tears. 'He managed to tell me all about you and the baby.' She stopped and fumbled for a tissue in her gold handbag, dabbing at her eyes and nose before she could continue. 'I'm so proud of him. Just fancy, Greg of all people delivering a baby, all on his own. I would never have believed it.' She sniffed again, then laughed. 'I don't think he ever changed so much as a single nappy when Lavinia was a little one.'

'I'm so grateful to him,' I said. 'Really I am. I don't know what would have happened if he hadn't turned up when he did. And I'm so relieved to hear he's going to be all right. Please thank him for me and tell him we are both doing well.'

'Oh, I will, you can be sure of that. It was the first thing he wanted to know when he finally regained consciousness. "Where's Amber," he said, "and where's the baby?" I didn't know what he was talking about at first. I thought he was still dopey from the anaesthetic.'

She leant forward and clutched my hand. 'He was in the operating theatre for five hours, you know. Can you believe it? His back, his leg, a shoulder, just about every bone in his body.' She dabbed her eyes again.

'Poor Greg. But he will recover, won't he?'

'Don't you worry about him, dear. He's strong as an ox. It would take more than a little fall like that to finish him off.' Pam was really smiling now. 'Lavinia's on her way over to see him. She'll be here later today, so I can't stay long. She said she had to see her daddy as soon as she could, now she's made it up with Vladi.' She tucked her tissues away in her handbag and stood up, ready to leave. 'Oh, and Greg was asking after James as well. Do you know how he's getting on? I understand he had a bit of a fall too. They're quite a pair, aren't they?'

'I haven't been able to see James since we got here,' I said. 'Did Greg say anything about him and how the accident happened?'

'Nothing that made any sense, dear. Something about what total chaos it was up there and how it was a blessed wonder you all got out in one piece.' She shook her hair back and repositioned her sunglasses on top of her bleached hair. 'I must dash. I've got to make sure everything's ready for Lavinia. She'll want to drop in and see her daddy as soon as possible.' She turned towards the door, then surveyed the other new mothers in the ward and said, 'I'll tell her to bring you some flowers, shall I? Can't have you being the only mummy in here without flowers now, can we?' Then, with a fluttery wave of her hand and a waft of Opium perfume, she was gone.

I watched her leave and thought that, much as I was grateful to Greg for his help with the birth, I would not be turning to his family for support once I was able to leave the hospital. And although I was now reassured that my husband was not a murderer, I could not rid myself of the knowledge that he was still a liar.

Chapter Seventy-One

19 June 1944

As they return to the farmhouse after visiting Zenia and her live-stock, Agata hisses at Georgiou, 'So, she has a regular visitor when the ram is brought to service the ewes! He will see us, see the girls and maybe ask questions. I thought we would be safe here, now I am not so sure. When is Saint Michael's Day?'

'November the eighth. I know because it was my father's name day. One month before the feast of Saint Spyridon. But calm yourself. She didn't say anyone else would come before then. He only comes to bring the ram.'

'But others may know he comes here. They may think there are rich pickings here if there is only one old woman to keep watch.'

'True. If things get any worse, people may venture further into the countryside to find food. But we are a long way from the town; there are many productive farms further south that they will raid before daring to brave the mountain paths.'

'Perhaps. But the Germans don't only take our food. People are frightened as well as hungry. They may well be willing to face the harsher conditions of the mountains if they think they will be safer.' Agata thinks as they walk, then says, 'I must tell the girls where to hide, if they have to. We must have another place where they can be safe.'

'Perhaps the cellar,' Georgiou says. 'I haven't checked it properly yet. But it is dry and there is ventilation. We'll look at it as soon as we're home.'

Agata squeezes his hand. There is so much work to be done in the house and she wants to sweep floors, wash windows and make beds, but the safety of the girls must come first. The children are holding hands, skipping along the path, singing in high voices, innocent of any threat to their well-being, until Matilde stubs her toe on a broken cobble and her song changes to a pitiful wail.

'There, there, my dear,' Agata says, bending over the wounded foot. 'We'll bathe it when we get home.' Anna clings to her legs and adds her cries to those of her sister. 'You're not hurt as well, are you?' She continues to cry until Georgiou picks her up and says he will carry her all the way back.

'If only they had shoes,' Agata says. 'How will they manage in the winter, without shoes? And their father a cobbler too.'

'Papa mended shoes,' Matilde says.

'He did, didn't he? But he never made any shoes for you and your sister?'

'Not for us, but he gave Rebekka shoes.' Matilde takes Agata's hand and they resume walking. 'Rebekka's our big sister. She had shoes so she could go to the bakery for Mama, to fetch bread.'

Anna overhears this remark and begins wailing again. 'Mama, I want Mama.'

'Where's Mama?' asks Matilde. 'When is she coming to take us home?'

'She's working hard so she can come back to get you soon,' Agata says, blinking back her tears. 'I'm sure she thinks of you every day and prays you are both good girls, eating all your food and going to bed when you are told. And she'll be so pleased to know you have grown big enough to need new dresses, won't she?'

Matilde nods and says, 'When can I have my new dress?'

Agata thinks again of the many chores she must complete before she can sit down at a clean table and take up her sewing again, the sewing so suddenly interrupted by that unexpected and unsettling visitor. 'If you and your sister can help me in the house, I will have the dresses finished very soon. So you must promise me you will do everything I ask of you.'

Matilde nods solemnly. 'And can I have shoes as well?'

'We shall think hard how we can find you both some shoes for the winter. The mountains can be very cold. There may even be snow.' And Agata wonders whether, within the ruined houses of the village, she may find some leather or even a little pair of forgotten shoes.

Chapter Seventy-Two

James

July 2008

'I want to see my wife. Where is she? And the baby, where's the baby?'

I think those were the first words I said when I woke from the operation to set my leg and arm. I hadn't expected to be knocked out for so long. I'd been in plaster once before years ago, but that was only a wrist fracture, caused by a stumble in the school gym. This time my leg was in traction and my arm was suspended too, because I was told there were complications with the elbow and wrist.

'Where's Amber? Where are my wife and baby?' I asked the nurses these questions every time they came to check on me, when they smoothed my pillows, held water to my lips or adjusted my leg. But all they did was smile and nod, until finally a nurse who spoke good English was at my bedside. 'I will find out for you,' she said.

I waited, I dozed, and I hoped Amber would suddenly appear, but it must have been more than an hour before the nurse returned. 'Your wife and baby are doing well,' she smiled. 'They are in the maternity ward with all the other new mothers and babies.' She looked pleased at this announcement. 'Would you like me to give her a message?'

'I'd like to go and see them.'

She shook her head. 'You are not allowed to move yet. You must stay here longer.'

'Then please tell her I am sorry. And ask her to come and see me here, as I cannot go to her.'

'Of course. I will do that for you.' She smiled again. 'Do not worry. They are both being cared for very well and you have a lovely baby boy.'

But I *was* worrying. I wasn't worried about their well-being, but I was worried about what Amber might be thinking; what she felt about me and all that had happened. I lay there, barely able to move, waiting for my next dose of painkillers and enduring the attentions of the nurses for my every intimate need.

When, after another day had passed, I had still not seen Amber nor even received a message from her, I really began to fret. I looked out for the English-speaking nurse all morning and when I finally saw her, I called out, 'Have you spoken to my wife yet?'

She came across to my bed with her beaming smile, saying, 'You have such a beautiful baby. You have seen him today?'

'No, I haven't. Are you sure Amber realised I can't go to her?'

'Of course. She understood very well. I told her, Mr Young must stay in his bed, so you will have to go to him when you feel able.'

'And what did she say?'

The nurse shrugged. 'I don't remember. I think she just thanked me. That is all.'

I had no other way of reaching Amber. I was helpless. Then shortly after lunch, a phone was brought to my bedside. 'Please. For you,' said a nurse whose English was not so good, passing the receiver across to my functioning left hand.

'Hi, mate,' said the voice on the other end. 'How're you doing?'

It was Ben, and I was so relieved to hear from him. 'I'm strung up and going out of my mind,' I said. 'They won't let me get out of bed to see Amber and the baby. It's driving me absolutely mad.'

'I've been holding off coming to see you. Thought I'd wait till you were feeling a bit more sociable. But I'll come up and see you both this afternoon if you like.'

He turned up later, bearing a couple of James Bond novels, a large bouquet and a bowl of fruit. 'Shaken, not stirred,' he said, setting the bowl down on the bedside cabinet. 'Thought you'd prefer that to flowers.'

'Oh, so the flowers aren't for me then?'

'They're for Amber. I'll pop down to see her next. Thought I'd come and see the invalid first though.' He ran an inquisitive finger down the traction wires, but caught my eye, my look warning him not to interfere any further.

'I still haven't been able to see her yet. Go and tell her I'm desperate, will you?'

'Sure thing. And I gather Greg's here somewhere too. Quite a family gathering, isn't it?' He laughed and pulled up one of the battered metal chairs that were all the general hospital provided for visitors.

'Greg?' My heart felt as if it had stopped for second or two. 'I didn't know he was here. I didn't even know he'd survived.'

'He's a tough old bugger, that one. Pam says he'll be in for a fair bit, but he'll pull through all right in the end.'

Ben ripped off the cellophane wrapped around the fruit and began picking at the grapes. 'Don't mind, do you?'

I waved my good hand at him. 'Go ahead, be my guest.'

He ate a couple of grapes, then said, 'What exactly happened up there in the village? No one seems to know how it all started.'

I sighed. 'No idea. It was just crazy.' Then I added, keen to change the subject, 'Toss me a grape, will you?' And for a few minutes, it was like we were schoolkids again, with Ben attempting to throw grapes directly into my mouth. He succeeded a couple of times, but the rest rolled down my gown and onto the sheets.

We stopped our game when one of the nurses walked past my bed and looked sternly at us both.

Ben gathered up the fallen grapes and quickly ate them himself, then pulled a face at me when she'd gone. 'Looks like I'd better go and deliver these,' he said, picking up the flowers.

'Can you come straight back once you've seen them? Tell Amber I have to see her. And the baby.'

'Of course. I'll pop right back.' He pushed his chair away and saluted to the nurse as he left.

I lay back on my pillows, hoping the next person through the ward door would be my wife with our child. I must have dozed off, because suddenly I felt a hand on my shoulder. I woke with a start to see Ben standing beside me, still holding his bunch of flowers.

'Did you see her?' I said. 'Is she coming here?'

'No.' He shook his head. 'She wasn't there.' He looked worried.

'Not there? Well, where was she?'

'I've checked with the ward sister and the hospital receptionists. She's not here in the hospital anymore.'

'Are you sure? Then where is she?'

'I don't know, mate. All they could tell me was that she'd discharged herself yesterday.'

'Could she do that? Was she well enough?'

'I guess so,' Ben shrugged. 'They wouldn't have been happy to let her go, otherwise.'

'But where on earth has she gone? She can't have gone back to Mountain Thyme.' My mind was in a frantic whirl, thinking of every possibility, everyone she might turn to. 'Her mother, you must call her mother. Maybe she's gone back to the UK to recover. That's probably what she'd do, isn't it? Go somewhere she'd feel safe, to be looked after.'

Ben was still frowning. 'Possibly. Do you have a number I can call for you?'

'No, I've nothing in here. I've no idea where my phone is and all our personal effects are still up at the restaurant. We brought nothing with us.'

He stood there by my bed, the bouquet hanging limply from his hand, his thoughtful gift now looking less like a cheerful greeting and more like the sad offerings arranged on roadside shrines. He shook his head again and said, 'But I don't understand. Why wouldn't she tell you where she was going? What happened to you guys up there?'

I knew I couldn't tell him or explain, for I barely understood it myself.

Chapter Seventy-Three

James

August 2008

As I was due to be in hospital for another couple of weeks, Ben popped in as often as he could when he was in town on other business. I called my parents to get Amber's mother's number and that was a conversation I'd rather not repeat, with my father baffled by what had happened and my mother fussing. 'What do you mean, there's been a fire, dear? Do you want us to come out there, darling? Bring you and Amber some clothes? The baby's due soon, isn't it? Do you want us to come out and help you?'

'No, Mum, don't worry. There's no need for you to come over here. I just can't get back up to the house to get my stuff. We're fine. I just need that number, that's all.'

And the call to Amber's mother was even worse. 'Whatever made you think she'd be here? Why on earth don't you know where she is? For goodness' sake, you'd better find out fast. She could be suffering from postnatal depression. It does happen, you know. The poor girl, she must be struggling. It's bad enough having the baby arrive early, but a fire as well, that's terrible. I'd better arrange to come out immediately.'

I eventually managed to persuade her not to catch the next flight by promising to call her again as soon as I had more news, but I thought Amber would have every right to feel depressed. After all, I'd destroyed everything we'd come here to achieve.

In two years we'd gone from finding the right location for our home and restaurant then launching the business and acquiring a fast-growing reputation to facing utter devastation – our home was nearly destroyed, our business in tatters for some time to come and our marriage on the rocks. The only good thing salvaged from this awful mess, thanks to Amber and Greg and with no thanks to me, was our baby, who I had only seen briefly on that first day and who I hadn't even seen being born.

Ben tried to make me feel optimistic, saying, 'Amber's a sensible sort of girl. She won't have done anything silly. I'm sure she's just taken herself somewhere quiet to think things over.'

'You're probably right, but I'd still like to know where she is and whether she's all right.'

'Eleni says Amber probably just wants a good rest. She says it's hard enough having a baby under normal circumstances in hospital, with people who know what they're doing, but the thought of having a maverick like Greg as your birth partner or whatever they call it, would be enough to send any woman into hiding for a while. She'll get in touch eventually, you'll see.'

But she didn't. I left it a couple of days and then suddenly, I don't know why I hadn't thought of it before, I remembered Inge and Marian. When Ben came that afternoon, bearing a pay-as-you-go phone and a DVD player for me, I said, 'Can you go down to that beach shop, the Mill, you know, the one run by the two lesbians, and see if Amber's there? She was very friendly with them before all this happened. I've suddenly realised that's where she might be holed up or that they might know where she is. They came to visit a few times while Amber was pregnant. Well, Marian did. Inge wasn't always up to it.'

'Sure, mate. I'll drop round and check it out on the way back.'

'And can you phone me and let me know if she's there?'

'Of course. Can do.'

It was a couple of hours later when he came back to the ward, instead of phoning. 'You were right about the Mill,' he said. 'She's fine and she's staying there at the beach shop with her friends.'

'So, did you see her then?'

'No, but I spoke to the older woman, Inge. She was sitting at the desk out the front when I got there. She said she would find out if Amber wanted to come down and see me. She took her time about it, but when she came back she said Amber was feeding the baby and didn't want any interruptions. I asked if she had a message for you and Inge just said there wasn't one.'

'What? Nothing? Nothing at all?'

'Apparently not. I asked how long she'd be staying there and Inge said they were happy for her to stay as long as she liked. Then I asked if she needed anything and was told that Amber and the baby had everything they wanted for now and Amber could get in touch if she needed to. It was pretty much an eff-off, really.'

I was stunned. This wasn't at all what I was expecting. I'd started to think Amber might have calmed down by now and that she might at least have given Ben a message for me. 'Didn't she even want to know how I was?'

Ben shook his head. 'Afraid not. You're still in the doghouse for some reason, mate.' He turned to leave, then said, 'Whatever you did, it must have been pretty bad for her to be digging her heels in like this.'

I couldn't bear to tell Ben why Amber was so pissed off with me, and let him leave. Once he'd gone, I began to brood on the situation. Amber was my wife and she was preventing me from seeing my first-born child. What right did she have to do that?

I was lying there on my bed, despondent and bored, knowing that the next event in my day would be the dreadful tea round (dreadful because the hospital could only offer limp Lipton's teabags, not strong English tea), when I was surprised to see a familiar but unwelcome face through the doorway to the corridor.

From my bed in the far corner of the eight-bed ward I had a good view of all the staff and visitors coming and going. Most were intent on reaching their destination, bearing baskets of fruit and bunches of flowers for patients, or pushing trolleys; some hovered at the entrance, wondering if this was where their friend or relative was recovering. But none of them stood on the far side of the corridor staring into the ward with such undisguised contempt. Like Dimitri was doing.

Chapter Seventy-Four

20 June 1944

'Matilde, Anna, come here. I have something to show you.' The girls come running indoors when Agata calls. 'We are going to play a game. I am going to show you a wonderful new hiding place.'

Their smiles fade and they look fearful. 'Are the bad men here?' Matilde asks. Anna sucks her fingers and looks as if she might cry.

'No, you mustn't worry, they aren't here. Don't be afraid. But remember how we had a safe hiding place before? You are used to hiding if need be, so if they were to come here and I told you to hide, this is where you must go.' Agata pulls back the table in the kitchen, then slips the rug to one side, uncovering a trapdoor with an iron ring handle. She lifts it open, revealing wooden stairs, then takes the lit lantern from the table and steps down. 'Come with me and see how comfortable it is in here.'

Matilde kneels down and hangs her head through the trapdoor opening, peering into the dim void. But Anna scrambles down the steps after Agata without hesitating, and her sister soon follows.

The cellar smells of the goods stored in its depths in the past: wine, oil and olives. One day it will be filled with these goods again, but for now it mostly smells of straw, as Agata has made a bed of stuffed sacking covered with a blanket, set on wooden planks supported by bricks. She has also swept the floor clean of dust and wiped the cobwebs from the walls. 'Look what a cosy bed there is for you. And here,' she takes the lid from a squat, bulging tureen, 'there will always be good things to eat. And you shall have water in a big flask as well.'

Anna reaches into the dish, takes out a dried fig and begins to munch it. Matilde is cautious and walks around the cellar, looking into every corner and up at the small air vents which allow a little light to filter into the gloom. She points at the old chute, once used for deliveries. 'Can we get out through there?'

Agata takes her lamp to look. 'Maybe,' she says. 'I'll have to see how it's shut outside. Would you be happier if you knew there was another way out?'

Matilde nods, then joins her sister, who is eating another piece of dried fruit. 'We shall see if we can find a ladder, so you can get out that way if you need to,' Agata says, thinking Georgiou could make one if they can't find one somewhere in the ruins of the village.

'I like it here,' Anna says, munching her fruit. 'Can we play in here?'

Agata thinks for a moment; it would be good if the children were used to the cellar and came to see it as a friendly rather than a fearful place. 'Of course,' she says. 'We could leave the trapdoor open all the time under the table. Then you can pop down here whenever you like. It would be a good idea for you to get out from under my feet when the bad weather comes.'

'Can we have a light down here?' Matilde asks.

'We'll see,' Agata replies. In time there may be flagons of oil, casks of wine and other vital goods stored here and she can't risk fire. 'If we can find a very safe oil lamp we might be able to let you bring down a light.'

'We'll be ever so careful. Promise.'

'I've said we'll see. Now come upstairs with me. I want you to help me finish cleaning the house. I can't make dresses in that dusty room with a dirty table.'

'I want to help,' shouts Matilde, scrambling back up the steps.

'Me too,' yells Anna, running to the steps then rushing back to the tureen to grab another dried fig, which she holds in her teeth as she grasps the rail at the side of the stairs.

Agata cannot help laughing at their eagerness. She hopes the cellar will always be a playroom and not a prison, but she knows she is wise to prepare, just in case. And now the girls are calling to her, telling her she must hurry, she must finish cleaning so she can complete their dresses.

Chapter Seventy-Five

James

August 2008

I was shocked to see Dimitri standing in the corridor, looking into the ward. From his confident stance I could tell he wasn't casually passing through, like the many other transient visitors with their gifts and expressions of concern; he was standing there opposite the ward doorway deliberately staring straight at me. It was quite obvious to me, from the intensity of his glare, that he wasn't searching for another old friend, he wasn't lost or unsure which bed to visit: he had come to find out where I was and how I was doing.

After what seemed an age, he gave a slight nod, then with a lift of his chin and a half smile, he walked off, not hurrying or scuttling away with guilt, but with a slow, arrogant swagger. And then I knew without a doubt that he had come to the hospital solely with the intention of looking for me, so he could see how I was recovering. And when he saw how disabled I was, laid up in bed with my plaster casts and with crutches by my side, he was satisfied that I couldn't possibly be any kind of a threat to him, at least not for quite some time to come.

I remembered our last encounter, the night of the fire, how I had thrown his car keys as far as I could. I'd barely thought of him since then, but now I recalled my empty promise to deal with him later. He must have scrabbled around in the brush searching for those keys – maybe he'd found them while I was running to the village in my desperation to find Amber. Or, more likely, he knew how to hotwire a car. Yes, of course, a man like Dimitri, with his many skills and underhand ways, would know exactly how to do that. The mere loss of keys wouldn't stop him in his tracks.

I wished I had dealt with him then and there, but my priority had been to reach Amber. And now what chance did I have of ever fulfilling that feeble promise? *I'll see to you later.* He was on his feet, looking fit and strong, and I clearly wasn't. And he could see that I wouldn't be back to full strength for weeks, maybe months. No, there was no chance he would be worrying about retaliation from me in the near future, if ever.

For the rest of the afternoon and into early evening I could barely take my eyes off the doorway, hoping he might decide to pass by again. It certainly took my mind off the tea trolley and its disappointments, but I couldn't concentrate on any of the books or DVDs Ben had brought. I'd scan just a few words and not remember what I'd read, or half watch a scene then find myself glancing at the door, expecting to see Dimitri's mocking, self-satisfied face staring at me again.

But finally, my vigilance paid off, though not in the way I had hoped. I was being helped back into the ward by one of the nurses after a visit to the bathroom when I heard the screeching tones of Greg's dreadful daughter, Lavinia. 'Sweetie,' she squealed, 'poor you, all in plaster, hopping around. You're nearly as bad as Daddy.'

'How is he?' I continued my lame progress, hoping she would soon go away.

'In agony, of course.' She pouted. 'It was such a terrible shock, seeing him laid up there like that. I couldn't sleep for at least a week.' Then she forgot her distress and smiled, saying, 'But he'll be back to normal by Christmas, the doctor says, so Mummy and I are planning a big welcome home party for him. You'll have to come. It will be such fun for all of us!'

'Thanks,' I muttered. 'I'll have to see what I'm doing around then.' And then it occurred to me that Greg might have had other visitors, as well as members of his family. 'I haven't been able to go and see your father yet,' I said. 'Do you think he could cope with a visit from me now?'

'Oh, sweetie, he'd simply love to see you. I know he would. He's only had me and Mummy fussing over him all the time he's been here. We're driving him simply mad. Do go and see him. He hasn't had any boy talk to cheer him up for ages.'

'You mean he hasn't had any male visitors while he's been here?'

She shrugged. 'No, I don't think he has.' She looked vague, fluttering her false eyelashes. 'Oh, wait a minute. Mummy said Daddy's assistant, or whatever he calls him, came round the other day. Mr Barberis, isn't it? But I don't think he went in to see Daddy, he just chatted to Mummy. She says he's Daddy's right-hand man and will do anything for him, or her, while Daddy's laid up.'

'I bet he will,' I muttered, as the nurse led me back to my bed.

Lavinia fluttered her fingers and blew me a kiss from the middle of the ward. 'Must dash, darling. Vladi's bringing the yacht across tonight for dinner.' I watched her saunter out, and noticed how every man in the ward was mesmerised by her swaying high-heeled totter.

So Dimitri had been checking up on Greg as well as me. But did that mean he was worried about Greg's opinion of him, or were they still partners in crime?

Chapter Seventy-Six

James

August 2008

There was only one way for me to find out whether Dimitri and Greg were still in partnership, and that was to visit my old friend myself. But that was easier said than done, as I still wasn't particularly mobile and Greg was being treated in the private section of the public hospital, on the far side of the building. Of course he was; he wouldn't be subjected to the crowded general wards with their constant round of loud visitors, like I was. He had to have the best.

I waited for the English-speaking nurse to come on duty and asked her if I might be taken in a wheelchair to visit a very ill friend, who had also been badly injured in the fire-gutted village where I'd had my accident. She was sympathetic and said she would find out if he was both able and willing to have visitors. She came back later, saying I could see him that afternoon.

I spent a tedious morning having some physio then passed the time alternately lying on my bed and sitting in a chair with my leg outstretched, watching a fly struggle to free itself from a web in a corner of the window. There was a view of the car park, hedged with pink oleander bushes, and I tried to amuse myself by observing a lot of hysterical shouting and bad parking as various cars manoeuvred into the tiny spaces.

When I arrived at Greg's room that afternoon, although I was prepared for his injuries, I hadn't expected him to look so frail. The bouncing joker full of bravado had been reduced to a pale and shrunken figure, propped up on his bed frame, his eyes still ringed with dark bruises and evident stitches on his scalp, where some hair had been shaved away. One arm was in plaster and I could see bandages across his chest, partially covered by pale-blue pyjamas.

'You made it here at last, then,' he whispered. His voice had but a vestige of its old cockiness, but still retained a hint of humour.

'Couldn't put it off any longer, buddy,' I said. 'I've been missing you. Sorry I haven't brought you any grapes. Thought you'd be sick of them by now anyway.'

'Can't stand the sight of them.' His eyes rolled towards the fruit basket on his bedside cabinet, piled with peaches and dripping with grapes. 'Pam thinks they're good for me.'

'She must have been worried sick about you.'

'Nah, pissed off, more like.' He paused to catch his breath. 'Gave me a right telling-off. Said I should never have gone racing up there. Should have left it to the professionals.'

'If we'd left it to the professionals, Amber and the baby might not have survived. I owe you a big thank you for that.' I paused for a second, mentally twiddling my thumbs, then said, 'Look, mate, I'm really sorry I pushed you that day. Never thought you'd end up in such a mess. Sorry about that.'

Even in his poorly state, he managed a half smile, then he said, 'Water under the bridge, old man. Anyway, how are they both doing? The little chap must have grown a lot by now.'

I was quiet for a moment, but then thought there was no point in being less than open with Greg. We had both suffered so much, shared so much, so I said, 'I expect he has. But the fact is, I haven't seen either of them since we were brought here in the air ambulance.'

'But that's… how long… two weeks? You've not seen Amber or the baby in all that time?'

'She doesn't want to see me or speak to me. She's totally pissed off with me. She blames me for everything.' I couldn't help giving a deep sigh. 'It's such a bloody mess. I think I've lost both of them for good.'

'She blames you for the fire? But that wasn't anything to do with you.'

'I know, but she feels I contributed to the whole situation that led up to it. And I have to admit I hadn't been completely honest with her about our plans for the site.'

He was silent. I could see him thinking as he gazed out of the window, then he spoke, without turning back to look at me, 'Well, we both know who's behind it all, don't we?'

I nodded. 'Did you know he popped in for a visit?'

Greg looked alert. 'What? Here?'

'I saw him hanging around near my ward, yesterday. And I understand he came up here to see how you were doing as well. I don't know if he looked in on you, but I think he spoke to Pam.'

'He's been checking out both of us, you mean?'

'Looks that way. But what are we going to do about it? You're laid-up and I'm barely able to walk. We're both pathetic specimens. Neither of us is in any condition to pay him back for what he's done. And if we go down the legal route, neither of us is likely to come out of it whiter than white.'

Greg managed a tiny croaking laugh in response, but couldn't speak.

'I damn well wish I'd dealt with him when I had the chance that night. All I did was try to thump him and chuck his car keys away.'

He managed another scratchy laugh. 'Bet that really hurt his feelings.'

'I know, it sounds stupid now, doesn't it? Bloody stupid. I wish I'd had the chance to slash his tyres at the same time as well.'

He gave another snort. 'It needs more than that, mate.'

'Like what?'

He managed a smirk, his bruised face lopsided. 'Well, Lavinia's back with her Russian, so we could call the heavies in.'

'Seriously? No, you're joking, aren't you?'

'Afraid so. If it's going to work, it's got to be subtle and it's got to be kept well away from the two of us.'

'Brilliant. Then we don't stand a chance.'

'I'll keep thinking.' He grimaced. 'At least I will if this bloody head of mine stops killing me.'

Chapter Seventy-Seven

20 June 1944

It is so hot that year, the year they finally leave Greece. The sun is merciless. The rays were scorching when they were crammed into the open boats, but Rebekka thinks that being at sea was more bearable than standing beside the railway lines on burning hot stones.

While the barges were being towed on the water, a slight breeze drifted across the waves and the sea spray was cool, dampening the clothes they had been wearing since they left home. But here in Haidari, in Athens, the intense heat radiates in searing waves from the concrete and gravel. It feels a little like the baker's ovens in Corfu Town, where from an early age Mama sent her to buy loaves of crusty bread, so fragrant she could smell them as she approached the shuttered green doorway near the harbour. And now there is no friendly baker's wife to greet her with floury kisses and no scent of freshly baked bread, there are just harsh shoves from brutal soldiers and the sour odours of sweat and fear.

Rebekka tugs at her father's sleeve and points. 'Papa, is that our train?' Ahead of them they can see a line of cattle trucks headed by a large steaming engine.

'I fear it might be, my child. But at least the cars are spacious. There will be plenty of room for us all to sit down comfortably.'

'But there are some proper train carriages further along down there, with windows and curtains. Why aren't they all like that?'

Papa frowns. 'Those carriages are only for the Germans. You don't want to go in one of those.'

And then Rebekka notices, ahead of them in the crowd, that a very pretty girl is being roughly dragged away from her family by two soldiers. She screams, her mother cries out and tries to hold her daughter back, but is struck on the side of her head by a pistol. Blood trickles down her cheek. The girl is manhandled down the track to the compartment and hauled inside. Several more girls and young women soon follow, all protesting loudly, although surely that carriage is more comfortable than the one Rebekka's family is being herded into. Mama puts her arm protectively around her daughter, saying, 'Lower your head, child. Hold your bundle close to your chest. With luck, they will think you are too young.'

More and more people are pushed into the boxcar. There is barely room to stand, let alone sit. Then the hefty doors are hauled shut and the bolts are slammed into position. The only fresh air comes from four narrow windows at the very top of the cattle car. If someone faints or expires, there might be a little more room, but not much. Rebekka tries to count how many are crammed into the carriage with her, but being so short, she can't see everyone's head. She guesses a hundred, or maybe less, all tightly packed in together.

All around her she can hear cries. There are the harsh orders of the Germans, hitting weary people as they climb into the cars, the feeble wails of hungry, dirty babies and the weeping of women. And above all these distressing sounds she hears the screams of those who have lost their shoes or have been barefoot ever since they left their homes, as the skin of their naked feet is burnt by the caustic quicklime that powders the carriage floors.

Chapter Seventy-Eight

Amber

August 2008

My days at the Mill fell into a comforting pattern of sleeping, bathing, feeding Theo, changing him and then resting again. I joined Inge and Marian for meals when I felt like it, but sometimes they brought me a tray in my room, or I sat alone on the balcony in the warm afternoon sun, just thinking about all that had happened and how my life would be in the future.

After a couple of weeks, I felt strong enough to help for a couple of hours or so in the shop most days, while Theo slept, and when Inge and Marian went into the town to hold their vigil and direct the tourists to the fort. The beach was busy and the days were so hot that the shop was generally quiet until the visitors began leaving late in the afternoon. When there were few customers, I found it quite relaxing to be folding caftans and bedspreads, stacking pottery and dusting shelves, sometimes with Theo sleeping in a basket by my side. The occasional tourist would drift in to buy an olive wood bowl or a scarf as a souvenir of their holiday, but mostly I just sat and watched the bodies baking on the sand, the windsurfers skimming the waves and the children cavorting in the sea.

One particularly quiet day, I was sitting as usual at the desk on the lower terrace, where Inge always positioned herself when she was minding the shop. I was gazing, chin resting on my hand, at the cafe across the road, where James and I had sipped cold drinks two years previously, when we had first noticed the beach shop. And as I looked around, from beach to cafe and back again, I suddenly became aware of being watched myself, in that skin-prickling way that sometimes happens. I let my eyes drift from group to group, from table to table, and then I saw him, at least I thought it was him, sitting at a shaded table right at the back of the cafe's terrace, too far away for me to be quite certain at first, but sure enough when I focused on that bearded face.

A night or two later, Inge and Marian invited me to have supper with them once Theo was settled and when I joined them, I saw anxious faces and felt that I must have interrupted a private conversation.

'Is everything all right?' I asked. 'I don't mind taking a tray upstairs if you'd like to be on your own.'

'It's nothing,' Marian said. 'Just business, that's all.' She gave a weary shake of her head and sighed.

'Anything I can help with?'

She gave Inge a despairing look, which conveyed far more than she had in words, then said, 'Just our old friend making a nuisance of himself once more, that's all.'

'More than a nuisance,' Inge said, frowning. 'He's been pestering Marian at the mountain shop again. He just won't take no for an answer.'

'By that, I take it you mean Dimitri?'

Marian nodded, then took a bottle of wine from the fridge and held it out towards me. I shook my head as I wasn't drinking while I was breastfeeding. 'Well, I'm going to,' she said. 'I need it after the day I've had.' She poured herself a large glass and diluted a little with water for Inge.

'I meant to say,' I said, 'but I'm pretty sure I saw him sitting over in the cafe the other day, staring at the shop. So what exactly has happened now?'

'He's been storing some construction machinery in a disused barn a little further up the track,' Marian said, 'and today he left a digger right on the junction, completely blocking the path to my storeroom.'

'Didn't you ask him to move it?'

'I would've done, if he'd been there.' She looked furious, frowning. 'I swear he did it on purpose. And I had some heavy pieces of furniture to shift today for an order, so it made life extremely difficult for my delivery guys. They couldn't back their vehicle right up to our barn, so they had to carry everything much further than they should have done. They weren't at all pleased with me.'

'Have you had problems like this before?'

She shrugged and looked at Inge, with that look that often passed between them, and said, 'Similar. It's usually something that I can't quite pin on him or blame him for.' Gulping some of her wine, she then said, 'And when I finally saw him coming back and asked him to move the digger, he couldn't have cared less. He just said a driver was meant to have collected it during the day, and if it was that inconvenient then maybe I shouldn't use the barn anymore, and I should reconsider his offer to take it off my hands.'

'What a damn cheek.'

'I know. He's got a nerve. He keeps going out of his way to make life awkward for us. There's been a constant stream of little problems that are irritating and inconvenient. Last week I found one of the recently delivered stone fonts was badly cracked, though I'm quite certain it was perfect when it was unloaded. And there were also several cigarette butts on the ground behind the shop the other day, as if someone had been hiding out there, spying on me.'

'But he hasn't done anything worse than this, has he? I mean, he hasn't actually threatened you?' I sat down at the table and began picking at the olives and tzatziki Marian had set out in small terracotta bowls. The olives were from the local groves, small and black, slightly bitter.

'Not so far,' she said, pushing a basket of fresh bread towards me. 'Why do you ask that?'

And then I knew that it was time to tell them both the whole story, insofar as I knew it and could understand it myself. I took a deep breath and then began. 'When James finally managed to find me in the cellar after Theo was born, he told me Dimitri had started the fire. He said he'd seen Dimitri lurking when he first reached the village that night. He blamed him for the fire. He said he believed Greg had given Dimitri free rein to obtain possession of the land by any means possible, and that was how he'd decided to do it.' My story was a highly simplified version of events, but I couldn't bear to say anything about James saying he wished he'd killed Dimitri, rather than Greg.

Both women were open-mouthed. Inge's face was even whiter than usual as she said, 'That awful man deliberately caused the fire that could have killed both you and your child? He knew that your time was near and that you were helpless. Surely he knew you always stayed the night at Mountain Thyme?'

Hearing her actually state this fact, in these stark words, even though I'd been aware of it myself for nearly three weeks now, pierced my stomach again and made me feel sick. I nodded. 'I'm only telling you what James told me. But there's no way Dimitri couldn't have known I'd be there that night. I was barely leaving the place by that stage – it was so hot and I was so tired and huge. I slept at Mountain Thyme every single night. He was bound to know that. And he must have known James often stayed overnight at Greg's house as well.'

I took a couple of deep breaths to banish the sickness, then said, 'I can understand that he might not have realised the fire would spread so fast, so I'm not saying he actually intended to kill me, but the fact is, he had no regard for my safety and he didn't lift a finger to help me when the fire engulfed the whole village. He didn't warn me or try to save me.' My eyes filled with tears. 'Greg may have been complicit in this whole mess, but at least he came to my aid in the end. He saved me and Theo and now I don't even know whether he's made a full recovery or will be marked for life because of his injuries.'

Marian came around the table and hugged me. 'You're safe now. Both of you are safe here.'

'And this man, this monster,' said Inge, 'what was his motive? What did he have to gain from such a terrible disaster?'

I shook my head as I replied, 'I guess he might have stood to gain financially, once the land was developed. Maybe he thought he could scare us away and then buy our property cheaply, but I don't really know.'

'It's such a callous way of clearing undeveloped land,' Inge said. 'Every year it happens. They know they aren't allowed to build on virgin sites, so they go out there and burn them. It may seem logical, but it's devastating and they can't control it, once it starts.'

Marian was pouring herself more wine and stood there thinking. Then she suddenly said, 'It's all about greed and resentment with him. He cannot stomach the fact that we own this shop as well as our shop in the mountains. It must have been the same for him with your place. I think he likes us to do all the hard work, establishing the business, then he wants to take it off our hands, as he puts it.'

'I don't know what you mean,' I said. 'Before, he was always so helpful to us, working on the renovation, managing the whole project. I really liked him. I've only ever seen him being considerate and utterly charming. The man James says started the fire is not the man I've known for the last couple of years.'

'But he's like that to get what he wants,' Marian said. 'He soon drops the act if it doesn't get him anywhere.'

'This so-called charming man,' Inge said in a quiet, tired voice, 'believes I am not the rightful owner of this shop and this house. My dear Georgiou and Agata left their entire estate to me in their will, but he has disputed this. He says they had no right to give me what he calls "family property". He has been pestering me and arguing his case for years.'

'I had no idea. I knew Marian had her doubts about him, but I never knew that he was the one questioning your inheritance and making your life so difficult as well. Can't anything be done about him?'

Inge sighed. 'I've taken advice from a local lawyer and been told the will is legitimate, but Dimitri Barberis has continued to contest it.'

'He just won't give up,' Marian said. 'He wants to wear us down until we can't go on any longer.' She shook her head in anger and poured herself more wine. 'Sometimes I think we should pretend to agree with him, give him a false sense of security and wait till we've got him on his own, then… *boof!*' She punched the air, spilling her drink over the table in the process.

I couldn't help but laugh and through my spluttering managed to say, 'Then what, once you'd bloodied his nose, you think he'd give in?'

'Or if I could get him out in a boat, and then whoosh, over the side!' Marian was laughing too.

'No, take him for a walk up one of those steep mountain paths,' I said. 'Then just the gentlest little push, rolling down the hill.'

Inge was gazing at each of us in turn, a tolerant smile on her face, as if we were two naughty children planning mischief. 'But we must fight fair, girls. He is far too clever to put himself in a vulnerable position. Let us wait and see.'

Marian was quiet for a moment, then she exploded. 'You'd think even a slimy character like him would have the decency to leave a terminally ill woman alone, wouldn't you?' She looked angry and drained her glass in one. 'I swear his bullying tactics have caused Inge's illness.'

'Darling, you can't say that,' Inge said, shaking her head. 'You know very well how much I used to smoke and drink.'

'Maybe,' Marian said, 'but he hasn't helped. And now we know what he is really capable of doing. He will stop at nothing to kick us out of here and out of the mountains.'

Chapter Seventy-Nine

24 June 1944

The old ewe does not have as much meat on her bones as the spring lambs, but she gives them a good kleftiko, flavoured with oregano and rich with tomatoes. 'It's as good as my mother's,' Georgiou says, his chin dripping with gravy.

'That ewe served me well,' Zenia says. 'A good lamb every year for ten years. And now she will feed us until we have the pig.'

Agata does not like these references to killing in front of the children, even though she knows they must learn the facts of survival in these harsh times. They too have greasy chins from the fatty meat, meltingly tender after long, slow cooking with lemon and potatoes added towards the end. But one meal alone cannot finish all the good meat this one beast has provided, so she is thinking how they can be sure this bounty will not be wasted. 'If only we had salt,' she says, 'then we could cure as well as smoking and air-drying.'

'But we do,' Zenia answers with a smile that reveals her toothless gums. 'We can make pastirma and salami. It is not the best with mutton, but it will feed us.' She slurps the finely chopped flesh and potatoes, spilling grease on her clothes. 'And I have enough to cure the skin as well. Then you may give these poor children warm boots for their little feet. They will not want chilblains this winter, when the weather turns.'

'I had been worrying about that,' says Agata. 'We have been looking through all the old houses to see if there was anything we could use to make shoes. But nothing has turned up so far.'

'Ah, there was much to find,' Zenia says with a sly grin. 'Over the years I've sifted through every corner, every chest and every cupboard. You won't find much of any use now, my dear, but tell me what you need and I may well have it tucked away in my little house.'

Georgiou roars with laughter. 'Zenia Vasilakis, you crafty old witch! Does nothing escape you?' He shakes his head and hugs his wife. 'This is how the old survive, with cunning like a vixen and her cubs.'

'What's a vixen?' Matilde rests against Agata, her greasy hands staining her dress.

'A very clever fox, my dear. Zenia has been very sensible. She has made sure that nothing the old villagers left behind here has been wasted. Why, we may even be able to give your dirty scratched toes something to keep them warm this winter.'

'And me,' says Anna, climbing onto Georgiou's lap. 'I want shoes and a dress.'

'You will have them, darlings. I will finish the sewing very soon. But as you are both so greasy and messy from eating so much kleftiko, I think you should stay in your old clothes for a bit.'

'They will need more than dresses for the winter,' Zenia says. 'You must come and see what I have stored away. There is wool, sheepskin and cloth, all of which you may put to good use. You are used to the winters of the coast. There may be storms there, but they are not like the biting winters of the mountains. We must all prepare.'

'And I will gather wood for our fires,' says Georgiou. 'There's seasoned timber to be found around the village and in the olive groves. I must lay in a store of dry wood before the rains come. And I'll stack logs for you, Zenia, so you have plenty to keep you warm through the winter.'

'Thank you,' Zenia says, with tears welling. 'Thank you, my family. I give thanks to God that I have a family again, after all these years alone.' Matilde and Anna are touched by her emotion and both go to her at her seat, patting her knees with their tiny hands. She sniffs, then says, in her usual gruff tones, 'And you, my boy, you will make up for all the cherries you stole and ate by pruning my grapevine as well as yours. Here, we do it before Apokrias in the middle of February.' She shakes her head and sighs. 'Ah, if you could have been here then, when I was young. The dancing and feasting we had at that time, before the 40 days of Lent.'

'Then perhaps this year we should celebrate a little,' Agata says. 'We are safe, we have plenty, we should be happy then and give thanks for our good fortune.'

'And I will teach the children how to dance like I danced in my youth,' Zenia says, standing up unsteadily and waving her arms, then grabbing the hands of the two girls. 'We shall all dance the rouga and feast like kings and queens. And we shall all wear our finest dresses.'

Chapter Eighty

James

August 2008

A couple of days after Greg and I had spoken, a nurse was helping me walk to my daily physiotherapy session. They wouldn't let me use a wheelchair now so I was managing with a crutch and a helpful arm. Halfway there, Pam came bustling along the corridor towards my ward. As soon as she saw me she called out, 'Oh, James, thank goodness, there you are. He says he has to see you today.' Her mascara was streaked, her lipstick was smudged and she had a crumpled tissue in her hand. 'I've been with him all night. He's in such a bad way.'

'I can come right now. But I thought he was getting much better?' I transferred my hand from the nurse's arm to Pam's, and we started shuffling towards the private rooms.

'He seemed to be improving, but he's had chest pains since yesterday morning and now the doctors think he might have a clot.' She dabbed at her eyes with the ragged tissue as we walked. 'I tell you, it's all too much for me. And Lavinia's only just gone back to Vladi as well. She'll be in absolute pieces, I know she will.'

'Maybe you should go home and get some rest. I can stay with him for now. I wasn't planning on going anywhere very exciting today.'

Pam didn't get my little joke and just said, 'I'd be so grateful, dear. Do you know, I'd feel so much better if one of his friends was with him today. I tried to call that nice Mr Barberis, but I can't seem to get hold of him, even though I've left several messages. He'd do anything for Greg, I know he would.'

'Did Greg say he wanted to see him?'

'Yes, he was asking about him and wanted to know what he said when he called by the other day, when Greg was still only semi-conscious. He said he's got some unfinished business with him, but I said darling, you can't go thinking about business matters in your state. You've got to concentrate on getting better. I thought he'd be feeling a bit brighter after I told him about the hotel. I was sure that bit of news would really perk him up.'

Her long nails clawed my arm as we made slow progress along the corridor, but I tried to ignore the discomfort and said, 'What's happened to the hotel?'

'They've had to close down, dear. Apparently, they've got a serious drains problem, so I've been told. I thought he'd be pleased to hear that, but he didn't seem to be the slightest bit interested. That's when I thought he must be feeling really ill, if that piece of news couldn't cheer him up.'

We reached Greg's private room and Pam helped me shuffle to his bedside, where Greg was lying back on white pillows, his eyes closed, looking even more drained than he had the last time I'd seen him.

'I've brought James to see you, darling, just as you wanted. He's going to stay with you for a bit while I nip home to freshen up.' He opened his eyes as she leant over his grey face and kissed the top of his head. He noticed me, but didn't say anything while she peered into her powder compact and applied lipstick.

'Bye for now, you two. Be good.' Her fingers fluttered at us both as she left the room, leaving a faint trail of scent.

I sat down next to the bed. 'You're looking a bit rough, mate. You've not been eating enough of that fruit, I expect.'

He fixed me with bloodshot eyes. 'Eat the lot, why don't you? Help yourself to the whole bloody bunch, for all I care.' He sounded exhausted, but there was still a little of his old fighting spirit left, I could tell.

'I was on my way to physio, but Pam said you wanted to see me right away.'

'Yeah, I've been doing a lot of thinking since we had our last chat.'

'About our mutual friend?'

'That, and other things.'

'Have you come up with anything we can use on him?'

'Nothing that's much use. Look,' he sighed, 'I know you blame me for this whole effing mess, and I'm not surprised. I'd have thought the same in your shoes. I've not lived a good life, you know. Been in trouble all my bloody life.' He let his head loll back against the pillow and closed his eyes.

'Yeah, I know. You're a crafty old rascal. But I know it wasn't deliberate and I forgive you.'

'Do you?' He opened his eyes and tried to reach for my hand across the crisp, tightly tucked sheet. I grasped his hand in mine and he said, 'I've done some terrible things in my time. Unforgiveable things.'

'Surely not.' I tried to laugh, thinking this was the old Greg, pulling my leg, but his hand was gripping mine with a force greater than I imagined such a sick man could muster. 'Go on, you're a bit of a bugger, but you're a bloody daft old bugger.'

'No, I mean it. When I was a boy... I never told anyone, I thought I'd killed her.'

'What? Who?'

He was silent for a moment, and then he said, 'I always was a hotshot with a catapult.'

I laughed as I still couldn't take this soul-baring seriously. 'I know, and you're still a bloody good shot. Like that night at the pool. We had a right laugh, didn't we? And hey, what's this about the place being shut down? Result, eh? Pam just told me. Good news or what?'

He managed a slight smile. 'Yeah. May have scored there.' He paused again, then said, 'But this was different. I've never told anyone about this before. She was one of my teachers. Miss Jones, taught us maths. Speccy Jones, we called her, cos of her glasses. She was on her bike.'

He released my hand and shut his eyes as if picturing the long-ago scene of his boyhood. 'It was near the end of the summer holidays. I'd been out in the woods all day on my own, building a den and shooting at birds, and then suddenly, on my way home, there she was. I was behind these bushes and I heard her bike coming.'

'You took a shot at her?'

'I was aiming for her front tyre. But I missed. Got her bang between the eyes. Knocked her right off her bike.'

'Blimey. What did you do?'

'Scarpered, of course. Ran home and hoped no one saw me. Then, when she didn't turn up at school for the autumn term, I was terrified I'd killed her. I was worried sick for weeks about what might have happened.'

'But you hadn't killed her, had you?'

'No, but she didn't come back to school for three months. When she did, she was limping. I couldn't look at her, knowing I'd done that to her.' He closed his eyes again and lay back, grey and withered, as if all his vitality and bravado had been deflated. Pam was right, he wasn't looking too hot.

'You feeling all right? Want me to call a nurse?'

He opened his eyes again and tried to smile. 'Nah. They'll only start making a fuss. I'm just tired, that's all.'

'Do you want me to go?' I was really rather worried about him. I didn't want to leave yet, as I'd been hoping he'd have something useful to add to our discussion about Dimitri, but I wasn't sure that talking was helping him right now.

He was silent, staring at me, then he said, 'The thing is, everyone has secrets. We all have something to hide.'

'Do you mean you've got something on Dimitri?'

'Wish I did,' he said. 'Mr Fix-it is too clever by half. He's probably been up to no good several times in his life, but nothing's stuck as far as I know.'

'We could report him though, couldn't we? Tell the police he's an arsonist.'

Greg sighed. 'He's probably got them in his pocket too. He's far too slippery to be caught out that way.' He gave a little cough, his forehead creasing in pain, then whispered, 'Anyway, he'd disappear the minute he got wind of any investigation. A quick little boat trip across the channel to Albania and they'd never find him in a million years.'

'Then I'll just have to deal with him when I'm back on my feet. I'm not going to forget what he did. He can't be allowed to get away with it.'

'I'd like to be around to see it when you do. Give me a good reason to get better.' He managed a small laugh, then grimaced, putting his hand to his chest. 'I'd like to see that. You, kicking the arse of the arsonist.'

Chapter Eighty-One

24 June 1944

Despite the horrors of confinement in the cramped, stinking boxcars, everyone grows to fear the stopping of the train. They long to be released, to stretch their limbs, to breathe clean air, but sometimes, when the train slows or comes to a complete halt, there are new terrors.

The first time it happens, Rebekka cannot understand why she suddenly hears agonised screams coming from the next car. Cries of terror combined with coarse laughter. Then, as the shrieks subside, she hears the ominous message being passed from one boxcar to another in her own language. 'Stand back from the doors. Pass it on. The brutes are stabbing at us under the doors with knives.'

Rebekka isn't near the door, although there is more air there. 'What are they talking about, Papa?' There are sobs and groans all around them.

The next time the train halts, those in Rebekka's group who are still able to move shuffle back from the door as far as they can. Only inches, but precious inches. Slithering, slicing noises are heard, accompanied by cruel laughter and harsh words in German.

'They didn't manage to cut anyone in here this time,' Papa says, as the soldiers pass down the train to see who else they can torment. 'Who can believe it? Men of a civilised nation, trained soldiers, amusing themselves by pushing knives under the doors to slash the feet of the helpless. Is there nothing they won't do for entertainment?'

About halfway through their journey, when the train stops again, they hear shouts followed by gunfire. They no longer know which country they are in or who might know about the cargo of this train.

'What are they saying?' Rebekka begs Papa, trying to understand the strange language she can hear.

He holds her even closer, trying to interpret the commotion outside. 'I don't think it's German,' he mutters. 'And it's not Greek or Italian… Someone's shouting that they're partisans, Balkan partisans attacking the train.' They hear more shots and then the sound of doors crashing open, and people shouting in Greek that they have nothing, that the Germans have already taken anything of value.

'Can you believe it?' Papa says. 'They are raiding the train and stealing from us. Stealing from dying people. How low can people get? Isn't it enough that we have been forced to leave our homeland and are suffering? Are we to be left with nothing at all, not even our dignity?'

Then he covers Rebekka's ears so the screams and shouts are muffled, but she can hear her father's heart beating fast and she feels his fear.

Chapter Eighty-Two

Amber

September 2008

I imagine he didn't have to knock on the door and ask to come in. The Mill à la Mer was never locked until late at night and the wide stone steps, lined with displays of pottery, led from the shop terrace right up to the kitchen and into the heart of the house. He must have walked straight in with an arrogant sense of entitlement, just because his family was distantly related to the original owners.

I had taken Theo into the bath with me and I suppose that, with the running water and the door shut, I never heard him arrive. But when I went back across the landing to my room, with Theo wrapped in a soft towel, I caught raised voices. Marian's was loudest, Inge spoke occasionally and there was a deep and insistent man's voice too.

I was only clothed in a bath towel myself, so I didn't go down immediately. I dried Theo and dressed him in a vest and nappy, then settled down on my bed against the plumped pillows to feed him. As I was patting his back to burp him, which seemed to be taking longer than usual, I heard a scream and a crash, like crockery breaking.

I stepped out onto the landing and listened from the top of the stairs. Now I could only hear the commanding rumble of the male voice. I laid Theo down in his drawer cot and covered him with a sheet, then pulled on a loose dress and tiptoed down the stairs. My room was at the very top of the house on the third floor, and the voices were coming from the kitchen two floors down. I crept slowly down the stairs, listening as I went.

I knew that voice. It was forceful and demanding, where it had once been charming and helpful. And as I grew nearer, I began to think I could also hear crying. I crept closer until I was at the bottom of the dark flight of stairs, just before the kitchen doorway. I couldn't see inside, but light fell through the half-open door and I could hear everything.

'But there was a will,' Inge said through tears. 'It was signed. I saw their signatures and I've been told the will was valid.'

'That means nothing. Without witnesses, it is worthless.'

'But it was all done properly. I know it was.'

'My lawyers say family rights take precedence. That is the law of this country and I am entitled to contest the will.'

'But Georgiou and Agata used a lawyer. I know they did.'

'Huh, old Theodakis from the village? He'd agree to anything for a bottle of ouzo.'

There was more crying, and then I heard Marian speaking. 'So what do you want us to do? You can't reasonably expect us to clear out, not with Inge in her poor state of health. You can see for yourself how ill she is. And we have every right to consult another lawyer and receive a decent period of notice if you turn out to be correct in the end.'

'Go on then, consult your lawyer. See if you can find one who understands Greek family law. You will find I am justified. This property belongs by right to the Barberis family. It was ours for years and should have stayed so.' There was the sound of a thump and a crash, like a fist being pounded on the table, followed by more crying.

I peered through the crack between the door and the frame and saw Inge seated at the kitchen table, her head in her hands. Marian was crouching down, sweeping up shards of pottery, then she stood up behind Inge and put her hands on her partner's shoulders. With his back to me was the tall, broad-shouldered figure of Dimitri. I didn't want him to see me, so I stepped back a little and carried on listening.

'I give you just one month, ladies. One more month and then you must go. I doubt you will find a true Greek who will help two ladies of your persuasion.'

'We're not going to accept this,' Marian said. 'We're fighting you every inch of the way.'

Dimitri laughed. 'Fight all you like, ladies.' He paused. 'But be careful. I know how to get what I want. You have the other shop too, remember. Up there in the mountains,' he shook his head, 'so vulnerable up there. I hear the fires this summer have been a terrible problem for some people.' He laughed again. 'It would be a pity if all your hard work was wasted. Such an interesting property you have there. Maybe it would be better for you if you sold it to me now. I would make you a very good offer.'

'Absolutely not,' shouted Marian. 'We're not giving in to your blackmail. Now clear off and don't come back.'

'One month, ladies, no more.' He turned away from them and, as he came to the threshold of the doorway, despite the dim light on the landing, he noticed me standing to one side. 'Ah, and what have we here?' he said with a smile. 'Is this where you have been hiding? I wondered why you were not tending to your injured husband.' He reached for my hand in his old manner, but I pulled away. 'Oh, that is a pity,' he said, still reaching out for me. 'But, I see now, is that what has happened? You are no longer interested in real men? The ladies here, they must have converted you.' He laughed and his shoulders shook.

'You are disgusting,' I said. 'Is there nothing you won't do or say?' I tried to look as dignified as I could in my loose cotton dress, with wet hair and bare feet. 'I heard everything that was said in there. I am a qualified lawyer and I am going to help my dear friends fight you for as long as it takes.'

'You have such spirit. I like that.' He put his forefinger under the point of my chin and tilted my face, murmuring, 'Such a pretty little blackbird.'

I twisted my head away from his hand. 'Don't you dare touch me. Don't you ever touch me.'

'Ah, you really don't like the feel of a man anymore, do you, my pretty one?' He came a little closer and I stepped to the other side of the long flight of stone stairs leading down to the shop. And just at that moment, I heard Theo crying. I instinctively lifted my head towards the sound and Dimitri also looked upwards. A slow smile came across his face as he said, in a soft voice, 'And you have a baby now. One more reason for you to be very careful, Kukla.'

I slapped his face, hard. As he put a hand to his cheek, he stepped forwards. But he wasn't looking at the stairs, he was looking at me. He lost his balance at the top of the wide staircase and fell, tumbling downwards step after step, knocking pottery and urns aside until he lay in a heap at the bottom.

I stood with my hand over my mouth and turned to see Inge holding a broom, staring at the broken body below. 'What have I done?' I gasped, holding tight to the newel post at the top, as if I too would fall without its support.

Marian rushed down the steps and bent over his lifeless form. She touched his neck, then his wrist and then looked into his eyes. 'I can't feel anything,' she called. Then she ran to the front of the shop and I could hear her locking the door. As she returned to him, we could see blood pooling on the stone flags beneath his head.

'He's not dead, is he?' I whispered in a shaky voice.

'I hope so,' Inge said. 'He deserved it for all his threats and all the harm he has done.'

I turned to look at her. She wasn't smiling, but there was an ethereal calmness about her.

Marian came back up to us. 'I think he's dead. I can't be absolutely certain, but I'm pretty sure he won't be going anywhere soon or causing any more trouble.'

'Leave him there till the morning,' said Inge. 'Then we'll know for sure.'

'But we can't do that, can we? How would we ever explain it?' I said, still looking down that long flight of stairs at the broken figure below.

Inge shrugged. 'We are such silly, absent-minded women. Always so forgetful. Sometimes we don't remember to lock the door at night. Someone must have come in to rob the shop and fallen on the stairs. We heard a noise after we had gone to bed, but thought it was the cats that have been getting in over the balcony. Such a nuisance, all these stray cats. Imagine our horror when we went down to unlock for the day and found we'd had an intruder in the night and the poor man had died without us ever knowing. Such a shock for all of us. Had we known, we would have called the police and an ambulance, of course.'

'Of course we would. But he had only himself to blame,' said Marian.

'But it's my fault. I made him fall.' I could feel tears starting to well in my eyes and I was trembling.

'No, you didn't, *liebchen*,' said Inge, standing to attention with her broom. 'Don't you remember, I pushed him? I'm sure I didn't mean to, but I was sweeping and he tripped over the brush.'

Chapter Eighty-Three

Agata has worked hard all day, cleaning and cooking, but now she has nearly completed the white dresses she has promised the girls, running her swift needle along the hems with tiny stitches. She rubs her eyes and yawns. The light is starting to fade, the children are fast asleep and she too will soon retire.

Ever since they arrived in the village, she has been scrubbing and washing, and now her bed and that of the children are laid with lavender-scented sheets, old and patched, but clean and cool nevertheless. Even up here, in the freshness of the mountains, the day has been relentlessly hot, as if they are nearer to the burning sun and further than ever from the cooling waters of the sea.

'You should stop now,' Georgiou says, patting the space on the bench beside him. 'It would be wrong to strain your eyes. Come sit with me till the light has gone. We may see the fireflies again as it darkens.'

She sits by his side, leaning back against the wall of the house, warm from the heat of the day. She rests her head on his firm shoulder. The far hills grow hazy as the setting sun turns to soft pink. Geogiou is tired too. All day he has gathered wood, turned hay for winter fodder and tilled a patch for their vegetable garden. He is working harder than ever before, but they are both at peace, satisfied their labours have been worthwhile.

'I'm very grateful to Zenia,' Agata says after a moment of quiet. 'She is so generous, but I worry about sharing everything with the children. She doesn't know about their parentage, but is it right that they should always have the same food as us?'

'I think you are worrying too much, my dear. All that matters is they grow strong and stay healthy.'

'But from the little I know of their ways, I know that they are not meant to have milk, yogurt or cheese with meat. And I've already broken that rule several times. So many of our traditional meals put everything in the kitchen into one pot! Moussaka, stifado, souvlaki – we use cheese or yogurt with everything. We even make dishes out of saganaki cheese alone! I had to stop myself adding cheese to the kleftiko the other day, just because my mother always cooked it that way. And what we'll do when you've butchered that pig, I don't know, really I don't.'

'Why, we'll all enjoy eating it, of course. Why wouldn't we? And why shouldn't we share it with the girls? If that is the only meat we have come the winter, we shall all be glad of it.'

'But will they be damned if they eat pork and ham and sausages? And will we be damned for letting it happen?'

Georgiou puts his arm around his wife and holds her tight. 'My love, I feel sure that their parents, their community and, above all, their God, will forgive them and us if they survive these difficult times. They will not be condemned just for staying alive, as their family have been condemned.'

'You mean, you think their parents and sister will not survive?'

'I fear so. In fact, I think there is very little chance they will return. The rumours did not give me much hope.' He is silent for a moment and they both sit still, watching as the light fades and the bats emerge from nearby roofs to flutter their night-time dance. 'Whole communities,' he says in a low voice. 'Whole villages taken away because of their heritage and beliefs. And who knows what they are suffering now?'

'How has it come to this? We have always been able to live together in spite of our different faiths.' Agata sniffs and wipes her eyes with her apron.

Georgiou squeezes her hand. 'My dear, if you feel you must avoid damnation, then go to the church to pray for forgiveness for yourself and the children, but add their family to your prayers, I beg you. I feel they are in need of them.'

Agata knows that the village church is still standing. She has knelt there briefly several times since they arrived. Its door is shut against vermin and birds, but not to the few people still living here. 'I will go tomorrow morning and every morning after that,' she says. 'I will pray for us and for them.'

Chapter Eighty-Four

Amber

September 2008

I slept no worse than any other new mother does every night, after it had happened. Marian made us cup after cup of tea, we ate the last of Inge's apple cake and we talked for at least an hour, until I felt calmer and more certain. Then Marian crept down the stairs to check again on our intruder and reported that he was quite cold and still, so we could safely go to our beds. I fed and changed Theo, fell asleep for a couple of hours, fed him again, slept some more and then woke with the sunlight. I could hear voices down below and when I went to the top of the stairs, I could again hear a male voice rumbling, interspersed with the voices of the two women. But this time it was not arrogant, it wasn't hectoring, it sounded calm and sympathetic.

I carried my baby down the stairs in my arms, holding him tight to my breast, and found Marian and Inge seated in the kitchen talking to a tall uniformed policeman. He stood up as I entered and bowed his head, saying, '*Kalimera*, madam. If I may please have a moment with you as well.'

I must have looked bewildered, because Marian came and put her arms around me. 'You'd better sit down, Amber. I'm afraid something simply awful happened last night.'

'Something awful? Why, what's happened?'

She sat next to me and, still with her arm around my shoulders and looking me directly in the eye, she gently said, 'It appears we had an unwanted visitor last night while we were all asleep.'

I gasped and looked across the table at Inge, who was calm but looked even paler than usual. 'Are you both all right?' I asked, aware that I was breathing fast.

'Don't worry, there's no need to look so alarmed. We're both fine.' She squeezed my shoulder, then added, 'But the intruder isn't. I'm afraid he's dead.'

I concentrated on looking at Inge and not at the policeman. 'Oh no, how?'

'The thief must have slipped on our stone steps,' Inge said. Her expression was hard to interpret, she always looked weary. 'Poor Marian found him very early this morning when she went downstairs. Such a terrible shock for her, poor girl.'

Marian shook her head in self-recrimination. 'I thought I heard a crash in the night. But I assumed it was those damned stray cats again. I should've got up to check.'

'I'm very glad you didn't,' Inge said. 'Just think, he might have turned on you and you could have been attacked and hurt.'

'If he hadn't already fallen down the stairs,' Marian added.

'Madam,' the policeman said, focusing on me, 'did you hear or see anything suspicious last night?'

I stared at him, blinking, then shook my head. 'No, I don't think so. I'm so tired with the baby. He wakes in the night, you see. And as soon as I've fed him, I fall asleep again.'

'Of course,' he said. Then he turned back to Marian. 'Have you noticed anything missing?'

'Our takings are locked away every night, but I haven't had a chance to check the stock properly yet or look around the house.' She stood up, as if intending to go down to the shop immediately, but the policeman waved at her to sit down again. 'All in good time, madam. Please do not distress yourself now. Stay here with your friends and I will check how far my colleagues have proceeded downstairs.' He left the kitchen and we heard his boots scuffing the stone steps as he made his way down, along with the occasional crunch or tinkle of a shard of broken pottery.

We stayed sitting at the table, not daring to talk about the true events of the previous night in case he returned. Marian made coffee, we ate stale croissants from the previous day and Theo snuffled, and then began to squeal, so I fed him again.

At last we heard those heavy feet on the stairs once more and the courteous policeman was back. He stood to attention before us, then said, 'He's gone, madams. We have dealt with the matter. There will be no more questions.'

Marian stood to thank him and shook his hand, then, in the doorway, as he turned to go, in a quiet voice he said to her, 'You may wish to deal with the mess down there without the mother.' She nodded, then came back to us once he had gone.

'Mess?' I asked.

'I can clear it up myself,' Marian said. 'It's not that terrible.'

'No, I want to help. I won't faint, I promise.' So I settled Theo in his basket, with Inge watching over him, while Marian and I carried pails of water and brushes down the flight of stone steps. We swept away the broken pots, then doused the pool of blood and brushed the stained water towards the side door and a nearby drain. Several buckets later, with the addition of bleach, the flagstones were relatively clean, glistening with damp, not death.

'That's enough, for now,' Marian said. 'If it's still stained when it dries, we can throw a mat over it. No one will ever know.' She stood with her broom upright, in a pose echoing the one Inge had adopted the night before. 'Are you sure you're all right?' she asked.

I was staring at the stones, remembering the broken figure that had sprawled there. 'The other night, we joked about wanting him out of the way. We talked about how we could bump him off. But we never really meant it, did we? I never really thought we would get rid of him.' I looked at her standing there, her hair and face damp with the effort of washing away all that blood. 'But I keep thinking I did this to him. And though I'm glad he won't cause trouble any more, I can't be glad he's dead.'

Marian propped her broom against the wall, reached out her arms and hugged me, holding me tight. I was shaking. 'Shush. You mustn't upset yourself. It wasn't your fault. He tripped, didn't he? And he had no regard for you or Theo. Always remember that.'

Chapter Eighty-Five

James

November 2008

On that stuffy train down to Cornwall, I thought long and hard about all that had happened. There was plenty of time to think on that tedious journey. The train was packed. I had to fight for a seat and the buffet car was closed. Five hours is a long time without sustenance for a man like me, so I was in a foul mood by the time I got to the pub where I'm now working.

But I kept thinking, how important is it to tell the truth? I was prepared to tell Amber every last detail of every conversation, to admit I'd been wrong and hang my head in shame, if it would have put everything right, but I never did. She's changed so much since that disastrous night and not only is she is preoccupied with Theo, but she's also obsessed with the need to talk about what she calls 'Corfu's Holocaust'. She goes to the Old Fort with Inge at least once a week, saying they have to tell tourists what happened and that she will go with Marian when Inge is no longer here. I've tried telling her the past doesn't matter, but she keeps going on about how the truth must be told, no matter how far back it goes.

We said goodbye at the airport. What it signified I'm not sure. Goodbyes can mean 'see you tomorrow', 'let's meet again soon' or 'farewell and good riddance'. I hate to think she meant the latter, but I fear so. She wanted to stay with Inge and Marian, helping them in the shop and in their mission in the town.

Theo was in her arms, chubby-cheeked, four months old. He looks more like Amber than me, with his dark hair and golden skin, and she looked so beautiful, my lovely Amber, my wife, mother of my first child, perhaps my only child. And how do I look to her? I know she still sees me as a villain, the destroyer of her dreams, and she is the saviour of the only good thing that has come out of this wretched mess – Theo.

We came to the island with such hopes and in the end our home and our business were destroyed, along with our marriage and any chance of living together as a family. I will never see my son's first tooth, witness his first steps or hear him utter his first word. Isn't that punishment enough? If I stay away from them, will I finally be absolved and forgiven?

As my plane soared into the sky towards a grey English November, I'd looked down at the clear blue sea and the marshland around the airport runways, and wondered if it would have made any difference to Amber if I had been able to demonstrate just how much I wanted to make amends. If I could have got even with the one person responsible for that terrible fire, might she have shown me some compassion? But I hadn't been able to even remonstrate with Dimitri in person, let alone punch him in the face or slash his tyres.

I didn't discover what had happened to him until I went to Greg's funeral in the last week of September. I was walking independently by then, with the aid of a crutch, and I was determined to attend the ceremony held at the white church on the hill above his villa. Pam was dressed all in black, a huge feathered hat shading her face, while Lavinia hovered around her mother, alternately clutching her arm and that of a dark-suited man with slicked-back hair and aviator shades, who I assumed was the notorious Vladi.

The service was ponderous and the church was stifling with the heavy scent of white lilies. As the family filed out, after the coffin was carried to a waiting hearse, Lavinia noticed me through the lace of her dramatic black mantilla and reached for my arm. 'Join us for drinks later, won't you,' she said in a breathy voice, which was either the result of her emotions or the restrictions imposed by her extremely tight corset-like dress.

When I met with the other mourners in the nearby restaurant, where the waiters were circulating with trays of wine and dishes of olives, I waited my turn to offer my respects to the widow. Pam was dignified and calm when she shook my hand. 'It's so good of you to come, James, especially when you are only just back on your feet yourself. Do you know, you were one of the last people to speak with Greg before the very end? He was so fond of you and always said how much he looked forward to your meetings, especially your little late-night heart-to-hearts.'

'I'll never forget him. He really was a great character.'

She smiled. 'Everyone's saying that about him.' She looked around the room, at the drinking and laughing crowd of bereaved. 'All these people here. I can't believe how many good friends he had. And everyone's been so very kind.'

I followed her gaze, scanning the heads and faces above the uniform of black suits and dresses. I knew hardly anyone there and I couldn't see the one face I was really interested in finding. 'I'm very surprised Dimitri isn't here to pay his respects,' I said. 'He and Greg had worked together for quite a while, hadn't they?'

'Oh, Mr Barberis, you mean? Haven't you heard?'

'No, heard what?'

'My dear, the most extraordinary thing. He died within a few days of Greg. His funeral is going to be held at the end of next week.'

I was shocked to hear this, but largely disappointed that even this opportunity to redeem myself had slipped through my fingers. Maybe someone else had taken his or her revenge before me. 'No, I didn't know that,' I said. 'Whatever happened to him?'

Pam shrugged, looking vague. 'A fall, I believe. I'd like to have gone to the funeral, but Lavinia wants me to go straight back to London with her next Wednesday.'

At this mention of her name, Lavinia turned to her mother and put a protective arm around her shoulders. 'Mummy can't be expected to cope with everything all on her own here any more. The strain of it has all been simply too much for her.' She lifted her lacy veil and looked at me with heavily made-up deep-blue eyes. 'If you've still got any business matters to sort out, you'll have to talk to Vladi.' She touched the arm of the dark man standing by her side, turning him towards me. 'He's handling all of Daddy's affairs now. It's so dreadfully complicated and he's awfully good at that sort of thing.'

Vladimir held out his hand for me to shake, saying, 'And you are?'

'James Young. I had a restaurant, Mountain Thyme, up in the mountains. Greg was a good friend and backed us when we were setting up.'

He frowned and said, 'This is the business involved in the fire and where Greg had his unfortunate accident?'

'I'm afraid so. It was pretty badly hit up there and we haven't been able to reopen the restaurant again yet.'

His eyes narrowed under his frown. 'Then we shall talk later.'

We did talk later. It wasn't the sort of conversation I enjoy having at any time, let alone in a fragile recuperative state. If Greg had recovered I could imagine him slapping me verbally, as well as physically, on the back and saying, 'Don't you worry, mate, we'll show them, we'll pick up the pieces and start again.' But Greg was no longer around to joke and be optimistic and Vladi wasn't interested in pipe dreams. 'My father-in-law was a most generous man,' he said. 'But business is business. His estate requires his investment to be repaid.'

'But I have nothing left,' I protested. 'There's no viable business there at present and there's unlikely to be any prospect of reopening for some time to come. We're still waiting for the insurers to settle before we can start the repairs.'

'That is most unfortunate,' he said. 'But I will be generous with you. I will require you to pay me at least a proportion of the insurance payout, equivalent to the share that was given originally.' He slapped me on the back, his heavy hand lingering as he finished speaking, but it wasn't a jovial, matey slap; it was proprietorial, insistent and belittling. 'That is a fair deal, I think you will agree. We shall talk again soon, my friend.'

In the end, when the insurance settlement came through, I was left with nothing. I'd hoped to salvage a little from the smoke-blackened walls and begin again, but there was barely any cash left once I'd satisfied Vladi's demands.

I turned to Ben, thinking I could carry on working for my old friend until I was back on my feet, both physically and financially. But he shrugged and said, 'I'm really sorry, mate. Things aren't looking so good. We've had a reasonable season this year, and usually by this time we'd already have a stack of repeat bookings and deposits for the coming year, but there's barely anything coming through. The usual punters are sounding nervous, the way the financial markets are going right now. We're going to be stretched to get through the winter at this rate.'

So I can't avoid the truth any longer and there can be no more lies. In pursuing my dream of being a great chef, running an acclaimed and starred restaurant, I sacrificed both my wife and my child. I never blame Amber, I never blame Greg; I blame myself for not seeing what would happen. I blame myself for trusting too much and for not facing the truth. But I want to go back to remembering the good things, the hope and the happiness we had together at first. I want to go back to smelling lemons and fresh oregano, not smoke and destruction. And when I can, I hope we will go back and start again.

And now, instead of working for myself in my own business, where I once shook the hands of grateful, appreciative clients and looked out over the idyllic mountains of Corfu, I fry fish in a pub in Cornwall. I'm still cooking, I'm working hard, but every day I have to face the fact that because of my arrogant deceit, I left my wife and son in Corfu. Back then, I wasn't afraid of lying, but I am now.

Chapter Eighty-Six

29 June 1944

'Papa, the train has stopped.' Rebekka's voice is a hoarse whisper, her throat is parched, her tongue so dry it seems to stick to the roof of her mouth. But Papa doesn't answer, nor does Mama. They slumped into an everlasting sleep days ago.

Mama insisted she wasn't hungry, giving Rebekka tiny morsels of food throughout their long journey: raisins, nuts, hidden away in the pockets of her clothes. Sometimes, when the trains slowed on the tracks, they heard the gushing of water and droplets sprayed through gaps in the loose boards of the crammed boxcars. Rebekka was crammed against the wall of the train, so she licked at beads of moisture to ease her thirst and pressed her fevered forehead against the dampened wood to cool herself.

'You are strong, you will survive if you work hard,' Mama said in a faint voice before she finally slept. Rebekka kept hold of her hand, which grew cold despite the stifling heat of the carriage, where the overpowering stench increased with every minute of their tortuous journey. No one could move unless their neighbour expired; everyone vomited, defecated, urinated and died where they stood and the floor was awash with slippery waste.

'Tell me more about my sisters,' Rebekka pleaded with Papa, hoping he too would not succumb to sleep. And he tried, he tried so hard, but he was so tired of standing day after day on their horrifying journey.

'Tell me more about Matilde and Anna, Papa,' she urged, trying to make him stay awake, so she could imagine she was anywhere but this stinking carriage.

'They live on fresh eggs from chickens that scratch around the cottage and the vegetable garden,' he whispered. 'There may not be lamb or beef, but they have chickpeas to make buttery fava, flour for bread and goat's milk to drink and make feta. They will be such big strong girls when we see them again.' When his soothing words finally ceased and she knew he could never comfort her any more, Rebekka repeated these reassuring phrases in her head, over and over, telling herself, 'My little sisters are safe. My sisters will be there, waiting for me when I return.'

And now the train has stopped. There are cries outside. Rebekka hears the harsh slam of bolts being drawn, doors crashing open and curt shouts from the soldiers, '*Alles da lassen! Alle heraus, schneller!*'

Those who are still alive and able to drag themselves from the stinking carriages are falling out of the train into the open air. Rebekka feels ashamed of her stained dress, but she drags her filthy bundle with her to the open door and looks out. Those who are not already dead and unable to leave are crawling, limping, stumbling alongside the track, guards watching over them. Is this where they are all going to live and work? There are men in striped clothes grabbing their sacks, throwing them into one big pile.

'*Schneller heraus!*' shout all the men and the soldiers. Rebekka doesn't know what it means, but she jumps out and staggers with the few who can still walk, wondering when they will have to start work and when they will all have a good meal after their long journey.

Chapter Eighty-Seven

Amber

October 2009

There was much laughter in the house when I returned from my late-afternoon walk with Theo. We go out every day at around 4 p.m. once I've woken Inge from her nap. She is still with us, but so much weaker, and I have taken over her duties in the shop. Theo loves to see the donkey, wave at the cats scavenging around the mini-supermarket and be admired by all the elderly ladies who sit outside the shops and houses on their white plastic chairs to see the world pass by. He gurgled and smiled as they told him what a handsome *bubala* he is and how he will break many hearts when he is older.

So we returned from our excursions in a cheerful frame of mind, Theo ready for his supper and me thirsting for tea. And once I'd taken him out of his buggy and carried him up that long flight of stairs, I heard shrieks of laughter followed by Inge's raucous cough. There, at the kitchen table, were two plump older women I'd never met before, but who were clearly well known to Marian and Inge. They were eating sticky pastries glistening with syrup and sipping strong coffee.

As soon as they all saw me and Theo, one of the women cried, '*Bubala!*' and stretched out her arms towards him. I smiled at her, but continued to hold him.

'Amber, we have unexpected visitors today,' Marian said.

'But most welcome all the same,' Inge added in her croaky voice. 'I must introduce you to our guests. They have not been back here for such a long time and it is such a great pleasure to see them again.' More murmurs followed, with kisses blown by both the women, then Inge said, 'Amber, I want you to meet two dear old friends. Their last visit to us was more than ten years ago, but you will know of their connection with this house.'

I believe I stared blankly and must have looked rather stupid, for Inge then said, 'These ladies are the two children I told you about. The children Agata and Georgiou saved all those years ago.' She waved her hand at each of them in turn. 'This is Anna and Matilde.'

Both ladies smiled at me and then Anna stood up, waggled her broad hips and, with an infectious laugh, said, 'I couldn't get in our hiding place now for sure, not with this big behind!'

Her sister laughed too, saying, 'Anna has eaten too many baklava. She always was the greedy one.' Then she stood and embraced her sister, the wings of flesh on her arms wobbling as she tried to reach around Anna's generous frame.

Inge was laughing and coughing at the same time, but managed to say, 'The first time they came back, they both tried to crawl in through the wardrobe. It was so funny. They almost got stuck.'

'How long ago was that?' I asked.

'Oh, the first time was 1976,' Anna said. 'When Georgy and Aggie were still alive and Inge had begun helping them.'

'And we still couldn't get inside,' Matilde shrieked, tears of laughter running down her cheeks. 'We were both pregnant again!'

'But we had our older children with us and they all insisted on trying out our hiding place. They loved it.'

'They wanted to sleep there, didn't they?' Inge said.

'They did. They thought it was a great adventure. But Anna and I can hardly remember the time when we first came to stay here and had to hide. We were both so very young then.'

'But we saw more of it later, when we came back from the house in the mountains, when the war was all over and it was safe again,' Anna said. 'We all came back to live here for – how long was it?

Four years? No, five years, I think.' She turned to her sister. 'Yes, five years, it must have been 1950 when Uncle Costas came from Athens to fetch us. You were eleven then, and I was nine.'

I took all of this in, then with some hesitancy said, 'So your uncle came to find you? Not your parents?'

Both women looked grave, then Matilde shook her head. 'Sadly, they went, along with all the others. Very few came back. We don't know exactly what happened or when, but we believe our mother and father died at some point during the deportation. Many people died on the way. The conditions were so terrible. But we know our older sister Rebekka reached the end of that dreadful long journey and arrived in Auschwitz.'

At this point I hoped there was a happy ending to the story, but Anna said, 'Unfortunately, she did not survive, like so many of them. Most of them were gassed on arrival.' She sighed. 'It sounds harsh of me to say it, but sometimes I think it was better she didn't have to endure any longer.'

Matilde hugged her sister and they both said something I didn't understand. I think it might have been a prayer in Greek or Hebrew. Then they both pulled delicate hankies from hidden corners of their clothing, Anna from her sleeve, Matilde from the depths of her generous bosom, to dab their eyes.

'But we are here,' Matilde said. 'We are the lucky ones. Our parents and sister loved us enough to give us away, to save us. If we had been rounded up with the others, we could never have survived. As it is, we are large of life, we have children…'

'And grandchildren,' added Anna. 'And we've had a good life, here and in the mountains. Come on, Matilde, let us show them all the dance we learnt there, from that old woman.' She grabbed her sister's hand and they both stood and then began to sway and sing, clicking their fingers, stamping their feet and turning around each other. Two broad-hipped, grey-haired ladies, shrieking with laughter and dancing to the tunes of their childhood, bracelets jangling on their wrists. Marian and Inge clapped their hands in time as they danced and I bounced Theo on my hip, making him giggle.

When their dance came to an end, they collapsed on the chairs and gulped glasses of water. 'Oof, I can't do it like I used to,' declared Matilde. 'We were young and nimble then, not fat old ladies.'

Her sister reached for another pastry and with her mouth full of honeyed crumbs, said, 'The first time we learnt that dance we were wearing the dresses Aggie made for us, do you remember?'

'Of course I do. White dresses. We were so excited to have new dresses. Dearest Aggie. And she was so proud of us. Like a grandmother, she was.'

'And darling Georgy, a grandfather.'

'And old Zenia, a great-grandmother. Our parents may have had to leave us behind, but we were so lucky. We gained another very loving family.'

'It sounds as if you lived happily, in spite of those difficult times,' I said.

'Oh, we did,' Anna said. 'And we learnt so much from them. When we came back here to the coast we even learnt how to sail Georgy's boat and catch fish. Georgy and Aggie told us we had to learn many skills in case we had to fend for ourselves.'

'So many orphaned children were not so fortunate,' Matilde said. 'When Uncle Costas finally came for us and took us to join the rest of the family in Athens, it was very different to the life we had here. We didn't know about it at first, because they didn't tell us everything, but there was terrible famine in Athens during the war. The Germans took everything. Thousands of people starved to death in their homes and on the streets. As we grew old enough to know all the facts, it became clear to us, that in spite of occasional hardships, we had been very lucky.'

'So lucky and so loved,' added Anna. 'Our years here and in the mountains were some of the happiest of our lives. We often say that, don't we?'

'Very happy,' agreed Matilde. 'My favourite time was in the mountains, with the sheep in the meadows and helping Georgy collect kindling for the stove. We haven't been back to the house there in all these years. We wanted to go this visit, but we hear there's been a terrible fire up there.'

'You've never told me where it was exactly,' Inge said. 'Amber and her husband had a restaurant in the mountains but it was destroyed last year by fire.'

'Beyond New Perithia,' Matilde said. 'There was a farmhouse that had been in Georgy's family for many years. I can just about remember arriving there and spending our first night downstairs while Aggie tried to make it habitable. She worked so hard, cleaning and cooking. But we didn't mind how it looked as long as we were safe and well fed. It didn't matter to us that it was rundown and dusty.'

'And we had the cellar, remember?' Anna added. 'Aggie said it would make a good hiding place if we ever needed to suddenly hide ourselves, but we loved it and played house down there all the time.'

'We even chalked pictures on the walls,' Matilde said.

'And Aggie marked how much we'd grown too,' Anna said. 'She was so proud that her good food was making us big and strong, so she chalked our height on the wall. Oof, she'd be surprised at how big we've grown now!' And both women hugged again and kissed each other's cheeks.

And at these words, my skin prickled and I knew. I pictured the cellar where I'd hidden from the fire, the cellar where I'd given birth to Theo. And I remembered the faint marks on the walls I'd puzzled over: the A and the M repeated, with dates scrawled beside them. I'd thought it was something to do with keeping track of goods stored down there, a tally of the barrels and sacks. But it was nothing to do with oil, olives and wine, it was simply a record of the childhood of two little orphaned girls, their time growing up, gaining strength and staying alive.

I felt tears prick my eyes as I managed to say, 'But I know where that is. I've been there. I saw the marks on the wall. It was the cellar at our restaurant.' They stared at me, then I took a sobbing breath and said, 'Your cellar saved me from the fire. And it was where I gave birth to my son.' I sat down quickly, feeling shaky, handing Theo over to Marian while I sobbed.

Anna and Matilde rushed to hug me, offering lace hankies, kisses and a glass of ouzo with water. 'Don't cry, little one,' Anna said. 'You and your son are very much alive. You must give thanks for your survival, like us, not tears.'

'You have a handsome boy, my dear. He will make you proud,' Matilde said. 'You have much to celebrate.'

I couldn't bear to tell them how the fire had started, or how it had destroyed the business and my marriage. I could only nod and accept their encouraging words. And once I was calmer, I said, 'I feel so overwhelmed to know that the place that could have saved you, that was meant to be your secret place of safety, saved us instead. It seems uncanny that we should be linked by this.'

Both sisters kissed my cheeks and hands and Matilde said, 'Aggie promised us we would always be safe while we were in her care. She prayed in the village church in the mountains every day for our well-being. I think perhaps her prayers were heard and their power has endured. God kept watch over you during the fire, while you laboured. God blessed you and your child.'

HISTORICAL NOTE

To help me gain an understanding of the horror of the deportation of the Jewish community from Corfu, I read a large number of survivor testimonies from various countries, including Greece. Very few were actually those of the Corfiot Jews, as so few survived, so it is hard to know precisely what happened, hour by hour, and therefore I have based some fictional incidents on the statements of others in similar horrific circumstances. However, all survivors, without exception, referred to the soldiers who ordered them to leave their homes as 'Germans', not 'Nazis' or 'Nazi Germans', so I have followed their lead when writing about the events of 1944.

Figures for the number of Jews deported from Corfu and executed by the Germans in 1944 vary according to different sources, so I decided to rely on the number quoted in a handout provided by the sole remaining synagogue, the Scuola Greca in Vellissariou Street in the heart of the old Jewish quarter. This states:

On June 9, 1944, 2000 Corfiot Jews were rounded up by the Nazi Germans to be deported off the island. 91 per cent of them, along with another 67,000 Greek Jews and 6,000,000 European Jews were executed in the concentration camps. The Corfu captives were first sent off in small boats, then loaded on trains, ending their journey in Auschwitz. The hardships, famine, beatings and forced labor they were subjected to cannot be properly or fully traced.

The Holocaust of the Corfiot Jews took place on June 29, 1944. 1700 people were executed in the gas chambers and crematoria. 300 people were subjected to forced labor.

150 of them died under the harsh and inhuman conditions and only 150 would survive and be released by the Allies. Half of the Holocaust survivors migrated then to Israel, the USA and elsewhere. The rest of them returned to Corfu, bringing their community back to life, which currently numbers about 60 Jews.

This statement does not mention those who escaped the deportation, nor those who were hidden, although that is documented in several accounts. Nor does it dwell on the length of imprisonment before the captives left the island, or the length of journey they endured. Knowing that the Jews of Corfu suffered the longest transport of any community to Auschwitz makes the simple restraint of this document all the more startling.

The fate of this community is also recorded in a witness testimony documented by the Holocaust Memorial Day Trust in *The Untold Stories of Lost Communities*. Dr Nyiszli, who was forced to work for the infamous Dr Mengele, stated:

Last night they burned the Greek Jews from the Mediterranean island of Corfu, one of the oldest communities in Europe. The victims were kept for twenty-seven days without food or water, first in small boats then in sealed cars. When they arrived at Auschwitz's platform the doors were unlocked, but no one got out to line up for selection. Half of them were already dead and half in a coma. The entire convoy without exception was sent to number two crematoria.

Yet another testimony reports that on arrival in June 1944, some male Jews from Corfu were ordered to work in the crematorium. They refused and were shot on the spot.

The Jewish characters I have imagined in this novel are entirely fictitious, but their names are those of real members of the Evraiki community who were deported. From the family names of the lost, I deliberately chose to use a surname that sounds more Greek than Jewish, to emphasise how the two cultures, the two religions, lived side by side in harmony.

Among the handful of survivors was one Rebecca Aaron, whose testimony, published by *Enimerosi*, Corfu's daily paper, gave details of the Mayor's collaboration and the actions of the Greek Resistance in the town at the time of the roundup. She was deported but somehow survived and returned to Corfu, where she lived to a good age till 28 December 2018. However, so many never returned. The synagogue displays a plaque recording the family names of those who left the Evraiki. These are the families lost forever, but they must be remembered:

Akkos, Alchavas, Amar, Aron, Asias, Asser, Bakolas, Balestra, Baruch, Benakim, Ben Giat, Besso, Cavaliero, Chaim, Dalmedigos, Dentes, Etan, Elias, Eliezer, Eskapas, Ferro, Fortes, Ganis, Gerson, Gikas, Haim, Israel, Johanna, Koen, Kolonimos, Konstantinis, Koulias, Lemous, Leoncini, Levi, Matathias, Matsas, Minervo, Mizan, Mizrahi, Mordos, Moustaki, Nacamouli, Nechamas, Nechon, Negrin, Nikokiris, Osmos, Ovadiah, Perez, Pitson, Politis, Raphael, Sardas, Sasen, Serneine, Sinigalli, Soussis, Tsesana, Varon, Vellelis, Vital, Vitali, Vivante.

Finally, to put the terrible events in Corfu in June 1944 into the wider context of the war, the Jewish community's deportation ordeal began on 8 June, two days after Operation Overlord (D-Day) succeeded in giving the Allies the upper hand in Europe. The Germans left Corfu in October 1944, just over three months after fulfilling their mission to eliminate the island's Jewish community.

A Letter from Suzanne

Thank you so much for reading *Burning Island*. I hope you enjoyed reading it as much as I enjoyed writing it.

If you did enjoy it, and want to keep up to date with all my latest releases, just sign up at the following link. Your email address will never be shared and you can unsubscribe at any time.

www.bookouture.com/suzanne-goldring

During the writing of this book I have received encouragement from the Elstead Writers Group, the Ark Writers, my Vesta friends Gail, Carol and Denise and the inspiring Melanie Whipman. I must also thank my editor Lydia Vassar-Smith for pushing me further and further into the past.

I have dedicated *Burning Island* to our very dear friend, now sadly departed, Paul Walford. With his wife Jacky, Paul introduced my husband and I, and our family, to the delights of Corfu soon after the millennium. We were enthralled by the clear waters, the dramatic landscape and the friendliness of the local people and began to return as often as possible. However, it was only after maybe our third or fourth visit that I began to wonder why the synagogue in Corfu Town was not marked on the tourist maps left in our rented villas. The many churches and monasteries were clearly identified, but the synagogue, which we had passed on our treks on hot days to the wonderful market to buy fruit, vegetables and fish, was not.

Once I had done a little bit of research, I discovered that this was the only remaining synagogue on the island and then, to my horror, I uncovered the facts about Corfu's Jewish community. I was haunted by their dreadful story and became determined to find a way to make their fate more widely known.

So few Corfiot Jews survived the deportation that it was not only difficult to research their terrible experience, it also, for a long time, felt intrusive. I wasn't sure I had the right to describe the annihilation of this peaceful community. I wondered whether I should focus on the present and show how the potential for boorish, cruel behaviour and destruction is present in relatively civilised societies. However, I was persuaded by my editor and writer friends that the story of Corfu's Jews should be more widely known, so that no one enjoying the island can be unaware of its shocking past.

I love Corfu and I love the people, who greet us when we return with cries of 'My family!' They were kind and generous the year I had a car accident, they always plied us with shots of limoncello at the end of many wonderful dinners, our hosts baked us cakes when we returned to our favourite villa and shared their own pressing of olive oil, while we tried to rescue scrawny, flea-ridden kittens every time we visited. My husband and I returned once more in order to complete this book, but this time we didn't rent a villa with a pool, overlooking the sea, we stayed in the centre of Corfu Town, on the edge of the old Evraiki so we could walk in the footsteps of the lost Jews to the Old Fort, where they were imprisoned for their last days on this beautiful island.

If you go to Corfu, I hope you will enjoy the food, the warm company and the clear sparkling seas, but I also hope you will find time to stand in the barren quadrangle of the Old Fort and think about the people who once lived here in harmony with their Greek neighbours, but were forced to leave.

While writing *Burning Island,* the following online resources and books were helpful to me in my research: The Untold Stories of Lost Communities – Holocaust Memorial Day Trust, Farewell My

Island – a recording of interviews with survivors (www.worldcat.
org). An old Holocaust secret newly told – article on Ynetnews.com,
Ahistoryofgreece.com – Greece during WW2, Armando Aaron's
account of leaving Corfu in June 1944 (Collections.ushmm.org),
The Auschwitz Album – Yad Vashem, Shoah Resource Centre –
Yad Vashem, Famine and Death in Occupied Greece – Violetta
Hionidou, Jewish Museum Greece, *The Holocaust in Greece – Giorgos
Antoniou, Auschwitz* – Laurence Rees. *Helga's Diary – A Young Girl's
Account of Life in a Concentration Camp, The Durrells of Corfu* –
Michael Haag and *The Corfu Trilogy* – Gerald Durrell.

Made in the USA
Columbia, SC
01 February 2020

87414424R00214